MERLINSLADE

Also by Willow Tickell

A Gift from Artemis

MERLINSLADE

Willow Tickell

Hodder & Stoughton

First published in 1995 by Hodder and Stoughton
A division of Hodder Headline PLC

10 9 8 7 6 5 4 3 2 1

A CIP catalogue record for this title
is available from the British Library

ISBN 0 340 63507 X

Typeset by
Letterpart Limited, Reigate, Surrey

Printed and bound in Great Britain by
Mackays of Chatham PLC, Chatham, Kent

Hodder and Stoughton
A division of Hodder Headline PLC
338 Euston Road
London NW1 3BH

To Alex

Acknowledgements

Many thanks to my agent, Sarah Molloy, for the best of front-line encouragement and support. Special thanks as well to Sue Fletcher for her perceptive and tactful editorial advice, and to her assistant, Marysia Juszczakiewicz. I was also greatly helped by Lance and Alex Tickell, Joss Kingsnorth, Geraldine Kaye and the members of her writers' workshop, Penny MacDonald, Serena Gledhill, Stella Bowen of John Lindley & Co, Clifton, Bristol, and John Levy of Stancombe Cider Farm, Sherford, South Devon. Julie Herbert and Jo Armstrong of the Bristol Old Vic theatre company were particularly generous with their time and professional information. Any errors are mine alone.

Chapter 1

For a moment Georgia thought she heard the angels sing. They clung like moths to the carved stone ladders which soared heavenwards on either side of the doors to Bath Abbey. Their newly cleaned wings were dazzling in the June sunshine. Above them the sky had also been washed by overnight rain to a clear limitless blue.

She listened again. Though the voices were singing a hymn, they were decidedly of this world. They drifted across the Abbey courtyard, the stronger one male, persuasive, dominant, and as penetrating as the scent of marijuana. She was sure she'd heard it somewhere before. The backing voice, a woman's, twined softly in a counter melody.

Georgia wedged her folder of costume designs under her arm, and began to weave purposefully towards the sound. A light breeze tugged at her hat. She put up her free hand to steady it. The floppy straw brim was caught back with a posy of scarlet silk poppies. It framed a vivid, sensitive face, and the tourists thronging the courtyard, at first indignant at being so adroitly manoeuvred out of the way, forgot their protests when they encountered her smile.

The voices were loudest opposite the classical façade of the Roman Baths on the south side of the courtyard. Georgia insinuated herself into a space next to a young girl at the front of the crowd, and followed the direction of her rapt stare. A man was sitting on the back of a bench, a guitar resting across his knees, a black suede jacket flung across his shoulders as negligently as an Elizabethan courtier's cloak.

He was in his mid-fifties, sallow-skinned, with heavy drooping

1

lids over dark eyes, and he was singing 'Amazing Grace' as though it were a love song. There was a seductive challenge in his voice, to which the women in the audience were responding like hounds on a trail. Georgia, at the front of the crowd, caught his gaze, and briefly he seemed to be singing to her alone.

His eyes moved on to the young girl by her side swaying dreamily to the music. She was about seventeen, the same age as Georgia's sister, Chloe, who was safely away at boarding school. She had the same look of trusting naivety too, the look which so often landed Chloe in trouble.

Gently Georgia shook her arm. 'Do you know who he is?'

The girl focused on her with difficulty. 'Some guy who was in the charts in the seventies, they say. Brilliant, isn't he?'

A middle-aged woman just behind Georgia, hair set in rigid curls and clutching a PVC shopping bag to her chest like a riot shield, volunteered more information as she kept her eyes firmly fixed on the singer.

'Not just someone, dear. I'll swear that's Morrigan. I saw his last concert at Wembley in '75.'

Now Georgia knew why the voice was familiar. When she was a child in Africa, the ayah, of whom she saw far more than her own mother, kept the radio on all day long. It always seemed to be playing Morrigan's songs. Even when she lay in bed in the tropical night listening to her parents arguing downstairs, a background of his music drifted from the city bars to the university campus where her parents worked and lived. He'd retired from the pop scene after some scandal or other, but she couldn't remember the details.

The woman with the shopping bag shifted her stance to ease her legs. 'He was in prison for a while because of something to do with drugs. He always swore he was innocent. Afterwards he went off to live in India. A wicked waste, I call it, throwing away a voice like his.'

The backing singer, who stood behind the bench with a group of solemn young men and women, was clasping a Bible and a handful of flowers. She was a few years younger than Morrigan, and had a sweet, earnest face, crowned with a pile of blonde hair from which the brightness was beginning to fade. Her ample body, burgeoning in a long classical robe of white cotton caught at the waist with a cord, reminded Georgia of an underdone cottage loaf.

The young men in the group wore white shirts and grey trousers. They looked as sober as Quakers among the brightly clad crowd. The girls in the group were dressed in the same way as the backing singer, and carried collecting boxes as well as Bibles. Their robes were fashioned with obvious enthusiasm but little attention to detail. Georgia, who only recently had designed the costumes for an off-Broadway *Coriolanus*, longed to redo them.

'Morrigan used to live near Bath when he was young,' the woman with the shopping bag went on. 'They say he's just bought a house in the Royal Crescent. Now he's back here at last, I don't know why he wants to spend his time with a lot of religious cranks.'

'They're not cranks. They're wonderful,' said the girl next to Georgia. 'I've been to their centre. The Sanctuary, it's called. I wanted to stay, but my dad wouldn't let me.'

'Quite right too,' the woman went on. 'You're far too young to know your own mind. And as for the singer with Morrigan, she ought to know better at her age. She was preaching earlier on, but it wasn't proper religion. It was all mixed up with this New Age stuff.'

Morrigan swept his hand across the guitar strings in a final flamboyant chord. The audience surged excitedly towards him in a kaleidoscope of colours. He swung his legs over the back of the bench, leaped to the ground, and the members of the group instantly fanned forward, shielding him from the throng. The girls began to collect donations. Money poured into their boxes while the young men distributed leaflets among the rest of the crowd.

Georgia saw a collection box coming towards her. It was plastered with a label showing outstretched hands, and the words 'Help to Heal', but there had been something so odd about the difference in attitude between Morrigan and the rest of the group that she dodged to one side. She was wary of appeals to her emotions these days, and in any case was more interested in finding out where Morrigan had gone. He'd vanished completely, almost as though spirited away.

One of the young men managed to thrust a leaflet into her hand as a couple of policemen appeared and cast an assessing eye over the crowd. The woman singer had seen them as well. Like a mother goose she rounded up her followers, and led them at a dignified pace across the courtyard and through the entrance to the Roman Baths.

Georgia looked curiously at the leaflet. The group was called the Disciples of the Fountain. It ran courses which promised an awesome mixture of self-discovery, psychic regeneration, and personal fulfilment, and seemed to make much use of local healing wells. Though the group was ostensibly Christian the leaflet had several enthusiastic references to the earth goddess.

As Georgia read she allowed herself to be drawn along with the crowd, which had continued to follow the group right up to the entrance to the Baths. When she reached the door she found herself moving almost automatically inside the foyer of the dignified Georgian building. She paused for a moment, diverted by the glories of the ornate plasterwork ceiling, then caught sight of the group again, this time buying tickets to enter the Baths.

Georgia looked at her watch. She mustn't be late for her meeting in the Pump Room restaurant with Zelda Stein, a visiting theatre director from the States who had good contacts in Britain, and might put some work her way. But there was still time to spare, and she was intrigued by the Disciples of the Fountain. Impulsively she moved to join the ticket queue.

Skirting a marble pillar, she began to thread along the outside of the room, where there were fewer people. Again she was diverted, this time by a stand advertising the Museum of Costume. The sheer panache of the Rifat Ozbek gypsy dress on display was irresistible. While she was making a quick sketch, the folder under her arm slipped. She caught it just in time, but a couple of designs slithered out across the parquet floor, and came to rest behind the stand.

As Georgia bent down an arm shot out and grabbed the designs. Startled, she looked up. Morrigan had reappeared, seemingly from thin air, and was leaning back on the wooden

4

bench which ran the length of the wall, his guitar by his side, leisurely studying the drawings.

She put out her hand but he held the drawings away, his gaze moving to her face.

'Not bad, not bad at all, Georgia Tremain,' he said.

At first she was startled that he should know her name, until she realised he'd read her signature on the sketches. She matched his assessing stare with one of her own. Seen close to he was older, his face more dissolute, but in a Byronic way which some women might find appealing. Georgia thought that the deepset eyes, long hooked nose, and springing black curls only faintly threaded with grey made him look exactly the wealthy international gypsy he was.

'I'll take those now,' she said in a brisk tone. She'd met people like him before in the theatre, people who thought that success gave them the right to behave exactly as they wished.

'What's your hurry?' he asked. 'There's no blessing in haste.' His mid-Atlantic voice was heavy with persuasion, like over-scented massage oil.

'There's no blessing in being late,' she returned. If they started to discuss religion she'd be here for hours.

'But you need blessing, don't you?' he remarked, almost casually.

She was staggered by his presumption.

'Most people do, I imagine. Will you give me those designs, please?'

'So you think it's a lucky guess? I've been watching you, Georgia Tremain. You looked self-confident enough in that crowd, but when you listened to the singing your face told me something quite different.'

'If you don't stop this Billy Graham spiel and hand them over now, I'll call a security guard.' Her voice was taut as she tried to conceal her frustration.

He didn't move.

'You're not happy, are you? Perhaps you need to talk to someone.' His glance flickered towards the leaflet she was still holding. 'If only you'd come to the group, tell them what's wrong, there's so much help they could give you.'

His voice had lowered, become confidential and cajoling, like a priest teasing out secrets in the confessional. He was trading on his charm, yet the subtle, undermining voice made her feel that if she surrendered to it even for a moment, all her self-confidence, held on to with such difficulty in the months since her divorce, might suddenly collapse. She tried to stay calm, telling herself her reaction was ridiculous.

'I'm quite capable of helping myself.' She snatched away the designs. 'Not that I need any help, particularly yours.'

He smiled, turned his palms upwards in a gesture of mock surrender, and unhurriedly got to his feet. His eyes were on a slightly lower level than hers. He seemed to be enjoying her reaction. Now he reminded her not of a priest, but of a mischievous Pan creating chaos among the world of mortals. The contrast was bewildering.

'I didn't say mine, I said *ours*. The Disciples of the Fountain have helped me. They can help you too.'

His expression became serious again.

'I've been there, to the deepest pit and back. I know what it's like. If you come to the group it'll give you all you need.'

This dramatic over-emphasis was turning her off even more. It reminded her too much of Blake, her ex-husband, when he was trying to persuade her that he couldn't help being unfaithful.

She slipped the designs safely into her folder.

'At least I've learned enough about life to realise that's impossible,' she said scornfully.

'So I was right. You *are* unhappy. It sounds to me as if you've had the wrong teacher. Everything's possible with a good one,' he said.

'Meaning you, I suppose? Look, can't you understand that I don't need you? I'm perfectly happy as I am.'

'I don't mean me, I mean Brighid, the leader of our group. She's a wonderful person, a mother to us all. I'm just a humble follower, like the rest. And if you're happy, why are you getting so riled?'

Arguing with him was like trying to catch a ball of mercury. Every time she got her grip on the debate it changed shape and slipped away.

'I'm not upset. I just don't like this kind of emotional persuasion. I've been had that way before, and I don't intend it to happen again.'

Now she was furious with herself. Somehow he'd already made her say too much.

He shook his head. 'It always happens again. You really do need us, you know.'

The hint of triumph in his smile made her angrier still.

'I can look after myself. And you can just back off and brainwash someone else.'

She turned on her heel, and almost ran towards the ticket queue. She no longer wanted to follow the Disciples of the Fountain, but at least if she went on a tour of the Baths it would effectively separate her from him.

Once she was safely surrounded by a horde of French schoolchildren, she looked back cautiously towards the statue. Morrigan was already talking to someone else, a young girl from the audience outside, who was gazing at him in fascination. She began to feel a little calmer, wondering how she could have let such a blatantly manipulative approach disturb her so.

The children, gaudy in their rainbow-coloured shell suits and T shirts, flocked ahead of her like parakeets. They slowed her progress through the colonnades framing the green waters of the Baths, and clogged the display galleries. She wasn't able to escape them until they lingered to throw their unwanted centimes into an artificial wishing pool, and by then the uneasy feeling left by her encounter with Morrigan had begun to fade.

The only part of the building she still hadn't seen was the source of the waters itself. She walked along the final gallery, and at the end, quite unexpectedly, came upon it and the Disciples of the Fountain together, just when she'd decided that they must have finished their tour long ago.

They were ranged in silence on a platform set slightly above an arched cavern whose dark mouth was veiled in shifting clouds of steam. From it water rushed into a stone channel encrusted with rusty orange deposits of iron, which shone beneath the flood like trapped sunshine. From there the spring cascaded over a ledge into a shallow pool fringed with a few hardy ferns.

7

The leader of the group stepped forward to the edge of the platform, leaned over and threw her flowers into the pool. Gravely she folded her hands in silent prayer. Morrigan had reappeared by her side, and stood gazing soulfully into her face. The only deity he appeared to be worshipping was Brighid.

For a moment Georgia was caught up in the sheer theatricality of the scene. The stately white-clad women, the grave young men, the strange light, and the hypnotic rushing of the waters merged to produce an atmosphere of total unreality. Even the schoolchildren erupting behind them on to the platform were caught up in the spell, and became silent, staring open-mouthed.

One of them, a girl of about ten with a brace on her teeth and a wispy plait, pressed a little too close to Brighid. Brighid didn't appear to notice, but when she finally emerged from her prayers, and started to lead the group from the platform, Morrigan's hand shot out. He grabbed the child's arm, and roughly manoeuvred her out of the way. When he released his grip Georgia could see the pressure marks of his fingers on her flesh.

Morrigan threw a vicious glance at the child, who was rubbing her arm and trying not to cry, and hurried away after the Disciples. The incident had happened so quickly that there was no time to stop him. Georgia was about to go and console the girl when she suddenly remembered her appointment.

She looked at her watch. It was a quarter past eleven. The highly organised Zelda would be fizzing with impatience, and might indeed already have left. Reluctantly leaving the child to her teacher, who had just caught up with the group, Georgia made hastily for an exit.

As Georgia paused on the threshold of the Pump Room, the dramatic change in her surroundings rapidly drove Morrigan and the Disciples of the Fountain from her mind.

She was back in Georgian England, in a large, elegant room hung with portraits of former Bath worthies. On a dais flanked by potted palms a trio played Mozart. Curtains of pink silk with sage green stripes were looped back from the long windows. At tables with cloths starched to an icy gloss a ballast of solid English citizens, firmly planted on Hepplewhite chairs, kept wary eyes on the tourists over their buns and coffee.

A voice like a slide of shale called to her. 'Hi, Georgia! Over here!'

A score of covert glances turned in its direction. Georgia knew the voice well. She'd heard it throughout last summer, the first and only summer of her marriage, while she and Blake were working for a theatre company in Baltimore. Zelda, a director renowned for her dramatic insight and superb cast control, had been one of the visiting artists.

She was sitting now in the middle of the crowded room, taking up the whole of a table for four, while the queue waiting for places shot her glances of envy and resignation. Georgia slid into the seat opposite, avoiding the disapproving eyes of a couple of matrons in box-pleats and buttoned-up collars at the next table. Being with Zelda in public was like being on a movie set.

Zelda's hair, wirier and more rampageous than ever, was only partly subdued by a couple of Spanish combs, and tinted a strange bronze shade. When Georgia last saw her it had been a rich brown plentifully scattered with grey. At least her eyes, in a face heavily tanned and sliding fast into middle age, were their usual piercing blue. Her blouse was adorned with a rope of amber beads. A deeply distressed denim jacket was slung over the back of her chair.

'You're looking great,' said Zelda affectionately, giving Georgia the airy kiss of the practised social greeter, and submerging her in a wave of Chanel 19. 'A lot better than you did in Baltimore.'

'Sorry I'm late,' said Georgia. 'I got sidetracked by some odd cult group in the courtyard.'

'A bunch of weirdos in bathrobes? I saw them too. Let me tell you, they're nothing compared to what goes on in California these days.'

She thrust a menu at Georgia.

'Let's order before we talk. My coffee level's down to zero. What'll you have?' She perused her own menu. 'Bath bun, scones, an Eccles cake? What's an Eccles cake, for Christ's sake? Some sort of crazy British cookie, I guess.'

She beckoned to the waiter who had just taken an order for more cakes from the women at the next table. The Pump Room specialised in young, good-looking staff, and he was no exception, tall and blond with narrow hips accentuated by his long white apron. The women bridled as he suddenly deserted them for Zelda.

'I'll have black coffee, and maybe a very small piece of shortbread wouldn't do any harm,' said Zelda. 'I need a sugar rush. It's been quite a week.'

'A cappuccino for me, please,' said Georgia, 'but nothing to eat.'

She shrugged off her cream linen jacket. Under it she was wearing a sleeveless silk camisole in a deep cinnamon brown. One of the shoulder straps had slipped down over a slender tanned arm. She pulled it up in a graceful, entirely unselfconscious gesture, and smiled encouragingly at the waiter, who was reeling under a fusillade of commands from Zelda. He was only about eighteen, and blushed violently, almost dropping his tray as he hurried off to the kitchen. Zelda looked after him with interest.

'Get that ass!' she said. 'But he's too young for me. I need my men fifty-something and longsighted these days, so they can't see the wrinkles.'

Georgia took off her hat, laying it on an empty chair. Her hair, in whose depths were mixed all the subtle colours of polished tortoiseshell, was cut in a sleek shoulder-length bob. Zelda looked quizzically at her.

'And how about you? I hope that two-timing husband of yours is history now. Is the divorce through yet?'

'Six months ago,' Georgia answered.

'How much alimony did you screw out of him?'

'Nothing to screw,' she said reluctantly. She hated talking about Blake, even to Zelda. 'We'd had no time to save, and the apartment was rented. But I did all right out of that TV mini-series contract while I was waiting for the divorce, and I had a good off-Broadway commission afterwards. My grandmother left me some money as well, and when I got home I decided to buy a place here in Bath. It's a good base.'

'I heard you'd set up your own business,' said Zelda. 'That's one of the reasons I wanted to see you. How're things doing?'

'Not too badly. Only small commissions at the moment, but I've been at it barely a month. It'll build up.' Georgia smiled brilliantly at Zelda. In the States she'd learned that confidence was half the battle. It was a hard-won lesson she didn't intend to forget, even though her bank balance was beginning to look like a vanishing oasis.

'Hmm,' said Zelda, with a long blue stare. 'Did you bring any of your latest designs?'

Georgia handed over the folder. One of the women at the next table tried to get a look, scattering crumbs from her second cake across the cloth.

Zelda leafed through the designs, studying each one carefully. Her hands were square and capable, ringless, the nails enamelled scarlet. On one wrist was a gold bangle as thick as a handcuff. She'd done well out of her own divorce a few years earlier. On the other wrist she was still wearing the ancient Donald Duck watch her son Howie had given her when he was small.

Georgia watched Zelda affectionately. Howie was the reason they'd become friends in the first place. A gangly twelve year old, he'd suddenly become stage-struck during Zelda's stay in Baltimore, and refused to go to summer camp. Instead he drove Zelda to distraction by hanging round the theatre, leaving a trail of Coke cans and blobs of chewing gum wherever he went. Georgia, remembering the interminable hours during her own childhood when she'd waited in vain for her own mother's affection, had taken pity on him and let him help in the costume shop. In so doing she'd earned Zelda's undying gratitude.

In return, when Georgia had just left Blake, and was feeling like a junked car which had gone through the crusher in a scrap yard, Zelda insisted Georgia stay with her till the end of the run. She spent long sessions listening with uncharacteristic patience while Georgia struggled to come to terms with the wreck of her marriage, braced her with affectionate humour, and finally rejoiced with her when she found a television job in California.

'What have you done with Howie this time?' Georgia asked. 'Is he with you?'

11

'He's crazy about sailing now, thank God. He's spending the summer with my parents on Lake Michigan.' Zelda carefully put the last design back in the folder, and looked up at her, smiling. 'These are great. Even better than the ones you did in Baltimore. How'd you like to work for me again?'

Georgia sighed. 'If only I could. But I can't go back to the States yet. It reminds me of things too much. This is a new start.'

'Not in the States. Here in Bath.'

'In Bath? But there's only one theatre, and that's rep. Stock theatre, I mean.' Georgia hurriedly substituted the American term.

'There are two now,' said Zelda.

There was a pause while the waiter brought their order. The music ended in a round of decorous applause.

'Jesus, listen to that clapping,' said Zelda. 'So damn' polite, and they played their hearts out. The audience'll have to do better at Merlinslade.'

'What's Merlinslade?' The name seemed familiar, but Georgia couldn't remember why.

'The theatre. I was telling you. Nico's setting up his own company there. Wait till you see it. It's only small, but pure Jacobean, designed by Inigo Jones, just a short drive from here, right on the tourist trail. And what do tourists want? Culture by the truckload, so that's what Nico and I intend to give them.'

'Real Inigo Jones? I don't believe it! And who is this Nico?'

'Christ, Georgia, you're so damned British sometimes. You have to believe this. Merlinslade is a country estate. The house goes back to the Tudors. It's one huge time-warp. It was owned by an old guy like little Lord Fauntleroy's grandpa, who hadn't changed anything since World War Two. As for Nico.' She shook her head and smiled. 'I could almost relax my fifty-something rule for him.'

'But who *is* he?' Georgia persisted warily.

'Nico Carwithen, the old guy's grandson. He's an actor, big in the RSC a few years back. You must know him.'

Georgia began to be impressed. 'I haven't met him, but I have seen him act. He did a stunning Cyrano before I went to the States. So has he inherited this Merlinslade?'

'Not Nico, but his older brother. Bron, he's called. There isn't much money around, and he's trying to make the estate pay its way. He comes over like General Custer at times, but Nico knows how to handle him. Nico could handle anyone.'

Georgia started to laugh.

'Have you gone completely crazy, Zelda? No money, and in England of all places? You always said you hated the climate here. You'd never survive the winter. What brought this on?'

'Well, I don't want it to get around too much,' said Zelda, leaning towards Georgia confidentially, yet scarcely bothering to lower her voice, 'but I'm undergoing severe menopausal stress.'

The women at the next table abandoned all pretence at eating. Their eyes bulged.

Georgia tried to control her smile.

'You won't think it's a bundle of laughs when it hits you,' said Zelda. 'Didn't your mother tell you anything about it?'

'My mother was never around long enough to tell me or Chloe things like that. She did give me a sex education book once, but I was the one who told Chloe about life, love and the universe. I thought HRT sorted out the menopause these days, anyway?'

'I should be so lucky. It had side effects for me. And why should I fuel the drug companies? I decided to go it alone, but the goddamned power surges began to wear me down.'

Georgia was puzzled. 'Power surges?'

'Hot flashes – hot flushes I guess you say over here. But power surge is the new name. It's more positive.'

The women at the next table were transfixed. Georgia gave them a quelling stare and turned back to Zelda, who was shaking out a cigarette from a packet of Camels.

'I just wasn't functioning at top capacity,' she said. 'I reckoned it was a case of shape up or ship out before my work suffered and the critics started slamming me. My gynaecologist said things would settle down in about a year, so I decided to take a sabbatical and look for work over here for while, where things go a little slower. I was sight-seeing when I met up with Nico at the Bath Hilton.'

'And what are you doing with Howie for the rest of the year?'

13

'Conrad's having him. It's about time he took some responsibility.'

Conrad was Zelda's ex-husband. He made hugely successful TV commercials, and had run off a few years earlier with a model from a chocolate advertisement.

'Well, it's great news that you'll be over here for a while,' said Georgia, smiling at Zelda affectionately, 'but you'd better buy some British underwear. I don't suppose Inigo Jones put in central heating.'

'How I am just now I won't notice the cold. Winter can't come too soon for me. And Nico's better than any therapy.'

The women at the next table gathered up their handbags and departed in an aura of disapproval.

'At last!' said Zelda. 'I thought we'd never be able to get down to business. Now I can tell you the deal I have in mind.' Suddenly she was completely serious, lowering her voice for the first time, and leaning towards Georgia across the table. 'A year's contract, designing the costumes for six plays at Merlinslade. I've signed up a young Irish set designer, but he's not free just yet, so I want you to do the sets for the first play as well. How about that for an offer you can't refuse? We open in September, which gives you plenty of time to set up a permanent costume workshop for the company, engage staff, and suss out the mechanics of the scenery. The theatre's beautiful, but not easy backstage.'

'Hold on a moment,' said Georgia, trying to absorb this battery of information. 'You're just a bit too fast for me. What about cash? You said there wasn't much around.'

'Nico's venturing most of his capital, and he's done all right for himself. He's worked on some major movies over the last few years. I'm taking a nominal salary. My alimony's more than enough for me, anyway. I really believe in this project, Georgia, and it'll be great if we can get it off the ground. Your payment wouldn't be huge, but it'd be solid, certainly enough for you to live on. And you should have time for small commissions on the side. It'd set you up nicely.'

'Maybe,' said Georgia. Her voice was cautious. The Inigo Jones theatre could be a wreck backstage, and once she'd agreed to join Zelda there'd be no escaping the whirlwind. She didn't intend to endanger her fledgling business working for a company which might go broke after six months. 'What's the first play?' she asked.

'*The Tempest*,' said Zelda. 'Nico especially wanted to open with something from the same period as the theatre.'

Georgia was instantly tempted. She'd always longed to dress Shakespeare's last play. Quickly she reviewed the plot in her mind. All the action took place on a desert island, where Prospero, the deposed Duke of Milan, had been marooned for many years with his daughter, Miranda, who had no experience of the ordinary world until shipwrecked outsiders arrived. The only other inhabitants of the island were the spirit Ariel, and the savage Caliban, both servants of Prospero.

The restricted setting would be perfect for a small stage. *The Tempest* had a magical atmosphere, wonderful effects, and the added bonus of a masque within the play itself. She'd not designed any sets in the States – in a large company they were usually contracted separately – but Zelda knew that, and presumably Nico was trying to do things as cheaply as possible. All the same, if it really was a Jacobean theatre, and she was stuck with the original stage machinery, the sets could be a nightmare . . .

'Come to Merlinslade and check things out for yourself,' said Zelda. 'Believe me, the whole place is to die for. I'll be there with Nico tomorrow. He'll fill you in on the actual payments. He saw those costumes you did for *Royal Hunt of the Sun* in Baltimore. He's your biggest fan. And you have to lay your luck on the line sometimes.'

'I've been doing that too much lately,' said Georgia. 'I've got to make my life work from now on.'

'Merlinslade's the perfect place for a fresh start,' Zelda encouraged her.

'You wouldn't ask for some minimalist modern dress version of *The Tempest*, would you?' Georgia asked. 'If the setting's as good as you say, it ought to be costume of the same period.'

'That's exactly what Nico and I want. You'll have a ball. And wait till you hear about the other plays. Let's order some more coffee, and I'll give you a full run-down.'

Zelda in professional mode was as unmenopausal as Mac the

Knife. Georgia finally exited into the Abbey courtyard nearly an hour later, head reeling from too much coffee and trying to concentrate on Zelda's plans.

'I'll fill you in on the rest when I see you tomorrow at Merlinslade,' said Zelda. 'You're going to love it.'

'Why don't you come and have lunch at the flat?' Georgia asked impulsively. 'I've just finished decorating. You'd be my first official guest.'

'Could I take a rain check on that? I must go back to the Hilton and get under a cold shower. My hypothalamus is acting up again, and I've got someone from *Vanity Fair* interviewing me at two.'

Georgia walked with Zelda as far as the entrance to the covered market, and said goodbye to her there. She watched her set off briskly in the direction of the Hilton, then turned into the covered market, pausing for a moment in the outer corridor to look at bolts of fabric and check through some cards of unusual buttons.

Once under the glass dome of the main hall she rashly bought an armful of tawny iris, and from a wooden-countered booth lined with lacquered storage tins, half a pound of jasmine and Lapsang tea. She was tempted at another stall by a punnet of early raspberries, succumbed, and finally escaped through the back exit.

She dashed across the road for a quick fix of the view above the Avon. The triple-arched bridge whose Adam façade so serenely spanned the green waters of the river was the nearest thing she knew to Venice in England. A few minutes later she had crossed it, passed the fountain in Laura Place, and was walking down the stately Georgian length of Great Pulteney Street.

As usual she was warmed by a sense of coming home, a feeling she'd never had in the impersonal service apartment in Baltimore. Her new home, which the estate agent optimistically described as a garden flat, was in reality a large, light semi-basement at the bottom of a flight of area steps. But it did have a back garden, and a cellar which Georgia was slowly turning into a studio. Best of all, it had been cheap, bought from a young executive who was desperate to take up a new job in London. She'd been able to fund her purchase with the proceeds from the sale of her grandmother's house, which she'd shared with Chloe.

All the way back to the flat Georgia had been unable to stop thinking of *The Tempest*. Even though she hadn't made any decision about the Merlinslade project she longed to sit at her drawing board in the ordered peace of her new home, and capture on paper the initial ideas crowding into her brain. She paused to admire the delicate ironwork tracery in the fanlight over the main front door, pushed open the gate at the top of the area steps, and began to descend into the courtyard.

She stopped abruptly. Someone was waiting for her. She stared. There on the bottom step, smoking, her feet propped up on a pot of pink geraniums, wearing the black Doc Martens that made her look like Minnie Mouse, was Chloe.

Dumped around her were an army surplus kitbag, a radio cassette player, and an old leather suitcase. She looked up at the footfall, and smiled the tentative, trusting smile which told Georgia instantly that she was in trouble.

'Hi, Georgy,' she said. 'I've come to stay.'

Chapter 2

'Why are you here? What's happened? What's wrong?' Georgia demanded, rushing down the remaining steps.

'Nothing's wrong.' Chloe slowly stood up, stubbing out her cigarette against the wall. 'I just need some space, that's all. I thought I'd crash out with you for a bit.'

'What do you *mean*, you need space?' asked Georgia. Chloe might appear nonchalant, but her hand wasn't quite steady on the cigarette. 'You can't just walk out of school. Do they know where you are? And don't throw that away here. I hate seeing fag ends in the yard.'

'You're such a control freak sometimes,' said Chloe. 'I thought you'd be pleased to see me.' Nevertheless she took a crumpled matchbox from her pocket, and with a martyred look stowed the cigarette end inside. 'They won't be worried yet at school. I got the morning off to go to the dentist. I needed to see you so much.'

She smiled hopefully at Georgia. The dark hair which framed her face was threaded with an assortment of tiny beaded plaits, but her wan face belied their jaunty effect. Georgia tried to harden her heart.

'That's not a good enough reason, and you know it. You should have talked to me on the phone first before doing something so drastic. I'm trying to start a business, you know. I can't just drop everything because you need some space.'

'I thought you'd be more pleased to see me than this,' said Chloe sulkily. 'But all right, I'm sorry I didn't warn you.'

'Then in that case you'd better come in and tell me what's happened,' said Georgia, trying to keep her voice brisk.

Chloe abandoned her nonchalant pose, and flung her arms round her sister. 'I knew you'd understand. You always do.'

Georgia, automatically returning the hug, and bracing herself for whatever revelations might follow, instantly detected that Chloe had lost weight. She stood back and looked at her suspiciously. 'Something's gone really wrong, hasn't it?'

'Well maybe, just a little,' Chloe answered, avoiding her gaze. 'But please, please, don't be angry again until I've explained. It's horrible when you get all steamed up as well. I've had enough of that at school.'

Georgia opened the front door. 'All right,' she said. 'But let's get it clear right away that you're not staying for long. I've a business to run, and you have A levels to do.'

Chloe followed Georgia into the hall passage, which she'd painted white and carpeted with grey-green seagrass matting. One wall was covered with a Chinese patterned paper of tiny scarlet birds flitting among wintery black branches, which Georgia had found in a junk shop.

Chloe followed her into the living room. She dumped her gear in the middle of the floor, and gazed around admiringly.

'You've made this place really, really smart. Lucky you, living here. And what a sofa! I love it!'

For a moment Georgia allowed herself a satisfied look round the room. It was spacious and surprisingly well lit. The curtains at the French windows into the garden were unbleached linen. She'd sanded the floor to the colour of clear honey and put down a pale yellow modern kelim scribbled with a grey design. The sofa, a vast four-seater with scrolled arms and a bow-shaped back, could have come straight from a Noel Coward play, and had been acquired in a mad moment at an auction. She'd used grey-and-white-striped mattress ticking to replace the original tattered satin cover, and loaded it with cushions in deep cranberry reds and thunder blues.

Chloe threw herself on to it, bouncing up and down a couple of times before kicking off her shoes and tucking her feet under her. She pulled a packet of cigarettes and a metal lighter out of her jacket pocket, and caught Georgia's eye.

'Just one,' she pleaded. 'Otherwise I eat too much.'

'Not even one,' said Georgia firmly. 'I don't want the flat full of smoke.'

Reluctantly Chloe put the cigarettes away, pulled off her jacket, and dropped it over the side of the sofa. She wore a drooping black cotton skirt with a fringed hem, and a baggy sleeveless T shirt which accentuated the thinness of her arms.

'I don't see why you should be so scratchy about it,' she said. 'Everyone smokes at school. I had to join in. They think I'm weird enough already.'

This sounded like one of Chloe's usual exaggerations. Georgia decided to ignore it. 'You certain don't need to lose weight,' she said.

Chloe looked down at herself, and grimaced.

'Yes I do, I'm gross.'

Georgia's anxiety increased. She decided to see what happened when she offered Chloe some food.

'Well, I'm going to have some lunch, anyway. Wouldn't you like some too?'

'Not, especially, but you go ahead. Don't mind me,' said Chloe. 'That's a stunning chair. It isn't really Charles Rennie Mackintosh, is it?'

Georgia glanced at the wooden armchair opposite the sofa. The high pointed back was painted ash grey with a design of curving black and mauve tulips. It was uncomfortable even with its velvet cushions, but she kept it because she'd made it for her first play at college. She dragged her mind away from that light-hearted production of *Mrs Warren's Profession* and focused on Chloe again. She was sitting neatly curled up, and with her green eyes and small pointed face looked as complacent as a cat who'd just settled down for the night.

'Don't change the subject,' Georgia said sharply. 'How can I not mind if you don't eat properly?'

She went into the small kitchen which looked out over tubs of flowers and a rampaging fig tree in the front courtyard. The original kitchen flooring had been scuffed vinyl, now replaced with terracotta tiles. There was an old built-in dresser which she'd spent hours dragging to a subtle shade of sea green, and a square table painted a glossy navy blue.

Quickly she assembled some pâté, a flat loaf of ciabatta bread, a couple of lettuce hearts and vinaigrette dressing. When she put the tray on a low table in front of the sofa, Chloe paled.

'Pâté! Oh no! It's the worst thing. It's bound to have liver in it, and liver's a mega toxin trap. I'm a vegetarian now. Didn't I tell you?'

'No, you didn't, and if you remember, I wasn't expecting you anyway,' said Georgia, wavering between deepening anxiety and irritation. 'If you'd warned me I'd have bought something different.'

She went back into the kitchen, and found some hummus at the back of the fridge.

'When did you become a vegetarian?' she asked Chloe, as she put the dish down on the table.

'Only this term. But the veggie food at school is yuk. That's why I need a break.'

'And that's the only reason?'

'Well, no, not just that. It's such a bloody heavy scene generally there. The other kids are going into hysterics about mock A levels already, and what's it all for in the end? There aren't any jobs anyway.'

'That's not the point,' said Georgia, thinking as she'd thought so many times before during Chloe's crises that this should be her parents' responsibility. Because Georgia was eleven years older than her sister, people assumed too often that she'd look after her. 'You need exams to get into art school. It'll be worth it in the end.'

She wondered how many more platitudes she'd have to trot out, when all she wanted to do was give Chloe a good shaking. Art school would be exactly right for her. Ever since she was a child she'd been interested in jewellery, making exotic necklaces from seeds picked up in the forest, and brooches of painted clay and wood. Lately she'd produced some stunning designs in enamel and silver.

'I suppose so,' said Chloe. 'But I honestly can't hack it at school for another year. I thought I could stay here with you, and go to a tech for my second year of A levels.'

Georgia only just managed to conceal her dismay. She was

expecting to have Chloe for part of the school holidays, but her sister in permanent residence was quite a different matter. Now especially, when she was starting to feel confident that she could handle her new life, and with a big commission on the horizon, Georgia wanted the flat to herself.

'I don't think that's a good idea,' she said gently. 'I need my space too. I really think you ought to stay at school. Let me ring the head and sort things out.'

Chloe looked at her piteously. She had a way of letting her eyes fill with tears, yet not brim over.

'It was just so great when you came back from the States, like a sort of miracle. I thought everything'd be all right at last. But it's the same as ever – nobody wants me. The olds couldn't give a toss.'

'Of course the olds want you. You know Dad and Karen asked you to live with them in Oz. Mother was quite willing to let you go.'

'You know I can't stand Karen. Phoney old cow! How could he choose a second wife like her? It was awful spending Christmas with them. And you bet Mother would have let me stay. Don't look so disapproving. You know exactly what I mean.'

Georgia did know what Chloe meant, though she couldn't say so. Beatrice, their mother, gave so much time to the African rain forest where she'd done her research for so many years, and which she was now trying desperately to save, that there was never enough to spare for her children.

'Of course she minds. You know how keen she is for you to go to college.'

'Yes, because then she won't have to think about me at all. Come on, Georgy, you know exactly what she's like, and you've had to put up with it for a lot longer than me.'

Their mother was a botanist, and her obsession with the rain forest had overshadowed their lives for as long as Georgia could remember. Her long absences in the field had contributed as much to the breakdown of their parents' marriage as the inability of Jim, their father, a busy surgeon at the African university hospital, to acknowledge that his wife's work was as important as his own.

After Chloe's birth and the divorce, when Beatrice had insisted on taking her daughters with her to the university forest research station, they'd received along with the other staff children a lack-lustre education from a series of tutors. Then, three years ago, when the forest was threatened with felling, their mother became completely absorbed in a conservation campaign. Chloe was sent to a cheerfully inefficient expatriate boarding school in the regional capital, where she got by on the minimum of work. The previous September she'd come to England to study for A levels, but had never seemed to settle down.

'I'm afraid she's not going to change. You have to learn to handle it.'

Though Georgia tried to sound bracing, she was thinking guiltily that at least she'd had her grandmother to help her when she went to school in England to do O levels. Grandma Baines, a widow, had lived in the unfashionable part of Bath, in a snug Victorian terraced house in Twerton. Life with her had been a revelation. Georgia returned home from the local school every day to find tea on the table, an atmosphere of calm, and a grandma who was gratifyingly anxious to hear about her latest exploits.

Chloe didn't answer. She'd only nibbled at a corner of bread and a couple of lettuce leaves. Now she was nervously fiddling with the beads in a braid, staring at Georgia with bush-baby eyes, and looking like an advertisement for *Les Misérables*.

Georgia sighed, thinking that if Grandma hadn't died, none of this would have happened. She'd just have to deal with Chloe as best she could, and get her back to school as soon as possible.

'All right, you can stay while I sort things out, but you'd better make up your mind that it's going to be for tonight only,' she said in a brisk tone. 'I'll show you where to put your bags, and then I must ring the school.'

She left a miraculously smiling Chloe inspecting the small spare room. It looked out on a sunken side alley overhung with brambles which ran down to Sophia Mews. There were a few basic pieces of furniture, and Georgia had slapped some emulsion over the fussy wallpaper until she could concentrate on redecorating more imaginatively.

Brandon Lodge, Chloe's school in the next county, hadn't even registered that she'd not returned from her dental appointment. Beatrice, actually having managed to notice Chloe's talent for making jewellery, and wanting to get her into A level courses in England with the least amount of resistance, had been attracted by the school's easygoing atmosphere and the excellent art department.

'We wouldn't have checked on her until evening roll-call,' said the headmistress. At the other end of the line Georgia could hear shouts from a game of tennis drifting in through an open window. 'We trust our sixth formers to behave sensibly.'

'I'm still not sure why she ran away, so it seems best for me to keep her here for tonight to sort things out. I'll put her on a train back to school first thing in the morning,' said Georgia, desperate to get the matter settled.

The head's voice took on a tone Georgia had heard many times before from people who were having difficulty with Chloe.

'I'm glad to have this chance to talk to you, Miss Tremain. It's so difficult to get any kind of lead on the best way to deal with your sister when both parents are so far away. I've felt for some time that she might be developing into one of our few failures.'

'What do you mean, failure?' said Georgia indignantly, forgetting that she ought to placate the headmistress rather than cross swords with her. 'She's bursting with talent. I think she's done marvellously well, considering her upbringing. And anyway, isn't the school supposed to specialise in helping people like Chloe?'

'Unfortunately Chloe came to us distinctly short on inter-personal skills, which so far she's made no attempt to improve. She has problems which she should have worked through long ago.'

The headmistress's voice deepened as she assumed the soothing tone of an air hostess about to issue a warning of severe turbulence ahead.

'Chloe still craves the attention she never had from two very busy parents. She tries to get it from her peers, but not surprisingly that hasn't worked. I must tell you that I've been having doubts for some time about the wisdom of her continuing with us.'

25

'But she's got to continue with you!' said Georgia, now thoroughly alarmed. 'She's only a year away from A levels. In any case you really should be discussing Chloe with my mother, not me. I'm not responsible for her.'

'It's almost impossible to get in touch with your mother on the phone, and she usually takes several weeks to answer letters, as you probably know. One very simple solution does occur to me, though. I wonder if you could possibly consider taking her in yourself, assuming you have the accommodation of course? There shouldn't be any difficulty over her completing her A levels locally, and I do get the impression that she's very fond of you. An older sibling can often do far more than teachers or a parent to help someone of Chloe's age towards a more mature attitude.'

With a sensation of panic, Georgia saw her independence disappearing just when she'd begun to enjoy it at last. Firmly she told herself that she wasn't in the market for anyone's emotional blackmail. She'd had more than enough of that during her marriage.

'It's absolutely out of the question. I've just started my own business here. I simply don't have the time to devote to her.'

There was a long pause at the other end. Georgia could hear a bell shrilling in the background. When the headmistress spoke again she sounded tired.

'Chloe simply needs firm but loving background support while she tries to establish her identity in the grown-up world. Unfortunately in a boarding school it isn't possible to give her that attention non-stop.'

Georgia resisted the temptation to tell the head of the hours she'd spent when she was younger trying to give Chloe just such support. Until she left college, and sometimes even after that, her mother had expected her to spend her vacations supervising Chloe. When her sister was small it hadn't been a chore, for she was an enchanting child. Chloe the adolescent could be enchanting too, but had become adept at self-dramatisation, playing her various minders off against each other in a succession of attempts to gain her mother's attention.

'I think she may be worried about something specific,' Georgia said, in a determined effort to put the ball back in the head's court. 'Have there been any particular problems at school?'

There was a pause at the other end of the line. 'Not what I'd call a problem.' The head's voice was cautious now. 'The sixth formers do tend to worry about A levels, but that's not surprising in today's economic climate, and Chloe didn't seem especially anxious. She had a sudden fixation on one of the boys recently, the sort of thing that often happens. I thought she'd worked through it. She appeared to accept the situation when he started going out with another girl.'

'Yet she's lost a lot of weight,' said Georgia. 'Didn't that concern you?'

'It didn't seem to be an undue weight loss, and many of the pupils have food fads. We try not to give eating problems too much attention. It often makes them worse.'

'She's smoking too. She never did that before.'

The head gave a resigned laugh. 'They have permission to smoke in the sixth form – quite frankly it's impossible to stop them – and in any case it's the least of our problems. I wonder if we could try a compromise? It's Thursday now. Keep Chloe till the end of the week, and see how you get on with her. If you genuinely still feel by Sunday that you can't cope, we'll take her back and try again.'

Reluctantly Georgia agreed. She couldn't afford to seem too unco-operative or the head might refuse to take Chloe back at all. They chatted a little longer, and she returned to the spare room with a feeling of deep unease.

Chloe had lost no time in making it her own. The patchwork coverlet Georgia had helped her make during an interminable summer holiday lay on the bed. Her aromatherapy essences were neatly lined up on a chest of drawers. Gérard Depardieu smouldered from a poster on the wall, and wreaths of necklaces hung from the brass bed rail along with her dearest possession, a genuine Edwardian parasol picked up in a London street market. The general effect of inconsequential charm was only slightly marred by the clothes she'd scattered over the floor in search of her treasures.

Chloe herself sat on the bed, clutching an ancient and beloved stuffed toy, a dog with floppy ears named Wooster because of his extreme soppiness. She looked up apprehensively at Georgia's entrance, forgetting to make any attempt at sophistication. Georgia tried to harden her heart.

'Well, that's settled then,' she said, knowing very well that nothing had been settled at all. 'You can stay until the weekend while we talk things over, but you have to go straight back to school on Sunday night.'

Chloe cast Wooster to one side.

'You're an angel! I won't bother you at all! I'll be so helpful, you won't know how you ever did without me.'

'Good,' said Georgia. 'So I hope this means you'll finish your lunch?'

Chloe leapt off the bed. 'I was going to all along. That hummus looked wonderful. Come on, Georgy, what are you waiting for?'

Chloe was asleep, cocooned in her duvet, when Georgia peered in on her after breakfast next morning. The radio sang unheeded on the floor by the bed, and her clothes were draped like prayer flags about the room. She'd spent the previous afternoon wandering round the shops, and the evening watching television. In spite of her words earlier on she'd eaten hardly anything.

Georgia had tried to phone Beatrice, but the operator on the field station switchboard said she was away for a couple of weeks. Georgia's father, at the end of a poor telephone link to Sydney, and on his way to a long operating list, said exasperatedly that he didn't see how he could do more than offer Chloe a home. In the end, desperate to get on to paper the initial ideas for *The Tempest* still seething in her head, Georgia had with combined guilt and relief postponed any immediate attempt to solve Chloe's problems, and firmly shut herself away in her studio.

But though her drawing pad and notebook were tucked in a folder by her side as she drove out of Bath to meet Zelda and Nico at Merlinslade, she'd purposely not brought the rough designs made the previous evening. She needed to see the theatre itself before she revealed any ideas. And besides, she still hadn't decided whether to take the commission.

Whatever happened, her journey wouldn't be wasted, for she was meeting Esther Hallen, a school friend she hadn't seen for

several years, for lunch. When she'd checked Zelda's instructions
for getting to the theatre she realised why the name of the estate
was familiar. Merlinslade village was where Esther now lived.
After leaving college she had worked at a mission in Bristol
where she'd joined the movement for the ordination of women.
She'd since become a deacon, and now looked after a scattered
country parish.

Though it was still cool, with a light breeze, the sky was a
steady, settled blue. When Georgia at last turned off the main
road into an undulating landscape of deep wooded combes and
limestone downland, she stopped to put down the hood of the
car, an old Triumph bought from the previous owner of the flat.

After a triumphant struggle with the mechanism she rolled up
the sleeves of her white cotton shirt, and undid another button at
the neck. With it she was wearing a favourite waistcoat made of
old brocade, and jeans and espadrilles in case she had to clamber
about backstage.

The side road unfolded for another couple of miles. Eventually
she passed a garage and car wash with busily whirling brushes on
the outskirts of Merlinslade, and a couple of minutes later arrived
at the village green. There was nothing modern here. It looked
like a tourist's dream of old England. The only sign of life was a
cleaner polishing the windows of a pub called The Mortal Man.

The turning to the estate ran by its side, and soon narrowed
into a long winding lane. The banks on either hand, twice as high
as the car, were thick with foxgloves and pink campion. The hazel
hedges crowning them had once been neatly laid, but now
sprouted wildly like green fireworks, almost meeting overhead.

As the car bumped along Georgia caught sight of a figure
ahead which seemed vaguely familiar. A woman in Wellingtons
with a long white dress hitched up to her knees was busily
gathering plants, inspecting each one with intense concentration
then laying it tenderly in a trug over her arm. It was Brighid. She
pressed herself back into the hedge as the car edged past, giving
Georgia a singularly sweet smile and holding up her open hand as
if bestowing a blessing.

Georgia guessed the group must live near Merlinslade. It was
odd, all the same, to meet Brighid again so soon. Georgia

wondered where Morrigan was. She couldn't imagine him traipsing along the hedgerows in muddy Wellingtons. For a near fatal moment the thought made her lose her concentration. She slammed on the brakes just in time to avoid a car parked carelessly askew in a passing place.

It was a car quite unlike her own, an open grey convertible with a heavy roll bar, grey plush seats like armchairs, and a stereo pouring forth Tammy Wynette over the English countryside. Grinding perilously to a halt by its side, she saw that the man behind the wheel was studying a copy of *The Face* magazine. A can of Budweiser was propped on top of the dashboard, and his legs were draped across the passenger seat. He had his back to Georgia, but swung round at the screech of her brakes. She'd pulled up so close to him that she was reflected in his mirrored sunglasses. As he slowly removed them she realised that it was Morrigan.

Seen in the strong sunshine he looked even more dissolute. His were the sort of overstated looks that did best on a stage. Unavoidably their eyes met. She'd been going to yell at him, but was so startled by the encounter and his sudden look of recognition that she accelerated wildly away, almost scraping the side of his car.

In a moment she was round the next bend and roaring along the lane, caught up in illogical panic in case he followed. After a minute or two, when she heard no engine behind her, she made herself slow down, and began to realise with wry amusement that what had really startled her was the way he'd seemed to appear in response to her thoughts. It was almost as if he'd been expecting her, when in reality he was simply waiting in comfort to chauffeur the toiling Brighid.

By the time the lane began to run alongside a high brick wall she'd almost regained her self-possession, and the need to find the turning into the Merlinslade estate soon forced her to file the incident at the back of her mind.

'Keep your eyes open as soon as you get to the boundary wall,' Zelda had said. 'You can't miss the entrance. You'll see a couple of crazy birds straight out of *Jurassic Park*.'

The birds, a pair of stone griffins, were unmistakable,

brooding beneath lichen-covered wings on either side of wrought-iron gates much in need of a coat of paint. As Georgia drew up an elderly man who seemed to be expecting her stumped on bandy legs round the side of a crumbling lodge. He unlocked the gates with a key worthy of a medieval dungeon, and waved her through, raising his cap in salute. Georgia wouldn't have been surprised to see a rosy-cheeked milkmaid bobbing a curtsey in the background.

The first part of the drive was lined with gloomy thickets of rhododendrons so impenetrable that they could have been growing in their native Himalayas. The banks of leaves were splashed like sixties wallpaper with blowsy pink flowers, whose petals were just beginning to carpet the drive. When Georgia opened the car window the scent of damp earth and rotting vegetation reminded her of her mother's rain forest.

She trundled on at a sober pace in case there were more aged retainers about, and began to curve round a gentle bend. As she emerged into the straight she almost hit a bike spreadeagled across the drive a few yards ahead of her. A boy was crouched over it, trying to prise off a tyre.

She just had time to slam on the brakes, but the shock of this second near collision was so great that she stalled the engine completely. The boy stared up at her. He looked about twelve, wearing jeans and a faded T shirt. The only sound came from dew dripping from the leaves, and the faint creaking of branches among the thickets.

He stood up, a tyre lever clutched in his hand. He was tall and gangly, his face just starting to change from child to man. Shock and defensiveness were mingled in his expression. He opened his mouth and shut it again.

'Do you have a death wish?' Georgia enquired.

'I wasn't expecting anyone, was I?' he said in an injured voice.

'Well, I certainly wasn't,' replied Georgia, 'so perhaps you wouldn't mind moving your bike out of the way.'

Though his hair had been cropped in a fashionably aggressive cut, his expression was still defensive. He stared at her for a few seconds longer, then finally lugged the bike to the verge.

'Is that all right?' he said, with a put-upon look.

Georgia relented, remembering how absorbed she used to become in her drawings when she was young, and how she hated being nagged. 'Do you need any help? Would you like a lift up to the house?' she asked.

This time he blushed when she spoke to him, then forgot his self-consciousness as he took in her car.

'Wow, is that a TR4?'

'Exactly right,' said Georgia. 'Well done.'

She'd always wanted a sports car, and the offer of the Triumph had been too good to miss, though it was so old that the floor was a patchwork of welding.

'Can I give you a lift somewhere?' she persisted.

He came towards her, wiping his hands on his jeans, which were a mass of carefully engineered rips. He walked round the car, ran his hand lovingly along a tail fin, and gave her a smile which transformed his face.

'That's a really sound motor,' he said seriously. 'A ride'd be well wicked. But there's no room for the bike, and my dad'll lose his marbles if I leave it here.' He studied her face again. 'If you're going up to the house maybe I'll see you later.'

'Maybe you will,' said Georgia. 'But I've come to talk about the theatre. I don't know how long it'll take.'

'Oh, the theatre.' He gave a dismissive shrug. 'My dad never stops going on about it. That, and the estate.'

'Who's your dad? Nico?' asked Georgia, thinking he hadn't sounded much like a candidate for fatherhood.

'No, Nico's my uncle. He's brilliant. My dad is Bron Carwithen.'

'And what's your name?'

He became solemn again, and stuck out his hand. 'Sorry. He'd really let me have it for not telling you who I am. I'm Ned Carwithen – Edmund really – what a crap name to stick on anyone, but Dad did it to please my great-grandfather.'

'And I'm Georgia – Georgia Tremain,' she said, formally shaking Ned's hand and thinking that Bron Carwithen, so concerned with convention, must be a dismal father. At least her own parents, whatever their shortcomings, weren't like that.

'Great to meet you.' Ned beamed at her. He went over to the

32

bike and heaved it upright. 'I'll start pushing back now, then I'm sure to see you at coffee time. Nico never misses it. He says coffee runs in his veins.'

He trudged off down the drive, head stuck doggedly forward. Georgia waved at him as she drove past, glad that Nico at least sounded normal, or she might well have turned round and gone straight back to Bath.

After another hundred yards the rhododendrons thinned, then gave way to tranquil parkland dotted with clumps of magnificent old trees. The chestnuts were so laden with waxen-flowered candles that their lowest branches almost touched the ground. Away from the verge the grass had not been cut. It was knee-high, heavy with dew, and tangled with a profusion of wild flowers. There were yellow-enamelled buttercups, sturdy spires of bee and pyramid orchis, ox-eye daisies, and rising over them all, cow-parsley like a delicate veil. A couple of shire horses, heavy fetlocks fringed with long white hair, grazed peacefully beneath a stand of oaks. Zelda had been right. It was exactly like entering a time-warp into rural England as it used to be.

As Georgia drove on through the park a manor house of pale gold stone slowly revealed itself through the trees, couched under an escarpment that rose steeply to open downs. The face of the escarpment was clothed in woods whose dense foliage, blue in the morning haze, looked like the billows of an island sea.

She came to a stone bridge over a stream running between banks of balsam and loosestrife. The water meadows on either side were criss-crossed with drainage ditches, now choked with reeds. She drove on down an avenue of limes whose fresh green leaves glistened in the sun, becoming increasingly astonished that all this splendour could have remained hidden so near to Bath, and have been kept to itself by one family for so long.

The drive ended at an ornate arched gateway, which gave on to a courtyard in front of the house. The long façade, an easy amalgam of Tudor and Jacobean architecture, was topped by a graceful curved pediment above a series of mullioned windows. Doves strutted on the stone-tiled roof. The front door was carved with panels of grapes and pomegranates. By its side the grey trunk of a wisteria twisted towards the eaves like an Indian rope trick, before cascading back towards the ground in a waterfall of mauve blossom.

Georgia got out of the car. The sun was warm on her back, the courtyard filled with the peaceful cooing of the doves. She was still taking in the scene as the front door swung open, and a man appeared. Zelda was close behind in jeans and a red T shirt, with a loudly checked tweed jacket flung over her shoulders.

The man paused. He seemed to pose unconsciously for a moment, one arm resting above his head against the doorway, and then he ran lightly down the steps towards her. A voluminous tan suede coat flowed about him. Georgia recognised his face at once. It was Nico Carwithen.

Chapter 3

Nico was about thirty, not much taller than Georgia, with a thickset body which would need constant exercise as he grew older. But now the lightness of his movements and his natural flamboyance were what instantly caught the eye. He had dark blond hair brushed back from a face not particularly remarkable in any way, though on stage it was as malleable as Plasticine to the demands of the character he was playing.

'It's great to meet you at last. Zelda's been singing your praises for days – not that she needed to. I managed to catch your *Coriolanus* in the states. I thought it was terrific.'

The smile he gave her was wide, open, almost clown-like. His eyes were as observant as a juggler's.

'I hope I'm not too late,' she said. 'I kept wanting to slow down and stare.'

Zelda came up by Nico's side. 'Vintage nostalgia, isn't it? I knew you'd be hooked.'

'Let's hope it hooks the audiences too,' said Nico. His voice had a slight huskiness, as distinctive as coffee spiced with cardamom.

'I met your nephew in the drive,' said Georgia. 'He was mending his bike.'

'That sounds like Ned. He's machinery mad. At the moment he thinks we're totally unreasonable for not giving him driving lessons in the grounds.'

'I couldn't see the theatre. Is it part of the house?'

'No, it stands on its own at the back. I thought we'd go and have a look at it before we get down to business. You'll want to know what's involved before you decide whether to join us. We can have some coffee later.'

Nico shepherded them across the courtyard, and through a gate in a high yew hedge. They began to walk down a terrace at the side of the house. He chatted easily yet very much to a purpose. Hidden in all the relaxed talk was an interview, conducted in the most subtle way, but an interview all the same. Georgia had been expecting it, but still found herself reacting uneasily, mainly because his manner reminded her of Blake's. He wasn't like him physically, but the charm was identical, the charm that had persuaded her to take Blake at face value. It reminded her of someone else too, someone she couldn't quite place just now.

The terrace looked across a lawn to a herbaceous border, where another gnarled old man in a troll-like knitted cap was laboriously pulling up weeds.

Zelda began to laugh. 'Christ, who's that? One of the seven dwarfs? Isn't there anyone under ninety working here?'

'That's Mr Samms. The whole place is full of staff pensioned off by my grandfather. They live in tied cottages on the estate, and most of them insist on carrying on just as before.' He turned to Georgia. 'I expect Zelda's told you my brother Bron inherited Merlinslade earlier this year? The old guard among the staff drive him crazy now he's trying to reorganise things, but so far he hasn't been able to come up with any tactful way of getting them to stop.'

'Bron's an unusual name,' said Georgia. 'Is it short for Auberon?'

'Better not let him hear you ask that,' Nico answered with a grin. 'No one's less like the king of the fairies. No, Bron's an old family name. It belonged to the first Carwithen. He was a Cornishman who settled here in Tudor times, and made his pile out of wool.'

He paused to open another gate which led into an unkempt knot garden, then turned again to her.

'Zelda said that when you left Baltimore you went to work for Colossus television in LA. How did you like it there?'

'I liked the money,' said Georgia with a smile, thinking it wouldn't do any harm to let him know this important fact. She wasn't a young, starry-eyed beginner who'd take almost any salary for the sake of experience. 'But I'm not so sure I'd want to be a permanent West Coast person.'

'The same with me. I did very well out of movie parts there, but it's good to be home.'

He continued to extract information until they'd emerged into a smaller courtyard, which had its own approach running from the main drive to the house.

Nico stopped. 'The theatre!' he said with a flourish worthy of a fanfare of trumpets.

It was an intriguing building, about the size and shape of a small church, with a steeply angled roof, and constructed of the same golden Cotswold stone as the house. It looked like a place with a secret, for the walls were almost blind with a few small windows mostly beneath the eaves. The end facing them was curved to accommodate the auditorium.

Masks of comedy and tragedy adorned the heavy outer doors, which opened into a spacious vestibule floored with chequered marble. The bust of a Jacobean courtier with a ruff and goatee beard smiled benignly from a niche over the auditorium entrance.

'That's an earlier Nicolas Carwithen,' said Nico. 'He was mad about the stage. He nearly bankrupted the estate building this place.'

He pushed open the auditorium doors, and they were in the theatre itself, standing in a wide corridor which ran round the back of the stalls.

'The decorators have just finished, so it's looking its best,' said Nico.

Georgia walked down a few steps between the seats, looking around her with astonished admiration. She'd been expecting some dim and dusty wreck, but the theatre glowed with subtle front-of-house lighting. It was small, intimate and absolutely perfect, a jewel box of red and gold and pure white. The only part that appeared to have been altered was the raked semi-circular pit, where the original benches had been replaced by Victorian seats upholstered in wine-coloured plush.

The ceiling was white, with ornate plasterwork like moulded snow, and a crystal chandelier hanging from a central rose. There were tiers of benches in the balcony, which was supported on veined marble pillars, their capitals ornamented with gold leaf. The rich russet wood of the balustrade had been carved with an intricate pattern of birds and flowers. Above the stage towered the proscenium arch, painted with cherubs disporting themselves in a gilded chariot which flew among puffs of silver cloud.

'It's astounding,' said Georgia when she could find words. 'So intimate, and yet so grand.'

'I hope the audiences'll think so too. We're aiming at the sort of people who go to Glyndebourne. To make a profit in such a small theatre we'll have to charge high prices for seats. Once Bron's got the house into shape we'll probably sell tickets in a package combined with dinner in the great hall.'

'Is that the original proscenium arch?' Georgia asked. 'Shouldn't it be heavier and more like the façade of a house?'

'Inigo Jones came back towards the end of his career, and put in this new one. He painted it himself. And at the Restoration old Nico's son hired Grinling Gibbons to carve those balustrades.'

Zelda, watching Georgia's face, gave her gravelly laugh. 'I knew you'd love it. But don't go completely ape yet. Wait till you've seen backstage. Sets in this theatre won't be easy. There shouldn't be much of a problem with a play of the same period like *The Tempest*, but I'm glad we have a specialist set designer coming in later on.'

They followed Nico down the centre aisle towards the stage. He ran up some side steps on to the proscenium.

'Wait there just a moment,' he commanded. 'You must hear the acoustics.'

He whirled into the centre of the stage, his coat rising like a magic carpet about him, and launched into the famous Henry Irving dream soliloquy from *The Bells*. He seemed to dwindle physically into the elderly, guilt-ridden Mathias. Though it was traditionally the ham actor's party piece, Nico invested the tortured burgomaster's character with a pathos she'd never seen in it before. It was a brilliant way of demonstrating the stage's potential. Georgia was almost persuaded by it alone, and yet a small warning voice still urged her not to commit herself before she'd been behind the scenes.

'Terrific!' said Zelda, clapping furiously. 'We'll be crazy if we don't put that on as a Christmas special.'

She was already climbing on to the stage. Georgia followed her through the proscenium arch, and was instantly in the other world of the theatre, a complete reverse of the glamour and gloss of the front of house, the world where the true magic was made. She sniffed the dry, rosiny smell mingled with the scent of paint and sawdust, and felt immediately at home.

Nico pushed a pile of woodshavings to one side with his foot. 'The chippies have been refurbishing as fast as they can. Zelda's right, though. The sets aren't going to be easy technically, but I'm sure you'll cope. There aren't too many scene changes in *The Tempest*, after all.'

In spite of this reassurance Georgia almost abandoned the whole idea as she began to appreciate the problems. For a start, there were no flies, the normal extension to the roof from which scenery could be lowered into place. Instead, flat pieces of scenery ran on stage in long grooves from the wings. They were set up one behind the other like playing cards. When one was no longer needed it could be moved to the side, and another rolled on in its place. Nor was there a backdrop but sliding shutters instead, again arranged in an interchangeable set which could be left open if necessary to reveal a small vista stage at the back. The stagehands would need the strength of Olympic wrestlers to haul everything into place.

The machinery for the special effects, which Nico was now enthusing over and seemed suicidally determined to use in the play, was even worse. Apprehensively she inspected the thunder machine, a metal tube which zig-zagged from a machinery loft to the stage floor. Down it ancient cannon balls, left over Georgia suspected from the Civil War, were rolled into a deep wooden tub.

There was a ramshackle winch for raising objects through the trap-door, and, most daunting of all, an unstable arrangement of pulleys and ropes at the back of the vista stage, suspending a cradle from a rough oak frame which looked horribly like a gallows. By this means Nico planned to convey a bevy of goddesses down from the heavens in a chariot during the masque.

'We're so lucky to have these effects,' he was saying. 'Theatre historians never stop pestering me for permission to study them. They'll be a tremendous draw.'

'Not exactly the sort of draw you want if the cradle crashes,' said Georgia.

'Don't worry. It's being overhauled. And at least the planning people had to let me install a decent lighting system, because of the fire risk,' he said, gesturing towards a reassuringly efficient-looking electronic console.

'And what about the wardrobe? I suppose there is one?'

'Not an original, I'm afraid. I was coming to that.' For the first time Nico looked wary. 'The Jacobean tiring house was partitioned by the Victorians, and turned into a green room and dressing rooms. A new wardrobe was built on to the back of the theatre, but it hasn't been used since the war.'

They negotiated a mass of ropes and abandoned pieces of scenery stacked like pieces of toast against a side wall, and proceeded down a dingy corridor lit by a single shadeless light. On the way they passed the green room and dressing rooms, where painters were busy covering the walls with emulsion.

'And this is the wardrobe,' said Nico, throwing open a door at the very end. 'I'm afraid you'll have to use your imagination, but it'll be perfect with a few simple improvements.'

The room needed every ounce of imagination Georgia could muster. Though it was a good size, the walls were masked with flaking paint in a hideous shade of spinach green. Cracked and buckled linoleum covered the floor. There was a range of ancient cupboards with warped doors, and under one of the windows, which overlooked a tangled orchard, taps black with age dripped into a shallow stone sink.

A well-maintained cattle shed would have been more promising, she thought gloomily. Apart from the natural lighting the only things in the room's favour were a new electric water heater over the sink, and some equally new power points.

In the middle of the floor was a deal table strewn with empty takeaway cartons and polystyrene mugs. Some paint-spattered chairs stood round it, cushioned with hessian sacks.

'Sorry about the mess,' said Nico. 'The workmen sometimes have lunch in here.'

Zelda, who'd said very little so far, had obviously decided that the time was ripe for a massive injection of optimism. She sat down on one of the chairs, clasped her hands behind her head, and smiled encouragingly at Georgia.

'Awesome, isn't it? And what a challenge! *The Tempest* in a setting like that can't possibly fail. It'll be magical.'

Georgia took her pencil and notebook from her shoulder bag. She was now veering even more towards caution. Nico had already been far too vague for her liking about the safety of the stage machinery, and she'd have a strike on her hands at once if she asked the wardrobe staff to put up with a place like this. She went over to the sink. The grey stone was encrusted with dirt.

'Not very magical for the people who'd have to work in here. Can you imagine what our union would say about it?'

She opened one of the cupboards. The interior smelt of mice. Nico sat down, propping a pair of elegant feet in boots made of pistachio green suede on an empty chair.

'I know it looks terrible at the moment,' he said disarmingly, 'but I swear you won't know the place by the end of next week. The painters are starting here tomorrow, and Bron's got some new plumbing lined up. Naturally you can have a free hand equipping it. Within the budget, of course.'

She looked round the room again. At least it was large, and had plenty of natural light. Some fresh paint would make an enormous difference, and if Nico really did let her have a free hand she might make something of it. But it wouldn't be easy, and in any case no mention had been made of her fee so far.

'So what do you think?' he demanded. 'Will you consider coming in with us?'

She resolutely refused to succumb to his smile, wondering if she could work with someone who reminded her so much of Blake. But she needed the commission and she had to be logical.

'What about money?' she asked.

He mentioned a fee for the whole season's contract which though adequate, was by no means generous. Zelda caught her look of doubt.

'Once the costume shop's up and running, and Liam takes over the sets, you should have plenty of time for other commissions.'

41

Nico lowered his feet and leaned forward. 'Look, I know very well that I'll be lucky to get you on those terms, but we're on a tight budget. The estate is almost broke, and any spare cash Bron's able to raise has to go back into the land. I'm doing this partly because I want to help him make a go of the estate, partly because I can't bear the prospect of the theatre becoming derelict. I've put in most of my capital, but I can't afford anything like London rates. I'm simply hoping that, like Zelda, most people will look on the opportunity to work here as part payment in itself.'

At last Georgia began to feel she was seeing the real Nico. Perhaps he wasn't so like Blake after all.

'I am tempted,' she said slowly. 'It's an exquisite theatre. A setting like that would enhance any play. But firstly it's only fair to tell you that I don't have the experience to attempt more than the most simple of sets. And I'm especially concerned about safety.'

'Normally I'd never have asked you to take on the sets. It's just unfortunate that Liam O'Grady isn't free yet. I swear the machinery'll be properly overhauled, and you can keep the rest as simple as you like.'

Georgia sat down next to Nico. It was becoming difficult to resist the challenge, but the matter of the workroom still had to be resolved.

'Secondly, I must be able to offer my staff reasonable working conditions. If I did take on the commission, this place would have to be refurbished to my own specifications.'

'I'm listening,' said Nico, lowering his feet to the ground. 'Tell me exactly what you'd want.'

'To begin with, walls and ceiling and woodwork painted white, the lino taken to a dump, and hardboard put down instead. After that, some simple partitions to section off a small office and a washing and dyeing unit. For the unit itself I'd need an industrial extractor fan, a new double sink and plumbing for a washing machine. And the workroom must be warm. It's impossible to cut and sew accurately with cold hands. Central heating's best, but convector heaters would do.'

Nico kept on smiling, though his face fell slightly. 'Isn't that all a little over-ambitious?'

'It's the absolute minimum, before I even begin to think of movable equipment. You'll be using it for many years, so you may as well get it right to begin with.'

Georgia had already worked in too many sub-standard costume workshops. She'd always sworn that if she was ever able to set up one of her own it would at least be comfortable. Wardrobe assistants cheerfully worked themselves into the ground for salaries a bank clerk would have scorned.

'If you want costumes by early September the refurbishments must be finished as soon as possible, at the latest by the middle of June.'

Nico pondered. 'I can fix most of it,' he said, 'but Bron won't be keen to take the plumbers away from their work at the house.'

'It's reasonable, Nico,' said Zelda, 'and we certainly don't want problems with the union over working conditions.'

'Right,' he said. 'I'll just have to twist Bron's arm. If Georgia joins us, it's worth the hassle.'

'You haven't told me yet what my budget's going to be,' said Georgia.

Nico consulted a page of scrawled figures taken from his pocket. After a masterly pause and a heavy sigh, he finally came up with a sum which would just cover the purchase of recondi-tioned equipment and second-rate materials, and provide mini-mum wages for her staff. She was sure he was trying it on, and in her annoyance forgot to frame a tactful reply.

'I couldn't hope to do it on that. I need reliable equipment, and the wardrobe staff must have decent salaries. The privilege of working here won't pay their rents. Half again on top of your estimate, and with care I could just about manage. Anything less, and it'd be a second-rate job. It's a wonderful theatre, and it deserves the best.'

She clasped her hands in her lap to conceal her nervousness, which wasn't improved by Zelda's making a warning face at her to back off. But Nico thought for a moment, and then gave a graceful shrug of resignation.

'You're right. The theatre does deserve the best. We shouldn't aim for anything less. The sort of audiences I have in mind ought to be wealthy enough to stand another pound or two on the price of seats if we have to spend a little more. So do we have a deal?'

Georgia looked down at the notebook in her hand, still hesitating. Nico, who'd begun to congratulate himself on having hooked her at last for a sum still less than he'd been prepared to offer, began to wonder if he'd completely misjudged her. He hadn't expected such a determined campaign to get her own way. Yet she was intriguing as well as exasperating, sitting there at the dusty table with a smooth curtain of hair falling provocatively over the side of her face, so that he couldn't quite see her expression.

She looked up and gave him a direct stare out of grey eyes whose irises were ringed startlingly with black.

'There's one other thing that bothers me,' she said. 'It doesn't seem as if there's going to be much chance for ordinary people to see the plays.'

He bit back his impatience. The profile of the audience wasn't her concern, yet he didn't want to lose her. Ever since he'd seen her work in the States he'd known that she was the perfect designer for Merlinslade.

'Look,' he said patiently, 'maybe I haven't made it clear enough that we're on a knife edge financially. If we don't show a profit in the first year the theatre will have to close. The only way we can do that is to go for the evening dress audience.'

'Couldn't you find some way of making it less exclusive? Why not put on some cut-price matinées? Just because people haven't much money it doesn't mean they're unable to appreciate a place like this.'

Zelda had warned Nico that Georgia could be stubborn, but he hadn't bargained for such prolonged resistance. As if in response to his thoughts, he saw Zelda throw another warning glance at her. Though she reddened slightly, she still persisted.

'I'd love to come in with you, but I really wouldn't feel happy about it unless you can widen the audience.'

She threw back her hair and stared at him defiantly under dark, level brows. Though she was so attractive, it was her personality that was starting to interest him now. It might well be worth giving way on this one point. He looked enquiringly at Zelda.

'I'm all for equality. Cut price matinées are a great idea,' she said, 'and it'll keep the cast on their toes to have a different kind of audience.'

'Right,' said Nico. 'We'll fix it somehow. It'll make great PR, and I might even get another grant on the strength of it. Bron's sure to kick up a fuss, of course. He's becoming a bore on cost-efficiency, but he's promised to let me have a free hand in the theatre, so there's not much he can do.'

He quickly held out his hand, before she could come up with anything else. Georgia took it, and gave him a look which had at last lost its remoteness. If she ever allowed herself to let up on the professional dignity he could imagine her smile melting glaciers.

'It's a deal, then. Welcome to the company,' he said. 'Why don't we make a list now of exactly what you want done in here? Then we'll go over to the house and celebrate with coffee.'

They entered Merlinslade by a back door. A glass case stood against one wall of the badly lit vestibule leading into the kitchen. It contained a stuffed fox whose eyes glinted wickedly in the half light. Above it hung an old oil painting of a balloon-like pig on tiny pink legs.

'Watch your step,' said Nico, picking his way through the jumble of boots and shoes cluttering the floor.

In a butler's pantry to their right an elderly woman in a flowered pinafore and brown lace-up shoes light years from Doc Martens was washing up in slow motion at another stone sink. A large tin kettle hissed on a gas ring to the side of the wooden draining board. Her back registered extreme long-suffering.

'We're here, Mrs Meads,' Nico called to her as they passed. 'Could you bring us some coffee?'

The kitchen was dominated by a cast-iron range like a black cliff, with a series of central heating pipes running from it which reminded Georgia of a ship's engine. A fire murmured some-where inside, doing nothing to heat the room to which winter had come again. Nico bent down and switched on the single element of a pre-war electric fire.

A long dresser was strewn with copies of *Country Life*, empty beer cans, a tangled nest of twine in a magnificent Chinese bowl, and an oily bicycle chain on a piece of newspaper. Tucked away at the side, sitting on the floor, Ned was mending his tyre. The contents of a puncture repair kit were scattered round him. He looked up and smiled at Georgia.

They sat down at a large, crumb-strewn table. It was covered with a grubby damask cloth the size of a double bed sheet. Marooned in the middle were some sticky jars of marmalade and honey. A dessert spoon was stuck in a coffee-stained sugar packet.

'I'd like to have given you coffee in the great hall,' said Nico, 'but the workmen are renovating the ceiling. That's where we're going to lay on the pre-performance dinners. I'm getting a quote from a banqueting firm which specialises in period food.'

'You mean roast boar's head and suckling pig?' said Zelda. 'The cholesterol count'll be out of sight.'

Georgia was listening to the conversation, and taking in her surroundings at the same time. With its general air of gloomy decrepitude the room would have made a perfect set for Cinderella's kitchen.

Mrs Meads shuffled in with a tray. She unloaded a Georgian silver coffee pot, and a heavily charred fruit cake. To them she added some delicate Royal Worcester cups and saucers from the dresser cupboard, then ruined the effect by bringing a brown earthenware milk jug with a chipped rim from a fridge by the door.

'This is Georgia Tremain, Meadie,' said Nico. 'She's going to design the costumes for us.'

'Pleased to meet you, I'm sure,' said Mrs Meads, nodding at Georgia. The red cardigan under her pinafore made her look like a geriatric robin. 'I baked you a bit of cake, Mr Nico, when you told me you were expecting guests. But I can't do this sort of thing every day. I've too much on my hands, what with the meals as well as the house.'

'It looks wonderful,' said Nico, as though she'd presented him with something straight from Harrods food hall.

Mrs Meads beamed at him fondly before shuffling away again through an inner door covered in moth-eaten baize. Over it was a row of bells, each neatly labelled with the name of a room. There must once have been a squad of servants to wait on the

Carwithens, Georgia thought, and clearly they'd never got over it. She longed to ask why one elderly woman should be looking after three young active males, but didn't quite like to. Zelda had no such scruples.

'Jesus, haven't any of you Carwithens heard of the reconstructed man? What did you do when you were in the States, Nico? Women over there aren't into domesticity any more.'

'Oh, I managed somehow,' he said evasively. 'Maid service came with my apartment, and a girl from studio catering used to make me meals now and then.' Across the kitchen yard the stable clock struck eleven. He looked at his watch. 'Bron'll be here in a moment, Ned. Don't you think you should take that tyre outside?'

Ned merely retreated further into his corner with an obstinate shrug. As he did so, the clock sounded its last stroke, the baize door was thrown open, and a man walked in, with a dog following close on his heels.

He was wearing an olive polo-necked sweater under a mechanic's overall of brown twill. The colours gave him a military look. He was several years older than Nico, and several inches taller. He walked straight over to the carver chair at the head of the table, sat down, and cast a glance round the assembled company as if they were on defaulters' parade. The dog, a red setter, padded silently to a basket near the range.

'This is my brother,' said Nico. 'Bron, I'd like you to meet Georgia Tremain. I've managed to persuade her to do the costumes for us. You know Zelda, of course.'

Bron stood up for a moment and gave Georgia's hand a brisk indifferent shake. His eye fell on the jars in the middle of the table.

'For Christ's sake, hasn't anyone put these away yet? Breakfast was three hours ago. It's about time this cloth was changed too.'

'Poor old Meadie's rushed off her feet,' said Nico.

'She wasn't asked to help. She volunteered, and you know she enjoys fussing. I wasted half an hour lighting the bloody range this morning, and I've got the estate to run. Anyway, whoever had breakfast last should have cleared away.'

Ned made an unwise movement in his corner.

'It was you, wasn't it, Ned? And haven't you been told not to bring bits of bike into the kitchen?'

He scrambled to his feet looking more resigned than per-turbed.

'I wasn't last, it was Nico. Besides, it's only a tyre and a tiny little chain.'

'I want them out in the stables now. And don't sneak.'

Ned gathered up his possessions and made a hasty retreat, pulling a face at Bron's back as he disappeared through the outer door. Nico had poured coffee for everyone. He began to cut into the cake.

'We'd better try this, but Meadie's cakes are as good as a depth charge. I recommend caution.'

Georgia was becoming increasingly irritated with the elder Carwithens' feudal attitude to Mrs Meads.

'Maybe she'd do better if she had a modern cooker and a washing-up machine,' she said.

Bron was transferring sugar from the packet to his cup with an expression of distaste. He gave her a cold grey stare.

'She's been offered them both, and she refused.'

'It's true,' said Nico. 'If Bron suggests anything new she thinks it's an insult to the dear dead days of yore. She worked here for forty years, and she's besotted with the place.'

Zelda took a minute piece of cake, and added two sweeteners to her coffee. 'She seems a nice old homebody, but you'll need someone with more pzazz than that to run the place once things really get going.'

'Zelda's right, Bron,' said Nico. 'Can't you think of some way of tactfully replacing her?'

'I'm working on it,' he said shortly.

He stirred his coffee and then sat back, drumming his fingers on the table. He was darker than Nico, with a deep tan. The blond lights in his neatly cut brown hair had presumably been produced by the sun, for Georgia couldn't imagine he'd stay a moment longer at the barber's than necessary. He looked as if he spent most of his time out of doors, and as if he could scarcely suppress his impatience to return there.

'Georgia's been inspecting the costume workroom,' said Nico.

'It's going to need a bit more work than I originally thought. Can you spare the plumbers for the next few days?'

'No, I can't,' said Bron. 'Not till they've overhauled the heating system.'

His gaze moved to the range.

'How many times do I have to remind everyone that this thing won't work efficiently unless it's riddled now and then?'

He got up, pulled open the fire door, and rattled inside vigorously with a long iron hook. A shower of glowing cinders fell into the ash tray as the fire burst into life. He kicked the door shut, and returned to the table.

'And I want the new bathroom finished as well,' he said. 'I've had enough of sharing with Ned. He's like an adolescent whale.'

'Come on, Bron, be reasonable,' said Nico. 'A few days' delay won't matter.'

'It'll matter to me, and in any case I can't move workmen at a moment's notice. It wouldn't be cost-effective. They'll have finished by the middle of next month. I'm sure Miss Tremain can find some way of managing till then.'

Georgia was staggered by this lordly disregard for everyone's needs except his own.

'I don't think you quite understand what's involved,' she said, trying to keep her voice as detached as his. 'By the middle of July we'll be in the thick of costume making. If we've only one small sink for dyeing and screen-printing, there'll be huge delays. Having to pre-wash fabrics by hand will make things worse. We'd never meet the first night deadline. It'd mean postponing *The Tempest*.' She forced herself to smile at him, and couldn't resist adding, 'I'm sure you'll appreciate how *un*cost-effective that would be.'

He gave her a long thoughtful stare, then looked at Nico enquiringly.

'Georgia's right,' Nico confirmed. 'We'll save a lot more money if we put up with Ned for just a little longer.'

Bron drummed his fingers on the table once more. There was a long pause, during which Georgia began to think she would have to pull out of the commission if he didn't agree. There were already far too many difficulties ahead without this

49

added complication. Then he nodded at Nico, avoiding Georgia's gaze.

'All right. I'll see what I can do. You'd better give me a note of what you want.'

It didn't sound like a particularly firm arrangement to Georgia, but Nico seemed satisfied, and at that moment Ned sidled back into the room. He drew a chair up to the table, scraping the legs on the floor, and reached for the cake. Bron's hand shot out and grabbed his wrist.

'Hold on a moment, Ned. Can't you see there's someone new here? You haven't said hello to Miss Tremain.'

'Georgia, please,' she said, smiling at Ned and pushing the cake his way. 'Ned and I met in the drive. He's already introduced himself.'

'You must have impressed him,' said Bron drily. 'And since you're back with us, Ned, perhaps you'd explain what you're doing at home during term-time?'

Ned gave an injured sigh. 'I told you last night, but you never listen to anything I say. It's a teachers' re-orientation day.' He pounced on a piece of cake, and began to devour it before he was stopped again.

'I should think they need re-orienting after they've coped with you lot,' said Nico, topping up his cup with coffee.

'So what exactly are you planning to do with your spare time?' persisted Bron.

'Me and Jason Mason and the rest of our mates have been making a new trials circuit for our bikes down on the set-aside land. We're testing it out this afternoon.'

'Who's Jason Mason?'

'I've already told you at least twice. He's just come to live in the village. His dad's got a Cosworth Sierra.'

'I see,' said Bron. 'Perhaps I should come over this afternoon and take a look at this circuit of yours.'

Ned's face fell. 'Do you have to? Jason'll think I'm a mega nerd. His dad never snoops on him.'

'Tough,' said Bron. 'His father doesn't have to pay the bills here. The last time you made a trials circuit you and your friends broke a huge hole in that hedge Mr Samms was starting to re-lay.'

'You always get crashes on a real circuit. We couldn't help it.'

Ned's face had reddened. Georgia was becoming ever more sympathetic towards him.

'Talking of hedges, on my way here I saw a woman gathering plants in the one along the road from the village,' she said. Ned sent her a grateful look as he crammed the last of his cake into his mouth. 'She was from that strange Disciples of the Fountain group. Are they neighbours of yours?'

There was an awkward silence, but at least Bron was frowning at her instead of Ned now. 'Yes, unfortunately,' he said after a long pause. 'And if they aren't monopolising the Grail Well with their half-baked ceremonies, they're tearing up the local vegetation.'

'The Grail Well! How fascinating! Has it anything to do with King Arthur?' asked Zelda.

'Nothing at all. The spring which feeds the well, the Merlinsfont, rises on the escarpment, and joins the river further down. The estate's called Merlinslade because there used to be merlins nesting in the cliff. Slade is the local name for a valley. But some romantic started a story that Merlin once stayed here on a journey with the Grail, and dipped it in the spring to drink. It's led to all sorts of nonsense.'

Ned was now looking happier, and Bron even more annoyed. Georgia was delighted with the success of her diversion. She decided to improve on it.

'I saw the woman in the courtyard of Bath Abbey yesterday as well. She had that singer Morrigan with her, the one who used to be a pop star. They seemed a rather unlikely combination.'

There was another silence, but this time full of some hidden tension Georgia couldn't place which seemed out of all proportion to her innocent remark. Bron looked thunderous, and when Georgia, puzzled, glanced towards Nico for enlightenment, he gave her an almost imperceptible shake of the head. Ned knew something too, for he opened his mouth to speak, caught a second head-shake from Nico, and took another piece of cake instead.

'I must get back to the workmen,' said Bron. 'You've had enough cake, Ned. Put it back and go and finish that repair,

51

instead of hanging around here.'

'It's been great meeting you, Ned,' said Georgia, trying to cheer him up as he retreated sulkily towards the door. 'Why don't you come and see me next time you're in Bath?'

'That'd be ace,' he said, looking as if he couldn't believe his luck, 'Where do you live?'

'Seventeen Sophia Street. It's right in the centre of town.'

'Catch you later then!' he said happily, bouncing out into the vestibule.

It was a relief when Bron got up from the table immediately afterwards, nodding a stiff-necked farewell to her and Zelda, and snapping his fingers at the dog to follow. On his way out he trawled the empty beer cans off the dresser and into a wastepaper basket with one irritable, accurate sweep of his arm. As the door closed behind him, Georgia caught Zelda's expression and just managed to control her laughter.

'Wow!' said Zelda, the minute he'd gone. 'Does your brother have an attitude problem, Nico! Is it women he dislikes, or just everyone?'

'Bron's all right really,' said Nico. 'The estate gets him down. He never expected to have to run it so soon, and now he's got Ned to cope with too.'

'Where's his wife?' asked Georgia.

'Hit the road, I guess,' said Zelda. 'Why should she stick around while he kicks ass?'

Nico smiled lazily. 'Got it in one about hitting the road. But she didn't leave for that reason.'

'So what happened?' said Zelda.

'He was very young when he married Imogen, and just starting in the regular army. He loved the life but she became bored with it, and with motherhood. Definitely not officer's wife material, our Imogen. So she cut loose, divorced Bron, and let him have custody of Ned. But in spite of all that I sometimes think he's still holding a torch for her. He's never had another serious relationship.'

'Did he take care of Ned on his own?' Zelda asked.

'Bron had several overseas postings, so our parents looked after Ned. When my father died my mother couldn't cope with

Ned on her own. Imogen suddenly decided to go on a motherhood kick, and offered to have him instead. Bron thought Ned ought to spend some time with her, and let him go.'

'Poor kid,' said Georgia, longing to know why Ned was now at Merlinslade, but not liking to ask.

'Bron's pretty good with him most of the time, but he's been up to here with the estate lately, and he wasn't exactly overjoyed at having to leave the army.'

'Anyway, I guess we're here to talk about the theatre, not to discuss your brother's hang-ups,' said Zelda. She frowned as she consulted her watch. Donald Duck's arms were already swinging towards eleven-thirty. 'We'd better get back to business. I have to go soon. I've a lunch date in Bristol.'

'Who's interviewing you this time?' Georgia teased her. '*Cosmopolitan?*'

'I'm meeting Redvers Monk. *The* Redvers Monk. How about that?'

Georgia stared at her. Redvers Monk had been one of the leading British stage actors of her parents' generation, as well known as Burton and Olivier, but he'd abandoned his career completely in the seventies. She'd only seen screen versions of his most famous stage roles.

'Redvers Monk? I thought he'd disappeared from the acting scene years ago because of a drink problem.'

'That's the understatement of the century,' said Zelda. 'The poor guy became an out and out lush. I was in the audience when he finally fell to pieces on stage, at the Broadway first night of *Dr Faustus*. It was awesome, like the collapse of some magnificent building. He's never acted since then.'

'So what's he been doing all this time?'

'He came from Bristol originally,' said Nico. 'He bought a house there, holed up, and drank away the years. I sometimes used to come across him in the Bristol Old Vic bar. He was always more than half cut, but still a spell-binder. He'd occasionally do radio work, but I could never persuade him to go on stage again.'

'I can't imagine anything much worse than having a talent like his, and not being able to use it,' said Georgia.

'That's what I thought too,' said Nico, with an approving look at her, and once again she felt she'd briefly seen the real Nico. 'In the end some of us clubbed together and sent him to dry out at a clinic in the States. He's a reformed character now, and raring to go.'

Zelda extracted a couple of large green vitamin capsules from a bottle in her bag, and swallowed them with the last of her coffee. 'He has a slight confidence problem, but we can soon overcome that. Redvers is the perfect Prospero.'

'Prospero?' said Georgia, now almost speechless. 'You mean you're actually considering him for *The Tempest*, here at Merlinslade?'

'Nico's already signed him up. As soon as he knew Redvers was back in Bristol, he made him an offer he couldn't refuse.'

'It was bloody hard work,' said Nico, looking complacent, 'but in the end I persuaded him that he owed it to his public. He couldn't have much better circumstances for a comeback – a small theatre, a sympathetic audience, and all on his home ground.'

Georgia felt a sneaking sympathy for Redvers, encountering the full force-field of Nico's charm.

'The prospect of Zelda directing him really clinched the deal,' said Nico, giving her one of his most engaging smiles.

'The publicity's going to be out of sight for the return of an actor with Redvers' reputation,' said Zelda.

'It'll be wonderful if it works – I can see that,' said Georgia slowly. 'But perhaps he won't want publicity? It's bound to be a terrific ordeal for him. And it's a huge risk for you, Nico. Supposing he fails?'

'We won't let him fail,' said Zelda, who had now assumed the absorbed, evangelistic expression which meant there'd be no stopping her. 'If we all support him he'll come through. That's one of the many reasons I wanted you to do the costumes – you're especially good with actors who feel spooked.'

In spite of the compliment Georgia couldn't completely overcome her misgivings. It would be the opportunity of a lifetime to work with someone of Redvers' stature, but putting him on in the first play was yet another gamble, and bound to affect the rest of the season if it failed.

Nico got up and started striding excitedly round the room.

'We've signed some really good actors from the big companies who don't want a huge salary as long as they can work with Zelda and Redvers. She'll tell you about them at the first director's meeting. Then there's a couple of brilliant kids who've just graduated from drama school to play Miranda and Ferdinand, the young lovers. And I've always wanted to do Caliban.'

'What about Ariel?' Georgia asked.

He paused by the window, intuitively standing where the light was best. 'That's the tricky one. We've auditioned at least twenty people, and got all the casting agencies looking out for us, but we haven't yet found a guy we like.'

'It isn't specified as a male role in the cast list,' said Georgia. 'I've always imagined a woman in the part. After all, doesn't Prospero call Ariel "my delicate sprite"? It's fiendishly difficult dressing a man for the role without making him look like a drag queen.'

Zelda gave a sudden gust of laughter. 'We'd get even more publicity that way. But Georgia's right, Nico, we should have a woman for Ariel. Let's strike another blow for the feminists. They haven't been doing too well lately.'

'A woman would make a better foil for me too,' he said thoughtfully, returning to the table. 'Right, I'll speak to the agencies again this afternoon.'

'I think that's all for the moment, then. I must run if I want to make it into Bristol by one,' said Zelda regretfully, 'but we'll have our first formal planning session in the theatre a week from today. Can you come along with plenty of preliminary ideas, Georgia? Give me a call at the Hilton if you have any problems.'

Zelda was still shouting instructions at them as she roared away in her hired car, which she'd parked outside the stables.

'I'd better go too,' Georgia said to Nico, 'if you can just remind me how to reach the front of the house again.'

He had propped himself against a bale of straw the exact colour of his hair. 'Do you have to leave so soon?' he asked. 'I thought you might let me buy you a pub lunch.'

'Sorry, but I've already got a lunch date with a friend at the rectory. Another time, maybe.'

'At the rectory? Who do you know among that bunch of no-hopers?'

'The curate, Esther Hallen. I was at school with her. What do you mean, no-hopers? I thought she lived on her own.'

'You'll see when you get there,' said Nico mischievously. 'I haven't met your curate friend yet, but some of the others come to the pub now and then. Are you sure you won't change your mind?'

'Quite sure,' said Georgia, wondering what she'd let herself in for with Esther.

'Then at least have a quick drink to set you up for the humble pie. I shall need something to help me face Meadie's Scotch eggs. You could have played cricket with the last lot. We can go down in your car, and I'll walk back.'

Georgia wavered. She still felt slightly uncertain about Nico, but she would be working with him over the next year, after all, and there was something very flattering about his openly admiring gaze. If Nico could look at her in that way, perhaps she hadn't entirely withered up after the divorce.

'Perhaps just a glass of wine, then,' she said.

The beams of the saloon bar were varnished with the blackest and glossiest of paint, a battery of horsebrasses shone above the fireplace, and there was a strong smell of draught ale and bacon-flavoured crisps. A couple of elderly men with equally elderly dogs at their feet were playing cribbage in an inglenook, while a farmworker obsessively punched the keys of a slot machine. At the bar a bunch of young executives and their secretaries on an office outing were having drinks while they studied the menu.

Nico steered Georgia towards a quiet corner, and went to place his order. When he appeared by their side the heads of the office group turned like a line of puppets. The landlord almost dropped a tray of glasses in his eagerness to serve him. In amusement Georgia saw the women at the bar surreptitiously look her way, one by one, to check the competition.

Nico brought the drinks over to the table, bestowing a dazzling smile on his audience en route.

'Sorry about the stares,' he said. 'It's been like that ever since I did those movie parts. Anyway, here's your drink. Personally I'd need something a lot stronger than that before a session with the curate, even a female one.'

'So you're not worried about the state of your soul?' said Georgia teasingly.

'The only thing I'm worried about at the moment is getting the theatre to run at a profit. Tell me what you think of Merlinslade now? You looked so shattered when you came backstage that I thought we were going to lose you.'

'The house is beautiful, what little I've seen of it so far. And the theatre's a dream. Are you planning to stay on indefinitely if things work out?'

'That's the idea. But it depends partly on whether Bron can pull the estate together. He reckons if he can get it into shape by next summer we'll be all right. The whole of the house will be opened to the public then, and the farm's going to be run as a working demonstration of pre-war agricultural methods. Combined with the theatre they should make a terrific tourist attraction.'

'He doesn't seem particularly keen on the task.'

'It's a bad deal for Bron. Thank Christ I'm not the older one. He was doing really well in the army, and he'd just got himself seconded to the UN military mission in Bosnia. It was exactly the sort of thing Bron likes – lots of command, lots of responsibility. He's already had several overseas postings. Merlinslade must seem very low-key after that. The main problem now is that he keeps forgetting he's not in the army still.'

'So I noticed,' said Georgia. 'Why did he marry someone who hated it so much?' Tales of other peoples' divorces held a horrible fascination for her these days.

'Imo married him, not the other way round. Bron had a reputation as a charmer who couldn't be caught, and she saw him as a challenge. Her father was a self-made tycoon, and she realised that Bron could give her the one thing she couldn't buy – entry into the world of the landed gentry. They were sleeping together, and she stopped taking the pill, didn't tell Bron, and when she became pregnant refused to have an abortion. Bron of course did the decent thing – I'd have let her get on with it – and the result was total disaster.'

'He doesn't seem much like a charmer now.'

'He's a good guy if you're in a real fix. Do you have any brothers or sisters?'

Georgia was halfway through her drink, and beginning to feel more at ease. She couldn't help liking the way Nico continued to stand up for his unappealing brother.

'I've a much younger sister. She's staying with me just now.'

'What's she like?'

'Very sweet, but she has a craze a minute. She's mad on aromatherapy and Gérard Depardieu at the moment.'

'And is there anyone you're mad on?' asked Nico casually, opening a bag of prawn-flavoured crisps. He took a crackling handful when he'd offered her some, and started to wolf them down. 'God, these are good. I'd better take some with me to cheer Ned up.'

'My art's the only thing in my life,' said Georgia, matching his bantering tone. 'I'm a very single-minded person.'

'Born to blush unseen in the wardrobe, are you? I don't believe it.'

'Well, not quite unseen perhaps.' Georgia was astonished to find how easy it was to be conducting this sort flirtatious conversation again.

'Then how about having dinner with me one day? Strictly to discuss our art, of course.'

Georgia had never intended things to go this far. She scrabbled for an excuse. 'I'm sorry, but I really am going to be much too busy from now on.'

'We could make it next week, after the first director's meeting. We'll need a break, and Zelda's going up to London that evening.'

Georgia hesitated. She found his persistence soothing to her battered self-esteem, and she'd been burned badly enough over Blake to make very sure the date didn't develop into anything serious. In any case, there was something she was curious to know.

'All right,' she said slowly. 'I will if you'll tell me something.'

'Anything,' said Nico with a melting smile. 'The secrets of my past are yours. God, that sounds like a line from a play. It probably is.'

'Then tell me about Morrigan. Why did Bron clam up like that when I mentioned him at coffee time? And why did you warn me off the subject?'

Nico looked surprisingly taken aback.

'Morrigan? Why do you want to know about him? You don't fancy him, do you?'

'Fancy him?' Now Georgia was startled. 'That's the last thing I thought of. In fact he scared me a little, though I'm not sure exactly why.'

Nico laughed. 'I suppose he does look slightly sinister, poncing about in all that black gear at his age. But you don't have to worry. He's the poseur of the century, and perfectly harmless really. The only really wicked thing about my dear uncle Gervase is that he's wasted his musical talent for so many years. In fact it's more than talent, it's genius.'

Georgia nearly dropped her glass. 'Your uncle? He's your uncle? You must be joking!'

But even as she said the words she was remembering how Nico's lazy smile and confident deployment of charm had reminded her when they first met of someone she couldn't quite place. That someone, she now knew, was Morrigan.

Chapter 4

Nico was both amused and pleased by Georgia's reaction. He'd been wondering what it would take to shake that somewhat daunting self-possession.

'He should have inherited Merlinslade, though my grandfather, old Edmund, never married Morrigan's mother. She was a landgirl he had a fling with early in the war. Morrigan took her maiden name when he went on stage. Soon afterwards my grandfather married someone else, but he did recognise Morrigan as his heir until he was sent to prison. Then old Edmund changed his will without telling anyone, and left the estate instead to his son by marriage, Bron's father and mine.'

'And I suppose your father didn't inherit because he died?'

'He had a heart attack only last spring, just after old Edmund, so Bron was saddled with Merlinslade.'

'It must have been awful for you all.' Georgia's face was brimming with sympathy.

'It was pretty bad.' Nico preferred not to remember his mother distraught with grief, Ned upset and miserable, and Bron haggard with anxiety as he tried to cope. 'But my mother's all right, at least. She's living with her sister now.'

Georgia frowned. The serious expression made her even sexier, Nico thought.

'But that was some months ago. I still don't understand why your brother should have been quite so short-tempered this morning.'

Nico decided that he was having to gloss over Bron's bad moods too often these days. He wouldn't be pleased if he knew all the family skeletons were being revealed, but he'd brought it on himself.

'Bron's always been bloody jumpy about Morrigan. He resents him for landing him with the responsibility for Merlinslade, and he's never trusted him. Morrigan used to stay here a lot when we were young. Bron was a quiet sort of kid. Morrigan resented him because he was very fond of our grandmother. He was always winding Bron up. I got on all right with Morrigan, though. He used to take me out for half days from boarding school, and he was good with tips. He seemed incredibly glamorous to me then.'

'Why exactly did he go to prison?'

'He was put inside for possessing heroin. There were rumours that he'd been dealing, but I don't believe them. When he was released he went on the guru trail in India, and started dabbling in various religions. He returned to England just after my grandfather died. I think Morrigan's rather a sad character these days, though Bron doesn't see him that way.'

'Does he ever come to Merlinslade now he's back in Bath?'

'Oh, yes, he's always turning up, trying to persuade Bron to let him be one of the family again, but Bron freezes him out pretty damn' quick. I have a drink with him from time to time. I feel a bit sorry for the poor old bugger. He ought to have another chance, like Redvers.'

Now Nico had captured Georgia's attention completely, he didn't intend to go on discussing his relations' hang-ups, which he'd had far too much of recently. Two of the women at the bar gave him the perfect opportunity to change the subject when they came over to ask for his autograph.

It was a bore not even to be able to drink in peace on his home ground, but the group looked well heeled enough to be potential theatre patrons. He signed the bits of paper thrust at him, and ran off the patter he reserved for these occasions, putting heavy emphasis on the opening of Merlinslade in September.

When he turned back to Georgia she was watching him with a strange expression. He wondered if she resented the interruption. It was odd if she did, because she must be accustomed to that sort of thing. He knew from Zelda that she'd been married to an actor in the States, though Zelda had refused to give him any details, beyond saying it had only lasted a few months.

'Sorry again,' he said, 'but there's not much I can do about the

62

fans unless I permanently wear shades and a wig.'

She gave a remote smile. Again she wasn't focusing on him, and he decided on more shock tactics.

'So now I've filled you in on the dark secrets of the Carwithens, how about telling me a bit about yourself? Zelda said you'd divorced recently. I gather that's why you left the States.'

He certainly had all her attention once more, but he hadn't meant his question to leave her looking so shaken.

'Zelda told you?' she slowly. 'But I'd asked her not to talk about it.'

Her hand was lying on the table. He put his own over it. She hardly appeared to notice.

'We weren't gossiping, if that's what you're worried about. But I am trying to run a business concern. I needed to know why you'd left the States before I took you on.'

'In case I'd run off with the takings?'

'Look, really, you're getting me wrong. I don't want to know the gory details. Christ, that's your business, and anyway it happens all the time these days, especially in the theatre. Marriages crumble as fast as anthills.'

'You think I don't know that?' she said wrily. She was beginning to look a little more relaxed.

'Personally I've never been brave enough to give it a try,' he said. 'I don't suppose I ever shall. The theatre's mistress and wife all in one.'

He became still more intrigued when this statement, which most women would have taken as a personal challenge, produced from her an expression of pure relief. He began to look forward even more to taking her out again.

She pulled her hand away carefully, and looked at her watch.

'The drink was perfect, but I'm afraid I really must go now. I don't want to be late.'

'Right,' he said, trying to hide his disappointment. It was still only a quarter to one by the clock over the bar. 'Just follow the road on the other side of the pub. You can't miss the rectory. It's next to the church. And don't forget we have a dinner date next Friday.'

She hesitated.

'You promised,' he said. 'It won't be any big deal, I swear. We can discuss business all evening if you want to.'

'That won't be necessary,' she said with a sudden prim, enchanting smile. 'I'm not a complete workaholic yet.'

Georgia had purposely left a little time in hand so that she could leave her car by the village green, and walk up to the rectory. She now needed a few moments to sort out her feelings about Nico as well.

She couldn't help liking him, though when he was signing autographs his manner had again been so similar to Blake's that it threw her for a moment. But unlike Blake, he didn't pretend to be what he wasn't. He'd made it very clear that he didn't want any long-term commitment. That suited her perfectly, and though she'd been surprised by her response when he touched her, it was easily attributable to being on her own for so many months.

As Georgia approached the small Norman church she wondered what Esther would make of Nico. She'd been one of Georgia's closest friends at school, part of a small group of girls who were all different in one way or another because of their upbringings or enthusiasms. Esther was the most different of all because she was so deeply and unselfconsciously religious. Yet everyone at school had liked her, in spite of her infuriating refusal to gossip or speculate on the teachers' love lives. People stayed friends with Esther even when she knelt by her bed every night on a school holiday, and publicly said her prayers.

Georgia was a little early still. To pass time she wandered through the graveyard and into the church. The nave was flanked by a double row of Romanesque arches. Stained glass splashed the grey flagstones with brilliant colour, as if a medieval pavement artist had been at work. From the carved oak rood screen Adam and Eve looked down hand in hand, not yet banished from a Garden of Eden where rabbits and unicorns frolicked together.

Georgia walked slowly round the walls, studying the memorials. Most of them had been put up to the greater glory of past Carwithens. It seemed that when they weren't cultivating their acres they were busy directing military operations or governing long-suffering colonial tribes. There was a tablet to a Carwithen who'd fought for the Royalists with the Cornish Sir Bevil Grenvile at a local battle in the Civil War, while the deaths of old Edmund and his second son were recorded on a stark slab of black granite.

Georgia finished her tour, and sat down in a pew before the rood screen. Outside she could hear the chatter of rooks squabbling over their nests. Someone was pottering in the vestry, probably arranging flowers. It was peaceful in the little church, and for the first time in a long while she allowed herself to think for more than a few seconds of Blake.

Meeting Nico had resurrected all her suppressed memories. After her separation from Blake she'd gone over them again and again, trying to understand how he could hurt her so much and yet say he still loved her. Finally, out of sheer self-preservation, she'd had to stop trying to solve the puzzle, and get on with her life.

Just for a moment she let herself recall his face when she first found out that he'd been unfaithful all along. He'd looked like a small boy who confidently expected to be forgiven. He'd tried so hard to persuade her to stay in the States.

'I can't desert Lyn now,' he'd said, 'but I still want to go on seeing you. I know you'll miss me.'

He'd somehow made her feel that she was the one at fault for not being more tolerant. And in spite of everything she *had* missed him. Missed his sensitive understanding of her moods, missed the way it was so easy to talk to him, missed the way he'd brought an extra warmth to everyday life. She'd slept with other men before, but he was the first she'd lived with. He wasn't a particularly passionate lover, but for a short time he gave her something she'd only ever had from her grandmother: a sense of at last being all-important to someone. In the first weeks of their marriage, before she'd found out, she'd felt herself blossom like the magnolia in the arid backyard of their apartment block. She still wondered if he really had loved her, or if it had all been a consummate actor's illusion. She'd long ceased crying over Blake, but every time she thought for too long of their wrecked marriage she had to fight feelings of inadequacy and despair. She tried without much success to banish them now by concentrating on the pattern of the kneeler at her feet. As she stared at the cross-stitching so hard that her eyes ached, she heard a voice saying her name.

Startled, she looked up and saw someone walking towards her between the choir stalls, a slim figure severely clad in a black cassock under which the curve of breasts was just visible. No one but Esther could have diverted her gloomy thoughts more effectively.

Georgia flew from the pew to hug her. With her cheek pressed against Esther's thin, intelligent face, she thought with relieved amusement that her clothes might look different, but she hadn't really changed. The blonde hair clustering round her head in cropped curls like shavings of newly cut wood, which had been Esther's main beauty, still smelt of baby shampoo, and there was another perfume lingering about her, one Georgia hadn't come across for years.

'Esther, you're impossible! Only you could use lavender water! And why are you going round dressed like that sexy priest in *The Thorn Birds*?'

Esther looked bashful. 'One of the old ladies in the almshouses gave me the scent. I couldn't hurt her feelings by not wearing it. And the cassock helps people to remember that I'm a pastor as well as a woman. It's necessary sometimes.'

She surveyed Georgia.

'Anyway, you look good enough for both of us. I'm longing to hear what you've been doing. Let me lock up, then we can go over to the house. I had to check on a few details for a wedding tomorrow.'

'You actually *marry* people?' said Georgia, as they went down the aisle.

'Of course. A deacon can officiate at most ceremonies, apart from communion. I'll be able to do that as well when I'm ordained next year.'

'I can see you're a woman of importance,' said Georgia, waiting while Esther paused to lock the main door behind them.

'I wish my parishioners thought so. Most of them treat religion as some sort of spiritual insurance policy. They come here at the beginning and middle and end of their lives, and I don't see much of them in between. Sometimes I think that if I didn't have the refuge to run, I'd be doing more good back in the inner city.'

'I didn't know you ran a refuge as well.'

'The rectory's so big, it seemed all wrong for me to be living there alone. I opened it to women with nowhere to go, some from round here, and some from Bath who needed to be out of the city.'

'How many are there?'

'Ten of us altogether. Two battered wives, Tracey and Maureen, with four children between them. Then there's Kim. She was living with some travellers till her van was set on fire. Michelle, who's just seventeen and dropped out of everything. And Sumitra Graham. She's Anglo-Indian, married to a local man who committed suicide last year after losing his money in a business crash.'

She tucked her arm through Georgia's.

'But you'll meet most of them at lunch, and I want to hear about you. I was in such a hurry when you phoned that there wasn't a moment for questions. What are you doing back in England? Somehow I assumed you'd stay in America.'

Georgia had mentioned briefly to Esther in her Christmas card that she was getting a divorce, but hadn't given any details.

'I didn't want to hang around there after Blake and I split up.'

'I was very sad to hear about that.' Esther gave Georgia a grave look which made her even more thankful that Esther didn't know the full story.

'There's really nothing to be sad about,' she said, making her voice purposely casual to discourage any further comment. 'It's all past history as far as I'm concerned.'

Esther gave her arm a sympathetic squeeze. 'It's wonderful to have you back, whatever the reason. Tell me exactly what you've been up to at Merlinslade? It must be something to do with the theatre.'

By the time Georgia had finished a brief account of her morning, they'd reached the rectory. Built of glaring red brick, it was mercifully screened from the church by a stand of cypresses, and had obviously been put up to accommodate a large Victorian family. Esther pushed open the front door.

'People have been so good giving me their spare furniture,' she said happily.

It was only too clear that she had no inclination towards the worldly art of interior decoration. The rectory was as gaunt inside as out, furnished with a dismal assortment of what looked like clerical cast-offs. The chilly, high-ceilinged entrance passage was carpeted with a threadbare Turkish runner. The plastic-veneered 1950s hall stand was flanked by a pair of Victorian chairs with nests of horsehair bursting from the seats. Yet there was a cheerful tangle of small, brightly coloured jackets on the stand, and the sound of children playing upstairs. And instead of the smell of mutton stew which Georgia remembered from Esther's vicarage childhood, a delicious aroma compounded of garlic and new bread floated towards her.

Esther led the way towards the back of the house into a large common room where a radio with a bent aerial was blaring out the Jimmy Young show. A poster of Michael Jackson in a purple satin jacket was tacked up next to an oil painting of some long-forgotten bishop. There were some sagging armchairs in front of a small gas fire, and pieces of Lego ranged along the window sill.

A girl in jeans and a studded leather waistcoat over a black T shirt looked up from laying the table. A lizard was tattooed on her upper arm. Her hair, dark with gel, had been cut very short and sleeked back from a strong, lively face.

'This is Kim,' said Esther, turning down the radio. 'She's doing the cooking until she can find a job. She used to work for a catering firm in London before she joined the travellers. Meet my friend Georgia, Kim. She's been at Merlinslade all morning.'

'Hi,' said Kim. Her hands were stained with beetroot. 'Nice to meet you. What were you doing there?'

'Looking at the theatre. I'm going to work in it for a while.'

'You want to watch those Carwithens. They're a right pain at times, aren't they, Est?'

'They've had a lot of problems recently,' said Esther.

'Their only problem is that they think they're a cut above everyone else. You can't get any decent service in the pub when

Nico Carwithen's having a pint. And his brother tore a strip off Maureen's Dan for making a hole in a hedge the other day. It's wrong for one man to own all that great pile when other people don't have homes. The young kid, Ned, he's OK, though.'

'I don't think Bron Carwithen ever wanted to own Merlinslade, but he's tied by family tradition,' said Esther. 'I get the impression he'd give it up tomorrow if he could.'

'Pigs might fly!' said Kim. 'I know his sort. All landowners are the same.'

She'd finished laying the table, and now brought from the kitchen a bowl of salad garnished with dandelion shoots, a rough round loaf of home-baked bread, and a chicken casserole. Esther picked up a brass gong from the sideboard, and beat it vigorously. The rest of the inmates started to filter in from their rooms upstairs.

Tracey and Maureen were two weary-looking women in their mid-thirties. Tracey had a stolid three year old, and a toddler whom she dumped in a high chair. Sumitra Graham, black hair knotted in a smooth coil at the nape of her neck, wore a drooping white cardigan over a sari, and held her arms clasped across her body as if she were standing permanently in an east wind. She gave Georgia a shy smile when introduced, and slid silently into her place at the table.

'Michelle's gone to the Job Centre in Bath,' said Kim. 'And Maureen's kids have the day off school. They took sandwiches and went over to Merlinslade to play.'

'We were given a couple of old bikes for them,' said Esther, 'but we desperately need more things for the children.'

'That's exactly what I mean,' said Kim, banging down a jug of water, and finally taking her own seat. 'It's not bloody fair that Ned Carwithen and Jason Mason should have the latest mountain bikes, and our lot have to make do with rubbish.'

'I'll just say grace,' said Esther firmly. She bowed her head and launched into a prayer.

Georgia, watching her composed, intent face, wondered if she ever felt passionately about anything other than her religion these days. Yet there used to be another side to Esther. At school she'd been equally passionate about acting. Her performances in the drama group had astonished everyone. In them she seemed to come alive more fully than ever she did in real life.

Georgia glanced round the rest of the table. Kim was sitting with an exasperated but amused expression on her face. Tracey was trying to keep the children quiet, Maureen looked as if she hadn't slept all night and could easily do so now, and only Sumitra had her hands together and her head bowed. The moment the prayer finished Kim grabbed a ladle and started doling out the casserole.

'Did you see round the house at Merlinslade, Georgia?' Esther enquired, as she cut chunks of bread for everyone.

'Only the theatre. It's perfect, hardly altered at all from when it was first built. You must come and see it. You used to be so good at acting. I'll never forget that terrific Perdita you did on television.'

'Esther? Acting?' said Kim. 'I don't believe it. You're a dark horse Est. Why didn't you tell us?'

At Oxford, where she was reading Theology, Esther had been seen in an OUDS play by an agent, and offered the part of Perdita in a television production of *A Winter's Tale*. She was hard-up at the time, and after much heart-searching she had accepted the role. But though the director had by some miracle been able to procure her a coveted Equity card, Esther, to the wonder of her friends, afterwards resolutely turned down all other offers of work.

She frowned as she piled the bread on a plate. 'I decided I was getting to love it too much – the praise, the glamour, that sort of thing.'

'What sort of screwy reason is that?' said Kim. 'If you like something, go for it, I say.'

'Nico's got some good ideas for the theatre,' said Georgia hastily.

'I haven't met him yet,' said Esther. 'He only returned to Merlinslade a few weeks ago, and he doesn't come to church. But Bron Carwithen's agreed to read the lesson once a month.'

'He didn't appear to be in a particularly Christian frame of mind this morning.'

'He was fairly cynical about it, but he does seem to have some sense of duty. I'm sure he'll do a lot more for the church eventually.'

'You'll be lucky,' said Kim, scraping up the last of the casserole for herself. It had been a very puny chicken, and even eked out with vegetables had only given them a small bowlful each. 'You trust people too much.'

'Our Lord trusted people,' said Esther.

'No offence, Est,' said Kim, 'but look where it got him.'

Esther's face assumed a troubled, stubborn expression. Georgia knew it well. When she was younger she'd argued about religion with Esther until they were both hoarse. After her own experiences in the Third World it was hard to believe in Esther's benevolent God, or in the perfectibility of the human race.

Esther seemed all set for a long wrangle with Kim, but her attention was diverted by the toddler overturning his mug of milk. She embarked on another subject obviously dear to her heart, the setting up of a village playgroup. By the time that was exhausted they'd finished the casserole and eaten their way through a rhubarb crumble spiced with ginger and orange.

Kim started to clear away the dishes on to a tray, refusing all offers of help with the washing-up. Esther went with the two mothers to settle some dispute over the children's bedrooms, and Sumitra, who'd hardly spoken, slipped away noiselessly after her.

Georgia finished stacking a pile of plates for Kim. 'That was a great meal,' she said.

'Yeah, not bad, was it? The refuge budget doesn't run to much, though, and Est's such a soft touch that she'll help anyone with a hand-out. Not that I should complain. She took me in, after all.'

'I'm surprised you can't find a job when you can cook like that.'

Kim gave a short laugh. 'I've got a record. Employers run a mile from someone like me. But I have to go to the Job Centre every now and then to keep the social happy.'

'Sorry,' said Georgia in confusion. 'I didn't mean to pry. What on earth did you do to get a record? Oh God, I'm sorry again. I shouldn't be asking you that.'

'No worries,' said Kim. 'It's best when people ask straight out. I duffed up the guy who torched my van. He owned the land we were camping on. We caught him doing a runner. He wasn't hurt

71

much, just a black eye and a few cuts. My mate, the bloke I shared the van with, pulled me off before I really took him apart. But the mean git laid a charge. Anyway, he got put away, and I got a suspended sentence.'

Georgia looked at Kim with respect. 'What a bastard. I don't blame you. What happened to your friend?'

'He buggered off to a squat in London, but I didn't fancy going back to life in the smoke.'

'Is there any chance you could get another van?'

'Not unless I find a job. Anyway, I'm OK here for a while, and this lot need someone to keep an eye on them.' She looked up as she heard feet in the corridor. 'That's Est back again. I'd better shut up. She thinks I should forgive and forget.'

She whipped away the laden tray and disappeared into the kitchen as Esther returned. Sumitra was still there like a shadow behind her, this time carrying a bag containing some embroidery. She went to the window seat, and began to sew, looking as neat and self-contained as Beatrix Potter's mouse tailor of Gloucester.

'What are you making?' Georgia asked.

'It is a blouse, my gift for Esther,' Sumitra said, holding it out for inspection.

The cutting was faultless, the stitches, all done by hand, tiny. The collar, which she was embroidering with flowers, was scalloped with picot-edging so regular that it could have been made by a machine. Georgia had rarely seen work like it outside a museum.

'Where did you learn to sew like this? It's absolutely perfect.'

Sumitra fixed sad brown eyes on Georgia.

'Of course it is perfect. I learned in my convent school. Before I married and came to England, I was a professional dressmaker with a big, big firm in Bombay. We copied only couture clothes. But all that is past now. My parents have gone, my husband has gone, and even my home.'

'You have a home with us,' said Esther firmly. 'You do have some blessings, you know. Just to be able to sew like this is a great gift.'

Georgia handed the blouse back to her. 'Esther's right. I'm sure you could set up your own business here.'

'I keep telling her that,' said Esther, 'but I can't convince her.'

Sumitra looked indignant. 'I was not trained for business. I am an artist. And my husband did not wish me to work. He did not wish me to be exposed to racist insults.'

'But with your own business no one would insult you,' said Esther, 'especially if you started here in the rectory.'

Sumitra picked up the blouse and folded it away. 'I have a headache,' she said. 'Please to excuse. I am going upstairs.'

She disappeared as quietly as she'd arrived.

'Oh dear,' said Esther. 'Poor Sumitra. I know she's had a bad time, but she will resist any attempt to help. She just sits here day after day turning out that exquisite needlework, and never looking any happier. It's almost a year since she was widowed, and she really ought to be thinking a little more positively by now.'

Kim came back into the room to collect the last of the dishes.

'Will you and Georgia be here for tea, Est? I could throw a cake together this afternoon.'

'I thought you might like to go for a walk and have tea with us afterwards,' Esther said to Georgia. 'I've a parish council meeting later on, but not till six.'

'You'd better watch out,' said Kim. 'Brighid and the Disciples of the Fountain are all over the place today. I met a gang of them by the stream gathering rushes while I was looking for salad stuff.'

'Do you know the Disciples?' Georgia asked Esther. 'I saw them in Bath for the first time yesterday.'

There was a pause. 'Yes, I know them,' said Esther cautiously.

'You don't sound as if you approve.'

'It's not exactly that. No one could be full of more loving-kindness than Brighid. She wants to look after the whole world. She has a gift for healing, and for mothering too. She makes people feel secure.'

'Huh, smother love I call it,' said Kim. 'And it's so phoney, the way she spells her name. Michelle dropped out of the Disciples recently, and she says it's really Bridget. She changed it to Brighid to sound more Celtic.'

Esther frowned. 'That's true at least. But I've a lot of respect for her. She used to be a deacon at the mission where I worked. She came from a very poor rural family near Glastonbury, and her early life was a tremendous struggle. That's why she loves to help young people.'

'She doesn't sound Somerset now,' said Kim. 'The way she speaks is even phonier than her name.'

'Brighid ran a Christian holistic therapy group in her spare time, until she was asked to leave the ministry,' Esther went on. 'She'd begun to incorporate New Age elements into her teaching, saying that the Virgin Mary was simply an aspect of the earth goddess, who was in her turn the female aspect of God. Strictly speaking that's heresy, but in one way I agree with her. After all, why should God be exclusively male?'

'Right on, Est,' said Kim. 'I'm with you there.'

'What happened when she left?' asked Georgia, fascinated.

'She'd been saving for years. She bought a tumbledown farmhouse and outbuildings near here, did them up, renamed them the Sanctuary, and formed her own sect. Several of the youngsters from the centre went with her, and she's attracted more since then. She's a genius with disturbed teenagers.'

'At least the kids seem happy enough,' said Kim. 'And it's a lot better for them than being on the funny farm.'

'Perhaps,' said Esther thoughtfully. 'In many ways she's been a great loss to the church.'

'She doesn't sound so bad,' said Georgia. 'Bron Carwithen got very worked up about the group this morning, but I suppose that's because of Morrigan's connections with it. Nico told me all about him. I gather he should have inherited Merlinslade.'

'You should hear what they're saying about Morrigan and Brighid in the village,' said Kim. 'But Michelle thinks he's got some sort of mother-fixation on her. Apparently he was nuts about his own mother.'

'I think we should stop gossiping,' said Esther firmly and infuriatingly. 'It's nearly three already. Shall we go for our walk now?'

Once past the rectory the road petered out in a wide rutted path. Esther hitched up her cassock, revealing a pair of surprisingly frivolous socks, and clambered over a wobbly stile. Georgia followed her through some meadows which had just been cut for hay.

'This is all part of the Carwithen home farm,' said Esther. 'Old Edmund tried to keep the public out by letting the stiles fall down and ploughing the footpaths, but it didn't work.'

The track narrowed. A cuckoo was flinging a broken call from the woods clothing the escarpment. They crossed the river by a wooden footbridge, beneath which the banks were yellow with kingcups, and continued on until they came to a large field of young corn. The path ran along its side towards another stile into the woods.

There a faint haze of withering bluebells still remained, and the scent of wild garlic was heavy in the air. Georgia followed Esther up a sunken track bounded by ancient limes. Their roots reached into the earth like gnarled hands. The wood grew taller and thicker, stretching almost impenetrably on either side of the track, choked with festoons of briony and old man's beard.

Eventually they emerged into a more open beech hanger. The ground was soft with last year's mast. Smooth grey trunks soared above their heads. The trees seemed like sentinels, not hostile but calmly watchful. As they continued to climb, the slope was steep enough to prevent conversation, but not steep enough to prevent Georgia's thoughts reverting to Blake again.

Halfway up the slope they sat on a fallen trunk to regain their breath. Esther undid a couple of buttons at her neck, and looked up at the calm blue vault of the sky through the trees. She loved the beech grove. It was one of the reasons why she'd brought Georgia here.

'It reminds me of a cathedral,' she said. 'The atmosphere's so solemn and peaceful. Don't you feel it too? I often come here when I'm worried about something. It's a good place to think.'

She transferred her gaze to Georgia, who was looking into the distance with the expression she'd worn when Esther first saw her in the church. That look was the other reason why she'd brought Georgia to the beech grove. 'You never explained why your marriage broke up,' she said quietly.

Georgia snapped her gaze back to Esther. Her expression

became wary. 'Why should I?' she asked.

Her voice was curt. Esther guessed the question had taken her off guard, as she'd meant it to.

'I just felt you might like to talk about it. Most people do. Because you hadn't said anything, I thought perhaps it was still bothering you.'

Georgia picked up an empty beech husk, breaking away a section of prickly shell to reveal the silky fur inside.

'There isn't much to tell. I made a bad choice, that's all. We weren't right for each other.'

'It seemed such a rapid decision,' said Esther. 'How long were you married?'

'Six months. Quite long enough.' Georgia's voice was expressionless. 'I only needed two to find out. And it's easy to get a divorce in the States.'

'Find out what?' said Esther softly.

Methodically Georgia began to dismember the rest of the husk. It was hard enough to tease out the real reasons for the breakdown of any marriage, Esther thought, but even more difficult in Georgia's case. Their lives had been so different. Her own tranquil, trusting relationship with John, a young chaplain in a northern university, seemed light years from Georgia's experience.

'Blake had someone else all along, and never told me,' Georgia said, still avoiding Esther's eyes.

For a few moments the only noise came from the breeze soughing in the tops of the beeches. Esther was puzzled. Infidelity was common enough, but it didn't usually lead to quite such a rapid breakdown in a marriage. People usually had another try, and Georgia had never been one to give up easily.

'Why do you think he didn't tell you?' she asked.

'It was an affair he wanted to finish. He was desperate to prove to himself that he could do without it. He thought being married would change things. He knew I loved him, he thought he loved me, and so he took the risk.'

'Didn't you feel like giving him a second chance?'

'No, I bloody well didn't! And anyway something else happened which meant he had to go back to the other person.'

'Poor Blake,' said Esther, still trying to probe for the truth. 'At least you're free, but presumably he's now in exactly the same situation as before?'

Georgia hurled the pieces of beech husk away. The cuckoo's mocking call echoed from deep within the wood. 'For Christ's sake, Esther, what kind of reaction is that? He used me to help him out of his own emotional mess!'

'Yet you said he thought he loved you. You must have believed him to begin with. You must have got something out of it as well.'

'Of course I did, at first. I thought the marriage was everything I wanted, till I found out . . . Even then I might have given it another go. But then this – this second thing I was telling you about – killed it completely.' She looked at Esther for the first time. Her eyes were wretched. 'And whose side are you on anyway? I'm trying to feel better, not worse.'

'I don't think one should take sides in a divorce. I'm just sad that you feel so resentful. People don't get over something like this until they stop being bitter.'

Georgia, looking at Esther's earnest, puzzled face, decided that there was no point in telling her more. She'd been a fool not to resist the temptation to spill out her anger and resentment. She knew from Esther's letters that she was conducting some virginal long-distance liaison with her chaplain in Leeds, so how could she possibly understand the lonely, humiliating aftermath of a marriage like Georgia's?

She stood up, brushing strands of moss from her jeans.

'The only thing that makes sense is that I've been a complete idiot,' she said, trying hard to calm her voice. 'The break-up unbalanced my whole life for a while. It could even now – look how I'm almost quarrelling with you. So let's just drop the whole subject. Shall we go on?'

Esther threw Georgia a sympathetic glance which made her want to scream with irritation, but said nothing more as they began to toil through the trees again. Georgia walked ahead, driving herself upwards as she tried to empty thoughts of Blake from her mind, dislodging showers of earth and decaying leaves with her angry footsteps. Gradually the beeches gave way to a straggly stand of yew, and they began to hear the sound of running water. Georgia stopped to wait for Esther, who reached her side looking infuriatingly composed.

'I thought you'd like to see the Grail Well,' Esther said. 'It really is a special sort of place.'

Georgia would have loved to answer that in her present frame of mind she could do without a visit to some holy well, especially as it would no doubt lead to even more good-intentioned pronouncements. But Esther's face was so full of innocent anticipation that she managed to suppress another dismissive remark. She searched around for a non-committal comment, and remembered something Bron Carwithen had said.

'I gather it's been more or less taken over by Brighid and the Disciples of the Fountain.'

'It's traditionally a healing spring, so she does rather consider it her personal territory.'

'You'd have to be in pretty good health to get up that slope in the first place,' said Georgia.

Esther had found an overgrown side path through the yews. She pushed her way along it, holding back the branches, into a large grassy clearing backed by sheer rock. It was like a secret outdoor room. Rowans arched gracefully across the bare limestone, forming a graceful backdrop to the pool at its base. The cliff towered above for another fifty feet to open downland, which was bounded by a line of hawthorn trees.

The well pool, wide enough to swim in, had long ago been edged with slabs of stone to form a raised parapet. Its crevices were packed with cushions of moss. More flagstones formed a platform between the pool and the rock face. From it steps led down into the water, which was too deep to stand in. Round the inner edge of the pool, about a yard beneath the surface of the water, was set a wide ledge, where pilgrims could stand to bathe in comparative safety.

At the back of the platform, a massive standing stone with shining green ribbons of hart's tongue fern growing round its base stood in a hollow gouged from the rock. On the stone had been incised a primitive representation of a woman, squat and pregnant, her face almost featureless apart from closed eyes and secretive mouth.

'People believe the carving's St Bride,' said Esther, 'but it's much older than Christianity – were Celtic, the experts say. The Church had it rededicated to the saint in the Middle Ages.'

The water in the pool was clear as the sea on a tropical reef. The pebbles in its depths shone in the dappled sunlight like polished agate. Among them a spring rose in a series of gentle bubbles which just shivered the surface. The water spilled out of a narrow overflow, and then plunged downwards along a rocky bed. Through a gap in the woodland made by the stream, Georgia could see Merlinslade and the surrounding estate dreaming in the afternoon sunshine far below.

She sat on the parapet to regain her breath after the climb. When she dabbled her hand in the water the cold stung her skin. She scooped it up in her palm and drank a few drops. It had a refreshing, slightly bitter taste. She glanced over at Esther, who'd gone to sit on the other side of the pool. Her hands were clasped in her lap, and her eyes closed. Probably praying for my redemption, Georgia thought wrily, but all the same there was something very calming about the atmosphere of the pool, the lulling sound of the stream, and the flicker of light in the water.

She sat in a sort of trance for a minute or two while Esther continued to pray, until they were roughly interrupted by something crashing about in the yew thicket. It sounded like a large and breathless animal. Esther looked up with a startled expression. The branches sprang apart, and an untidy figure burst into the clearing.

It was Brighid, her hair escaping from a loose plait, with twigs clinging to the bottom of her long white robe. Her broad, slightly flat feet were crammed into leather sandals, and she was carrying some empty wine bottles in a wicker basket.

She stopped abruptly when she saw them. Georgia glanced at Esther, who'd risen hurriedly to her feet. The contrast between the two women was striking: Esther slim, almost asexual in her cassock, Brighid like some burgeoning fertility goddess.

Brighid's large, soft mouth stretched into a smile. She put down her basket on the grass. 'Esther, my dear, how good to see you here. The peace of the fountain be with you.'

Georgia suppressed the frivolous thought that it sounded like a line from *Star Wars*. She watched Esther nearly disappear as Brighid wrapped her flowing white sleeves round her in a comprehensive embrace, and then saw her advancing, arms outstretched, in Georgia's own direction.

Before she could escape Brighid had enfolded her as well. Georgia braced herself, expecting to be overwhelmed. Instead she had the impression of being received into a soft, infinitely comfortable feather bed which had about it the enticing scent of summer flowers and freshly mown grass. She felt almost like a baby in the embrace, as if Brighid were inviting her to become a child again, to resign all her cares into her keeping. It was an alluring but unnerving sensation, and one she didn't like.

She managed to pull herself away, but not entirely, for Brighid had somehow got hold of her hands, and was holding her at arm's length, gazing searchingly at her with cloudless blue eyes.

'Didn't I see you at our meeting in Bath yesterday, then again along the road this morning?' she said. 'And now you're here at the well.'

The coincidence obviously had some deep significance for her which Georgia, wondering how soon she could disentangle her hands without seeming rude, couldn't begin to fathom. Luckily Esther came to her rescue with brisk introductions.

'And what do you think of our holy well?' Brighid asked.

'It's very peaceful,' said Georgia diplomatically, at last managing to pull herself away.

Brighid's wide, guileless eyes seemed to reflect the light from the pool. 'The presence of the Grail is with us still, leading us to harmony with nature, making us at one with the mother god, the female aspect of the deity which has been denied so long.'

'There is only one indivisible God, Brighid,' said Esther gravely, 'and the Bible says "Thou shalt have no other gods before Me".'

' "In My house are many mansions",' Brighid instantly quoted back. 'The goddess and the god are equally part of one great whole.'

'The Holy Spirit can have no gender,' said Esther. 'The Testaments only spoke of God as male because they were written in the framework of a patriarchal society. Your concept of a

Christian earth goddess is completely misguided.'

'It's completely logical. It explains exactly why we've gone wrong,' said Brighid eagerly. 'We've almost ruined the natural world because we forgot that there was a goddess as well as a god. If we listen to her, copy her wise and gentle ways, nurture the caring part of ourselves, above all forgive ourselves, we can find fulfilment. It's never too late to make ourselves new.'

Brighid's eyes were shining with excitement. Her voice had fallen to a deep contralto. In spite of her untidy hair and mud-spattered robe she conveyed so much passionate conviction that for a moment Georgia could almost believe her. Might indeed have believed her if experience hadn't told her nothing was as easy as that. But she began to understand the influence Brighid could have on someone very young and unhappy and confused.

'Not in the way you mean. You've taken the wrong path,' said Esther, looking all set for an absorbing theological discussion.

Georgia wondered how long this would go on. She was beginning to think longingly of Sophia Street and a long relaxing bath and even of Chloe's chatter. Merlinslade, Nico, the refuge, the discussion of her marriage, and now Brighid had been almost too much to take in one day.

'You're tired,' said Brighid in a voice heavy with understanding, turning her blue gaze on Georgia. 'How selfish I am to keep you here. You must go home and rest. Take some well water to drink on your way. I'll gladly lend you one of my flasks.'

'There's no need for that. We shall be having tea at the rectory shortly,' said Esther, to Georgia's relief. Brighid's uncanny intuition of her mood had startled her, and she'd no desire to lug a heavy and no doubt leaky bottle of water all the way downhill.

'I shall expect a visit from both of you at the Sanctuary very soon. I especially want you to meet Morrigan, Esther. You must have heard he's joined us. He was heaven sent. He's started to do so much for the group already.'

'What I've heard makes me think you should be very careful,' said Esther. 'You have young, susceptible souls in your care.'

'Don't you remember our Lord's words? "Judge not lest thou shalt be judged".' Brighid picked up her basket and went over to the pool. She began to set out her bottles on the parapet. 'Morrigan has become a different person. Long ago, when he was still in India, he'd already begun to realise that he was on a false path. His dearest wish is to join us now in making the world a safer and more caring place.'

Esther hesitated.

'Maybe,' she said slowly. 'But it seems odd that he should return to a place where he's already caused so much distress.'

A look of pained resignation came over Brighid's face.

'Where better than to show how much he's changed? Who are we to question his motives when he has a genuine intention not to err again? To forgive is divine. I'd have expected more understanding from you, Esther.'

She rolled up her sleeves, revealing plump, sturdy arms with the flesh dimpled at the elbow, and began to fill the bottles from the pool.

Esther's face set in an obstinate expression.

'Don't forget you're working without the safety net of the Church, Brighid. If something goes wrong it can't help you.'

'Nothing will go wrong,' she said, with a seraphic smile. 'The goddess will see to that.' She started to cork the bottles and lay them in the basket. 'Stop worrying, Esther. You should relax, trust your own feelings, get in touch with the real person within yourself. It's the only way you'll realise your true potential.'

Esther gave a sigh of exasperation. 'I'm worried about the real person within Morrigan,' she said.

'Then why don't you come and talk to him yourself?' asked Brighid. She stood up, looking like a figure from a Greek frieze with her basket balanced on her hip. 'And now I'm afraid I must leave you both. I've remedies to make up before supper. So many people are beginning to rely on them. But don't forget there's always a welcome for you at the Sanctuary.'

They watched her blunder cheerfully out of sight among the trees. Georgia was struggling not to laugh, and even Esther was smiling as she shook her head.

'A good woman, but a misguided one.'

'She's certainly persuasive, but she seems fairly harmless,' said Georgia, sitting again to shake a stone from her espadrille before she and Esther moved on. 'I can see that Morrigan must make a huge difference to the group.'

'He's definitely not the sort of person Brighid should be associating with, even though he is supposed to be a reformed character. I'm always wary of dramatic conversions. His was certainly that, and well publicised too. The press loved it. Straight from Buddhism to Christianity – it seems unlikely, though I suppose it is possible.'

'So what do you think his real motive is?' Georgia asked, as she eased her foot back into her shoe. Esther paused to consider her reply. She still looked as neat and cool as the pied wagtail poised on the parapet at the far side of the pool.

'It's hard to say, but I've a suspicion he could be intending to impose his own rules on the group.'

'What makes you think that?'

'Michelle left the group recently after some sort of argument with him. She was going to become a full member at a ceremony of baptism Brighid holds here at the pool, until Morrigan began to drop hints about changing the financial organisation. I did wonder if he could be after their money.'

'Why should he need it, though? He's made millions out of his recordings. I can't stand the guy, but it doesn't quite make sense.'

'Exactly. I dislike him as much as you. I've seen his public performances with the group, and the way he manipulates the audience. But he doesn't need the money, and you know I hate this sort of conjecture. The village is buzzing with enough rumours already. I don't want to add to them.'

Esther pressed her lips together in a way that Georgia knew of old heralded her imminent refusal to discuss the subject any more. She shook out the folds of her cassock, and the wagtail flew on to a rowan branch with a impudent flirt of its black and white wings.

'I've been far too indiscreet as it is. Let's drop the subject. Tell me more about Chloe. Have you decided yet whether to send her back to school?'

Esther began to pick her way determinedly down the narrow path which led away from the pool along the bank of the stream. Georgia started to follow, but she turned briefly, curious to know if the wagtail had gone back to the pool.

A different movement caught her eye. On top of the escarpment, not quite concealed by a thorn tree, she saw the glint of light on field glasses, and then a figure in a black jacket. She stared again, and before it disappeared had a long enough glimpse to be certain that she'd just seen Morrigan. But whether he'd been keeping watch on Brighid, on Esther and herself, or even Merlinslade, was not clear at all.

Chapter 5

The Sophia Street flat was empty when Georgia got home, but Chloe had left a note peppered with exclamation marks on the kitchen table.

'Met Natty in town this afternoon!!! Her dad's just got a job at the university!!! She asked me to stay the night at her house, so don't wait up.'

Georgia frowned at the smiling face drawn in the huge C of the scrawled signature. Chloe had carefully omitted to say where Natty lived, so that she couldn't be summoned home, and had thus successfully evaded a discussion about her future for a second day. More worrying still, Natasha, who'd at one time been Chloe's best friend at the research station, made trouble as unthinkingly as a muddy puppy let loose on a newly washed floor.

When Chloe was eleven Natty had scared her half to death by persuading a local witch doctor to let them watch one of his ceremonies. And when Natty discovered some cannabis in her parents' bedroom drawer and persuaded Chloe to smoke it with her, they'd both ended up completely stoned for twenty-four hours. Everyone was hugely relieved when Natty's father moved on to a new scientific post in the Far East.

Chloe's defection did have one compensation, though. It left Georgia free for an essential concentrated read-through of *The Tempest* before she put her thoughts together for the first director's meeting the following week. She made herself a light supper, put on an old Dylan tape, and settled down with the play.

She read quickly and intensely, the music weaving in and out of her consciousness, and as she made notes her earlier impressions began to take on added depth and richness, like water tinged with slowly falling drops of wine. Images of the African reefs, of the ancient woods at Merlinslade, and of the paradise carvings in the church, all swam through her mind. When she got to bed in the small hours her ideas for the sets were beginning to take firm shape.

In the morning the images were sharper still after sleep. She sketched all day and finally emerged in the late afternoon to make herself a cup of tea. After a fruitless search in the fridge she realised that Chloe must have drunk all the spare carton of milk the previous day, and was forced to sally out into the town for a replacement.

Great Pulteney Street was thronged with tourists drifting about happily and aimlessly in the sunshine. Georgia found some milk in a corner shop, and then, realising that she'd missed almost the whole of a glorious summer's day, turned into the cool greenness of Henrietta Park.

The flower beds were full of roses. Bumble bees blundered among them, almost too weighted with pollen to take off for another flower. Lovers seemed to be everywhere: entwined on the grass, sitting in absorbed conversation under the trees, walking totally engrossed in each other along paths lined bridally with mock orange blossom.

She sat down on a bench, feeling intensely alone in spite of the people around her. She remembered walking with Blake in the park opposite their apartment, lying in his arms under a flowering cherry, looking up at the tent of white and a cardinal bird perched like a scarlet brush stroke in its midst, and thinking it wasn't possible to be happier. She'd been living since the divorce in a cocoon of unremitting work which she'd spun to prevent the outside world harming her any more, and sent up a short prayer to whatever god might be listening that her sister would have more luck than herself.

At five o'clock Chloe telephoned from a call box to say she was staying on for supper with Natty. She conveniently let her money run out just as Georgia was warning her not to stay too late.

Georgia went back to the studio, and started to work on a list of equipment for the wardrobe at Merlinslade. Again the time rushed by, until at about ten o'clock she heard a faint movement in the flat, and realised Chloe must have sneaked in unobserved. She crept upstairs, intensely disliking having to monitor her in this way. There was a faint line of light under the spare bedroom door.

When Georgia threw it open, Chloe was sitting in bed in a baggy pink T shirt with Tintin on the front, laying out her Tarot cards on the duvet. A new poster had been tacked to the wall, of a woman with streaming hair, presumably meant to be Gaia, embracing the globe. Instead of the Crowded House tape which had played nonstop on her first night, the room was filled with the unearthly songs of the blue whale.

Chloe looked up with a start, her eyes vast and shining in the rays of a scented candle stuck in an eggcup by her side. Georgia snapped on the central light. The cards slithered on to the floor. Chloe dived out of bed and began to rush round picking them up.

'Look what you've made me do!' she said in a shrill, accusing voice. 'You're supposed to treat the Tarot with respect. I'll never get a proper reading now.'

Georgia took the cards out of her hands and put them firmly on the chest of drawers. Chloe grabbed the silk handkerchief and laid it tenderly on top of the pack before leaping back into bed. Georgia just had time to see how thin her legs were below the T shirt. Chloe pulled up the duvet, wound her arms round her knees and glared at her.

'It's no good looking at me like that,' said Georgia. 'We have to talk, and you know it. I don't want another day of disappearing tricks tomorrow.'

'I thought you'd like me out of the way. You keep telling me how busy you are.'

'I told the headmistress you'd be back at school on Sunday evening. I haven't changed my mind.'

Chloe stared at her as if she'd said she'd got to go to jail.

'You're not really going to send me back? Everyone hates me there. How could you, just when I've met Natty again, who was my best friend *ever*?'

Georgia sat down on the edge of the bed. 'What do you mean, everyone hates you? You seemed to have masses of friends when I visited the school.'

'That was then,' said Chloe darkly. 'Everything's different now.'

'I'm warning you, Chloe, nothing I've heard from you so far is going to make me change my mind. And especially not wild statements about people hating you. Why should anyone hate you, for heaven's sake?'

'Because I'm different, because I haven't done all the things they've done. The boys especially think I'm useless. No one wants to go out with me.'

'But the head said you had a boyfriend till a little while ago.'

'Exactly. He finished with me because I wasn't like the others.'

'I wish you wouldn't keep saying that without telling me what you mean.'

Chloe picked up Wooster from the side of the pillow, and clasped him in her arms, resting her head on his chin. Tears began to well into her eyes. She sniffed.

'Just get on with it, will you?' said Georgia irritably.

Tears were flooding down Chloe's cheeks. 'There's no need to come on like the Inquisition. All right, I will tell you, and then you'll be sorry. I'm the only girl in the sixth who's a virgin! It's so uncool!'

There was a temporary silence while Georgia veered between a strong desire to laugh, and anger that Chloe should have been made to feel so anxious about something which was her own private choice.

'Darling Chloe, you are an idiot,' said Georgia, trying to keep her voice unconcerned, and putting her arms round her. 'I'm sure the other girls are just having you on. I really don't believe you're the only one. They simply want you to think they're women of the world. And anyway, it's far more laid-back not to go with the crowd. It's your decision, you know, no one else's.'

'But it's not just the girls,' said Chloe, her voice muffled against Georgia's shoulder. 'It was the boys too. Even Martin, the one I was going out with. He was fantastic. He looked just like Daniel Day-Lewis. I was such a dumbo. He said it was uncool not to go all the way. I told him I was a virgin. I thought he'd be pleased. Men are supposed to like virgins, after all. We'd sort of – sort of gone a bit far one evening. It was in the library store room.'

Georgia, who was already disliking the sound of the marvellous Martin intensely, just managed not to say she hoped he was cool enough to use some sort of contraception.

Chloe wiped her eyes on Wooster's ears. 'He was mad, really mad with me. He said I was trying to get him into trouble, and he couldn't possibly do it with me now because virgins made such an awful noise, and someone might hear. Then when I cried I think he was a bit sorry, and he said he didn't mean it, and it was just that I was too fat, and he didn't really fancy fat girls. I felt a million times worse then. Being fat is worse than being a virgin.'

She started crying again in good earnest. Georgia, feeling she'd give anything for five minutes in which to tell this unpleasant schoolboy stud exactly what she thought of him, kept her arms round Chloe and murmured encouraging noises.

'Anyway, when I told the other girls what had happened, they all said I'd better find some one else to lose it with, and go on a diet double quick. Then I might get him back. But I don't want him back. I hate him forever.'

Who were these other girls to tell her sister when or when not to lose her virginity? Georgia thought furiously as she felt Chloe's thin shoulders shaking with sobs. 'I never heard such rubbish. They were probably jealous because you went out with him, and not them. And someone like Martin isn't worth going out with anyway.'

'Do you really think so?' said Chloe in a doubtful voice.

'Of course I do. You'll meet someone much nicer very soon. Is that why you weren't eating?'

'Partly, and partly because I felt so uptight all the time.' She looked hopefully at Georgia. 'So you do see why I couldn't possibly go back? And now I've met Natty again it'd be even harder. You don't know what it's like not to have friends. You were never sent to boarding school with a lot of stand-offish rich kids. You were so lucky going to a comprehensive and staying with lovely Grandma Baines.'

Georgia felt herself wavering. If she did let Chloe stay it would mean the end of her privacy and independence. But the thought of her sister being railroaded into losing her virginity was even worse. And she really was worryingly thin.

'If I did let you stay,' she said slowly, 'you'd have to swear to behave yourself. I don't have the time to sort out any more problems. I don't want you hanging about here all day, either. You'd have to find a temporary job.'

Chloe gave a huge gulp, and pulled away from Georgia. She was smiling like a rainbow.

'You're so good to me, Georgy! And a job's no problem at all. Natty can get me one at Fruits of the Earth. She works there three days a week.'

'I'm not so sure I want you to see too much of Natty. And what's Fruits of the Earth?'

'Natty's really, really responsible these days. You wouldn't know her. Fruits of the Earth is a brilliant shop here in Bath. It sells organic food and herbal remedies and crystals. Everyone's so sweet and friendly there. You'd approve the minute you saw it. They're always wanting staff.'

'Why? What's the snag? I suppose they don't pay much.'

'Oh, Georgy, you're so suspicious. Natty says it's a privilege to work there. It does so much good.'

'All right,' said Georgia. 'I'll make a bargain with you. You can leave school, for the rest of this term at least, and we'll see how you've got on by the end of the summer. If things work out, and the parents give their OK, you can go to the local tech to finish your A levels in September. But if not, you must promise you'll go back to school for a final year. I'm sure we can find one you'd like more than Brandon Lodge.'

'Of course I promise!' said Chloe, now radiant. 'And I do understand about needing your space, especially after the divorce. But it is a bit hard for me when you won't tell me anything. People are always nagging me to be more adult, but they don't treat me like one. We are sisters, after all, yet you've never told me why you and Blake split up. He looked so fabulous from his photos I just couldn't understand it.'

Georgia hesitated. Perhaps it wasn't fair to Chloe not to tell her what had happened. If she didn't hear at least a little bit about it, how was she ever going to learn that you could survive something far worse than a schoolgirl romance?

'He was gorgeous,' she said. 'But that wasn't why I married him, though it certainly helped.'

'I expect he was a terrific lover,' said Chloe in a worldly voice.

'It depends what you mean. He wasn't particularly dynamic. He was a gentle sort of person in many ways. But he made me feel I mattered to him more than anyone else, and at the time that was more important than the most earth-moving sex.'

She smiled at Chloe's puzzled look.

'You and I had an odd sort of upbringing. We didn't get a lot of the ordinary steady background love that other kids take for granted. It makes us more susceptible to people like Blake and Martin who seem to be offering us what we've missed. Do you understand?'

Chloe was knotting and unknotting Wooster's ears.

'Yes, I suppose so. But I understand even less now why you got divorced, and after such a short time too. He was gorgeous-looking, and he made you feel great, so what could go wrong?'

'He was still in love with someone else. He thought if we got married he'd find the strength to break with the other person,' said Georgia, wondering if it would ever get easier to explain. She wished sometimes she could make a video of herself describing what had happened, and sent enquirers off to look at it in an anonymous cubicle a hundred miles away.

'What a ratbag! And who was this other woman? An actress, I suppose. Did you have a confrontation? Was it terrifically dramatic?'

'There was a confrontation, but it wasn't what I'd expected,' said Georgia.

Even now she could hardly bear to re-run that meeting in her mind. She'd gone to it brimming with angry resentment. When she left, the resentment had been joined by guilty pity and a fear so profound that it made the next three months a living nightmare.

'What do you mean? I don't understand,' Chloe persisted.

'I'm sorry,' said Georgia desperately, 'but I still can't talk about it too much. And I don't want to, now I'm beginning to forget a little at last. That's something else you have to understand if we're going to share the flat successfully. I'll tell you one day, but not yet.'

To Georgia's surprise the first week with Chloe in residence was less difficult than she expected. Chloe remained good-tempered, and ate satisfactorily large meals. By mid-week she'd started a part-time job at Fruits of the Earth. Georgia was able to retire thankfully to her studio to finish another small commission for a museum. Afterwards she still had time to vet and sign the contract Nico sent her, and to complete her list of equipment for Merlinslade in time for the director's meeting on Friday.

It took place in the theatre green room, which had last been used during the war by visiting entertainers when Merlinslade was an officers' mess for a nearby army camp. Like most green rooms it was a shabby, comfortable place. A couple of utility sofas upholstered in faded blue moquette and some battered leather library chairs were grouped round a low table whose original surface was almost obliterated with cigarette burns and the rings of innumerable coffee mugs. On the wall there were damp-stained Angus McBean shots of the pre-war London Old Vic, and a signed photo of Gertrude Lawrence, in a backless bias-cut dress which revealed almost every vertebra, dancing with a heavily brilliantined Noel Coward.

'I'll just get out my Power Book,' said Zelda. 'I want to give you both my thoughts so far on *The Tempest*.'

She produced a lap-top computer from the depths of her shoulder bag and propped it on the table. Nico winked at Georgia. He was dressed more casually today, sitting on the arm of one of the sofas in washed-out jeans and a white T shirt with a Pernod logo. A navy blue beret was jammed on the back of his head.

Zelda called up a page of notes, and they plunged into the sort of early exchange of ideas Georgia loved, when anything and everything was still possible and suggestions became more and more crazy and inspired. The discussion began to flag only after an hour of concentrated talk.

'Time for coffee, I think,' said Nico, going over to an electric percolator which was a far cry from the standard green room issue.

Zelda sipped hers cautiously at first, and then with increasing enthusiasm. 'Not bad for an English brew,' she said.

'How did you get that fancy machine past your brother?' Georgia asked, when she finally put down her mug.

'I didn't,' said Nico. 'It's in the equipment schedule as a second-hand electric kettle. He's unlikely to come in here any-way, now the painters have finished. And he knows very well I can't function without decent coffee. I've got to have some respite from Meadie's concoctions.'

Zelda opened her copy of *The Tempest* again. 'If you've both finished, can we get back to the play?' she asked. 'To sum up, the central theme is the reconciliation of Prospero with his brother who stole his dukedom, and the reconciliation of Miranda with the modern world. The island's rather like Merlinslade, in that it's a place out of step with time. Prospero, the creator of visions and dreams, can make anything happen there. The sets must convey that atmosphere. What ideas have you come up with so far, Georgy?'

Nico had almost reached the end of a cigarette. He held it bunched in the fingertips of his right hand. The mannerism made him look more than ever like the off-beat hero from some French cult movie. His eyes, sharp and lively, turned on her.

'Shakespeare was supposed to be inspired by early accounts of the Bermudas. I'd like to make it an island with a tropical beach, but darker inland, perhaps a sort of rain forest. That way we could have some terrific sound effects.'

'Sounds good to me,' said Zelda. 'And how about the cast?'

'The four main characters are all inhabitants of the island, so their costumes could be completely imaginary, produced by

Prospero's magic. Redvers will be wonderful to dress. He's tall, and he has tremendous presence.'

'He *did* have tremendous presence,' said Zelda. 'I damn' well hope Nico's right, and he can get it back again, or we're all in shtuck. He wasn't overly confident when I met him.'

'Of course he will. He just needs a bit of encouragement, poor old sod,' said Nico.

'I'd like to put the court and the sailors into Jacobean costume,' said Georgia, 'but design something right over the top for the clowns, Trinculo and Stephano. Can you tell me what the woman who's playing Miranda looks like?'

'Fiona Hughes? Young, of course, blonde, medium height, nothing outstanding till you see her on stage. She's got a terrific range. I want a Miranda who can cope with the brave new world, not just a daddy's girl. Sean Marchant who plays Ferdinand is a real hunk.'

'Ariel you can't tell me about, presumably,' said Georgia.

'I'm still interviewing. That's why I have to go up to London this evening. I've a full list tomorrow. But obviously I'm not going to choose a two-hundred-pound grandmother with a replacement hip.'

'Then of the main characters that just leaves Caliban.'

'Aha, yes, Caliban,' said Nico. 'Come on Zelda, tell me the worst.'

'Again I leave the dress to Georgia. But I don't want him played as a straight horror. I want him slightly likeable.'

'Thanks a lot,' said Nico. 'So what's it to be, Georgia?'

She shot him a mischievous glance.

' "Part fish, part man", that's what Trinculo says when he first sees him. But he is drunk at the time. Some people think Caliban was a wild man of the woods, like the ancient green man.'

'I refuse to go on in a mermaid's tail. I must be able to move easily. I'm putting lots of biz into the part.'

Georgia smiled. Biz or business was all the little extra effects an actor used to flesh out his role.

'Nor do I want to wear arty bits of fishing net,' Nico went on. 'And I'd prefer not to look like a gorilla either. I saw a terrible

Caliban a few years ago who wore a sort of fake fur jump suit.'

'You'll like it, I promise,' said Georgia, busy making notes. 'But you might be glad of some fur in this theatre in the winter.'

Nico's demands didn't upset her. They weren't unusual, and it was important for an actor to feel completely at ease in his costumes. The main thing at this stage was to exude confidence. Major problems normally didn't arise until the first fitting stage.

'Right,' said Zelda, 'now we've done a quick trip round the main characters and got Nico settled, shall we go on to the minor ones? We can have another general discussion after lunch.'

They talked all morning, decamped to The Mortal Man in Zelda's car for a brief break, and worked again into the mid-afternoon. Towards four o'clock Zelda stretched, and shut down her lap-top.

'I have to crash at the hotel for an hour or two before I go to London,' she said. 'Shall we meet again here in a couple of weeks to see Georgia's designs? Say two weeks next Tuesday?'

'Fine,' said Nico. 'I've got a lot of PR to do.'

'You'll need a little time to equip the wardrobe and engage staff, Georgia. When do you plan to have it all up and running?'

'Just as soon as I can find the right people. I'd like to have a look at the wardrobe before I go, just to check the improvements.' She looked enquiringly at Nico.

'Let's leave it till after the weekend, shall we? It's been a heavy day,' he said, stretching his arms and yawning deeply.

It was a textbook yawn, conveying terminal exhaustion; so textbook that Georgia instantly suspected he was concealing something.

'I want to make sure the partitioning's in the right place,' she said, 'and that the plumbers remembered about the washing machine.'

'It's a bit late to start on all that now. And I rather wanted to show you the house before you left.'

With difficulty she resisted the bait. She'd been longing to see the rest of Merlinslade.

'I'd love to go round the house,' she said, 'but the wardrobe really is more important just now.'

Nico sighed and unfolded himself from the depths of his chair.

'Then I suppose I'd better come with you. There may be one or two small points I need to explain.' His voice was blandly vague.

'I'll leave you both to it,' said Zelda, with an amused look. 'I told you Georgia wouldn't let things pass, Nico.'

When Nico threw open the door of the wardrobe, everything seemed perfect at first. The walls and ceiling were freshly painted, hardboard covered the floor, and the partitions were in exactly the right place. Even the windows were fairly clean, with only a few smears. But when Georgia went into the washing and dyeing area the old stone sink was still in place, the taps still dripped dismally, and there was no sign of plumbing for the washing machine.

She turned to Nico angrily. 'Your brother said this'd be done by now. It's not a huge task, for heaven's sake.'

Nico spread his hands and gave her a disarming smile. 'I'm abjectly sorry, truly, Georgia. I did keep on reminding Bron.'

'He's had a week to fix it, and he's obviously got no intention of hurrying. Supposing I said it didn't matter when you got the costumes? Doesn't he realise actors have to wear something?'

'Of course he does. But things have been a bit difficult for him lately. I'll speak to him again, and I'm sure it'll be just as you want next week.'

'Look, Nico, there isn't any room for delay. I must start bringing in the heavy equipment as soon as possible. I suppose he thinks making costumes is just a matter of handsewing some simple seams and buttonholes, dashing away with the smoothing iron and then adding a few feminine touches at the last minute? In fact, that's probably the whole problem. He's classified it as women's work, and therefore it goes to the back of the queue. I'm right, aren't I?'

'Bron's not really a chauvinist. I think he's just got too much on his hands at the moment, and this seems rather trivial.'

'Then he has to be made to realise that it isn't. I'd better talk to him myself. Where is he?'

Nico wandered over to the cupboards and began to open the doors one by one. 'I don't advise it,' he said, with his back to her. 'The more you nag him, the more bloody-minded he gets. Come and take a look over here – the carpenters have done a brilliant job on these doors.'

'I'm not going to nag him,' said Georgia, ignoring the diversion, 'and I won't involve you. All you have to do is tell me where I can find him.'

Nico shut the door, and came back to sit on the edge of the table.

'You're really keen to play Russian roulette, aren't you?'

'Better now than later,' said Georgia firmly.

Nico shrugged and smiled. 'All right, but I'm keeping out of it. Bron's in the carpentry workshop today, next to the stables. He's working on one of the old wagons. I'll take you over there now.'

There had been a shower at lunchtime, and the cobblestones in the stable yard still gleamed with rain. Georgia and Nico dodged through the puddles to the far end, past loose boxes and an open barn crammed with ancient farm machinery. A chicken hopped down from a harrow, and picked its way fastidiously round a patch of mud. Nico stopped near a partly open door.

'That's the workshop,' he said. 'I'll grab another cup of coffee, then wait for you in the front courtyard, just in case you need first aid. Just look at those puddles, will you? I feel a severe attack of the Gene Kellys coming on.'

Whistling the theme tune from *Singing in the Rain*, he bounded away across the puddles, only pausing at the corner of the yard to twirl by one arm from a drainpipe and wave his beret at her before he disappeared.

Cautiously, still smiling, she pushed open the workshop door. Her footfalls were hushed by a silt of sawdust and woodshavings. Spiders' webs curtained the windows, except for one which overlooked a carpenter's bench. It had been polished with considerably more enthusiasm than the windows in the wardrobe. From an old radio in a walnut-veneered case the last part of Sibelius's Second Symphony spilled into the empty room.

Through an open door into the wagon shed she could see part of a hay wain. It had a faded blue body, and the tail board was outlined with yellow stringing. The rear axle had been wedged up on a section of tree trunk. One of its wheels, with a section of the wooden rim removed, lay across an upturned barrel in the workshop, and another was propped against the wall.

Some wooden-handled chisels and gouges were lined up at the back of the bench beneath a rack of saws. Motes of dust floated in the light reflected from their blades. The old-fashioned tools were small works of craftsmanship in themselves, their spare lines immensely pleasing to the eye.

Idly, as the music flowed over her, Georgia picked up a chisel. The beechwood handle fitted snugly into the palm of her hand; its squared-off blade was razor sharp. A new rim section for the wheel lay on the bench. The scent of freshly honed wood made her remember the African woodworkers in the village near the research station, who produced miracles of carving with even simpler tools than these.

Her mind was so far away that for a moment she didn't realise someone else had come into the workshop. Bron stood by the bench, watching her. He was wearing the same overalls as before, and a khaki shirt with rolled-up sleeves. His forearms were powdered with sawdust, and he had an open spring-loaded rule in his hand.

'Do you want something?' he asked in a voice which demanded a negative reply. He let the steel rule whip back shrilly into its case.

Rapidly she assembled her thoughts. 'Yes. I want to know why the wardrobe isn't finished. You promised to have it done by now.'

He put the tape in his pocket, and went to the radio, listening to it for a few moments before he fractionally turned down the volume.

'I promised nothing of the sort. I simply said I'd try,' he replied.

He came forward, and took the chisel from her. She wondered how he could go on wearing such hideous overalls day after day. She decided he must be the sort of dauntingly worthy person to whom appearances meant nothing.

'That's not for playing with,' he said, and put it firmly back in the rack. He looked as if his mind was still more on the music than the subject of their discussion.

'Your brother is paying for my time and expertise. You appear to want to waste them. It doesn't make sense.'

He took the new rim section from the bench, and went over to the wheel lying across the barrel. The music was gathering into the final movement. She thought angrily that he might at least have turned the volume down a little more.

'You've got most of what you wanted. You'll just have to make do for a little longer, that's all,' he said.

He picked up a lever and with immense concentration began to coax the spokes into position, so that they'd fit into the opposing sockets on the inside curve of the new rim joint. She'd only seen a description of the procedure in a book on forgotten country crafts, but she knew enough to understand how tricky it was.

'Could you mend that wheel without the proper equipment?' she demanded, dredging in her memory for the specialised vocabulary of the wainwright. 'Could you lever the staves into the felloe mortices without the spoke dog? But you have no problems, of course, because *your* workshop's got everything you need.'

As the symphony drove towards its towering conclusion, she wasn't sure if he'd even heard her. He'd manoeuvred the spokes a little way into their sockets, and was lining up the rim dowels to fit the body of the wheel.

'I could do it,' he said, taking up a mallet to hammer the rim into place. 'But it'd present a slight problem, I suppose. Where did you pick up all that jargon?'

'I designed a farmyard set for a college production of *Tom Jones* a few years ago. We made a replica of a haywain.'

'So that makes you an expert, does it?'

'Of course not. But I do remember quite a lot about the wainwright's craft. I might even be able to tell you something you don't know about the carts next door.'

She didn't intend to argue with him through the noise of the mallet as well as the music. Deliberately she went through the inner doorway into the quiet of the wagon shed.

He hesitated, clearly not wanting to miss a minute of the Sibelius, but eventually put down the mallet and came towards her. He walked easily, like Nico, but without Nico's panache. He seemed to be concentrating on her at last.

'All right,' he said, 'you're obviously not going to let me listen to the music until you do.' He put his hands on the side board of the blue cart. 'Tell me about this box wagon.'

'You've got the name wrong,' she said, beginning to enjoy herself. 'It's a bow wagon, because the sides are curved to accommodate the wheels. It's smaller than the Suffolk wains I copied for the play, to make it easier to manoeuvre on the hills round here. For the same reason it has a full-lock. You ought to paint the wheels red. It's the traditional colour in this part of the country.'

Even now he wouldn't acknowledge her expertise. He stood with his hands on his hips, gazing at her in a way that made her feel as if she was showing off. She decided to have one last shot at cutting him down to size.

'If you're really so pushed for time, I could fix the other wheel for you,' she said sweetly. 'I've got half an hour to spare.'

She couldn't imagine anything more unpleasant than having to work alongside him, but at least there was now a satisfying expression of appalled disbelief on his face.

'That won't be necessary,' he said in a stiff voice. Everything about him urged her to leave his territory.

'Then we've nothing more to say to each other. You leave me no alternative except to ask Nico to cancel my contract. I wouldn't be able to finish the costumes and sets by the due date, and I never promise what I can't deliver. I'll go and speak to him now.'

She marched back into the workshop to collect her notebook which she'd left on the bench. The symphony was drawing to its last majestic notes. He followed her, and stood with his hand resting on the radio, as if he wanted to feel the music as well as hear it.

She was still too angry to experience the regret which she knew would come later in good measure. She lingered for a moment, half caught up in the music herself, wondering if she could have handled the interview in any better way. Her eye went the tools for a last time. Almost instinctively, drawn once more by the craftsmanship, she picked up a box plane, feeling the perfect balance and the smooth grain of the polished wood beneath her hand.

As the music came to an end she laid the plane carefully on the bench, and when she looked up he was watching her.

'I'll have what you want done by the beginning of next week,' he said abruptly. 'I can't promise more than that.'

While she was still struggling with her astonishment, he extracted a small notebook from the top pocket of his overalls, and proceeded to make some notes with a pencil stump in a cursive, compact script. Before she could decide how to reply without actually having to thank him, he snapped the book shut, turned off the radio, nodded to her, and went back into the wagon shed. He was obviously finding it equally difficult to beat a dignified retreat.

Out of sheer relief she started to laugh as she made her way to the courtyard at the front of the house. Nico was waiting for her, lounging on a mounting block by the door. He was flatteringly impressed by her success.

'I shall have to move you on to PR. How did you do it?'

'I don't honestly know what decided him. I thought I'd blown it all, but he suddenly gave way. He actually promised the work'd be done by next week.'

'Then you can count on it, even if he has to finish it himself. He probably will, come to that. The plumbers haven't been very co-operative about overtime.'

'Is he some kind of DIY freak? It'd fit in with that sort of solitary, obsessive character.'

Nico began to laugh. 'You've got him all wrong, you know.'

'Have I?' said Georgia wrily, as she got into her car. Nico looked in through the window to say goodbye.

'Bron was in the Engineers in the army. He can throw up a bridge or build you a road any time. He actually enjoys all that practical stuff. I'm a much more imaginative character, as you'll find out tonight. You haven't forgotten our date, have you? I'll pick you up around eight.'

Chloe hadn't arrived back from work when Georgia reached the flat. She ran a bath, poured in the last drops of her White Linen bath oil from her wealthy days in the States, and had a long wallow while she congratulated herself on the surprisingly successful end to her afternoon. She'd almost finished drying her hair when she heard Chloe come in. Georgia pulled on a kimono, and went to see what she was doing.

Chloe was in the kitchen, slowly and dreamily slicing a heap of vegetables for a moussaka while she listened to a Kate Bush tape. Some pieces of tofu like bits of singed rubber were cooling in the grill pan.

Georgia knew she'd asked Natty over for the evening, and that she'd hired a video of *Les Liaisons Dangereuses*. John Malkovich was the new light of Chloe's life. Georgia had seen a large packet of henna in the bathroom, so presumably there was also to be a hairdressing session.

'How was your day?' she asked cautiously.

'Fabulous!' said Chloe. 'I've been saving it all up to tell you.'

Georgia sighed and prepared to listen. Chloe's account of her work earlier in the week had consisted of an interminable inventory of every single item she'd sold, and a word by word repetition of what each customer had said to her.

'All right,' she said, moving over to the kettle to make herself some coffee. 'You'd better tell me before I get dressed, but quickly this time. And if you and Natty are planning a hairdressing session, I don't want to find the washbasin plastered with henna when I get back.'

Chloe picked up a lump of cheese Georgia had expected to last a week. She began to grate it haphazardly over the first layer of vegetables.

'You might at least try to sound a bit more interested. Something really, really wonderful happened at work.'

'What?' asked Georgia, her mind engaged on deciding how much she should dress up for dinner with Nico.

'This truly sweet woman came into the shop. She wanted us to

102

put up a notice about her centre. She runs holistic therapy courses there. She was terrific, Georgy. I've never met anyone I could talk to like her – she seemed to understand how I felt almost before I'd spoken.'

Georgia's mind came abruptly off clothes.

'What was the name of this centre?' she asked, with a sudden deep foreboding.

Chloe's face was radiant.

'It's called the Sanctuary. Natty and me are going to suss it out tomorrow, but I've already decided to sign up for some courses. So you see, you needn't have worried about my days off after all!'

Chapter 6

When Nico called for Georgia she was still recovering from an unproductive argument with Chloe about the wisdom of attending courses at the Sanctuary. Any inclination she'd felt for a tête-à-tête dinner had disappeared completely, and she was relieved to find that the restaurant he'd chosen made dining together as intimate as dining on stage.

La Veneziana, staffed by a bevy of Italian waiters in gondoliers' jackets, overlooked the Avon at the back of Walcot Street. The decor, all mulberry red walls and gilt woodwork, with marble-topped tables and black bentwood chairs, was an ersatz version of one of the older restaurants behind St Mark's Square in Venice. Nico, wearing a white linen Armani suit, blended perfectly with his setting.

They were ushered to one of the best tables, placed near the river, and so positioned that they could see and be seen. Nico ordered white Vermouth for them both. While they chose their orders from oversize menus bound with gold-tasselled cord, a stream of his acquaintances visited them, greeting him with peacock shrieks followed by mutual exchanges of flattery and large dollops of PR for the theatre from Nico. As he was monopolised by a particularly flamboyant freelance journalist who was promising to do a piece about Merlinslade for one of the Sunday magazines, Georgia began to wonder if he'd asked her out merely as part of a general publicity exercise for the theatre.

A collection of casual drinkers sat with their backs to the room at a crowded bar, where they could nevertheless keep an eye on the diners in a long mirror. Georgia was sipping her Vermouth and thinking that she might as well have brought a book with her, when she was startled to see the reflection of Morrigan's long, sardonic face. He was talking earnestly to an extremely pretty young girl, who appeared to be well below the legal drinking age and was trying to look sophisticated in a minute black dress and heavy carmine lipstick.

Georgia had no time to look away before his glance met hers. To her dismay he got up immediately and came with a self-advertising swagger towards their table. He was wearing tight blue jeans, and a white T shirt under a black jacket, with an outsize crucifix on a heavy gold chain slung round his neck. The journalist had only just left, and Georgia, glancing anxiously at Nico to see if he'd registered this new development, was even more alarmed to see a huge smile of welcome on his face.

'Uncle Ger! You're the last person I expected to see. You've met Georgia, haven't you?'

Morrigan slid into a spare chair. He gave Georgia a beguiling smile which seemed to have no spontaneity behind it at all. She looked away deliberately, but could still sense his gaze flickering over her like an adder's tongue.

'So what are you doing here?' Nico demanded. 'I thought you'd given up riotous living.'

'One needs to keep an eye on the enemy,' he said.

Nico, who'd evidently been more aware of what was going on than Georgia realised, glanced over to the bar, where the girl was being chatted up by a bartender with a Michelangelo profile, while she kept her eyes fixed anxiously on Morrigan.

'She doesn't look much like an enemy to me,' he said.

'The Disciples gather their harvest even in the most unpromising spots,' said Morrigan. 'Places like this are fertile ground. The poor child appeared to be searching for some kind of romantic encounter here. She was ripe for saving.'

Georgia wanted to giggle, and yet it wasn't amusing. The girl was much too young to be with someone like Morrigan. She'd seemed mesmerised by him.

'Are you sure she isn't ripe for something else?' said Nico. 'Come off it, you old faker. Tell us what you're really up to.'

'My dear Nico, I'm completely serious,' said Morrigan. 'How

106

often do I have to tell you and Bron that this is for real? I'm a changed person.'

His voice sounded genuine enough, but his eyes were so dark that it was hard to deduce their real expression. Turning to Georgia, he laid a hand bearing a knuckle-duster of rings on his crucifix.

'And I know you're going to change too. I pray daily that you'll join us at the Sanctuary,' he said in a voice dripping with concern.

Nico laughed at him and at Georgia's expression.

'Better try your holy rollering elsewhere, Ger. Or better still, stop letting down your public, and go back to making the sort of music you're best at. You keep telling me you want Bron to recognise you as one of the family again, but you'd stand a far better chance of getting him to take you seriously if you stopped playing around with religion.'

'But I couldn't be more serious about the Disciples!' said Morrigan. Now his voice was steeped in martyrdom. 'Only Brighid truly understands the suffering I've been through, the pain of being denied the friendship of my family, and the solace of my childhood home. With her help I've changed so much. And I'm relying on your support too, Nico. We were good friends when you were young, and we are still, I hope. I like to think I was some help to you when you were a homesick kid at boarding school.'

Nico laughed, but there was a note of genuine, if exasperated, affection in his amusement.

'Yes, all right, I'll have to give you that. Those London weekends saved my sanity more than once. It was just a pity you didn't do something for Bron too. He hated boarding school even more than I did.'

Morrigan ignored the remark about Bron. He looked slant-ways at Nico beneath lowered lids. 'Didn't I make up the shortfall in your grant at RADA as well?' he said softly. 'You owe me, Nico.'

'OK, OK, I know,' said Nico, with a hint of rising irritation. 'But I paid you back after my first film part. Give it a rest, Ger, and I'll see what I can do. I've got a plan in mind, but I haven't worked it out properly yet. Let's have a drink in The Mortal Man tomorrow morning. Or will you be preparing your Sunday sermon?'

'Our kind of worship is spontaneous, as you'd see if you visited us,' said Morrigan.

Nico grinned. 'You can give up that idea straight away. I've better things to do with the Sabbath.'

He glanced over to the bar, where the girl was drooping disconsolately over her untouched drink.

'Shouldn't you go back to your convert?' he said. 'She doesn't look particularly happy to me.'

'She'll be fine as soon as she gets to the Sanctuary,' said Morrigan. 'I'm taking her there now.'

'With purely spiritual intentions of course,' said Nico.

'Of course,' Morrigan answered blandly. 'I shall leave her in Brighid's care. I can see you don't believe me still, but helping the Disciples of the Fountain is the best thing I've ever done. It's brought so much purpose and happiness to my life.'

He stood up, and the girl, watching him like a dog longing for a walk, straightened and broke into a smile. 'See you tomorrow morning, then, Nico. You're lucky I'm free. I'm going to London for the next two weeks, to organise rehearsals for an aid benefit.'

'So you've decided to sing again after all? You're really into good works in your old age, aren't you, Ger?'

'It's just a one-off for charity. You know I renounced the professional stage long ago when I resolved to search for spiritual enlightenment. But the concert might bring some indirect publicity for the Disciples. I'm hoping to convert the group into a self-financing foundation, in the simplest way of course. Brighid doesn't want anything money-grubbing. I do hope you'll both change your minds and visit us at the Sanctuary when I get back.'

As they watched him go Georgia tried to reassure herself with the thought that by the time he returned from London Chloe could well have become bored with the Disciples of the Fountain.

'I can't help admiring him,' said Nico. 'Now he's home he's managing to reinstate himself in the most amazing way after all that scandal. He'll have the press on his side again in no time. It's all good news for Merlinslade.'

'I know he's your uncle, but surely you can see what an operator he is? Brighid must be trusting to the point of naivety. How can anything to do with him be good for Merlinslade?'

'You'll find out soon enough,' said Nico mysteriously. 'If the idea I'm going to put to him tomorrow works, he might even get back on speaking terms with Bron. And it's not Ger's fault that people fall for him in droves.'

'But he can't resist exploiting their adulation, can he? It may come under the guise of charity, but he's still doing it.'

'You're a bit hard on the poor guy. He's not been able to lead a normal sort of life for years. I think he knows this is a last chance to sort himself out. I feel I ought to help.'

'Nico the social worker?' Georgia teased him. 'I don't believe it!'

'Just one of my many talents. You've seen nothing yet!'

The conversation was interrupted by the arrival of their meal, an hors d'oeuvre of small violet-leaved artichokes, followed by a seafood risotto. The waiter filled their glasses with a deliciously dry Soave, brandished the pepper mill over the risotto one more time, rearranged Georgia's table-napkin, which had fallen to the floor, his hand staying a little longer on her knee than necessary, and disappeared with a hummed burst of 'Sorrento'.

Georgia caught Nico's eye, and they began to laugh together.

'I know, I know,' he said ruefully. 'The place is total kitsch. But you must admit it's fun, and it *is* good PR.'

By the time they'd finished the wine and come to the end of strawberry granitas, Georgia had begun to enjoy herself. The food was excellent, and Nico had a huge fund of scurrilous anecdotes about the theatre. Their mutual love of the stage made him easy to talk to, and he tactfully didn't mention her time in Baltimore.

'Let's have coffee on the terrace,' he said. 'It should be warm enough still.'

Outside the evening was perfectly calm, the water below them flowing silently in a darkening green stream. A replica of a gondola was moored beneath the terrace, with a lighted lamp at its prow. There was still some light in the sky, suffusing the façades of the houses on the other side of the river with a soft ochre glow.

The waiter set down a tray of coffee, two glasses of Strega liqueur, and a dish of fresh figs. Nico pulled out his cigarettes, watching Georgia surreptitiously over the flame of his lighter while she poured out the coffee.

When he'd called for her she was clearly on edge. She'd introduced him to her teenage sister, who scarcely seemed to be on speaking terms with Georgia and from whom it had been hard work to coax a smile. If they'd had the sort of row he'd been having with Bron lately he could understand Georgia's jumpiness. But she seemed more at ease now, her hair falling like a handful of satin round the curve of her face as she handed him his coffee. She was wearing a dress with the inky bloom of a black tulip which made her skin seem almost translucent.

'Sorry again about bringing you to a place like this,' he said. 'I only chose it because Bron's so uptight over spending these days. I feel guilty if I don't combine a bit of business with pleasure. But we can concentrate solely on the pleasure now.'

'I'm sure he wouldn't like the idea of your entertaining a mere costume designer,' said Georgia. 'I don't suppose he approves of anything that isn't useful. I'm surprised he even likes music.'

'Poor old Bron,' said Nico. 'He's probably sitting there on his own at Merlinslade with his CD player, getting a huge buzz from listening to some operatic diva pour her heart out. He's had a few girlfriends since the divorce, but though he's got a flat in London which he used on leaves, none of them ever lived there with him. Bron's a fairly private sort of person, and he was badly burnt over Imogen.'

'Tell me some more about her,' said Georgia. She picked up a fig and started to quarter it.

Nico thought about his easily bored, easily diverted and astoundingly selfish sister-in-law, who with her ice-queen looks had dominated the other army wives like a lily in a cabbage patch.

'She's the goods to look at, but a manipulative bitch, though that wasn't quite so apparent when she was younger. She's got a sizeable private income as well. The divorce lawyers advised Bron to claim maintenance from her. He refused, of course, but he'd be sitting pretty today if he had.'

'It seems odd that she should have fallen for someone like Bron.'

Nico dragged his gaze away from her lips as she transferred the fig's scarlet inner flesh to her mouth. She really was the most luscious girl. It was amazing that no one else had snapped her up by this time.

'When I was still a teenager, Bron was a serious handicap. Every time I brought a girl home she'd end up chasing him. You can't imagine the relief when he married.'

'Does she work at all?'

'She runs her own PR agency in London. She must be pretty mad that Bron's got Merlinslade now. When they married it seemed as though Morrigan would inherit.'

'What's she like with Ned?'

'I think she's genuinely fond of him. But it's all a bit unbalanced. When he was small and cuddly she'd drag him off on holiday with her occasionally, with a nanny to do the hard work. He used to adore her, but now he's growing up and seeing her more clearly it's different. The poor kid's pretty mixed up, really. It isn't easy for Bron sorting him out.'

Georgia had finished her liqueur while she listened to Nico. The swallows had gone to roost, and bats were flitting through the dusk.

'Anyway,' said Nico, draining his glass, 'it's bloody unfair really. She's sitting pretty, but the divorce screwed Bron up completely.'

'It does,' Georgia said. 'I should know.' The words were out before she could stop them.

She couldn't see his eyes in the dark, only the glow of his cigarette.

'But you aren't going to let it stop you enjoying yourself forever, I hope,' he said.

'No,' she answered slowly. 'No, I'm not. Of course I'm not.'

Someone inside the restaurant was beginning to turn on the terrace lights one by one. Their reflection wavered in the water. She blinked and shivered.

'That's a good enough resolution for one evening, then,' said

Nico, 'and quite enough talk about my brother. I seem to remember we ended up discussing him last time.' He drained the last drops of Strega from his glass. 'Perhaps I'd better walk you home. It's starting to get chilly out here.'

The town was still busy with people like themselves slowly drifting through the summer night to their homes or hotels. Nico had left his car outside the flat. He stopped at the top of the area steps.

'Well, here you are, safely back at the nunnery,' he said.

Georgia hadn't intended to ask him in, but the note of teasing resignation in his voice made her feel unreasonable. After all, hadn't she just told him that the divorce wasn't going to stop her enjoying herself?

'Come in and have a last cup of coffee,' she said. 'My sister should be back from a visit to the movies quite soon,' she added, thinking that for once Chloe's presence would have some use.

It was the first time Georgia had invited a man into the flat. She deliberately switched on the central lights in the sitting room, and slotted a brisk Vivaldi concerto into the cassette player. She'd half thought that Nico would seem like an intruder, but he disarmed her by heaping praise on the decor, and immersed himself in her books while she went off to make the coffee.

When she re-entered the room she was taken aback by the change in atmosphere. A discreet single lamp shone on a side table, and instead of Vivaldi, a Cole Porter tune was swinging gently from the cassette player. When she'd asked Nico in she knew very well what might follow, but now she felt a rush of panic. He was disposed elegantly in a corner of the sofa, again looking as though the setting had been planned for him. As she gave him his coffee, and he brushed her hand with his, she told herself furiously not to be an immature fool.

Nico was amused to see that she took her own cup to a distant armchair. 'Won't you have yours with me?' he asked. 'It's like sitting on the Forth Bridge here.'

She hesitated, then came and sat down at the other end of the sofa, holding her cup carefully in front of her.

Nico gave her a quick glance. In spite of the insouciant notes of

'You're the Tops' coquetting into the air, a perfect background to what he planned next, she looked as if she'd taken a seat in a dentist's chair. He knew he'd have to act fast to get anywhere before the arrival of her grumpy little sister. He slid gracefully sideways, transferred Georgia's cup to a table, and insinuated an arm round her shoulders.

'This must be the original casting couch,' he said.

He had the feeling that she was forcing herself not to resist. That made the situation even more interesting. As she gave him a nervous smile, he lifted the curtain of hair from the side of her face, and began to kiss the pale, secret skin behind her ear.

Georgia felt him gently bite her ear lobe. His lips moved onwards to her cheek. Her only emotional reaction was that the sensation was pleasant and soothing. She let him kiss her mouth, and after a few moments began to enjoy it a little more, but as mindlessly as she might have enjoyed sunbathing on a Mediterranean beach.

Nico's reaction seemed to be the same. He drew back to look at her. 'You have the most delicious lips,' he said, as gracefully as a line from a play, and exactly as though he were still eating the strawberry granita.

But it wasn't a play, it was real. And because it was real, it should surely mean something more to her than this. She began to panic at her lack of response, struggling to pull herself upright.

'Nico, I'm so sorry, but – but – I don't think I can. It's just too soon.'

'Of course you can. People often feel like you after a divorce. It's the same as drying on stage. The longer you wait for your next entrance, the more difficult it seems.' He stroked her hair. 'You've just got to give a little, that's all.'

'But how can I when it means absolutely nothing to me?' she burst out. 'I just don't feel anything. Not deeply, I mean.'

He began to laugh. 'Darling Georgia, neither do I! At least, not in your earth-moving sense. But I do think it's the best game in the world, and that's how you have to look at it if you don't want to get hurt – simply as a game, or even as a very special sort of acting, if you like.'

'Maybe you were never hurt anyway,' she said. 'I don't think you could say that, otherwise. *Were* you ever hurt, Nico?'

He forced himself to think for a moment, and remembered the pangs of an infatuation for a much older woman in his first West End production. But he'd known that his part in that play would make his reputation, and he'd learned to control the anguish, to turn it to his own use. As he gained confidence in his craft, and came to realise that women would always be available for him, he'd assumed the same light-hearted approach to sex as the French film actors he so enjoyed working with.

'There's no mileage in that kind of reaction,' he said airily. 'Life's too short.'

She was gazing at him as though she couldn't quite decide if he was Confucius or Machiavelli. Rapidly he began to undo the buttons down the front of her dress. He slid his hand inside, and met a layer of silk. He tried to guess whether it was a camisole or a teddy. If the latter, it would be hell to infiltrate without scaring her off. He explored further, and had just discovered a promising area of bare skin when the front door banged shut with a tremendous crash.

He realised at once that the sister must be back and swore under his breath. He might as well give up completely on the de-frosting programme now, he thought resignedly. It would be impossible for either of them to relax with a temperamental teenager roaming round the flat. As it was, Georgia had already shot away from him to the far end of the sofa like a nervous yearling from a starting gate, and was doing up her buttons at lightning speed.

While Georgia fumbled with the last button, listening anxiously to the noises outside, she prayed that Chloe was alone and still sufficiently annoyed with her not to come in and say goodnight. Her relief was intense when she heard her go into her bedroom and shut the door with another loud, meaningful bang.

Now she could only think of getting Nico out of the flat as fast as possible. To her surprise he forestalled her. He calmly drank down his coffee, then rose and pulled on his jacket.

'I guess that was your sister. And from my long experience of family rows, it sounds as if she's giving you a hard time. You'd probably like me out of the way.'

'It's been a terrific evening, but perhaps it would be best for you to go,' she said, with a surge of thankfulness for this unexpected co-operation. 'I had a big grouch at Chloe earlier on, and she obviously hasn't forgiven me yet.'

'Sounds like a Bron and Ned scenario. I'll stay if you think it'd help. Sometimes I can make Ned see the light when Bron can't.'

'No, really, I can manage, thank you,' said Georgia hastily.

Nico's voice had not been enthusiastic, and if he did try to win over Chloe she'd probably fall in love with him on the spot, though even the repercussions from that might be preferable to her joining the Disciples of the Fountain.

'Right, then, I'd better go,' he said. 'I must say heavy teenage scenes aren't really my line.'

She led the way to the front door. 'It was a terrific evening. I did enjoy it, truly,' she said, as he stepped into the front yard.

'Even the end? Good. We must continue as soon as I get back.'

'I didn't know you were going away,' she said.

He caught her unawares with a rapid farewell kiss. 'How nice. You're looking disappointed.'

He bounded up the steps, but turned when he was halfway. 'Yes, I'm off to the States on Monday to persuade the Americans to visit Merlinslade. I'll look forward to seeing the wardrobe all set up by the time I get back. And don't forget, this evening was just the overture.'

Throughout the following week, as Georgia assembled equipment for the workshop, she kept telling herself that at least her lack of emotional reaction made the relationship easier to stop. An involvement with such an influential member of the company had enormous potential for trouble, especially if the other members of the wardrobe staff became resentful. And yet in some ways she didn't want it to stop. Nico's sympathy and sense of humour were exactly what she needed, especially now when Chloe was in full prima donna mode.

When Georgia refused to advance her the fees to attend courses at the Sanctuary, she'd spent the weekend behaving like a wronged heroine in a silent movie, only to appear after work on

Monday full of smiles, announcing that she'd got an advance on her wages and had paid the fees that way. Georgia, in the thick of buying and transporting equipment for the wardrobe, had neither the time nor energy for another confrontation, and decided to deal with the next lot of problems when they arose.

Now it was Thursday, Chloe's first day at the Sanctuary. Natty had called for her at eight, and they'd set off together for the bus station looking heart-breakingly innocent and eager. Georgia worked all day in her studio on last-minute adjustments to the models for the sets, totally absorbed in the perfect miniatures she'd fashioned from cardboard and balsa wood.

The creation of imaginary worlds had delighted her even as a child. When she was very young her father, attending a professional conference in London, had for once remembered her birthday, and in a fit of guilt-induced generosity bought her a fully stocked replica of a Victorian doll's house. She'd played with it for years, changing the decor over and over again, re-dressing the doll family, and inventing endless stories for them, which invariably featured improbable but deeply satisfying parents who never, ever left their children alone.

At five o'clock she heard Chloe arrive, but was too absorbed to try to find out what had gone on at the Sanctuary. She was deciding how to pack the models for the journey to Merlinslade, when she heard the studio door open, and the clattering of china.

A moment later a tray containing a plate of bread and honey and a cup of tea clattered down by her side, perilously close to the models. The bread was so dark and full of bran that it looked as if it had come from a Russian prison. A quarter of the tea had already slopped into the saucer.

'I've brought you a treat,' said Chloe's voice happily. 'I thought I'd make tea for you, for a change.'

Georgia wondered if she was hearing aright. Apart from the one effort at moussaka when Natty came to supper, Chloe hadn't lifted a finger in the kitchen since she arrived. The mere effort of keeping her room tidy seemed to exhaust her.

'I've just had the most important day of my life!' said Chloe, with an expression on her face Georgia normally connected with the aftermath of pop concerts. She launched into an impromptu pirouette round the studio, her skirt spiralling about her.

'You'd better tell me about it,' said Georgia, resigning herself to the interruption. 'But sit down first, before you break something vital.'

Chloe cast herself into a chair, picked up a piece of bread and honey, and began to devour it.

'When we got there some of the Disciples showed us round. You wouldn't believe how nice they were. It's a fabulous set-up. Brighid designed everything herself. They have a holy glade where they tune into nature, and a sweat-lodge, and a real stone circle for empowerment ceremonies. There's the sweetest little chapel too. Brighid baked the bread herself – she sent you some especially to try – and we had bean sprouts with sunflower seeds, and an apple cake for lunch. Apples cleanse and strengthen, you know. Brighid says the apple is the goddess's own fruit.'

'Which particular goddess is that?' Georgia enquired.

'Gaia, of course, the earth mother.'

'But I thought the group was supposed to be basically Christian.'

'It's Christian as well. Brighid told us loads about St Francis and the animals, and about St Bride. She's the Sanctuary's patron saint.'

Chloe looked so happy that Georgia didn't have the heart to criticise any further.

'Morrigan's away, isn't he?' she asked cautiously.

'Yes, he's gone to London to fix up a charity concert. The others say he's terrific, but he doesn't have anything to do with the teaching. He just helps with publicity and organisation, and takes part in some of the ceremonies.'

So Brighid still retained control over the most important part of the set-up, Georgia thought with relief. 'And what did you do after lunch?' she pursued.

'Natty and I each had a special counselling session of our very own with Brighid. It's not psychotherapy or anything weird like that. She just lets you talk for as long as you want about your feelings, and then she sort of suggests how to reorganise your life. She says I've got the most amazing sensitivity, and a huge potential for making the world a better place. Those were her actual words! She says I have to channel my bad feelings away from myself by helping others and developing my artistic gifts.'

'I hope this isn't going to channel you away from doing A levels in the autumn.'

'Of course not! She wants me to go to college. She says I'll be able to spread the message of the goddess there. She says that if Natty and I do well this summer we can become real Disciples like the others. I'm going to make some decorations for the chapel.'

Chloe burbled on for another fifteen minutes. The more Georgia listened the more muddled Brighid's philosophy seemed. Yet there didn't seem to be anything positively harmful about the activities at the Sanctuary, and if Brighid's methods produced only a tenth of what they promised things might not work out too badly. All the same, she decided that as soon as there was a slight lull in her own work she must inspect the Sanctuary for herself.

By the middle of the following week the workshop was nearly ready for action. Georgia felt almost satisfied as she unlocked the door, dumped some rolls of brown pattern paper in a corner, and cast a critical eye over her domain.

Two long sturdy tables stood in the middle of the room, and sewing machines had been installed on side benches. Soft board ran the length of one wall for pinning up call notices, designs, pattern pieces, swatches of fabric and general reminders.

The second-hand industrial shelving was already half stocked with bolts of fabric, as well as holding tiers of clear plastic boxes filled with thread, buttons, and a hundred other vital items of haberdashery. There was an assortment of adjustable models, some hat blocks, and a couple of large ironing boards. A corner of the room had been turned into a fitting area with a winged Victorian cheval glass and a small sofa.

Nico was due back from the States today, and next week the cast would arrive. Georgia stood for a few moments longer, enjoying the brief sensation of having the room all to herself. She'd created exactly the atmosphere she wanted, the atmosphere of her grandmother's house, one of comfortable unassuming order. It was the perfect antidote to the ramshackle, decaying grandeur of the rest of Merlinslade.

She put away the pattern paper, tacked up some posters, and surveyed the fitting area, which was to be curtained off with a pair of beige velvet drapes found in a car boot sale. The colour was so dismal that she decided to dye them in the new twin-tub washing machine.

The extractor fan hadn't arrived yet, and she opened a window to let out the clouds of acrid steam rising from the tub. It was a glorious day. Zelda was probably at this moment startling the carthorses with her daily jog through the park before going to her own room in what had once been the estate offices.

As Georgia prodded down the heaving mass of fabric she looked idly out over the orchard. When she arrived Bron had been there in deep consultation with Mr Meads, who was bearing a scythe larger than himself and was about to mow the long grass beneath the trees.

When she waved to them, Mr Meads had given her a gap-toothed smile, but Bron barely acknowledged her. He disappeared almost immediately, and Mr Meads had by now, despite his age, already laid a long line of swathes across the orchard.

The air was full of the scent of newly mown grass. A thrush was repeating his song over and over, as if he were calling her to come outside. She felt an instinctive desire to sit for a little while under one of the apple trees with the sun on her face, and simply enjoy it all, but she knew that in her present state it was far safer to remain where there was plenty to do. She sighed, and went back to the curtains.

Zelda, who'd just emerged from one of the dressing-room showers after a jogging session from which it felt as if her knees would never recover, pushed open the wardrobe door, intending to cadge a cup of coffee. Georgia was standing over the washing machine in a PVC apron, gauntleted to the elbows in rubber gloves, inspecting a piece of steaming fabric held up in a pair of wooden tongs. Her hair was tied back from her face with a piece of black tape. She looked completely absorbed, but not in her work, judging by the wistful expression on her face, one which was there far too often, in Zelda's opinion.

'Any chance of some coffee before I go back to dragging this place into the twentieth century?' Zelda asked. 'I spent most of yesterday reorganising my office. Every time I ask Albert to move something that's been in the same spot for the last hundred years, he goes into terminal shock.'

'Who's Albert?' Georgia enquired, peeling off her gloves and apron.

'Mr Meads. I'm trying to loosen him up a little.'

Georgia filled an electric kettle at the sink, and took it into her office. Zelda followed, thinking that her muscle tone definitely wasn't what it used to be. She eased herself into a sagging but supremely comfortable country house armchair, its faded cretonne disguised with an Indian bedspread in soft pinks and browns.

'You look pooped,' said Georgia. 'Do you have to go at the jogging quite so hard?'

'It takes a while for the endorphins to peak. You ought to jog with me. It'd do you good. Think of Bron's face if he saw both of us spoiling the view!'

'It's the one thing that might make the agony worthwhile,' said Georgia with a smile. 'Maybe I will when the wardrobe staff arrive, and I'm not quite so pressed for time.'

Zelda looked round the office while they waited for the kettle to boil. Georgia had worked her usual transforming magic even on this unpromising space. A green-shaded library lamp on a brass pedestal adorned an old oak desk. Buttercups and ox-eye daisies filled a brown earthenware jug. There was a basket chair with a couple of patchwork cushions, and she'd lined one wall with a fascinating range of small drawers, a throw-out from a chemist's shop judging by the Latin names painted on them. A couple of vivid Bakst designs for the Ballets Russes hung above a shelf crammed with reference books.

As Zelda had hoped, Georgia had made her office into a haven. Most of the members of the cast would come to it at some time or other with deeper anxieties concealed beneath questions about costumes, and leave with their self-confidence restored. If only, thought Zelda, as she watched Georgia pour boiling water into a cafetière, she could perform the same witchcraft on herself.

'How was your dinner with Nico?' she asked. Georgia had so

far not said a word about it.

'Rather too public.' Georgia took down a pair of mugs from a shelf. 'But it suited me. I'm not into heavy dates any more.'

'Don't give me that corny old line. It went out with women's girdles. You're quite capable of keeping Nico where you want him and having a good time.'

'I did have a good time.' Georgia calmly offered Zelda a tin of what looked like genuine home-baked peanut cookies. 'But it certainly wasn't accompanied by the sound of a thousand violins. Nico and I are just good friends.'

'Huh, that went out thirty years ago as well. For heaven's sake, Georgy, you're being dated by a guy who gets as many fan letters as Ken Branagh, and you act like he's the boy next door! I don't get it. You can't stay in the freezer forever, you know.'

'You didn't after your divorce, did you? Neither shall I,' said Georgia.

'I didn't stay there because some good friends hauled me out before it was too late. You'd better listen to me, Georgia. Someone has to talk sense to you.'

Georgia handed over a mug of coffee. Zelda took in the aroma appreciatively. It was her third cup that day, and she'd probably get the jitters, but it was worth it. Georgia sat down at the desk, doodling on a spare scrap of paper while her own drink cooled.

'OK, OK, I'll think about it,' she said in a casual voice. 'How are things going in the theatre? I haven't seen you for a while.'

'Don't ask! I still haven't cast Ariel. I've wasted too much time in London on auditions this week. And it's hard to get anything done properly while Nico's away. I tried to check the catering arrangements for the company with Mrs Meads. Nico said he'd ask her to lay on a simple daily lunch at the house, but when I mentioned it to her she almost went into orbit.'

'Perhaps Nico's found you an Ariel in the States,' said Georgia soothingly. 'And he could ask an outside caterer to do the lunches.'

'He can't persuade Bron to release any more funds,' said Zelda. 'I hadn't realised just how short of money the estate is. And yesterday, when I went to see Redvers again in Bristol, his feet were so cold, they were solid ice. You've got to pull out all the stops for his costume. I can see him chickening out completely if he doesn't like it.'

'He'll like it, I swear.'

'Who'll like what?' said a voice from the office entrance that was unmistakeably Nico's. He sauntered into the room, and dumped a cabin bag still bearing its flight tags on Georgia's desk.

'Jesus! Do you have to creep up on us that way?' said Zelda, almost choking over her coffee.

'I thought you'd be pleased to see me,' said Nico, with a wide grin. 'I can see I needn't have bothered to hurry home.'

He opened the cabin bag and pulled out a bottle of bourbon for Zelda, and one of vodka for Georgia, waving aside their thanks.

'Coffee!' he said, collapsing in the basket chair. 'That's all I want.'

In spite of his rumpled business suit and the long drive from Heathrow he looked remarkably cheerful.

'Jet lag seems to suit you, Nico,' Zelda said. 'I wish I could get across the Atlantic in such good shape. How was your trip?'

'Terrific. The PR guy over there had set up meetings with most of the big travel agencies, and I did some TV interviews as well.' He smiled his thanks at Georgia for the coffee she'd just put next to him, and lit a cigarette, blowing out the smoke with a huge satisfied sigh. 'That's not everything, though. I've just pulled off the biggest scoop of all time!'

He gazed at them with a mischievous, triumphant look, clearly determined to keep the suspense going as long as possible.

'Come on, then, Nico, spill the beans!' said Zelda. 'My nervous system won't take much more today. What've you done? Signed up Michelle Pfeiffer as Ariel?'

'Something almost better. Just before I left, I made Morrigan an offer I was pretty sure he wouldn't refuse. He faxed his answer to me in the States. He's agreed to become musical director at Merlinslade!'

Chapter 7

Georgia sat down suddenly on the desk. She felt as if a trapdoor had opened at her feet. Worse still, Zelda, from whom she'd expected a similar reaction, was looking delighted.

'Christ, that's a master-stroke, and so obvious, too! Why the hell didn't I think of it? But I understood that he'd decided to give up professional work completely after that prison episode. Wasn't it supposed to be some sort of atonement? How did you get him to chuck his scruples?'

'He hasn't got any,' said Georgia indignantly.

'Whatever the reason, it was a pushover persuading him,' said Nico. 'I only needed to point out that he'd have a legitimate reason for being at Merlinslade again, and the chance of finally proving to Bron that he does have the family's interests at heart. He saw the sense of it at once. And he's not taking a fee. All he's asked for is a small donation to the Fountain Foundation.'

'To the *what*?' said Georgia, with growing disbelief.

'It's some scheme of his to get more recruits, and train them for a world-wide fund-raising campaign. He really does seem to be hooked on Brighid and the group.'

Zelda was pacing about the office, all signs of fatigue gone.

'Remember that amazing album of Elizabethan folk music he did? Maybe he'll come up with something even better for us. Doesn't he have his own recording studio?'

'Yes, at his house in Bath. He's got a huge sound system in the basement there.'

'Let's have him sitting at the side of the stage in contemporary costume, just as the courtiers used to do. That way he'll get maximum exposure,' said Zelda eagerly.

Georgia tried to halt her before she became even more suicidally visionary.

'I think you're both insane, letting someone like Morrigan loose in a small, intimate set-up like this. He won't be easy to handle.'

'I can deal with a guy like that standing on my head,' said Zelda. 'Where's your sense of adventure these days, Georgia? And you'll only have to design one costume for him, for heaven's sake. No, I agree with Nico, we must go for it.'

'I do think you're becoming a tiny bit paranoid about Morrigan, Georgy,' said Nico more temperately. 'It really isn't fair to judge him on something he did so long ago.'

'But he's so clever, so insinuating,' she said, desperate to convince them. 'He could easily unbalance the cast if he wanted. I've seen the way he handles a crowd.'

'So have I, at pop concerts, lots of times when I was young,' said Nico. 'He's just what we need. You're worrying far too much about my old uncle. He's perfectly harmless these days, just an ageing swinger who hasn't quite given up strutting his stuff. You wouldn't grudge him that, I know.'

'I suppose not,' she said reluctantly, angry and frustrated at her inability to persuade them. The situation was hopeless with only her intuition on her side. 'But you won't ever persuade me to trust him.'

'You're worrying about nothing,' said Zelda. 'He won't make the slightest difference to you personally. He'll hardly need to come to the wardrobe, and when he does you can get your staff to deal with him.'

She looked out of the window, where Mr Meads had just laid low the final swathe of grass. 'I must catch Albert to move some more things for me. We'll talk about this another time, Georgy. Can you come over to my office this afternoon, Nico, so we can discuss the music in depth before Morrigan appears? And don't forget, both of you, that there's another director's meeting on Tuesday to discuss the designs.'

She departed from the office like a minor tornado.

'When will Morrigan appear?' asked Georgia. 'I'd like to have some warning.' She was well aware of the resentment in her voice, but she couldn't control it. Nico got up and put his arm round her shoulders. She was so preoccupied that she let it stay there.

'It'll be all right,' he said. 'Trust me. Ger's really not the big bad wolf you think. I'll be the first to say I was wrong if the experiment doesn't work, but the theatre can do with every bit of pull at the moment. We need a full house every night to make it into next season.'

He pulled her closer to him. His jacket still smelt of the aircraft cabin, but the gesture was reassuring. She decided there was no point in making any more fuss. She was too deeply involved by now to resign. She moved away, and began to collect up the coffee mugs.

'I'll just have to take your word for it, then,' she said.

Nico followed her outside to the sink. She put down the mugs, and donned her apron before hauling the curtains into the spin dryer.

'Putting on your armour, are you?' he said. There was relief at her compliance as well as mockery in his voice. 'Then I'd better let you get on with it. I need a shower and some more coffee before I break the glad tidings about Morrigan to Bron.'

Georgia eased her hands into the rubber gloves, trying to look distant and business-like to deter Nico from approaching her again. 'I can imagine his reaction,' she said. 'Wouldn't it be safer for you to go straight back to the States?'

'Bron can't stop me over this. He's agreed to let me have a free hand in the theatre.' He took her gloved hand. 'So when can I show you the house? Are you working here tonight?'

'I shall be tied up at home, doing the designs,' said Georgia, snatching away her hand.

'Would I were tied up with you, Georgy darling, rubber gloves and all,' he said, laughing at her. 'I'll just have to show you it on Tuesday, then, after the meeting. So no sloping off home next time!'

Chloe cleaned the flat on Saturday, leaving a trail of dirty dusters and lidless polish tins in her wake. On Sunday morning she used the last pint of milk in the fridge to make a pudding with macrobiotic rice from Fruits of the Earth. After lunch she shut herself up in her room to do some homework for Brighid. This consisted of reading Khalil Gibran's *The Prophet*, and learning the Little Prayer of St Francis by heart. Her studies were accompanied by the song of the whale played at full blast.

By five o'clock Georgia had almost completed the preliminary costume designs, and was desperate for tea. When she remembered the dearth of milk she set out to buy some at a small shop near the bridge which was open all day on Sundays.

For once the traffic was light, and as she began to walk back with her shopping along Great Pulteney Street towards Laura Place, a boy came scudding along the almost deserted road on a bicycle, wrenching the handlebars upwards in a lighthearted succession of wheelies. Just as she approached the pagoda-roofed Victorian letterbox on the corner, a beaten-up Cortina plastered with decals, rock music pulsating from every cranny, scorched past. The cyclist swerved, wavered and toppled spectacularly against the letter box, while the Cortina screeched round the fountain in the centre of Laura Place at forty miles an hour, and roared on down Great Pulteney Street.

Georgia rushed up to the boy, who was sitting on the kerb holding his arm, and staring at the retreating car. The wheels of the bike were still spinning. He turned his head in her direction, and she saw that it was Ned.

He was very pale, but struggled to his feet, leaning against the letter box. Miraculously he appeared to be still in one piece.

'Jesus! You gave me a fright, Ned,' she said. 'You've got to stop doing this to me. I thought that Cortina had finished you off. Are you all right?'

He inspected his arm. Blood was oozing from a large but superficial graze. He summoned up a wobbly smile.

'No worries, I'm OK, really. I was on my way to see you. Did you catch the Cortina's decals as it went by, Georgia? Mega brilliant, didn't you think?'

'Mega. But that's hardly the point. You were an idiot to be doing wheelies there.'

'Pretty good, aren't I? I can keep going on one wheel for ten seconds. Jason tested me with his dad's stopwatch.'

'You'd better come along to the flat,' said Georgia, 'but on your feet this time. No more cycling until we've checked the bike over.'

Ned secured the bike to the railings outside the flat with a hawser-like cable, and followed her indoors, clearly delighted with the success of his mission.

'Hey, smart city!' he said, looking round him as they entered the kitchen. 'If only Dad could see this. Our kitchen's the pits.'

'Sit down,' commanded Georgia, 'and let me look at your arm before we start discussing the decor.'

She took a first aid box from a cupboard in the dresser, and began to clean the graze. 'I'd better ring your father, and let him know you're here,' she said, when she'd stuck the biggest plaster in the collection over it.

Ned had only just managed to sit still, and was now out of his chair and inspecting the kitchen again.

'You don't need to,' he said, making faces at himself in a heart-shaped wall mirror. It was set in a purple papier maché frame studded with an assortment of sparkly buttons, and had been a handmade childhood Christmas present from Chloe. 'He knows where I am. I left a note on the kitchen table. And anyway he's got to read the lesson in church this evening. I don't suppose he's even noticed I've gone.'

This didn't sound much like Bron to Georgia. 'Are you absolutely certain?'

'It's the truth, honest. If you do get him on the phone he'll just think I'm bothering you, and tell you to send me back. You don't know what it's like on Sundays at home. Dad's idea of fun is going for a million-mile walk. All the other kids I know get taken to the adventure pool at Swindon, or Castle Combe circuit.'

'Really? All of them?' said Georgia in amusement.

'Well, not quite all, but you know what I mean. Castle Combe's ace. I went there once with Jason and his dad. I bet you had terrific Sundays when you were young.'

'I must tell you about them sometime, then you can judge for yourself,' said Georgia drily. 'All right, I'll take your word for it that your father knows where you are, but I'm going to drive you home. I'll ask Nico to collect your bike when he's next in Bath.'

'In the Triumph? Terrific!'

'Would you like something to eat first? There's a slice of quiche left over from lunch and some carrot cake.'

'Great! I'll have both!' said Ned. 'Thanks very much,' he added hastily. 'I guess you wouldn't want to waste them.'

He continued his tour of the kitchen while Georgia put the quiche on the table, and took a can of Pepsi from the fridge.

'What did you mean about your Sundays when you were young?' he said, after briefly testing some old-fashioned brass scales, and scrutinising a Robert Doisneau photo of some French children hanging on to the back of a water cart.

'I lived in Africa then. My parents were always busy, and I stayed with an ayah most of the time – that's a sort of nanny. When I was eleven they split up, and my mother took me and my sister to live in a forest research station with her. Most of the time we did have fun, but we were left on our own a lot, too.'

He pulled up a chair to the table with a hideous scrape, and started to gulp down the Pepsi. 'My parents are divorced. But I expect you know that already.'

'I had heard,' she answered cautiously.

'It's better living with Dad on the whole,' said Ned, impaling a piece of quiche on his fork. 'At least he's always there, and Nico's great. My mother lives in London, but I used to stay with my grandparents most of the time in the country. I moved in with Mum when my grandpa died, but she sort of freaked out after a while over the bike and my drum kit. I had an ace little dog called Conan, and she didn't like him much either.'

'Merlinslade must be just right for him,' said Georgia.

Ned's face clouded. 'Mum had him put down. I came back from school one day, and he just wasn't there any more.'

'Christ!' said Georgia, temporarily abandoning all attempts at remaining impartial. 'What a bloody horrible thing to happen. Poor old Ned.'

'It was fairly bad.' He tried to look nonchalant and didn't quite succeed. He hacked off another piece of quiche. 'I bunked off school, and got the train to Merlinslade next day. I thought Dad would really go for me, but he didn't. He said I could stay.'

He stuffed the quiche into his mouth. 'When Rusalka – that's his dog – has her puppies next month, he's giving me one. I think Mum's sorry now. She keeps sending me dosh, anyway, and she says she'll come over in the summer holidays.'

Georgia thought Ned's childhood sounded even more disrupted than her own. Hastily she diverted him with questions about Castle Combe, and he launched happily into an account of his day there with Jason Mason. He was describing a multiple pile up with the appropriate sound effects when he became unexpectedly silent. Georgia looked up from opening the cake tin, and saw that he was gazing open-mouthed out of the window.

'Holy cats! It's Dad,' he said. 'He would turn up and spoil everything!'

Georgia followed his gaze. Parked in the street outside the flat she could see the lower half of a very muddy Range Rover. A pair of legs in immaculately pressed trousers and highly polished leather brogues was descending the steps. A moment later the rest of Bron came into view. He looked as if he was about to quell a particularly nasty native uprising. As he rang a long belligerent peal on the bell, Ned appeared ready to crawl under the table.

Georgia went as slowly as possible to the front door. Bron had flung his suit jacket across one shoulder. He was wearing a blue and white striped shirt which Mrs Meads had no doubt slaved over for hours, and a regimental tie.

'I assume Ned's here, since his bike's outside,' he said.

'Yes, he's here. He came to tea. You may remember I invited him,' Georgia replied icily.

'I'd like to speak to him.'

Silently she stood aside to let Bron in. As she shut the front door she saw him give the Chinese wallpaper a disparaging look, as if mentally noting it down as evidence of weakness of character on her part. Every step he took into the flat made him seem more like an intruder. Unlike Nico he did absolutely nothing to fit in with his surroundings.

She led the way to the kitchen. Ned looked up at his father with a hangdog expression.

'What the hell do you think you're up to?' Bron demanded in a voice straight from Alaska. 'You know you're not allowed to leave Merlinslade without telling someone where you're going.'

'I did tell you. I left a message on the kitchen table. It's not my fault if you didn't see it.'

'Would you like a drink?' said Georgia, thinking it might sweeten his temper as well as divert attention from Ned, who was scarlet and gnawing his thumbnail.

Bron looked at her as if she were the lowliest of attendants in the lowliest of hamburger bars. 'No thanks. I've wasted too much time already. I don't believe you, Ned. You'll have to do better than that. You must have realised we were bound to raise the alarm when you didn't show up for lunch or tea.'

'I did leave a note. It's not my fault if you didn't look for it properly.'

'Do you realise just how much trouble you've caused?' said Bron. 'We'd have got on to the police by now if Nico hadn't remembered you'd said something about visiting Miss Tremain.'

'You never believe anything I say. It's not fair.'

'Is it fair that I've had to waste hours scouring the estate for you? Is it fair that I've had to cut reading the lesson? Nico's doing it instead, and he's not too pleased, I can tell you.'

'You ought to be glad. You're always saying what a drag it is,' said Ned, who now seemed to be regaining his composure.

Georgia thought that the congregation would probably enjoy basking in Nico's charm far more than having Bron glowering at them from the lectern. She couldn't have completely concealed her amusement, for Bron suddenly turned on her as well.

'And quite frankly I should have thought you'd have the foresight to ring me as soon as he turned up here,' he said.

She hastily adjusted her face, trying to work out a reply which wouldn't create even more trouble for Ned. 'I didn't think there was any special urgency. He seems to have coped very well on his own, and I'd planned to drive him back to Merlinslade myself. I'm surprised you didn't have the foresight to ring me, then all this could have been avoided.'

'I did ring you, some time ago, but there was no reply. For Christ's sake, do you really think I wouldn't be concerned about a twelve-year-old boy wandering round Bath for hours unsupervised? And if he coped so well, what's he done to his arm?'

'I just had a slight skid, that's all,' said Ned, quickly putting his arm behind him.

'Bath on a Sunday afternoon isn't exactly a den of iniquity,' said Georgia. 'Don't you think you're over-reacting just a little? Perhaps Ned's note blew away. Your kitchen is rather draughty, to say the least.'

'Yeah, that's right,' said Ned eagerly. 'I bet that's what it was. I wish you'd get our kitchen done like this, Dad. It's ace, isn't it?'

Bron gave his surroundings a boot-faced look. His gaze moved over Chloe's mirror and then on to a handful of Japanese paper sunflowers crammed into a spaghetti jar on the dresser.

'It's unusual,' he said. 'Go and wait for me in the Range Rover, Ned. You can put your bike inside, but don't you dare to lay a finger on the ignition.'

Ned got up reluctantly and took the car keys Bron was holding out to him. 'It's been great. Thanks a lot,' he said to Georgia.

'I've enjoyed it. Come again soon.'

She thought Ned would sulk, but as he passed his father on the way to the door he looked up at him with a tentative smile. Bron's expression relaxed fractionally. He put out his hand and ruffled Ned's hair.

'Get on with you, you skid artist,' he said.

Georgia, startled by this evidence of affection, had the crazy thought that maybe if she jumped on the table and did a tap dance she might even raise a smile from Bron. But as soon as Ned was out of sight another frown started to gather. He turned to Georgia. 'I'd really rather he didn't visit you again.'

'Why not? He enjoyed himself, and he doesn't seem to have had much fun lately. He could come on the bus next time, and I'll bring him home.'

'He has to settle down at Merlinslade. Racketing round Bath won't help.'

'I'd hardly classify coming here for tea as racketing. If you allowed him a bit more freedom, you might get better results.'

Bron stared at her. One of the taps was dripping, and in the tense silence the noise sounded huge. He went over to the sink and turned it off impatiently.

'How I deal with Ned is none of your business,' he said.

'Don't you see he's trying to grow up? You should give him some space, not criticise all the time.'

Georgia could feel her voice becoming louder, but she was unexpectedly relishing the role of matador. She was about to hurl another dart, when the kitchen door opened, and Chloe, accompanied by the sound of Kate Bush warbling gently from the bedroom, again made an appearance at exactly the most inopportune moment.

'Can you hear my homework?' she asked Georgia. 'I'm sure I know it now.' Her gaze slid round and alighted on Bron, who was staring at her like a hanging judge with gout. Her eyes widened, and she recoiled slightly.

'Sorry, did I interrupt something?' she said.

Georgia forced herself into an attempt at politeness. 'Ned Carwithen's been here for tea. His father came to collect him. Bron, I'd like you to meet my sister Chloe.'

'Hi,' said Chloe with an uncertain smile, stepping past him warily as she made for the fridge. She was barefoot, and her toenails were painted silver. She took out a packet of sunflower seeds and began to eat them one by one, looking more than ever like a startled marmoset as she kept her eyes nervously on him.

'How do you do?' said Bron stonily. He picked up his coat. 'I must go. I can find my own way out. But I meant what I said, Miss Tremain.'

Georgia aimed a parting barb. 'So did I. Maybe you should think about giving Ned a little more of your time. Otherwise, when he grows up, he might not want to spend time with you.'

'So you're an expert on child psychology, are you? I think you should wait till you've had one yourself, and know what you're talking about.'

'I do know. My own parents split up when I was young.'

He didn't reply, but as he left gave her a look designed to raze her to the ground. Through the window a few moments later they saw him go up the steps, ramrod-straight and radiating determination.

'Wow, you really socked it to him!' said Chloe, draping herself on a chair, and picking at crumbs from the cake. 'What a drongo! No one, but no one says how do you do any more. He's not really related to the scrumptious Nico, is he?'

Georgia sat down with her. She felt as if a tank had just powered its way out of her kitchen.

'He really is,' she said, 'and unfortunately that means he's going to be very hard to avoid.'

Perhaps as a result of her encounter with Bron, or the race to complete the costume designs, Georgia woke next day with the dull throb over her left eye which heralded a headache. Migraines had been another unwelcome result of the break-up of her marriage. The first had descended on her with the disintegrating effect of a computer virus at the time of the divorce, but they'd been so much better since she came to England that she'd rashly ignored the early warning of jagged lines of light floating across her vision the previous night, and not taken the medicine which sometimes cut off an attack.

As she drove to Merlinslade, she was still thinking hopefully that if she disregarded the ache it might go away. She carried the set models into the wardrobe workshop, locking them away in the largest of the cupboards. Tomorrow she'd bring over the costume designs for the meeting with Zelda. And on Wednesday the wardrobe staff would arrive to take up their posts.

Her wardrobe mistress, Annie Archer, a tough forty-year-old veteran, had recently lost her job when the backer of the West End musical she was working on went bankrupt. She was so desperate to find more work to fuel her mortgage that she'd agreed to let her London flat for a year and come to Merlinslade.

The cutter and general assistant, Kevin West, had been recommended by Annie. He was only two years out of college, but he'd seemed to know instinctively what Georgia wanted, and had produced a perfect test pattern and calico toile for her. She'd also hired a young Bristol girl, Jenny Oakley, unemployed since leaving college, and ecstatic at the chance to break into wardrobe management. She'd be responsible for maintaining the costumes, helping to dress the actors, and completing all the minor jobs which the others wouldn't have time for. Georgia was going to hire additional part-time staff only when they were needed. She already had an idea for one of them, which she intended to discuss with Esther after her visit to the Sanctuary.

For the Sanctuary had to be visited today, headache or no headache. It was Georgia's last chance before work began in earnest. Once Zelda had given the go-ahead on the designs there'd be virtually no let-up until the first night. Annie and her staff would take over much of the practical side, but Georgia would need to be constantly available for consultations and general problem-solving. In addition, she'd soon have to start the designs for the next play.

As she drove up the winding road to the top of the escarpment it was clear that the migraine had no intention of going away. Every time the car jolted over a pothole a stab of pain shot through her head, and when she stopped to look at the map her brain seemed to have gone into slow motion.

The Sanctuary lay in a fold of downland above Merlinslade woods. Outbuildings on either side of a rambling old farmhouse formed an open square round a grassy courtyard, where a group of Disciples sat in sober conversation beneath the shade of a drooping ash tree. Georgia had left her sunglasses at the flat, and as she got out of the car the full blaze of the sun hit her aching eyes like an interrogator's lamp.

One of the young men, wearing an informal uniform of neat navy blue shorts and a white tennis shirt, left the group to ask if he could help her. When he heard that she wanted to see Brighid, he led the way sedately through the house, and ushered her into a stone-flagged kitchen at the rear.

She stood for a moment enjoying the absence of glare. The only primary colour came from rows of neatly labelled bottles glowing upon shelves which ran the length of one wall. Bunches of fading plants hung to dry from ceiling racks. The floor was covered with worn earth-coloured tiles, and the long refectory table had been scrubbed so often that it was bleached drift-wood white. The small diamond-paned windows and a garden door were wide open, and the muted elemental colours in the room made it seem a natural extension of the landscape outside, rather than a separate entity.

Brighid stood at the far end of the table with her gown covered by a long green apron, her sleeves rolled up, vigorously pounding the contents of a mortar. In a shallow copper pan on the stove behind her a murky liquid bubbled gently, releasing a strong smell of stewed hay.

Georgia's escort had already silently disappeared. Brighid looked up, not a trace of surprise in her smile.

'Georgia, my dear, welcome! When your sister joined us I knew it wouldn't be long before you came our way.'

'I'm here to talk about Chloe, not myself,' said Georgia, although she knew that she was in no condition to start an argument with Brighid. Her head felt as if it was being slowly crushed.

Brighid went to the sink under the window, and washed her hands. As she shook the drops from her skin they spun through a shaft of sunlight, and crossed Georgia's vision in arcs of fire. Even the white huckaback towel on which Brighid dried her hands seemed blindingly bright.

Georgia hastily sat down in an oak wheel-back chair which faced away from the windows, resting her eyes on the dim light in the recesses of the room. Brighid placed herself opposite, and folded her hands in her lap.

'Chloe has so much potential,' she said. 'She simply needs to be taught how to channel her energies. Once she finds herself you'll be amazed by what she achieves.'

'Chloe does tend to fling herself into new enthusiasms, and she's only just getting over a relationship that went wrong at school. I should hate her to hurt herself rather than find herself.'

Georgia hadn't meant to be quite so blunt, but it was difficult to think of anything apart from the headache.

'It's natural for you to worry about your sister. But we shall listen to her, give her space to grow, and above all make her believe that we'll be there for her whenever and for however long she needs us.'

Georgia tried to think of a tactful way of pointing out that rather than helping Chloe grow up, Brighid's kind of care could turn into an emotional security blanket which she might never want to cast off.

'Perhaps you're afraid she may become too dependent,' Brighid went on, 'but the goddess wants us to learn to be strong and stand on our own. Chloe will know when she's ready to leave the Sanctuary.'

As at the well Brighid had uncannily echoed her thoughts. Georgia, struggling to find a reply, wondered if there was any point in arguing with her at all.

'Yet I'm told that some of the Disciples have been with you for several years,' she countered.

'None of them will stay here permanently. As soon as our new training centre is ready, they'll go into the world to spread the gospel of the goddess.'

'Chloe has to take up her A level courses again in the autumn. She's starting art college next year. I get the impression that she's being encouraged to work for the Disciples of the Fountain instead.'

'Naturally I don't expect Chloe to become a full-time evangelist, but when she goes to college I'm certain she'll find other lost children to send our way.'

Georgia's mind balked at the thought of Chloe as any kind of evangelist. She pressed her fingers to the side of her aching head. All she wanted was to lie down somewhere completely quiet and dark, instead of having to conduct this bizarre conversation.

'How can you possibly know something like that?' she said desperately. 'People of Chloe's age change so fast.'

'I do know. It's my special gift,' Brighid said softly. 'Just as I know that you have a headache, and that if you let me I can take it away for you.'

Even the limited light in the room was becoming intolerable. Georgia shut her eyes, thinking that it wouldn't have taken outstanding powers of deduction to work that one out.

She heard Brighid get up, heard the swish of her robe and the flap of her sandals on the floor. A moment later she felt Brighid's hands come round the back of the chair, and rest on her forehead, cool fingers moving softly from side to side, exactly as if they were easing out the creases in a piece of crumpled paper.

Brighid began to murmur some sort of incantation. It might have been a prayer, but Georgia couldn't catch the words. Gradually her hands, which always became icy during a migraine, began to tingle as though they were being held towards a gentle fire. The warmth seemed to creep downwards to her shoulders and the taut muscles of her neck. This time the sense of comfort was too strong to resist. Just for a moment she gave in to the impulse to let her head fall back against the pillow of Brighid's apron bib, and she slept.

When she woke she felt completely normal once more, and as if she'd been resting for hours. Yet when she glanced at the round-faced wooden clock on the wall a few minutes only had passed. Brighid was back in her seat, tranquilly stripping the blossoms from a bunch of dried flowers on to a square of paper. In front of Georgia was a small glass of pale green liquid. Brighid looked up and smiled at her.

'Infusion of feverfew,' she said. 'It won't harm you.'

Georgia was so astounded by her recovery that she drank the liquid without thinking.

'If you'd like to lose your headaches for good, all I ask in return is your attendance at a simple course of instruction in the ways of the goddess,' said Brighid.

The bitter taste of the infusion was already jolting Georgia's thoughts back into action. For a few minutes she'd been completely under Brighid's control. She wasn't sure how, but she was sure that she didn't want it to happen again. However good the result, she deeply distrusted such a wholesale handing over of her being.

'It's kind of you,' she said. 'But my doctor's already given me some medicine. I simply forgot to take it this time.'

'Drugs are only a temporary cure. The goddess can bring you permanent freedom from pain, permanent peace of mind. I know you've suffered lately, but bitterness is corrosive, you know. It eats away the soul.'

Like Morrigan's voice when she first met him in Bath, Brighid's too was deeply beguiling, but unlike his it did seem genuinely concerned. Her blue eyes radiated compassion. Georgia wondered if Chloe had told Brighid about the divorce, or if it was another inspired guess, the sort any seaside fortune teller might make. It was probably a little of both, for Chloe still knew very little about the break-up of her marriage.

All the same, Georgia was briefly tempted. It would be wonderful to banish the destructive self-doubt that still lingered after the divorce. Then her independence reasserted itself. It might be wonderful, but nothing was worth losing her freedom of mind.

'Thank you,' she said, 'but I'd rather try to manage alone.'

'We all need someone to help us,' said Brighid. 'Even I do.' A beatific smile spread over her face. 'The goddess truly blessed me when she sent me Morrigan.'

Georgia forced herself to plunge into the real subject of her visit.

'I can't help wondering if you're wise to let someone of Morrigan's reputation become involved in an organisation of this sort.'

Brighid gathered up a handful of flower heads and funnelled them into a storage jar.

'There's no need for you to worry on that score, my dear. He's a changed man. I should be very wrong to deny him access to the true light when he's repented so deeply. But because of his past I should naturally never let him become involved in the actual instruction of the Disciples.'

'I hear he's taking over the administration of the group. Surely that's not a good idea?'

'He's helping me to raise money for the Fountain Foundation, a magnificent new complex of buildings at the Sanctuary, a power house from which news of the goddess will spread world-wide. Morrigan's contacts are invaluable, though of course he consults me in everything. I persuaded him to become musical director at Merlinslade. I made him see that it could help publicise the Foundation.'

'But your group could lose its reputation entirely if things went wrong.'

'If I didn't give Morrigan the same loving trust that the goddess gives me, I wouldn't be worthy to serve her,' said Brighid simply.

With these last words Georgia was finally persuaded that Brighid at least was sincere. It would have to do for the moment. Chloe was over sixteen, she couldn't prevent her from joining the

Disciples, and it was quite clear that Brighid couldn't be talked out of championing Morrigan.

'I wonder if I could see round the Sanctuary? I'd like to know how Chloe spends her time here.'

'Of course. We have nothing to hide. It's very informal. All the disciples learn the art of herbal medicine in this room, for instance. I live in the house with the resident girls, and the young men have a dormitory across the courtyard. But we share a refectory and common room, and we meet together throughout the day.'

The accommodation in the house was perfectly ordinary, the bedrooms like the rooms of young girls anywhere, except that each had a table-top shrine of some sort, a picture of Gaia with a vase of flowers before it, a plastic statuette of Aphrodite surrounded by candles, a painting of St Francis among the animals and birds set in the centre of a rosary made of shells.

'All religions are one,' said Brighid, adjusting a palm leaf cross over a bed. 'I'm basically a Christian, but through my gift of healing St Bride has led me towards a deeper appreciation of the goddess. When you see the rest of the Sanctuary, and especially our chapel, you'll begin to understand.'

After she'd shown Georgia the men's dormitory and the refectory, both monastically austere, she led her towards a round stone building whose tiled roof was covered with a tapestry of lichens and stonecrop. Georgia guessed it had once been a grain store.

'This is our chapel,' Brighid said, 'the Sanctuary's living heart.'

The circular room inside was painted white and floored with amber-coloured pine. At one end was a deep alcove. In it, on a plinth above a semicircle of lighted candles, stood a huge piece of uncut amethyst, split to reveal a hollow core. In the amethyst's heart stood a figure of the goddess cut from rock crystal, her arms outstretched to form a shining, translucent cross.

A handful of Disciples sat cross-legged on cushions, their hands in their laps, gazing towards the shrine. The room was absolutely silent, almost womb-like, and filled with the scent of roses floating in shallow glass bowls on either side of the shrine.

Brighid beckoned her outside again, noiselessly shutting the door.

'We mustn't interrupt. It's vital not to disturb the process of visualisation.'

'Visualising what, exactly?' asked Georgia, still slightly bemused by what she'd just seen.

'Visualising the goddess imbuing them with strength and hope.'

'It sounds more like self-hypnosis to me.'

'It's the surest way to rebuild a shattered self-image. It works best in a completely relaxed and secure setting. The process can take several months, allied to other remedial treatments, of course.'

'What do those involve?'

'The groves of ancient trees in this area are particularly dear to the goddess. We hold dance ceremonies among them and at the stone circles on the downs. We tap into their ancient forces at the full moon. When a Disciple decides to become a permanent member of the group, I baptise him or her in the name of the goddess at the Grail Well.'

'But I thought you said you were a Christian?'

'I am simply reaffirming the power of other older, lost forces, just as fundamental as Christianity, and using them to fortify and heal.'

'And what part does Morrigan have in these ceremonies?' Georgia couldn't imagine him joining in some ethereal dance.

'He sings with us, of course,' said Brighid solemnly. 'Our ceremonies have been enriched beyond belief since he joined us.'

'Where does he stay? In the dormitory with the other men?' Georgia couldn't envisage that either. The spartan room she'd seen wasn't his sort of setting at all.

'Naturally he doesn't stay here,' said Brighid, turning an innocent face towards her. 'That would be most unwise until the public has fully accepted that his change of heart is genuine. He's said himself that he wouldn't want to endanger the reputation of the group in any way. He always goes back to his house in Bath.'

Georgia headed back down the hill towards the village and the rectory feeling moderately reassured. Though Brighid was eccentric and illogical, she did seem to retain a stock of basic commonsense. Georgia had seen no real evidence that Chloe could come to any harm, and indeed the atmosphere of peace and healing had been so strong that she couldn't help admiring what Brighid had managed to establish in the twentieth-century world. Though the Disciples were perhaps unduly sober for people of their age, a little seriousness might do Chloe good, and it was only for the summer. But she'd be glad to talk things over with Esther, all the same.

Tea had just finished in the rectory sitting room. The older children were watching the six o'clock news on a black and white television and doing their homework at the same time. Tracey and Maureen were discussing the latest iniquities of the Job Centre with Kim, Esther was making notes for a sermon, and Sumitra sat quietly in her usual place on the window seat.

They listened interestedly to Georgia's account of her visit to the Sanctuary. When it came to an end, Esther drew a neat line under her notes, and looked up with a serene face.

'I'm sure Brighid's telling the truth about Morrigan not living there,' she said. 'She can be very firm if she puts her mind to it.'

'Morrigan was the king of the ravers in his day, though,' said Kim. 'I'm not so sure I'd trust him.'

'We have to have some faith in others,' said Esther, 'or the world would be a dismal place indeed. I shouldn't worry, Georgia. Chloe will probably grow out of the group in a few months' time, and I'm certain Brighid'll look after her.'

'Nico's signed up Morrigan as the theatre's musical director,' said Georgia. 'He's convinced he's reformed too.'

'Well, at least Morrigan can't make a hash of things at the Sanctuary while he's working at Merlinslade,' said Kim.

Georgia felt more cheerful. The homely, matter-of-fact atmosphere of the rectory was a perfect antidote to the other worldly surroundings of the Sanctuary.

'Brighid didn't say anything about wanting a cook, did she?' Kim went on. 'I went for another job interview today, and the minute the guy heard I was on probation he shot out of the room faster than Polaris. I'd even work somewhere as whacky as the Sanctuary.'

'Sorry,' said Georgia. 'They seem to take it in turns to do the cooking. It's probably all soul food, anyway.'

'Most of them look as if they could do with a good steak,' said Kim. 'I'm not anti-veggie – far from it – but when I see them wafting about the hedgerows looking so sodding ethereal and self-righteous, it really gets to me.'

Esther frowned at Kim. 'That's not fair,' she said.

Kim shrugged and took her tea over to the television to watch the rest of the news. 'Why should I be fair?' she said. 'Life isn't.'

'How's the theatre?' Esther asked Georgia, filling in an awkward silence.

'Fine. The wardrobe's all set up, and the staff arrive the day after tomorrow. That's another reason why I came to see you.' She glanced over at Sumitra, who was still sitting in exactly the same position, her smooth head bent over some intricate drawn-thread work. 'I wondered if you'd like to come and work at the theatre, in the wardrobe, Sumitra?'

She lifted her head and stared expressionessly at Georgia, needle poised, a minute silver thimble on her finger.

'Just for a trial period, of course,' Georgia hurried on, 'just so that you can see if you like us.'

'What a marvellous idea!' said Esther in a brightly enthusiastic voice. Sumitra still said nothing.

'It doesn't have to be full-time,' said Georgia, 'though there's plenty of work.'

'What sort of work?' said Sumitra, in whose face suppressed interest was warring with suspicion. 'I am a professional, you know.'

'You're exactly what we need. Could I tell you a little about what's involved? I expect you know the story of *The Tempest*?'

'Of course.' Sumitra's voice was crushing. 'Every secondary school pupil at home learns Shakespeare through and through. They are not ignorant like the children here.'

Tracey and Maureen bridled. Esther threw a beseeching glance at them.

'The costumes I've designed for Ariel and the goddesses in the masque are extremely demanding technically,' Georgia hurried on. 'Our wardrobe mistress, Annie, won't have enough time to cope with all the details, and Kevin, her assistant, has quite enough on his hands with the cutting and tailoring.'

'It would be just ladies' clothes, then?' said Sumitra. 'I am not accustomed to sewing for men.'

'Just ladies' clothes,' said Georgia, detecting a definite wavering on Sumitra's part. 'The fabrics for Ariel's costumes in particular are so delicate that I must be able to trust the person who makes them up.'

'And you would pay me a proper salary? People think that because I haven't worked in this country before, I'll take anything they offer. It is not so.'

'A proper salary,' said Georgia. 'Union rates.'

'First I come to see,' said Sumitra. 'I am not saying yes, just maybe.' Nevertheless she gave a rare smile, revealing a row of small, brilliantly white teeth.

'Why don't you come along to the theatre with Esther tomorrow afternoon, and decide when you've had a look round?' said Georgia.

'That's an excellent idea,' said Esther. 'I've religious education classes most of the day at the primary school, but we could easily visit Merlinslade around teatime. It's all settled, then.'

'Perhaps,' said Sumitra, but she was still smiling as she returned to her embroidery.

'Hey, you guys!' Kim's voice broke in excitedly. 'Come over to the telly, and get a load of this! It's all about that charity concert Morrigan's organising.'

They reached the television just in time to see some closing shots of the Wembley rehearsal.

'And to conclude our report we have a very special item,' the presenter was saying. 'Morrigan himself is here in the studio to give us an exclusive interview, his first on television for twenty years.'

The camera moved to a woman in an angular scarlet jacket. It was Meredith Bell, the doyenne of the Channel Six current affairs team, an interviewer whose questions were as searching as a dental probe. Opposite her sat Morrigan, most untypically dressed in a sober grey suit, his hair sleeked back from his face.

Meredith Bell's eyes glittered behind a pair of metal-framed granny specs as she allowed the full force of her gaze to fall on him.

'We're all more than interested to know why you've decided to go public again, after declaring your permanent retirement from the pop scene when you came out of prison twenty years ago,' she challenged him, referring to the notes before her. 'Perhaps I could quote your own words at the time: "I intend to devote the rest of my life to atoning for my mistakes and pursuing the private path of inner light." A concert at Wembley Stadium doesn't seem particularly private.'

Morrigan looked modestly down at his hands.

'During my travels in Asia, I knew that one day I must do something to help the Third World. When I came home, and received so many amazingly supportive letters from my public, asking me to return to the stage, I felt profoundly selfish for having denied them for so long the only gift I have to offer. Through this concert in aid of World Heartbeat I shall be able to repay them for their wonderful loyalty, and, even more importantly, do something to help the poor and suffering.'

Georgia heard Esther give a sigh of approbation, but Meredith Bell still looked disbelieving.

'You're a very wealthy man. Wouldn't it have been simpler to make a donation to a charitable organisation while you were actually in the Third World?'

Morrigan hesitated, and cast his gaze up to the ceiling. As a display of reticence it couldn't have been bettered, yet Georgia sensed that he was bursting to talk about himself.

'I am not a rich man, believe me, Meredith. My legal expenses at my trial were colossal, and I had to ensure that my backing group was financially secure when I left the stage.'

'What a load of bullshit!' said Kim. 'His house in the Royal Crescent must be worth half a million, and if you're skint you don't drive around in his sort of car!'

'Shhhh!' chided Esther. 'Just hear him out.'

'These days my only wealth lies in my friends,' Morrigan continued. 'I recently became a member of a wonderful west-country group of Christians called the Disciples of the Fountain.

144

It changed my whole outlook, as I hope the concert at Wembley will help to change the world of the underprivileged.'

Like Kim, Meredith Bell was still not convinced. 'Yet I'm sure you're not averse to the excellent publicity the concert's bringing you?'

Morrigan looked shocked. 'I have to discharge my debt to society somehow. Singing is all I can do.'

'In the most visible way possible, by appearing at Wembley and on network television?' she persisted.

'I wonder if you realise exactly how much I lost through that one indiscretion twenty years ago, Meredith? Because of it, Merlinslade, one of the most beautiful estates in England, my inheritance, part of my life's blood, was willed away from me by my father in what most people consider an inordinately judgemental act.'

Meredith Bell pounced again. 'So you think it's judgemental to disapprove of hard drugs?'

'No one disapproves of them more than I do. That was another Morrigan twenty years ago, a different person, I assure you. And losing Merlinslade was far worse than being sent to prison.' He gave Meredith Bell a wounded smile. 'Don't you think I've been punished enough?'

Georgia could imagine handkerchiefs being taken out all over the country. Even Meredith Bell had begun to look slightly rattled.

'But the Lord in His goodness has once more tempered the wind to the shorn lamb,' Morrigan continued. 'He's given me yet another opportunity to demonstrate how much I've changed. I'm delighted to reveal that I've taken the post of musical director at Merlinslade's historic theatre, which is being revived by my nephew, the actor Nico Carwithen.'

'So this means you will be performing for money after all?' queried Meredith Bell hopefully, though she was clearly grasping at straws.

'My work for the theatre will enable me to atone for the wrong I did my family, and I shall be donating my salary to the Disciples of the Fountain, who are specifically dedicated to healing young, damaged souls.'

145

Meredith Bell's spectacles flashed dangerously as she tried a last line of attack.

'Some people might say that's a little ironic, since the prosecution at your trial alleged that you distributed drugs among some of your fans.'

'That was just a cruel rumour put about by those who were jealous of my success. It was never proved. I find it extremely sad that people as intelligent as yourself should still be repeating false accusations against a man who has been trying to expiate his mistakes for so long.'

Morrigan swivelled round to face the camera fully.

'And now I've talked enough about myself. I would like all of you youngsters out there who are sad, solitary, or distressed in any way, to know that I am constantly thinking of you.'

His face had assumed an expression of such solemn concern that even Tracey and Maureen were showing signs of approval.

'Very soon,' he continued, 'when the Fountain Foundation is set up, together with the many regional groups we have planned, there will be healing and sanctuary available for you wherever and whenever you need it. Perhaps I can best express my feelings in one of the most sacred songs of all time, which I dedicate to every young person who is lonely and oppressed.'

He picked up his guitar from a table by his side, swept his hand over the strings, and broke into 'Come unto Me, all ye that are heavy laden' from *The Messiah*. His voice vibrated with emotion. It was like being doused in a stream of warm, sugary glycerine, and yet it was strangely effective, so effective that as the piece ended Meredith Bell had actually taken off her spectacles and was gazing at him with eyes that looked suspiciously moist.

Morrigan smiled directly at the camera for the first time.

'I appeal to all my wonderful, generous friends out there. I implore you to send every penny you can to World Heartbeat, and please, please remember the marvellous work of the Disciples of the Fountain when our appeal campaign begins. God bless you, everyone.'

Chapter 8

Zelda was wearing cowboy boots when Georgia met her and Nico on stage next day.

'You're looking very all-American,' Georgia teased her.

'So I should. The Fourth of July's coming up, and by Thanksgiving I mean this theatre to be the best in the west. We have just over two months to first night, longer than the usual rehearsal time, but don't forget it's an untried company, and an unfamiliar theatre.'

'God help us all,' said Nico.

Zelda skewered him with a severe glance. 'No kidding, Nico. Life's serious from now on. This afternoon Redvers'll be here to look round the theatre before the others arrive, and discuss his costumes. I've got three actors coming from London for a final audition for Ariel as well. None of them's ideal, but I shall have to make a choice today. I'd like you to sit in, Georgy.'

'Would you like to go over to the wardrobe and see the designs now?' she asked. 'I've already laid out the models for the sets.'

She led the way along the corridor at the back of the theatre, past the silent green room and dressing rooms, soon to echo with voices.

She'd opened the windows of the workshop, letting in wafts of warm, hay-scented air. In the orchard Mr Meads was nimbly turning swathes of drying grass with a long pitchfork. The set models were laid out on one of the tables. Zelda and Nico began to prowl round, inspecting them in silence from all angles. This was the most difficult moment of all, Georgia always found, this exposure of her ideas to the critical gaze of the outside world.

'I like them. Yes, I like them very much indeed,' said Zelda after an interminable silence, slowly revolving round them yet again. 'The contrast between the two parts of the island is really great.'

The first set was a beach, framed in a mysterious tangle of mangroves, and backed with looming grey baobabs. Skeleton branches and huge multi-coloured shells lay scattered across the sand. Among the mangroves Georgia had constructed a grotesque platform of driftwood as a den for Caliban.

'I thought we'd have the sound of waves breaking on a reef to introduce the beach scenes,' she said.

The second set was a tropical version of Merlinslade woods, a grove of gnarled and ancient trees hung with flowering lianas, and penetrated by dark receding pathways. She'd built more platforms into the branches, making them as outlandish as jackdaws' nests.

'I can't wait to use those hideaways,' said Nico.

'It shouldn't be too difficult for the lighting designer to dream up some fireflies for the night-time scenes, and I want to use a tape of birds and bell frogs calling in the background.'

'I love the tree houses too,' said Zelda. 'They give me so much more scope for moving the actors around. I was worried that the old-fashioned flats might cramp the action.'

The final set, Prospero's cell, was dominated by a telescope trained through an archway on to the midnight sky. Books were everywhere, toppling from the shelves, stacked on the floor, and forming yet more hiding places for Caliban. A table groaned beneath a jumble of chemical apparatus. In one corner was propped a huge distorting glass.

'The glass is great. Lots of good biz with that,' said Nico. 'If you need extra props for the cell you can borrow things from the house. You'll see what there is when I show you round.'

'We'll use the vista stage for the night sky,' said Georgia. 'And I must show you how it works in the masque.'

She demonstrated the lowering of Juno's chariot, a marvellously baroque affair drawn by peacocks, to the floor of the vista stage.

'Loads of atmos, Georgy, and you've done wonders with those grooved flats,' said Nico. 'I adore the chariot, too. Morrigan's

148

music should add the crowning touch.'

'As long as he doesn't do it rock-style,' she said.

'Don't worry,' said Nico smoothly. 'He has some fabulous ideas, all perfectly appropriate. He's coming over this evening, and I'll show him the sets then.'

'The shipwreck at the beginning of the play can be played at the front of the stage, with the rest in darkness. We can use that lethal thunder machine, Nico, if you're still absolutely set on it, but I'd prefer to have recorded sound effects.'

'Of course we must use it,' said Nico. 'It's going to be a highlight of our backstage tours. I'll take full responsibility.'

'I like the idea of managing the shipwreck that way,' said Zelda. 'It cuts down changing the flats to a minimum. The less we use them, the better. The stage hands need to get used to them slowly.'

When they'd finished discussing the sets, Zelda went over to the other cutting table.

'So, let's see the costumes now,' she said, sitting down expectantly. Nico joined her, his eyes fixed inquisitively on Georgia's portfolio.

'I'll show you the main characters first,' she said. 'But don't forget these are only pilot designs.'

She set out two pen and gouache paintings, the first of Prospero in everyday wear. She'd given him a long robe and over-gown of brown velvet edged with purple. His cloak was indigo silk, embroidered all over with cabalistic signs, with a black lining. On his head he wore a close-fitting high-crowned academic hood.

'You've even managed to cover up Redvers' hair. The poor guy worries terribly about his thinning patch. He'll look just like Dante in that hood,' said Zelda.

'The lining of the cloak is purposely dark, so that he can reverse it to signify invisibility,' said Georgia.

'Did you know there's a family tradition that Shakespeare himself once played Prospero here, in the great hall, before the time of the theatre?' said Nico. 'We've a drawing in the library which is supposed to show him in the role, though it's never been authenticated.' He gave Georgia a challenging glance. 'You must

149

see it today, before you complete the designs.'

'And when Prospero becomes "absolute Milan" again, for the betrothal at the end of the play, he'll wear full court dress,' said Georgia, determinedly ignoring Nico, as she produced her next sketch for Redvers.

'The old bugger'd better not upstage me,' he said, when Zelda had finished enthusing. 'I only hope Caliban's going to look half as good. Don't keep me in suspense any longer, Georgia.'

She placed the design for his costume in front of him, watching his face closely. Few actors were able to hide their reaction at seeing their costume for the first time. It was a green Lycra body suit, with a subtle irridescence like the scales of a fish. Glaucous bladder wrack trailed down the arms and body. She'd painted in webbed feet, and a shock of pallid anemone-like tentacles in place of hair. Caliban held a fistful of black sea-slugs in one hand. As a final touch, she'd given him a huge abalone shell, lined with mother-of-pearl, which he could use to draw over his head like a hermit crab and peep through the row of holes in the side.

'I thought you could have some good biz with the sea slugs,' said Georgia mischievously. 'You could even eat one of them if you felt the audience was up to it.'

'It's magnificent, a real knock-out,' said Nico. His voice was absolutely sincere. 'And thank God I shall be covered. Body make up is such hell to do.'

'Your fans'll be disappointed at not seeing more of you,' Zelda joked. 'No, seriously, Georgia, I think it's tremendous, too. Tell me exactly how it'll be made.'

Georgia ran through the technicalities of the construction, then spent ten minutes trying to dissuade Nico from adding eels and coconuts to his props.

'Definitely not,' said Zelda ultimately. 'I know you, Nico. You'll make it far too Freudian. Let's move on to Miranda.'

Georgia laid out more drawings.

'I've put her in Moorish dress, muslin harem pants, and a loose blouse under a long green embroidered waistcoat. You wanted a liberated Miranda, and this costume'll give her more freedom than usual. But the wedding dress is formal, latticed with pearls, and it'll have a standing collar of silver lace.'

150

'So now, out of the principal roles, we're just left with Ariel,' said Zelda, after another lengthy perusal and discussion.

Georgia produced the first design. It showed a brief tunic of pale grey chiffon, soft and clinging as filaments of ash, the sleeves and legs of the leotard beneath it embroidered with narrow lines of silvery beads.

'The beads are placed to glitter in the beam of a single spot as Ariel moves about the stage. The arm draperies can be folded round her like a bat's wings when she needs to become invisible,' Georgia explained. 'I've done another in pale blue for when she receives her freedom, and melts into the air.'

Zelda was almost overwhelmingly enthusiastic by now.

'I can only think of one major snag,' she said. 'There's a huge amount of detailed embroidery. Will you have the time for it?'

'Don't worry. I'm hoping to take on a brilliant part-timer. Her work's out of this world. She's coming to have a look at the place this afternoon. She should be able to cope with the lace work as well.'

'Do show us dear Uncle Ger's costume before you go on to the lesser mortals,' said Nico. 'I hope you've made it suitably showy.'

Though Georgia knew her attitude was unprofessional, she'd hated designing Morrigan's costume. But all designers had to work with performers they disliked at some time or other, and at least she wouldn't have to do the physical fitting of it. That doubtful honour would fall on Annie.

Yet in spite of disliking him so intensely, the actual design of the costume had gone like a dream. She'd produced a black doublet and breeches of cut velvet, with a short, immensely flamboyant cape. The sleeves were puffed and slashed, caught at intervals with jet beads, the waist drawn down in an exaggerated V, as if it belonged to some predatory black wasp, and the hose fitted like a second skin.

'Wow!' said Nico, when he saw it. 'It's hugely flattering, and it's even got that slightly melodramatic air he loves so much. Not the sort of character I'd care to meet in a back alley, though.'

'I really wonder if it isn't a bit over the top, even for Morrigan,' said Zelda.

'My guess is that he'll love it,' said Georgia. 'He's so vain he won't even notice the overtones.'

Zelda had arranged to meet Redvers for lunch in Bath. Georgia ate a sandwich in the workshop as she wrote up the morning's notes for the final costume designs.

Afterwards she went backstage to look again at the machinery for the chariot. The cradle was raised on ropes wound around a massive ratcheted cylinder laboriously cranked by hand, and lowered with the aid of a counterweight. For some reason which still eluded her the rachets kept slipping, so that the cradle ascended in a series of terrifying jolts.

She'd wanted to dismantle it to find out where the fault lay, but the nails were thoroughly rusted into place. She tried several small adjustments, got a splinter in her thumb, and began to wish she were sitting in The Mortal Man drinking a long glass of lager. Nico had invited her to join him there, but he'd been so proprietorial since their dinner at the Veneziana that she was trying to avoid seeing too much of him, in spite of all Zelda's advice to the contrary. She had made Georgia feel as if there was something cowardly about not getting involved with Nico.

Crossly, she cranked the handle again, and this time a small but vital-looking block of wood flew out of the centre of the winch.

'Sod the wretched thing!' she said, and gave it a childish and extremely satisfactory kick. The whole construction shuddered crazily, releasing a fine shower of debris.

'That won't help,' said a cool voice.

She looked up from brushing dust from her clothes, and saw Bron standing by a stack of flats. For once he was dressed fairly normally, in jeans, a blue shirt with rolled-up sleeves, and desert boots. The boots surprised her most of all.

'What's it got to do with you?' she said. 'It's my problem, not yours.'

'I do actually own this theatre, you know,' he said. 'I'm the one who'll be sued if this contraption breaks someone's neck.'

'It's not going to. I'm working on it now. And if you're looking for Nico he's down at The Mortal Man.'

'I wanted to see you, not Nico.' He bent and picked up the

block of wood, turning it in his hands. He wore the unnecessary kind of watch that worked faultlessly five hundred feet below the Arctic ice-cap, kept time with split-second precision, and depressingly implied perfect punctuality and reliability in its owner.

'Why?' she asked. 'You don't own me, you know.'

He squinted along the block of wood, then looked up at her again. She saw that his eyes were not grey as she'd thought originally, but a deep slate blue.

'I came to apologise,' he said.

She stared at him suspiciously. He didn't look particularly sorry. She decided to make him work a little harder. 'So I'm meant to curtsey and say thank you. Is that it?'

'Of course not.'

'Well, that's how it seems to me.'

'I simply realised that I was perhaps rather – abrupt with you the other day when I came to fetch Ned.'

'Abrupt! You were bloody rude! And you didn't even bother to consider that Ned and I might be telling the truth.'

'Mrs Meads found Ned's note under the dresser this morning. I had another word with him, and I gather he'd told you I knew where he was.' He seemed about to choke with the effort of the apology, but ruined Georgia's pleasure with his next words. 'I wouldn't have blamed you if you'd made that clear in the first place.'

'Yet I seem to remember from something you once said to Ned that you dislike sneaks. So I can't win.'

He was looking delightfully uncomfortable again. 'I'm sorry you're taking it that way. It's not what I intended.'

'So this means Ned can visit me after all?' she asked, determined to wrest some more concessions from him.

'Yes,' he said abruptly. 'It's very good of you.'

'It's not good of me!' she exploded. 'You talk as though I'm performing some charitable obligation. I invited Ned because I like him. Stop patronising me. I may work here, but I'm not your servant.'

His expression was thunderstruck.

'I honestly didn't mean to give that impression.' He was almost stammering.

'Well, you do.' She held out her hand. 'May I have that block of wood, please? I need to fit it back into the winch.'

He looked so relieved at the change of subject that she almost began to laugh, but he didn't return the block. 'It's warped,' he said. 'It looks like a replacement. Someone botched it out of unseasoned wood, and it's got worse over the years. The only way you'll make the machinery work is by forcing the block into position.'

He rammed it back into some mysterious place in the middle of the winch, cranked the handle, and it began to revolve smoothly at last, though squeaking dismally as it did so.

'Candle wax'll stop that noise,' he said. He retrieved the block of wood. 'But this isn't safe. I'll make you another. I've got a piece of old oak in the workshop.' He gave her a sideways look. 'Dare I ask if you're replacing the ropes? They look fairly unsound to me.'

'Of course I am! Look, you really do have to understand that I know my job. You can come and inspect the hoist before rehearsals if you like.'

'I intend to. And who's being patronising now?' he said smoothly.

He threw the bit of wood into the air, caught it, and walked away towards the front of the house, whistling 'La Donna è Mobile' to the empty stalls.

Georgia came into the theatre again later that afternoon to find Zelda and Nico in the front row, talking to Redvers Monk. He had aged far more than the years that had passed since his last performance. Then he'd been a passionate and virile Faustus. Now he was more like King Lear.

His deepset, pouched eyes, set in a face with seamed and rumpled skin, had a weary look, as if they'd seen out too many nights in too many bars. He wore a baggy linen suit with narrow Edwardian revers and a cornflower in the buttonhole. He must have recently lost weight, for his trousers looked too big for his rangy body, and were held up by the sort of striped belt schoolboys used to wear.

He got up as Zelda introduced Georgia. His smile was singularly engaging, but had a strong hint of sadness in it.

'So you're Georgia Tremain. Nico's given you a splendid write-up. He tells me you'll even be able to make something of this old hulk of mine.'

'It's an honour to have you here,' she said. 'We're all certain your Prospero's going to be even better than your Faustus.'

'Ah, yes, my Faustus. "Where are the snows of yesteryear?" Where indeed?' As he took an amber cigarette holder from his jacket pocket, and started to fit a cigarette into it his fingers shook very slightly. Georgia was amazed that Nico didn't stop him. The no smoking rule in the auditorium was inflexible. He caught her enquiring look, and gently shook his head.

'We're going to do great things here, Redvers,' said Zelda in her most bracing voice. Georgia guessed she'd been having a hard time boosting his self-confidence. 'I thought you might like to sit in on the final auditions for Ariel, and generally get the feel of the place.'

Redvers nodded sleepily. His eyes were half closed as he drew on his cigarette. It had evidently been a good lunch.

'Could you call the first on the list from the green room, Nico?' said Zelda, in a voice which only just concealed her exasperation.

Redvers dozed on and off through the audition. The first candidate launched into Ariel's opening speech with tremendous confidence, but gave it such a strong Stanislavskian treatment that the meaning was almost thrown away. There was a long silence after Zelda asked her to wait in the green room, then Nico began to laugh.

'Talk about tearing a passion to tatters!' he said.

'Poor kid,' said Zelda. 'She must have been working on that interpretation for days.'

The second candidate had different problems. Though her voice was glorious, she was built more like a shot-putter than a sprite. Nico fidgeted all the way through her speech, but Zelda was plainly impressed, and Georgia began to replan Ariel's costume mentally to accommodate another fifty pounds of flesh.

'You don't really expect me to act with a tank like that?' Nico asked Zelda, as the girl disappeared with a self-satisfied smile.

'I don't expect you to condemn her simply because she's body-challenged,' said Zelda tartly.

The final candidate, though pretty enough to suit even Nico, was thrown completely in the middle of her speech when she suddenly realised that Redvers was in the audience. Her performance at once went into disastrous overdrive. As she disappeared towards the green room looking completely shattered, Zelda sighed.

'Christ, I must be losing my touch. They seemed so promising in London. The first one's method of interpretation is all wrong for this theatre, but she'd probably improve once I'd worked with her. We can't risk number three. She could freak out in the same way on the first night. The second had the best voice.'

'I never knew Ariel looked like Arnold Schwarzenegger,' said Nico in a gloomy voice.

'I could ask her to diet,' said Zelda doubtfully, 'but that's a risk too.'

She put on a pair of gold-rimmed half spectacles, and tapped into her lap-top, reviewing the list of actors she'd already auditioned in London. 'I must have seen about thirty Ariels now, no one's been exactly right, and time's run out. We really do have to choose one of these. Let's go for the first, and I'll do a heavy make-over.'

Towards the end of the auditions Redvers' head had drooped on to his chest until he appeared to be fast asleep, a state of affairs which would have called forth a biting reproof from Zelda in anyone else. But unexpectedly he now opened his eyes and sat up, looking like an ancient and moulting owl.

'Not worth it,' he said. 'None of them's worth it. They've no feeling for verse. I can't work with an actress who speaks Shakespeare like a laundry list.'

'Actor,' said Zelda, only just restraining her impatience. 'They're all called actors these days, Redvers. And a lot of the new generation believe that by de-constructing the text they reveal its true meaning. They're doing some interesting work.'

'Bollocks,' said Redvers. 'They throw away the meaning. The speeches lose their heart. Shakespeare is poetry. The two are inseparable.'

'Jesus,' muttered Zelda, rummaging in her bag, extracting some Vitamin E pills, and rapidly swallowing a couple. 'This is not good for my hypertension.'

'You've both got a point,' said Nico soothingly, 'but the main thing is that we really don't have time for any more auditions. I think Zelda's right. She'll just have to do some rapid reconstruction work on number one.'

'A feeling for verse isn't something you can teach overnight,' said Redvers scathingly. 'She's either got it, or she hasn't. And in my opinion, she hasn't.'

'I don't like to impose my authority as a director outright on anyone,' said Zelda in a tight voice, looking meaningfully at him, 'but in this case I may have to.'

Redvers subsided in his seat, muttering something under his breath. Nico was beginning to look worried. Georgia wondered if she should suggest a coffee break, when there was a sudden banging noise behind them as the auditorium doors swung open at the back of the stalls.

They all turned. Esther, dressed as usual in her cassock, was walking down the aisle between the seats, with Sumitra, wearing her old cardigan over a pink sari, stealing noiselessly behind her.

Georgia hadn't thought they'd arrive so early. She made some swift introductions.

'I'm so sorry. We've been auditioning for Ariel, and the final decision's taking longer than I expected. Would you mind waiting here for just a few minutes longer? Or perhaps you'd rather go over to the wardrobe and start looking round on your own?'

Nico was giving Esther a surreptitious appraisal of which she seemed totally unaware. He looked puzzled.

'No, wait, don't go just yet.' He spoke directly to Esther. 'I know I've seen you somewhere before.'

'I was in church, officiating with the dean, on the Sunday you read the lesson.' She gave him a level look. 'But possibly you didn't notice me? You did leave before the end.'

'No, no, I don't mean then,' said Nico impatiently. 'It's just that now I see you in the theatre, I'm certain I've seen you act somewhere.'

157

'I was once on television in a very minor way,' said Esther quietly.

'I've got it!' said Nico. 'You did that fabulous Perdita for the BBC! Everyone raved over you.'

'That was a long time ago. I never act these days.'

'But there's no reason why you shouldn't, is there?' Nico's voice became even more excited. 'I mean no church rule that actually forbids you to go on stage?'

'No,' said Esther, 'but I have my own rules and not acting is one of them.'

Though she was standing perfectly calmly, her hands clasped in front of her, Georgia sensed the underlying wariness in her stance.

'OK, I understand that,' said Nico, 'but I wonder if you'd agree to break it, just this once? I'd be so interested to see what you'd do with Ariel. Only a short reading, simply to give us all some new slants on what to do next, you understand. It might somehow break up this casting log-jam. You don't mind, do you, Zelda?'

'Be my guest,' she said. 'But I don't think you should hassle Esther if she doesn't want to do it.'

Esther sent her a grateful look. 'I really would prefer not to.'

Redvers, well into a second cigarette, seemed to have regained his composure. While all this was going on, he too had been watching Esther closely. He obviously liked what he heard and saw.

'I remember your Perdita as well, my dear,' he said. 'I haven't acted for many years either, so we're in the same position. I expect you've heard about my lapse from grace? I'm finding it extraordinarily difficult to begin again. Would you do me the greatest of favours by helping me to break the ice? Perhaps we could just run through one short piece together – maybe the opening scene between Ariel and Prospero?'

Nico leapt in at once. 'Won't you agree to that one small thing for us, Esther? As Redvers says, it'd help him so much.'

He gave her one of his most melting smiles. Georgia could see Esther's resolve beginning to crumble slightly under the double onslaught.

'I completely understand your scruples,' said Redvers, 'but it would be an enormous act of Christian charity.'

'Well, if you put it that way,' she said slowly, 'I suppose it wouldn't matter just for once.'

'Marvellous,' said Nico quickly, thrusting his Arden text of the play into her hand.

Esther went composedly up on to the stage, followed by Redvers, who was now looking distinctly uneasy.

'Jesus, Nico,' said Zelda in an undertone. 'I hope this isn't going to wreck everything. I don't see how anyone as uptight as she is could come over well on stage. I wanted Redvers to have longer to acclimatise. If she can't deliver he'll find it impossible to respond, and that'll make him even more jittery.'

'She's a marvellous actor,' Georgia broke in indignantly. 'And this makes it easier, not harder, for Redvers. He'll be concentrating on Esther rather than himself.'

'The sooner he plunges in, the better,' said Nico. 'He's been in agonies for days about starting again.'

'But it doesn't help the central problem,' said Zelda. 'We still shan't have an Ariel.'

'Don't jump the gun,' said Nico. 'I think she'll surprise you.'

Esther, waiting under the glare of a single spotlight for Redvers to find his place in the text, was feeling a great deal less composed than she looked. The brilliance of her surroundings, the atmosphere of the theatre, as if it was waiting for something hugely exciting to begin, the warmth of the beam bearing down on her, made her feel as if she was emerging from a long spell of sensory deprivation.

All over again she felt the old sensation of her personality expanding, becoming something she'd already decided long ago she didn't want it to be, something that always felt exactly right for her at the time, but which she knew from bitter experience wasn't right at all. Acting could never ultimately satisfy her like the more steady, enduring rewards of her present calling.

For a moment she felt like running from the stage before the spell caught her up even more deeply, and then she looked at Redvers and knew it wasn't possible. Unlike herself he appeared uneasy under the spotlight, not pulled together, his limbs seeming unconnected, like a puppet whose strings were loose. She caught a look of sheer panic on his face, and a deep sense of compassion took over.

She opened the book, found Ariel's first speech, and launched into it.

> ' *"All hail, great master! Grave sir, hail! I come*
> *To answer thy best pleasure; be't to fly,*
> *To swim, to dive into the fire, to ride*
> *On the curl'd clouds, to thy strong bidding task*
> *Ariel and all his quality."* '

At the sound of her voice, clear and compelling as a high-pitched bell, Redvers visibly relaxed, and like a lizard catching the first life-giving rays of the early morning sun, began to bask rather than cower in the spotlight.

'It's working, it's working!' Esther heard Nico whisper excitedly.

And she too felt as if something magical had happened. Redvers' voice, strong, dynamic, persuasive, had lost none of its old allure. To act with him was like being part of one great, harmonious verbal dance. When the dialogue finally came to an end she felt a profound sense of disappointment, as if some glimpse of paradise had suddenly been snatched away from her. She made her way off stage, blinking in the quieter light of the auditorium, Redvers close behind her.

'That's it, that's it!' said Zelda excitedly. 'Bravo, both of you. The part's yours if you want it, Esther!'

Esther sat down in one of the seats, gripping the plush arm rail, and trying to bed herself into reality again. She began to realise exactly what Zelda was saying.

'Now wait a moment,' she said. 'No one said anything about auditioning for the part. All I agreed to was a read-through to help Redvers.'

'But you were absolutely marvellous, the perfect Ariel!' said Nico eagerly. 'I knew you would be. And if you were on television, you must have an Equity card.'

He gave her a smile which disturbed her in a way that John's calm trusting smile never did. It was good to remember John, for thinking of him reminded her why she'd decided never to act again, and why she shouldn't consider the offer for even one moment.

'Well, yes, I do have a card,' she said. 'But really, the whole idea's quite out of the question.'

'If you're worried about your work for the Church, we'd do everything we could to accommodate your schedule,' said Zelda. 'It's only a six-week run, mostly evening performances, and no Sundays at all. So what's your problem?'

'It just wouldn't be appropriate,' said Esther. 'I'm hoping to be ordained next year.'

'Old Mr Nimlett, your predecessor, was always turning up in plays at the church hall,' said Nico.

'But this is professional theatre,' said Esther. 'It's quite different.'

'Exactly. You'd get a fee,' said Nico. 'You should be able to do a lot at the vicarage with it. Bron told me you were trying to drum up funds.'

He mentioned a sum of money which made Esther begin to waver. The thought of a timely injection of cash providing the children with toys, equipment to set up a nursery group, a new fridge for the kitchen, and some outings for the poorest pensioners in the parish was hard to resist.

'Georgia's designed some fabulous costumes for Ariel,' Nico went on. He gave Esther an irresistible glance. 'And all in perfect taste. Even the dean would approve.'

'I'm so sorry, but it really is impossible,' she said, finding it more and more difficult to produce a valid objection. 'I told you, I've given up acting.'

'I personally would be delighted to have you with us,' said Redvers gently. 'You have a great talent. It seems a crime to waste it.'

Georgia agreed with him, but, watching Esther, and guessing her feelings, she was almost as torn herself. She too would love to have her friend in the company, but she also knew what it was like to be persuaded against her will, especially by Nico.

'Why don't you come back to the wardrobe and discuss it over a cup of coffee while Sumitra's looking around?' she asked.

'That's an excellent idea,' said Zelda warmly. 'Please do think about it for a little longer at least.'

Esther gave way. 'All right,' she said with a resigned expression, 'but I'm afraid the answer's still going to be no.'

Back in the wardrobe Georgia ensconced Esther in her office, and then went outside to talk to Sumitra before filling the kettle. She had been wandering round as if she'd entered a cavern of delights, and was now stroking a bolt of grey chiffon with a longing expression.

'Let me show you the designs you'd be working on,' said Georgia craftily. 'When you see them, you'll realise how much you'd be appreciated here. This chiffon's for Ariel's costume. Only an expert could cope with beadwork on such delicate material.'

She spread the designs with their attached swatches of fabric out on the table, and went back to Esther, leaving Sumitra immersed in the drawings. Esther was dreamily gazing at nothing.

Georgia plugged in the kettle, and sat down.

'Come on, Esther,' she said, 'admit you enjoyed that run-through. You don't know how right you looked on stage. I can't see any reason why you should deny yourself this one small pleasure, unless it's out of sheer perversity. It's for such a short time, too, and you were saying yourself the other day that you needed more to do.'

'It's the thin end of the wedge,' said Esther ruefully. 'I just feel it's dangerous. I can't quite explain how it takes me over, but it does. My whole personality seems to change.'

'Perhaps that's good for you.'

'It's not. It's frightening. I worry in case I endanger everything that's really most dear to me. John knows how I feel, and I'm sure he wouldn't approve.'

'But it's your decision,' said Georgia. 'Not his.'

'I don't want to spend too much time away from the rectory, either. The others need a lot of support.'

'But wouldn't it be good for them to start to learn to do without you?'

'Perhaps. I'm not sure.'

When Sumitra suddenly appeared in the office doorway, Esther looked as relieved as if she'd been reprieved from agreeing to a life of sin. Georgia got ready to deal with another demonstration of self-denial, this time from Sumitra, but was astonished to see a huge smile on her face.

'I have been thinking most seriously,' she said, perching neatly on the arm of a chair, 'and I have decided to accept Georgia's kind offer.'

'That's wonderful!' said Esther and Georgia in startled unison.

'But on one condition. It is too, too hard for me to begin again all on my own. But if Esther takes the part of Ariel, if I know she is here if I need her, I will do it.'

Georgia glanced questioningly at Esther. She looked dismayed.

'But you really don't need me now, Sumitra,' she replied, sounding almost panicky, and going back completely on her earlier words. 'You're quite capable of managing on your own. And Georgia'll look after you.'

'Please, Esther,' said Sumitra. 'I know it's difficult for you, but it is for me too. Georgia is a good person, but it wouldn't be the same.'

Esther rested her elbows on the desk, folded her hands, and leaned on them with her eyes closed. Georgia wasn't sure if she was praying or trying to shut out Sumitra's pleading expression. Finally she looked up. She gave a defeated sigh, yet Georgia was certain that somewhere in its depths she caught a trace of relief.

'Then if you need me so much, and as long as the Church doesn't object, I suppose it's my duty to agree.'

Chapter 9

'Now,' said Nico, putting his head round the workshop door, 'how about a guided tour of the ancestral pile?'

Georgia hesitated. It was six o'clock. She'd spent the rest of the afternoon reassuring both Esther and Sumitra that they'd made the right decisions, and discussing Redvers' costume with him. Even when she went home to work on the finished sketches she'd still have Chloe to deal with. The final thought decided her. A civilised tour of the great house would be infinitely preferable to listening to the latest happenings at Fruits of the Earth.

Though the shadows were lengthening as they went round to the front of the house, the walls of Cotswold stone still gave off the heat absorbed during the day. Nico pushed open the carved front door. They passed through a stuffy anteroom, and stepped into the great hall.

It was dominated by a Jacobean refectory table so large that it must have been made on the spot. The surface, a dark river of gleaming wood, was decorated with a pair of magnificent but lop-sided silver candelabra and a cloisonné vase filled with a painfully stiff flower arrangement. Orange gladioli and purple lupins were crammed together with gloomy spikes of laurel, and no regard for form or colour.

There was a huge stone fireplace partly filled with a yellowing fan of pleated card stuck in a battered gilt pitcher, and heavy seventeenth-century furniture placed haphazardly about the room, the woodwork impressively polished but the upholstery like the tapestries in urgent need of repair. A series of portraits of past Carwithens was in equally urgent need of cleaning. A smell of damp, beeswax, and the white emulsion with which the walls

165

and ceiling had recently been painted, lingered in the room.

The impression was one of casual grandeur and distinct discomfort. Nothing in the room was designed for ease, and nothing had been done to show its contents at their best. Georgia longed to paint the walls a subtler colour, to fill the vase with tumbling roses, fling aside the half-drawn curtains, open the windows to the sun, and bring it all to life.

'I can guess exactly what you're thinking,' said Nico, 'but as you know, Mrs M goes into fits if we try to change a thing.'

'I suppose she's been wearing out the furniture and herself at the same time with all this polishing?'

'You're a great egalitarian, aren't you?' said Nico teasingly. 'But you're right. She never stops. We'll probably find her having the final session for the day somewhere about the house.'

The equally shabby but magnificent library appeared to have no twentieth-century books at all. Nico went over to a locked case, felt on top for a key, and drew out a portfolio of red Morocco leather. Carefully he opened it on a side table, and withdrew a pen and ink drawing.

'The first Nicolas is supposed to have done this picture of Prospero,' he said. 'Tradition has it that he saw the performance of *The Tempest* in the great hall as a child, and never forgot it. It could be Shakespeare, don't you think?'

The drawing, though amateur, was amazingly vivid. Prospero did indeed look a little like Shakespeare, but the most remarkable thing about him was his cloak, which he was holding before him in matador fashion as he goaded Caliban. The front panels were embroidered with the Tarot symbols for the Lords of Science and Harmony, and the back bore the full-length figure of the Queen of the Thrones of Water, her arms outstretched above the sea.

'I'm not so sure about Shakespeare, but those embroideries must have been magnificent,' Georgia said, still scrutinising the cloak.

'The cloak was left here after the play, an heirloom and reputed to be Merlin's, but it was destroyed in a fire in the eighteenth century. I wonder if you could make a copy for Redvers.'

Georgia put the picture down regretfully.

'It's a fascinating design, but I'm really too busy now to research the colours at the V & A, and I'd hate to produce a copy that wasn't as authentic as possible. If only you'd shown me the drawing earlier.'

'If only you'd agreed to look round the house earlier!' said Nico meaningfully, as she gave him back the picture. He slipped the drawing into the portfolio. 'Right then, we'd better get on and do the rest of the house.'

They trailed through a series of smaller reception rooms, crammed like the great hall with a clutter of furniture and bibelots arranged with little regard to display and a lordly imperviousness to comfort.

'Do you use these rooms yourselves?' asked Georgia. 'They're not exactly homely.'

'That's putting it mildly,' said Nico. 'Sometimes we have a formal dinner party in the great hall, but that's it. We've all got bedrooms in the Victorian south wing, and we live in the kitchen. Ned's covered his room with posters, but Bron hasn't done a thing with his, mainly I think because he can't bear to acknowledge that he's here to stay.'

'And what about your room?' said Georgia. 'Californian minimalist, or Italian nouveau rococo?'

Nico grinned at her. 'I've collected a few bits and pieces over the years, and they soften the edges. Would you like to see upstairs now? It's much the same as down here. There's really only one attractive room.'

They went up an oak stairway, and through a series of dark, interconnecting bedrooms, with dull yellow plasterwork and the pictures hung in the worst possible places. They just managed to slip by Mrs Meads unseen as she lovingly polished a Sheraton commode.

'Imogen would love to get her hands on all of this, of course,' said Nico when they were safely back in the corridor again. 'Bron's going to have fun restraining her when she arrives. She'd have it looking like a Harrods catalogue in no time. I hope you'll like this room at least. It's my favourite – the red boudoir.'

He flung open yet another door. The walls of this room were covered with faded rose-coloured watered silk, the curtains too were silk, sumptuous swags of lemon and pink, but papery thin when Georgia examined them.

'It belonged to Letitia Carwithen,' said Nico. 'She was an eighteenth-century beauty who became bored with her husband – he was one of the farming Carwithens, not an actor, needless to say – and took herself off to France every winter. She was a great hit at Versailles. That's the delicious Letitia, over the chimney-piece.'

Painted by Boucher, she sat on a swing, in a mass of flying silks and ribbons, displaying a pair of elegant ankles and nearly all her breasts. A shepherdess's crook lay on the ground beside her.

'I presume her flock was male,' said Georgia with a smile.

'That's one way of putting it,' said Nico with an answering grin, 'though she became very devout in her old age, and devoted herself to embroidery and good works.'

The room was dominated by a Chippendale bed as frivolous as its first owner. Slender mahogany posts supported a delicate pagoda-like canopy with carved wooden frills. The centre and four corners were adorned with tiny brass bells. Pillows of red damask lay against a massive tasselled bolster on a red damask coverlet.

Georgia wandered around admiring the carved gilt dressing table and chairs, then suddenly became aware that Nico was looking at her with the sort of concentrated, expectant gaze which could only lead to one thing, the thing she'd been trying to ignore, the need to make some kind of decision about where her relationship with him was going. His expression made it absolutely clear that he'd brought her here for quite another reason than sight-seeing.

To play for time she went over to the window. It was tightly shut, and a fly in the last stages of desperation buzzed fitfully against the glass. The declining sun was painting long stripes of dark green across the lawn beyond the courtyard. Bron and Ned were playing cricket, Ned's arms flailing like a windmill as he bowled. When she turned Nico was standing next to the four-poster.

'This is the only comfortable bed in the whole of Merlinslade,' he said. 'Bron dared me to try them all one school holidays. I nearly scared myself to death thinking of ghosts.'

Still she didn't know what to do. The atmosphere in the room was exciting in an odd way, as though it had been designed for clandestine encounters, everything bathed in a soft rosy glow reflected from the walls, and the rays of the westering sun. It made her feel as if it didn't really matter what they did. And perhaps it didn't. Nothing seemed straight in her mind these days.

Nico looked amused and excited at the same time. He peeled back the coverlet, revealing a much-patched sheet beneath, and sat down.

'Come and try it,' he said.

She went and sat next to him. She was wearing a shirt with the sleeves rolled up, and a pair of loose linen shorts. The sheet was cool against her bare legs. Nico smoothed his hand gently up her thigh.

'I'm sure you'd be more comfortable lying down,' he said in a voice as reassuring as a physiotherapist's inviting her to prepare for some soothing treatment.

She found herself lying back against the pillows, gazing up into the underside of the canopy, a mass of intricate pleats radiating from a central boss carved with a ring of drunken-looking cupids. Nico had already pulled off her sandals, and was now lying by her side, alternately kissing her and undoing the buttons of her shirt in a practised sequence clearly perfected during the course of many seductions.

'This is the best sort of guided tour,' he said.

His arm sneaked under her back and a couple of seconds later her shirt and bra had been tossed over the side of the bed, followed equally rapidly by the rest of her clothes. He paused for a moment, gazing at her as if he'd drawn some unexpectedly sumptuous present from the bran tub at a village fête.

'Christ, you're gorgeous. Gorgeous Georgy.'

She started to remonstrate, holding him off with her hand on his chest. Gently he put it to one side.

'Just trust me, sweetie. You're going to enjoy this.'

He began to kiss her breasts. She looked down at the smooth, amber-coloured head, and felt no response at all. She tried to force a response, to drum up some fantasy that might make her feel something, but not even that worked. She began to wonder if she'd become completely frigid. Frantically she kept telling herself that she mustn't go on like this, that it wasn't honest.

There was a brief respite while Nico stood up, went over to the door, and locked it. The action heightened the erotic atmosphere, but still she felt nothing. Rapidly he threw off his clothes. She looked at him dispassionately, at the stocky limbs, at the broad chest and thick russet pubic hair, and felt as much emotion as if he'd been a statue.

With a mischievous smile he began to draw the curtains of the bed.

'Now this is the sort of thing Bron never dared me to do,' he said.

It was like being in a warm red cave. Her sense of unreality increased. Nico slithered through the curtains, and started to kiss her again. She kept telling herself that she was in bed with a man half the women of England were in love with, but it made no difference. She remembered the last time Blake had made love to her, and that forced her to remember something else. She struggled to a sitting position, pushing away Nico's encircling arms.

He lay back against the pillows, his eyes searching her face. He gave an exasperated sigh. 'So what's wrong now? I thought you were enjoying it.'

'Nico, I'm sorry, but you'll have to – to use something if you want to go on. You know what I mean.'

He sighed again, running his hand lazily over the curve of her breast. 'Everyone's so twitchy about safe sex these days. Trust me, darling. You've nothing to worry about.'

'I'm not on the pill, anyway. I'm sorry, but that's how it is.'

'There's no need to get ratty about it. When's your period due?'

She thought for a moment. 'In two days' time.'

'It's all right, then.'

'I still want you to use something,' she persisted.

'But it's so much more fun without.' He was beginning to sound aggrieved.

'I told you, I just don't want to take any kind of risk.' To her dismay she heard her voice beginning to tremble. More and more the whole situation was bringing back everything she'd tried for so long to forget.

Nico pulled himself up on to an elbow, looking at her curiously.

'When you keep going on like this, you almost make me feel I'm taking some sort of risk as well. I'm trusting you, after all. I don't get it. What exactly did go on in that marriage of yours?'

'Nothing – nothing you need worry about,' she said desperately. 'And there's nothing wrong with me. I just want you to do what I ask.'

To her horror she felt tears gathering. She longed to tell him everything about Blake, the things she hadn't even told Zelda, but couldn't face coping with his rejection and disgust if she did. A tear ran down her cheek and fell on to the damask pillow, leaving a mark as dark as blood.

Nico's expression relaxed. He pulled her into his arms again. 'Don't cry, sweetie. I didn't mean to wind you up. We can do whatever you like, just as long as you try to have a good time.'

He leaned over the side of the bed, felt around for his jacket, and came up holding a packet of condoms, which he pushed under the bolster.

'Ever ready,' he said with a grin. 'So you don't have to worry about a thing.'

She'd never felt less like making love, but now, weak with relief, she felt she owed it to him. As his hands roved expertly over her, she couldn't fault a thing he did. It was the perfect arousal, and yet it didn't arouse her.

He was the only man she'd ever known who was able to put on a condom with panache. He accomplished it with one graceful movement, and began to drive carefully but purposefully into her. She gave up worrying, and determinedly tried to fake the perfect response. Nico was an athletic lover. The bed began to rock to his thrusts, and with it the bells, ringing rhythmically like a crazy call to prayer, and then becoming one long frenzied jingle, all mixed up with her faked moans, and his ecstatic cries.

Eventually, as she was beginning to worry in case Mrs Meads heard them, he pulled out of her, and rolled to one side, falling instantly into sleep. She bit her lip, staring up at the canopy, counting the pleats and the cherubs and the wooden scallops on the border, doing anything not to weep. The legacy of the divorce had been as harmful physically as mentally. And she'd now proved that sleeping with a man simply as some sort of sexual aerobics would never work for her.

Nico opened sleepy eyes. 'Why so solemn, darling? Just let me get my breath back, and we'll have another round.'

She sat up again, pulling the coverlet across her, and pushing back her hair.

'Nico, I'm sorry, but I can't do this again. It's nothing to do with you personally. I just – just don't think I'm ready for it yet.'

He leaned over the side of the bed again, felt in his pocket for his cigarette and lighter, and hauled himself up against the bolster. He lit a cigarette, staring at her steadily.

He exhaled. 'It's the best smoke of all,' he said, 'the first one after sex. You don't have to be so uptight. You're only feeling like this because you haven't done it for a bit. If we just keep at it I'll have you cured in no time.'

'Cured of what?' she said slowly. 'Cured of ever feeling deeply again? I think I'm already cured of that.'

'So it's all right, then,' he said cheerfully.

She drew back the bed curtains, swung her feet over the side on to the Aubusson carpet, and started to dress. Her body was hot and sweaty, and the fabric dragged against her flesh.

She went over to the window, and after a wrestle with the latch finally managed to open it, dislodging a shower of petals from a rose clambering along the ledge. She breathed in long draughts of the scented evening air. Ned had become the batsman now, and Bron was bowling to him with an expression of fierce concentration. There was no noise, apart from the smack of wood on the cricket ball, and the cooing of pigeons.

She turned back into the room. That was all she wanted, peace, and all she seemed unable to get. She thought she had it, for a few brief months, but then Chloe and Nico had arrived in her life at the same time, and she didn't have it after all. She could distance herself from Nico, though, and she would.

He was now dressed as well. He came up behind her, and put his arms round her, pressing his cheek against hers. Bron looked

172

up from polishing the ball on his trouser leg, and saw them at the window. He frowned, and hurled down a delivery which sent the stumps flying, and called forth a pained protest of unfairness from Ned.

'Poor Ned. Bron's been bloody uptight ever since I signed Morrigan,' Nico said.

She didn't answer. His arms tightened round her.

'Don't worry,' he said. 'We'll take things slowly. I'll make it all right for you, you'll see.'

'Nico, you must understand, I don't want to do this again. I'd rather simply be friends. I mean it,' she said.

He laughed softly. 'Women never mean it when they say a thing like that. We're going to be great together.'

As Georgia prepared the final costume drawings, exquisite cameos of line and gouache, she kept thinking what a fool she'd been to go so far with Nico. He was maddeningly persistent. When the cast arrived it became slightly easier to avoid solo encounters, but he found far too many opportunities for pouncing on her in dark corners backstage, and bombarding her with requests for more dinner dates.

The wardrobe staff appeared on the same day as the cast. Annie was the first, a stumpy figure in jeans and a sweatshirt, with a cap of greying hair, and a bulging bag of professional equipment in the back of her old Vauxhall. Kevin roared into the stable yard five minutes later on his motorbike, looking more like a Hell's Angel than a wardrobe technician. Jenny, a neat, dark-haired girl, arrived breathlessly on a bicycle from a village a few miles away.

Georgia took them almost immediately to London in search of supplies she'd been unable to find in Bristol or Bath. Annie, whose judgement she trusted entirely, hunted with Kevin for materials still needed for the court designs. She and Jenny plundered the oriental shops of West London for fabrics for the masque, then bore off their packages, still smelling faintly of incense, to the haberdashers of Covent Garden and Soho for elusive buttons and trims.

Morrigan didn't attend the design presentation to the cast, or the first read-through, though everyone was longing to meet him. He'd asked Nico to send him a photo-copy of his costume design before he went to London for a final concert rehearsal, and it had come back with a scrawled page of measurements which Georgia could only hope were reasonably accurate.

Esther caused some wry comments by turning up for rehearsals in her cassock, but her appearance was forgotten as soon as she started to act. Annie and Kevin began to translate Georgia's designs into patterns on yards of crackling brown paper, producing miracles of drawing with their curved French rules, then slicing their scissors smoothly along the confident pencilled lines.

As the toiles, the first mock-up garments of calico, emerged, the cast came into the wardrobe for their first fittings. There was the usual agonisings among the younger actors who weren't quite able to believe that the stiff, unwieldly toiles stuck with pins would be translated into the gorgeous creations of Georgia's drawings. The more experienced said very little, waiting till the second fittings when they would try on the real garment.

Georgia treated Redvers with kid gloves, guessing he'd hate to have an audience. She asked the other staff to stay in the background until she'd finished with him, and took care to have the materials for his finished costumes on display in the fitting bay, the designs tacked up by the mirror, and copious coffee and sympathy on hand.

He walked over from the theatre in a shabby but still splendid Sulka dressing gown of figured brocade. Apart from worrying obsessively about whether one of his shoulders was higher than the other, and insisting that she tried several sets of shoulder pads, most of his anxieties seemed to centre on the cloak.

'I look like a senile druid in this calico. Are you sure it's going to be supple enough when it's made up?' he said anxiously. 'Prospero's whole persona is in the cloak. I've lots of business with it, you know. I wonder if it isn't too traditional, as well.'

'It'll come to life when the embroidery's put on,' said Georgia soothingly.

'Will *I* come to life, though?' said Redvers in a gloomy voice. 'That's the question everyone's asking, isn't it?'

'Nonsense,' said Georgia. 'They're all worried in case they

don't live up to you. Even Nico, though he wouldn't admit it.'

'But I'm nothing but an old bag of bones now, a sad old bag of bones.' He repeated the phrase with the lugubrious look of an elderly bloodhound, rolling the words off his tongue and investing them with immense pathos.

'You've more presence than the lot of them put together,' said Georgia. 'Believe me, no one could carry off this costume like you.'

Carefully she began to release pins so that he could be free of the garment, and held out the dressing gown for him. He'd cheered up at her praise, but his face fell again as he saw himself in the mirror before the dressing gown went on again.

' "The lean and slippered pantaloon",' he remarked bitterly. 'Shakespeare said it all about old age, didn't he?'

He tied the cord round his waist, and sank into a dispirited-looking heap on the sofa, lighting another cigarette as she put the toiles back on their hangers.

'Sometimes I think I must have been mad to let Nico talk me into this,' he said.

Georgia gave him a cup of coffee. 'It's only because he admires you so much. And you're not the only one. He talks everyone round.'

'You too?' said Redvers, with an interested glance.

'Not entirely, but he's trying hard,' she said unwisely, sitting down with him.

Redvers began to look more animated. 'So that's how the land lies!'

Georgia was so relieved at Redvers' change of mood that she didn't immediately contradict him. She started to roll up the bolts of fabric she'd put on display.

'You're a kind girl, my dear, and not only kind, but talented too. Let me give you a small word of warning. Our Nico's a charming boy, but he isn't husband material. Not that I blame him, of course. I played the field in my day as well, to even more effect, I flatter myself.'

'I'm not looking for a husband,' she said. 'I don't think you'll find too many professional women who are.'

'So terrifyingly independent, you modern young things!' he

said. 'And tantalising as well. "If youth only knew what age cannot do" – it's the truest saying in the world.'

'You can do plenty still,' she rejoined. 'You just got to believe it.'

'You remind me of my wife,' he said. 'That's the sort of thing she would have said.'

Georgia was silent, not liking to comment. She'd read that his wife had left him, but she couldn't remember why exactly.

Redvers stood up, and pulled his dressing gown round him. 'I'd better go back to my lines. As fast as I learn them, they disappear. I used to be such a quick study twenty years ago. I could rattle off the whole of Romeo even now, though I'll never need the part again. Why can't our minds discard all the useless memories, all the unwanted baggage?'

He ambled towards the door, looking like a motheaten but still regal old lion. Georgia began to put one of the toiles on a dummy for Annie to work on, wishing she didn't know what he meant.

Redvers had almost reached the exit. He paused to throw his cigarette end into a fire bucket of sand, and as he did so Morrigan, who'd been in the theatre that day for the first time, sauntered through the door. Zelda had warned Georgia earlier that he'd probably come along for a fitting, and she'd also mentioned that Redvers seemed worried by his presence at the morning rehearsal. Even so, Georgia was surprised by Redvers' reaction now. He seemed to shrink into his dressing gown like a tortoise into its shell.

'Hi, Redvers,' said Morrigan. He threw an appraising glance at the older man's wrinkled neck and bony collar bones. 'You know, I was thinking when I saw you earlier that you really don't look after yourself.'

Georgia saw Redvers struggling to retain his poise.

'These days the public like people to look good,' Morrigan went on blandly. 'In our sort of work it's vital to keep in shape. I could introduce you to a great fitness studio.'

Redvers regained his self-control. He drew his dressing gown about him in a kingly gesture, and said in a voice laden with meaning which Georgia didn't fully understand, 'Keep your suggestions to yourself, Morrigan. I know only too well what your introductions involve.'

Morrigan shrugged as Redvers stalked out of the door. 'Sad to see someone losing his grip like that,' he remarked.

'I hadn't noticed it,' Georgia snapped, as Annie, who'd been hovering at the office entrance waiting for Redvers to leave, came forward with an expectant smile to meet Morrigan.

A sense of professional duty had already made Georgia reluctantly decide that she couldn't chicken out entirely at the first fitting. Nevertheless, after the introductions she kept well back from Morrigan as Annie hovered about him with pins and tape measure.

He peeled off his sweatshirt and jeans, and stood in black silk briefs which were scarcely more than a posing pouch, his eyes shifting from her to Annie to assess their reaction. His body was uniformly tanned, as if he spent hours basking on a sun bed, his chest covered with a pelt of curling hair which arrowed down to his briefs. The sturdy, commonsense Annie looked slightly faint as he pulled on the tights he'd be wearing beneath his doublet and breeches, and she began to crawl round on her knees, adjusting the seams on the inside leg.

Luckily the shirt was loose and needed few adjustments, but the toile for the doublet called for a skin-tight fit on the forearms and waist. There was so much re-pinning to do that Georgia was forced to work on one sleeve while Annie dealt with the other. All the time he kept up a flow of chat which Annie clearly found entrancing.

'It's so rare to find a fitter who really understands an artist's needs. You do have magic in your hands, Annie, absolute magic.'

He glanced sideways at Georgia.

'And I love the design. It's magnificent. I've been trying to persuade Brighid that the Disciples really need something more striking to wear. Perhaps you could have a word with her when you visit us.'

'I've already been to the Sanctuary, while you were away,' said Georgia.

'You mean I missed you?' he said, sounding as though he'd been deprived of a meeting with the Queen. 'Then you really must come again. You'll join her, won't you, Annie? I'm afraid there's an upper age limit of thirty for the Disciples, but we desperately need more mature people to help with the general administration. I'll give you both a very special tour. How about this weekend?'

'I'd love to,' said Annie, whose line of pins was acquiring a marked wobble as she gazed at his face.

'I'm busy,' said Georgia abruptly.

'Then at least let me buy you both lunch at The Mortal Man today. We can go down in my car.'

'I've too much to do. But I'm sure Annie would be delighted to go with you.'

Annie began to re-pin the waist, looking as if she might swoon away. Morrigan gazed down indulgently at her.

'Then maybe we'd better leave it to another day, when Georgia's free.'

'I don't have any spare time,' she said flatly.

'What a shame. Wouldn't you like to have some more news of your sister's progress at the Sanctuary? I shall be there after lunch to start reorganising the administration. I've been so busy with the concert that I haven't had a chance to meet her yet, but I'll make a point of it now. Still, if you're not interested in what your sister's doing . . .'

He shrugged, plainly expecting her to capitulate at once.

'I'll get in touch with Brighid if there's anything I need to know,' she said curtly. 'And that's enough alterations. You can get dressed. If you have any more queries about your costume Annie will be glad to deal with them.'

She escaped to her office, keeping a wary eye on the proceedings outside through a window in the partition. As soon as he'd strolled from the room, Annie rushed into the office.

'What a fantastic-looking guy, even at his age! So unassuming, too! No wonder the press rave about him. I can't wait to see this Sanctuary place.'

Georgia had hoped to have the flat to herself when she got home, but she found Chloe in the sitting room, wearing a pink leotard and practising Tai Chi movements to an Enya tape.

The moment she appeared Chloe rushed to take her portfolio from her, and almost pushed her into a chair. Georgia looked at her suspiciously. She began to wonder if this happiness had anything to do with Morrigan.

'How was the Sanctuary this afternoon?' she asked.

'I don't know,' said Chloe carelessly. 'I couldn't be bothered to go.'

'You didn't go? What happened?' Georgia was still more suspicious. Chloe had been making it very clear for days that she'd instantly go into a deep decline if denied access to the Sanctuary.

'I just didn't feel like it.' She danced over to Georgia's chair, sank down beside her, and laid her head on her sister's shoulder. 'I've been thinking how nice it would be for you if I came to help in the wardrobe sometimes. You wouldn't have to pay me anything, and I am good at jewellery, really good. You said so yourself.'

'What's all this about?' Georgia was incredulous now.

Chloe looked as if she was going to burst. 'Guess who I met at the bus-stop on the way to the Sanctuary? Sean Marchant! The actor who plays Ferdinand in *The Tempest*! I recognised him from those publicity photos you showed me, so I told him I was your sister, and after that we sort of took off.'

'He's a nice guy,' said Georgia encouragingly. Unlike Morrigan, Sean appeared to be refreshingly free from vanity and self-importance. 'So what happened next?'

'He was going to London to see his agent, but his bus was cancelled at the last minute, and he had ages to wait. He asked me to have a drink at the Crystal Palace. We got on really, really well, and he said he hoped he'd see me at Merlinslade sometime.' She looked anxiously at Georgia. 'He seemed to like me, Georgy. Wasn't that amazing?'

'Of course it wasn't amazing. Not everyone's like Martin. You just have to believe in yourself a little.'

'That's what Brighid's been saying too. So you will let me come and help, won't you?'

'I suppose I can't pass up a free offer like that,' said Georgia, smiling at her. 'But if I do say yes, you have to promise me to take it easy with Sean. Just because you got on with him for half an hour doesn't mean he's going to fall in love with you. He could have a girlfriend in London.'

'He doesn't! He told me so!'

Chloe spun round the room like a child's top. Georgia could almost hear her humming with happiness. 'Don't worry, Georgy. I'll be so sensible you won't know it's me.'

Chloe flopped down by the chair again, and looked earnestly at her.

'I want something nice to happen for you, as well. Why won't you go out with Nico again? He was on the phone just before you got here, asking when you'd be home.' She hesitated. 'We had a bit of a talk. He wanted to know about Blake.'

'About Blake!' Georgia looked at her distrustfully. 'I hope you didn't say anything tactless.'

'How could I, when you never tell me anything? I just said I thought Blake had hurt you very badly, and that you needed someone to help you get over it.'

Georgia groaned. 'Chloe, how could you? That'll simply encourage Nico. And it's not true, anyway. I am over it.'

'Then if you're over it, why aren't you nicer to Nico?' said Chloe. 'I don't see how I can possibly take your advice if you don't take it yourself!'

Nico had been watching for Georgia's arrival from the house next morning. When she drew up at her usual parking spot in the courtyard he came running down the steps. He'd phoned again the previous evening, and made her feel completely unreasonable when she still refused to go out with him.

'It's all fixed for tonight,' he said, as she stepped out of the car. 'It's a fabulous place. You're going to love it.'

'I'm sorry, Nico, but I'm not having dinner with you,' she said, angry at his continued pestering.

Some of the warmth left his expression. 'Come on, sweetie, don't be coy. I know you've a hang-up because of your divorce, but that's no reason to be such a wet blanket.'

'I've already explained how I feel, and the answer's still no,' she said, standing with her portfolio clasped to her breast.

'You haven't explained properly. You got hitched in a hurry, the guy was playing around, and so you split. End of story. You were hardly married at all, so I don't understand why you're making the divorce into such a big production.'

'There's no need for you to understand.'

'I don't see how I sodding well can, since you seem to have more secrets than the Pentagon,' Nico flung back at her. 'Any other man'd have called you a prick-teaser.'

She knew he was hurt, but the crudeness of the accusation infuriated her.

'And any other woman would have realised that you're nothing but a bloody make-out artist,' she shouted at him.

To add to her distress, Bron chose that exact moment to emerge from the garden gate, carrying the scythe she'd seen Mr Meads use a few days earlier in the orchard. She wondered frantically how much he'd already heard. He stopped and hesitated, glancing from Nico's face to hers. Nico made absolutely no concessions to his presence.

'OK, forget it,' he yelled at her, 'but we were a million bucks together, and you know it!'

'We weren't, we weren't,' she shouted back, even more angry that he was humiliating her in front of Bron. 'That just shows how little you know me!'

Nico shoved open the front door and disappeared into the house, shutting it with a bang that sent the pigeons wheeling up from the roof. She answered him by slamming the door of the car, and marching off towards the theatre. There was no other way to go except through the garden gate. As she went past Bron he didn't move but stood gravely watching her.

She looked up at him. Nico had come too close to the mark. Rage and frustration made her lash out blindly at the nearest target.

'Now you can disapprove of me even more,' she said angrily. 'So at least I've made one Carwithen happy.'

At lunchtime the rest of the wardrobe staff went to join the cast in the kitchen, where Mrs Meads, with the help of a crony from the village, provided lunch. Today it was mince, processed peas and boiled potatoes, with soggy supermarket quiche as a concession to vegetarians. Georgia couldn't face any of it, or seeing Nico.

She'd started to go jogging with Zelda, and she decided to take a turn round the park for half an hour on her own, to see if she could shake off her feeling of wretchedness. Once outside, however, it was far too hot for anything but the most sedate amble. She was wearing a pair of shorts made from sawn-off jeans, and a vest top, and her unprotected skin began to burn after only ten minutes in the midday glare. In spite of the note Bron had tacked up the green room, asking joggers to keep to the estate roads, she decided to head off towards the river in search of shade.

The whole of Merlinslade seemed asleep, swallows silent, cows and horses as motionless beneath the trees as painted toys, and only the collared doves keeping up a somnolent exchange of descending coos. The downs shimmered in a haze of heat. As Georgia crossed the meadows even the butterflies had ceased their dance, though an orchestra of crickets still played in the long grass.

It was cooler by the river. She wandered along the bank beneath a canopy of ancient willows which had been pollarded so many times that their heads were huge mops of rustling wands. The clear water flowed swiftly over a gravel bed, tugging at sheets of crowsfoot and wild cress. Damsel flies hovered on gauzy green wings above the stream. She plucked a stem of meadowsweet from the bank, and sniffed it as she walked along, the feathery blossom brushing her skin. Though she was doing nothing, for once she didn't begin to think of Blake.

She came eventually to a narrow wooden bridge, a sort of sluice with three open hatches through which the river poured. The water before the bridge had deepened into a pool, ringed occasionally by a rising fish. The banks were thick with the heady pink flowers of Indian balsam.

She kicked off her trainers and sat down under a willow, leaning back against the trunk. For the first time in a long while her mind was completely peaceful, occupied by nothing but the sound of a myriad tiny insects humming in the tree above her.

Sleepily she thought that perhaps this was a part of what Brighid was trying to teach.

She was jolted out of a semi-trance by the sound of rhythmic splashing, and the creak of oars in rowlocks. Then there came the rattle of oars being shipped. Through a gap in the balsam she saw Bron balancing in the prow of an elderly skiff as it glided along the bank. He threw a plastic carrier bag and a pair of waders on to the grass, stepped ashore and moored the boat to a tree stump. Rusalka leaped out of the stern, instantly putting up a mallard, and dashed off downstream in enthusiastic pursuit. Georgia flattened herself against the tree-trunk, trying to look invisible.

Bron's eyes were still on Rusalka. It was too hot to shout after her, and he decided to let her go. He congratulated himself on finding the perfect retreat. The daily lunch-time invasion of actors into the kitchen with their unending shop talk had begun to grate on him, though he enjoyed talking to Redvers, whose acerbic views on the world scene appealed to his present state of mind. He might just have put up with the chatter if the meal had been reasonable, but Mrs Meads' cooking had gone to pieces completely since she'd begun to cater for such large numbers.

Today he'd bought himself some food for a picnic in the village shop, but before eating he walked on to the bridge to inspect the woodwork. Several planks were rotten, and when he tried to lower the sluice hatches one of them refused to drop more than halfway. He went back to the river bank and pulled on the waders, then lowered himself carefully into the water, holding on to the frame of the bridge, and began to investigate. As he'd thought, the grooves of the hatch were jammed with debris.

He began to clear them, mentally offsetting the speed and volume of water against the present state of the bridge, and trying to work out the probable cost of repairs. As he worked another part of his mind was raging, as it did too often, over having to waste his life on something that seemed completely irrelevant to the needs of the modern world.

For the hundredth time he toyed longingly with the idea of simply renouncing his inheritance, instructing the family solicitors to put the management of Merlinslade in trust, and letting Ned sort it all out when he came of age. And for the hundredth time he decided he couldn't do it. He might, if he were very lucky, just manage to rescue the estate now, but if it were left in a state of minimal management for the next few years Ned would inherit an impossible task.

To make the whole situation still more unendurable, Imogen was threatening to visit, something he couldn't well deny her since Ned was now living permanently with him. As if to echo his gloomy thoughts, the cold was beginning to radiate through the waders. He compelled himself to empty his mind and concentrate on the business of pushing back through the water to the side.

Georgia hadn't dared move, hoping he'd return to the boat. But at that moment Rusalka, her legs and tail soaked, came racing back along the river bank, and unerringly detected her presence. She lolloped through the bank of balsam straight up to Georgia, and thrust a long cold nose into her hand. She began to wag her tail in broad sweeps, casting a shower of drops as effectively as a garden sprinkler from the saturated feathering on the underside.

Bron caught sight of Georgia instantly, and a look of indignant disbelief came over his face. She guessed he was as unwilling as herself to admit visitors to this secret spot. But there was nothing she could do, except wait for the first rush of the dog's greeting to subside, and for him to emerge from the water.

Bron clambered out on to the bank, letting the water stream off the surface of his waders as he tried to decide whether to order Georgia away. She merged so perfectly with her surroundings, her arms and long brown legs freckled with the sunlight sifting down through the waving mass of silvery leaves, that she might have been a dryad.

Until he recognised her he thought he'd surprised a trespasser. Nico had been taking her out recently, and to judge from the conversation he'd overheard this morning, was now hassling her in order to bring her to heel. Except that, unlike the usual run of Nico's girlfriends, she hadn't shown any signs of coming to heel at all.

He dragged off the waders and threw them into the skiff. She stood up, gazing at him, her hand on Rusalka's head. Her bare feet, untouched by the sun, were startlingly white against the lush grass.

He recalled the scene in the courtyard again. It hadn't bothered him particularly when she'd lashed out at him. He knew how infuriating Nico could be, and he was used to far more vicious accusations from Imogen. She'd clearly been shaken by the argument, and he was sorry now that he'd disturbed her.

Bron dried his hands on his trousers, picked up the carrier and moved towards her, meaning to call off the dog, and leave her in peace. He snapped his fingers at Rusalka, but unexpectedly, for she didn't normally care for other females, the dog stayed at Georgia's side like a russet shadow. He decided to make the best of a bad job, and began to unknot the handles of the carrier bag.

'I didn't see you there at first,' he said casually. 'I was going to have a picnic. Would you like to join me?'

Georgia was taken off guard as he set down the contents of the bag on the grass. There was a wedge of farmhouse Cheddar, a handful of tomatoes, some crisp buttered rolls, and a couple of cans of lager.

'Well, how about it?' he asked. 'But if you'd rather be alone, that's fine by me. I can row back upstream and find another place.'

'No – no – it's all right,' she stammered, startled by this unexpected sensitivity to her wishes.

He opened one of the cans of lager and handed it to her. She subsided into her original place, and began to drink. The liquid slipped with refreshing bitterness down her throat.

He sat on a fallen branch, and took a clasp knife out of his pocket. He sliced a tomato, cut some slivers of cheese, packed them neatly into a roll for her, then began to do the same for himself. For the first time she was able to study his face properly. She'd always been too annoyed at their earlier meetings to do more than register a general impression that it seemed to be composed entirely of straight lines: dark, decisive brows, a nose which could have been drawn with a ruler, and an uncompromisingly resolute mouth. It was the sort of face usually seen only in Victorian military paintings of desperate last-ditch stands. She decided it would be easier to apologise for the scene in the courtyard while he was concentrating on something else.

'I'm sorry about what happened earlier,' she said. 'I shouldn't have yelled at you.'

'Forget it,' he said briefly.

He looked up at her and smiled. The transformation was startling.

'What are the sluices for?' she asked, grabbing at the first safe subject she could think of.

'They divert the stream along a culvert into the water meadows. You probably missed it because it's choked with weeds. A series of smaller channels runs off it to irrigate the meadows in winter, and encourage new grass. I want to see if I can make the system work again. But ideally it needs Wiltshire horn sheep for grazing and they're not easy to come by.'

She got the impression that he'd been afraid she'd want to talk about Nico, and was relieved that she hadn't.

'And supposing you can't build up a flock?'

'I'll try short rotation coppicing. Growing willow and poplar to convert into fuel. They'd do well here. I'd probably make more profit out of that anyway, but it wouldn't show any returns for five years, and we need money fast. We ought to try to conserve the water meadows anyway. They're part of the estate's history.'

'Couldn't you do the coppicing somewhere else, perhaps on set-aside land?' she said, remembering a recent radio programme.

He looked astounded that she'd even heard of it. She managed to keep on the subject of farming for a full ten minutes, until, just as she was running out of things to say, he equally deftly changed the subject to the theatre. He too was surprisingly knowledgeable.

'Nico never talks about anything else,' he said with another smile. 'Some of it was bound to sink in. And I was once in charge of a battalion pantomime – almost as bad as going into action.'

'Have you ever been into action?' she asked curiously.

'Only in the Falklands and the Gulf. I was very young the first time, and scared out of my wits to begin with. But it was what I'd chosen, so I had to get on with it.'

He closed the clasp knife with a snap, and began to collect up the empty paper bags. She suspected he got on with most things in the same way, and yet she was starting to think that he wasn't entirely the unimaginative martinet of her first summing-up.

'I'll leave you in peace,' he said. 'I'm off to Trowbridge to see a firm of thatchers. They're interested in buying our organic straw. They say it's easier to work than the ordinary stuff.'

He picked up his lager can, drank the final drops, and packed that away too. He didn't look at her as he spoke the next words.

'Nico's not usually like that, but you might find it more effective to cool things for a while.'

Georgia wanted to deliver a biting warning not to interfere in her affairs, but she remembered how often she'd tried to justify Chloe's behaviour to other people.

'I am. I meant what I said to Nico,' she said curtly. 'But it isn't easy when we work together.'

He frowned, as if he didn't quite believe her. She was getting ready to defend herself again, when her attention was diverted by the sound of singing drifting through the still air.

Rusalka sprang up and stood with her head pointing in its direction, her body quivering with anticipation. Bron let the carrier bag drop, concentrating just as intently. The singing increased, until an untidy column of walkers appeared from behind a bank of reeds some way along the opposite shore, and the words of 'Green Grow the Rushes O' could plainly be heard.

First came Brighid carrying a trug filled with wild plants, her robe kilted to her knees, her sandalled feet splashed with mud and pieces of grass stuck between her toes. She was followed by a straggling band of Disciples, all bearing similar loads.

' "I'll sing you four O, Four for the Gospel makers",' Brighid carolled blithely, beating time with a willow wand held in her free hand, accompanied raggedly by the Disciples. And joining in with them, but still behind the reeds, was another voice, one Georgia knew only too well by now, the voice of Morrigan, giving the ancient song a strangely disturbing quality.

Bron looked as if he couldn't quite believe what was happening. Brighid hadn't seen him. She'd got through another two verses and was almost level with them, before he finally made a move.

187

'Christ almighty!' he exploded, and with Rusalka streaking after him, shot across the bridge which creaked alarmingly under his tread. He was brought up short on the far side by the appearance of Morrigan himself, wearing his usual black clothes and mirrored sunglasses. His jewellery glittered in the light.

Again he reminded Georgia of some unpredictable insect, perhaps a black dragonfly this time, like the ones poised so showily above the water. He sauntered up to the bridge, his jacket swinging from one hand, and placed the other on the rail, finishing the stanza when the voices of the others trailed away.

' "One is one and all alone, and ever more shall be so",' he sang, staring directly at Bron, and as usual managing to load the words with double meaning.

The bleak underlying message made Georgia feel cold. He made it sound like a curse. Rusalka growled, straining against Bron's hand on her collar. Bron ignored Morrigan completely.

'You're trespassing,' he said to Brighid. 'Not only that, but you're stealing plants again. I've warned you about this before.'

'The gifts of the earth belong to everyone,' she said with her usual sweet smile. 'I take to give, to give the gift of healing to others.'

'At the rate you're taking, there'll soon be nothing left to give,' said Bron.

'There's really no need for all this, Bron,' said Morrigan. 'They're my guests, and you won't miss a few weeds.'

'Not weeds,' said Brighid in a shocked voice. 'Simply another form of nature's art.'

'Of course.' Morrigan gave her a saccharine smile. 'How good it is that I have you to put things in proportion for me.'

'Your so-called guests have no right to be on the estate,' said Bron.' You're here only because you work at the theatre, and like the rest of the company you've been asked to keep to the gardens and the estate roads.'

'Yet Georgia hasn't done so,' said Morrigan, his eyes fixing on her.

Bron again ignored him. 'Next time I find you taking plants, I'll prosecute,' he said to Brighid. 'I want you off the estate now.'

The Disciples were already beginning to move away, looking

188

nervously over their shoulders. Brighid shook her head at Bron.

'Such anger!' she said. 'It corrodes the soul. I shall pray for you.'

'Pray for whoever you like, as long as you get out of here,' he said impatiently.

Brighid began to follow the Disciples, but Morrigan lingered for another few seconds.

'Yes, we shall pray for you, Bron, indeed we shall,' he said before he sauntered away. 'And soon you'll discover how strong we can be.'

Again there was a hidden meaning in his words, as if they were the opening shots in some sort of battle. Bron looked after him, still restraining Rusalka, and when they'd finally disappeared crossed back to Georgia, all his former good humour gone.

'He may be my uncle, but he's nothing but bad news,' he said, taking up the carrier bag. 'God knows what Nico sees in him. Or perhaps you're one of his fan club too?'

Georgia disliked Morrigan so much that she couldn't be tactful. 'I loathe him. I think Brighid's all right, though. She doesn't mean any harm.'

'I agree with you,' said Bron, 'and if I could persuade her not to dig up half of Merlinslade I might just manage to go along with her. But the association with Morrigan I can't take.' He got back into the boat, and undid the painter. 'I'd better make sure they really are on their way out.'

'Thanks for lunch,' said Georgia.

He pushed off from the shore. Rusalka flopped down in the stern, and lay with her muzzle on the gunwale, watching the water. Bron began to row vigorously away against the stream, something she suspected he thoroughly enjoyed. As if he guessed her thoughts he looked up before he rounded the bend, lifted his hand briefly in salute, and glided away beneath an arch of overhanging alders.

Chapter 10

Georgia spent the afternoon showing Jenny how to construct a lace standing ruff for Miranda's wedding dress, strong enough to withstand rapid costume changes. The wire framework had to be wound round with bias binding, the lace drawn tight as it was sewn into place, and then the whole thing sprayed with a flexible coating to stiffen it. The rest of her time was employed in converting men's Wellington boots into Jacobean footwear by adding wide turned-down tops of leather, lined with falls of lace.

She was tired when she got home, and when she'd poured herself a glass of Moselle, threw open the French windows and stretched out on the sofa. Chloe was in her bedroom. Her window was open too, for music from her cassette player drifted round the side of the house. As Georgia idly listened it began to dawn on her that she was again listening to Morrigan's voice.

She put down her drink, and tiptoed along the corridor to Chloe's room. Cautiously she opened the door.

Chloe lay on her bed, smoking. The poster of Gérard Depardieu had been replaced by one of Morrigan that was almost as famous as Che Guevara's in the seventies. He was standing in a skin-tight suit of black wet-look vinyl, jacket slashed to his waist, long curling hair flying out from a head thrown back in ecstasy, guitar jutting above his crotch. His throbbing voice filled the room.

'Hi, Georgy,' Chloe said dreamily. 'Isn't he brilliant? I never realised what the oldies were going on about till now.'

'He's a brilliant faker,' said Georgia shortly.

Chloe didn't seem to hear her. 'Brighid had to go into Bath this morning, and he took a hymn practice in the chapel. He asked me to stay behind afterwards. He was really, really impressed by my voice. He told me he's having a party at his house for all the theatre company next week, and he said of course I must come too.'

Georgia sat down on the bed, reeling at this onslaught of unwelcome news. She knew about the party, and had already decided not to go.

'I'm not at all certain you'd like his sort of party,' she said cautiously.

'Not like it?' Chloe stared at her as though she were simple-minded. 'Of course I will. Everyone says it'll be fabulous.'

'Surely you don't think he's more brilliant than Sean?' Georgia was getting desperate. 'Sean really likes you, but you'll turn him off quicker than anything if you go overboard about Morrigan.'

'You've got a disgusting mind!' said Chloe indignantly. 'The Disciples look on him simply as a father. And I'm going, whether you like it or not!'

Because Chloe had already started working part-time in the wardrobe, Georgia was forced to conclude an uneasy truce with her over the party. The company was already in a frenzy of happy anticipation, especially when the normally level-headed sound technician went over to Morrigan's house to listen to his prelimi-nary work on the music, and came back ecstatic about the general sumptuousness of the place. Annie and Jenny spent all their spare time discussing what to wear, and Zelda, who never appeared in anything but trousers, dragged Georgia into half the boutiques in Bath to help her find the perfect dress.

Chloe paid a visit to what Georgia considered the most alluring shop in a city where all the shops were a source of temptation, one which sold antique clothes. She spent most of her savings on a thirties black chiffon slip dress scattered with grey flowers, and held up with ribbon straps. Under it she wore a shrunken white vest, and on her legs pale grey tights and a pair of clumpy platform sandals. Her hair, brushed out into a hennaed cloud, was threaded with tiny jet beads. She looked a disturbing mixture of waif and siren.

When Georgia saw Chloe in the full ensemble, she decided

irritably that she'd have to go to the party after all to keep an eye on her. She chose a black dress she'd bought in the States, one she'd never liked, but it suited her mood, and her role as duenna.

Chloe was still complaining about being chaperoned as they drove up through the city to the Royal Crescent. The streets basked in the last golden glow of evening, and the slate rooftops had become a hazy blue in the gathering twilight. Couples were still sitting under the plane trees on the green in the centre of the Circus, but a few windows in the great surrounding circle of Georgian houses were already lit.

As they came to the end of Brock street the self-assured magnificence of the Royal Crescent unfolded before them. Georgia thought that Morrigan must be one of the very few people to own a whole house there, and again the incongruity between his city lifestyle and the sort of life led by the Disciples puzzled her.

A heavy-weight butler answered the front door and checked their names on a guest list. The contents of the entrance hall could have been repeated in any large Bath town house, except that the Chippendale chairs appeared to be real Chippendale, and the chandelier had the irregular lustre of antique glass.

They arrived firmly back in the twentieth century as they entered the first-floor drawing room. The three tall windows which ran from floor to ceiling were uncurtained, and looked across a broad sweep of grass to the city below whose lights twinkled like a spaceship in the dusk. The walls and pargeted ceiling were pale grey, and the pine floorboards had been replaced by some exotic tropical wood with a deep watery gleam.

Opposite the door was one of Andy Warhol's disaster paintings, the grim images only partially slicked over with a wash of Day-Glo mauve. On the wall at the far end of the room a pair of Francis Bacon nudes, painted in decomposing pinks and greys, were engaged in a coupling which was more a death struggle than an embrace. There was no furniture apart from a few low tables and long cushions of charcoal-coloured suede against the walls.

The room was crammed with people, the air full of cigarette smoke and the scent of cannabis. Morrigan waved at them from a circle of admirers which included the lead singer from a group currently at the top of the charts, and a stunningly beautiful woman who'd recently been the mistress of two cabinet ministers at once.

Chloe was so overcome by her surroundings that she didn't even remark on the yards of rain forest covering the floor. Sean homed in on her almost immediately. As music pulsed into the room from a concealed sound system, and a strobe light began to rake the dancers, Georgia retreated to a window seat. For once she didn't mind the role of chaperone. She'd had the beginnings of another migraine in the afternoon, and though her usual medicine seemed to have caught it in time, her brain felt slow and lethargic.

As she looked out into the dusk someone came and sat quietly next to her. To her surprise it was Esther, in a dark blue dress with a white lawn collar.

'I thought you wouldn't be here,' said Georgia. 'I used to love this sort of bash, but it's doing nothing for me tonight. Perhaps it's because of Morrigan. Or perhaps I'm getting old.'

'Not old, but wiser perhaps,' said Esther, looking round the room with a faint smile. 'I only came because I didn't want to seem stand-offish. The cast think I'm odd enough, as it is.'

'Unusual, not odd. But funnily enough, they like you in spite of it.' Georgia gave her a mischievous glance. 'I wonder what John would say if he could see you here?'

'I hate to think. Not that he's stuffy, of course,' Esther added hastily.

Georgia remembered the one time she'd met John, when she'd visited Esther at Oxford. She'd never come across anyone quite so serious. It had been agony to resist teasing him.

'Kim keeps telling me I've changed since I started playing Ariel. I hope it isn't true.'

Georgia looked at her affectionately. 'You've loosened up a bit, but that's not bad. You do tend to keep on the sidelines as far as enjoyment's concerned.'

'My job isn't to enjoy myself, it's to help people. And aren't you staying on the sidelines at the moment, Georgy? I'm sure Nico's interested in you. It'd do you good to go out more.'

'Maybe, but not with him,' said Georgia, watching Nico, who, dressed in his Armani linen suit and a wine-coloured shirt, was engaged in a long conversation with the parliamentary mistress.

As the lighting dimmed, and the sound system began to pump out a fifties waltz, Esther was asked to dance by the actor who played Trinculo, and before she had time to decline was borne away into the crowd. Georgia suddenly envied her. At least Esther didn't live on a permanent emotional see-saw, for that was all her own life seemed to be these days. She began to feel so desolate that she was almost glad when Nico appeared at her side.

'Darling, we can't go on like this!' he said, sending himself up in a perfect Noël Coward voice. 'How about a cease-fire? Or at least a dance to discuss a truce.'

He held out his arms to her with a confident smile. She wavered, remembering what Esther had said. Perhaps she was right. Perhaps if she talked to Nico she could persuade him to give her more space, and they could try again. Silently she allowed him to take her on to the floor.

He pulled her closer. 'Why the duenna's dress this evening?' he asked. 'It's lucky I know what's underneath.'

She tensed. 'You've got to forget that, Nico. I shouldn't have let it happen.'

'You've been talking to Esther too much, I can see.'

'Nico, I'm serious,' she said warningly, wondering if she'd have to leave him in the middle of the dance. To make things more difficult Morrigan was watching them.

'Of course you are, sweetie, seriously classy,' Nico replied, holding her even closer. 'Look at Uncle Ger. He's up to something. Probably working out how he can pinch you off me.'

Georgia shivered. 'God, I hope not.'

'No need to worry. The minute he'd got you he'd lose interest. He's like that. It's a sort of game he has to keep playing to prove he can win, especially now he's getting older. Bron doesn't believe me, but Ger's pretty insecure under all that flash exterior.'

'I can't say I'd noticed. And what about you, Nico? Is it a game for you?'

He whisked her into a series of tricky reverse steps he'd learned in the course of some long-forgotten play while he considered his reply. Through the back of Georgia's dress her body was warm and supple beneath his hand. Since the row with her he'd been surprised to find he was suffering from feelings of regret, and even, more unusually, from self-doubt.

'Maybe not this time,' he said. 'Anyway, I've booked us a table at Popjoy's for later on. I think we need to discuss this again.'

'I've told you, there's nothing to discuss. I still need space. It's nothing to do with you personally. I'd feel the same way about any man at this stage.'

She disengaged herself firmly from his arms, and walked back to the window seat. He followed her, startled to realise that if he lost her now, it would actually hurt. He began to wonder if the terrible settling-down syndrome was beginning to afflict him. He told himself bracingly that he was being ridiculous, that she'd soon come round if she saw how easy it was for him to find someone else.

Esther was back in the window seat too. His gaze rested speculatively on her. Her demure white-collared dress and short hair made her look like a choirboy in drag. He'd always been curious about her, about the reserves of emotion which only surfaced on the stage, and he'd idly wondered if any man had ever succeeded in bringing them out in real life. Now was a perfect chance to find out.

Nothing would demonstrate more clearly to Georgia what she was missing, and the thought of putting over a fast one on Bron made the idea even more appealing. Surprisingly, for he never usually interfered in Nico's affairs, he'd suggested after the argument in the courtyard that it might be a good idea to cool things with Georgia, but he certainly wouldn't approve of Nico switching his attentions to Esther.

Georgia watched her solemnly accept Nico's invitation to dance. Though she told herself she didn't care, she had to struggle with self-pity. Morrigan's party was going to be even more of an ordeal than she'd anticipated. She looked round worriedly for Chloe, and was relieved to see her still dancing with Sean.

The headache hadn't disappeared. She wandered from the drawing room with her empty glass in search of water. Downstairs the butler directed her to a basement cloakroom. As she paused outside to make sure that her pain killers were in her purse, and not in the car, the heavy door of the recording studio opposite flew open.

Morrigan burst through it, propelling before him one of the pop group. The musician was about eighteen and deathly pale. Morrigan, his back to Georgia, slammed him up against the wall. The boy was trembling uncontrollably. His eyes stared at something across the hall which Georgia couldn't see. She shrank into the cloakroom doorway.

'They're there! There in the corner! They're waiting to get me! Fucking great sharks with razor fins. For God's sake, Morrigan, why won't you give me something to take them away?'

His knees buckled, and he began to slide down the wall. Morrigan grabbed him by the front of his shirt and hauled him up once more.

'Pull yourself together, you little shit-bag,' he hissed. 'You needn't think you can freak out here.'

The boy was weeping, saliva drooling from his mouth. 'You've got to help me. You've got to get me a fix.'

'There's no got to about it. I don't help babies like you who can't handle things on their own. You're out, sonny!'

He twisted the boy's arm behind him, and proceeded to frog-march him, still sobbing wildly, upstairs and out of sight.

Georgia had been terrified in case Morrigan saw her. Pity for the boy, together with shock over Morrigan's callousness and the knowledge that there must be hard drugs somewhere in the house, were all combining to make her feel as if her own knees were about to give way.

She retreated through the cloakroom door, and collapsed on to a chair. While she waited for her legs to feel less rubbery she frantically tried to work out what to do. Eventually she decided that she had to find out for certain what was going on in the recording studio. After a few more minutes she managed to proceed cautiously outside into the basement hall.

A riff of music was coming from the studio. Though the red warning light was on above the door, it was very slightly ajar. Cautiously she peered round it. The lighting in the studio was subdued, the walls lined with grey sound-absorbing felt. A small performance stage was crammed with digital equipment: electronic keyboards, drum machines, sequencers, samplers, even a couple of hyper-violins, strange angular creations with tiny computers built into the bow.

Morrigan wasn't there, but the rest of the group she'd seen upstairs were gathered with their drinks round a low table. The lead singer was carefully shaking some rough grey crystals from a paper wrap into a pipe with a glass bowl. Georgia froze as he held it over a candle flame, and began to draw in the smoke. The other singers already looked bombed out of their minds.

Shakily she retreated into the hall. She'd seen people smoking crack in the States so often that she'd almost become accustomed to the sight, but she hadn't expected it to be so openly in use here. She'd made her own decision about drugs long ago, and normally she would simply have distanced herself, or left the party. But she couldn't do that while Chloe remained in the house.

Though she was fairly sure Chloe hadn't experimented with hard drugs, she'd never been in a setting like this before, where to do so could easily seem the height of glamour. She thought feverishly that Chloe might even have no choice. She'd seen people after their food or drink had been spiked with dope. Yet there was very little she could do to stop total strangers taking drugs at a party unless she reported them to the police, and she didn't have a single witness.

She turned to go back to the drawing room, preparing to chaperone Chloe even more closely. But as she paused, one hand on the bottom of the banister, her sister and Morrigan arrived together at the head of the stairs. Chloe was flushed and laughing. Behind them Sean hovered frustratedly, clearly exasperated at Chloe's defection.

Morrigan's hand was under Chloe's elbow. 'Has anyone ever recorded your singing voice?' he was saying. 'When I heard you in the chapel at the Sanctuary I thought it had immense potential. We desperately need another soloist for the Disciples' promotional video. Why don't we try a test track now in my studio?'

Chloe looked as buoyant and potentially unstable as a hot-air balloon in a high wind. Morrigan glanced back casually at Sean.

'Sorry,' he said, 'but this isn't really your line. You may as well go upstairs again. We'll probably be some time.'

'Are you sure that's what you want, Chloe?' Sean said stubbornly. 'We were going to have supper together, remember?'

'Yes, yes, it's all right,' said Chloe. 'Stop fussing so. I'll be back in a little while. We can eat then.'

Sean turned away without a word. Georgia was infuriated. Chloe had been raving about him for days, everything seemed to be going perfectly, she was even losing interest in the Sanctuary, and now in five minutes Morrigan had reversed everything. But foremost in Georgia's mind was the urgent need to stop Chloe entering the studio.

She stepped out into their path.

'Georgy!' said Chloe happily. 'Did you decide to go home? Is your headache bad? You don't have to stay for me. Sean'll walk me back.'

'Yes, I'm going home. The migraine's much worse,' said Georgia. She was horrified to find she was shaking. 'I need you to come with me, just to drive me there. And I want to go now.'

She sat down on a handy chair, and pressed her hand to her forehead in a gesture Nico couldn't have bettered.

'Can't you take some aspirins?' said Chloe impatiently. 'It's not convenient now, it really isn't.'

'I'm sorry you're ill,' said Morrigan, looking as if he didn't believe a word of what she'd been saying. 'Why don't you lie down for a while? My housekeeper'll look after you.'

The thought of lying on any bed belonging to Morrigan made Georgia feel queasy. She decided to make the most of the sensation.

'I must get home. I must have fresh air,' she said, clutching her stomach and giving a deep groan. 'I think I'm going to be sick.'

A look of extreme distaste passed over his face.

'In that case, perhaps you should go with your sister after all,' he said to Chloe hurriedly. 'We can set up the recording as soon as you return.'

Georgia produced another groan. Morrigan looked nervously at his pristine plush pile carpet.

'Oh, all right, then, I suppose I'll have to,' said Chloe, scowling.

Georgia grabbed her hand, and dragged her upstairs before she could change her mind. Once outside she rushed along the road to the car, fell into the passenger seat, and thrust the keys at Chloe.

Chloe got in, and started the engine. She stared at Georgia.

'You do look a bit odd,' she said. 'You've gone a sort of pale green.'

'Just get on with it,' said Georgia, having little difficulty making her voice suitably faint. 'And for heaven's sake remember to switch on the lights before you start.'

Luckily the streets were almost deserted, for Chloe had only just started driving lessons and annoyance made her careless. Georgia lay back in her seat, trying to look too ill to notice the sound of clashing gears, but the moment they reached Sophia Street she whipped the keys from the ignition. Taking no notice of Chloe's indignant protests, she marched into the house.

Chloe rushed after her, and caught up with her in the hall. 'You're all right! You were faking! It's not fair! Just when I was really, really enjoying myself. Why did you do it?'

Georgia went into the kitchen. She filled the kettle, and plugged it in. The familiar sequence of movements calmed her a little. She turned to face Chloe.

'I don't want you to go back there. I want you to promise me you won't ever go there again.'

'What are you on about?' said Chloe in a tone of utter disbelief. 'Of course I'm going back. I'm going to ring for a taxi now. It's the best party I've ever been to. And Morrigan's waiting for me.'

Georgia sat down at the table, drawing patterns on the cloth with the tip of a spoon which had been set out for breakfast.

'Chloe darling, I'm not doing it to upset you. You've got to believe me. Bad things were happening there, things you knew nothing about.'

'I suppose you're upset because people were smoking grass? But everyone does it, even at school.'

'It wasn't just grass,' said Georgia. 'I don't want you mixed up with hard drugs ever. I've seen what they can do in the States.'

'Why won't you realise I'm grown up now? I know all about stuff like that. Can't you trust me not to try it?'

'Yes, of course I can, normally,' said Georgia in desperation. 'But Morrigan's so persuasive, and everyone there was older than you. It might be very hard for you to say no.'

'I've never seen him use any sort of drugs. Brighid wouldn't let him near the Sanctuary if he did,' said Chloe indignantly. 'I'm not surprised Blake ran out on you, if you went on at him the way you go for me!'

Depression began to flood in on Georgia that Chloe of all people should use such an argument against her.

'And anyway, there was a girl at school who'd snorted coke, and she said it didn't do her any harm,' Chloe went on.

'Then she's a fool. But it wasn't just coke I saw. People were smoking crack in Morrigan's studio.'

Chloe looked momentarily taken aback. She quickly recovered.

'So what? I wouldn't have joined in.'

'Lots of people say that, but they do,' said Georgia vehemently. 'Coke's bad enough, but believe me, crack messes you up so fast you don't even know what's happened. It destroys your mind. And I'm not going to let that happen to you. You're not going back to the party.'

'I am!' said Chloe wildly. 'Just because you don't want to have fun any more doesn't mean I have to live that way. I'm phoning for a taxi now.'

Georgia knew that Chloe in this hard-done-by mood would soon become impossible to control. The only way to stop her was to shock her, but to shock her sufficiently would involve a threat she wasn't sure she had the nerve to carry out. She took a deep breath.

'If you go back to the party, I'll ring the police and tell them what's going on. You've never been in a place that's being busted. You wouldn't like it, I can assure you. It's no fun being arrested on suspicion. Don't you remember Annie's story in the workshop the other day, about that friend of hers who'd had a body search?'

Chloe paled. Annie's story, told in full anatomical detail, had greatly impressed her, though she'd tried to appear blasé at the time.

'You wouldn't dare! All the cast are there, Nico as well! How could you do such a mean, sneaky, horrible thing to them?'

Georgia still wasn't at all sure she could do it, but at least she seemed to be getting through to Chloe at last.

'Easily,' she said, 'if it keeps you away from crack.'

'But the publicity would be awful. It'd affect the whole theatre company. You might all lose your jobs. You're not like that, Georgy. I know you wouldn't do it.'

'Try me,' she said levelly, holding Chloe's gaze with her own.

After a moment or two Chloe's eyes began to fill with tears. 'All right, then, if it means so much to you I won't go back. But I hate you forever! Just when everything's starting to go right for me, you spoil it all. Just because you're getting all shrivelled up and bitter yourself, you don't want anyone else to have any fun! You're as bad as the olds! I'm never, ever going anywhere with you again!'

Chloe spent all next day, a Sunday, at the Sanctuary, and went to Fruits of the Earth early on Monday morning. She hardly spoke to Georgia, giving her instead meaningful and reproachful glances designed to wear down her resistance. She was clearly having second thoughts about her behaviour to Sean, and rushed to the phone each time it rang. She was even finally reduced to communicating with Georgia to ask her when he was next coming to the wardrobe for a fitting.

Georgia worked late all week to keep out of Chloe's way. On Friday her car was being serviced, and just after six she started to walk down the estate road to the village to pick up the last bus into Bath. It had been a hard day, and she was tempted to call in at the rectory. Kim would willingly have given her something to eat, and Esther would have driven her home afterwards. But the need to water her more fragile flowers, and the lure of an empty flat, for Chloe had rung to say she was having supper with Natty, drove her homewards.

The road which usually rushed by when Georgia was driving or jogging along it seemed to go on endlessly tonight. Her shoulder bag of African sisal was crammed with a plastic box of raspberries from Mr Mead's own garden, several reference books and a large pot of rubber solution for making masks at home. A long way off thunder was grumbling along the horizon, where clouds were slowly piling up into a towering anvil. The air was oppressive, and she felt hot even in her T shirt and wrap-over skirt, a soft blue cotton faded from many washings, and the most comfortable in her wardrobe.

Apart from the twitter of swallows sweeping low across the park, the only other sound came from a hornet making a foray among the flowers in the hedge lining this part of the road. She hated hornets. She'd seen her ayah attacked by one when she was small. The Merlinslade hornets weren't quite as menacing as the African variety, but they were big enough, and equally unpredictable.

To her alarm, even when she increased her pace the hornet kept up with her, zooming over her head like some miniaturised reconnaissance plane, buzzing away to blunder among the curled flowers of honeysuckle in the hedge, but always coming back. She began to wonder if it was attracted by the smell of the rubber solution.

She was trying to brace herself with the thought that the storm, if it did materialise, should at least drive the hornet way, when she caught another noise above the insect's buzzing wings. She looked behind her. A car was travelling in her direction, a gun-metal grey convertible with the hood down and a man in mirror sunglasses at the wheel.

Morrigan drew up by her side in a dramatic screech of tyres. 'Would you like a lift? I'm going into Bath, and there's a storm on the way.'

She looked up at the sky, though she'd already decided that she'd rather get wet than accept a lift from him. But as if Morrigan had personally ordered it to do so, the hornet swooped so close to her face that she could feel its wings fanning her cheek.

'That's a nasty-looking beast,' he said. 'It said in the local paper that a man from Trowbridge died of an insect sting on his mouth last week. His tongue swelled up and choked him.'

He leaned over, and opened the passenger door for her. The hornet had retreated for a moment to hover above the hedge, but now launched itself into another approach run, aiming straight for her head. Georgia's nerve failed. She got in beside Morrigan, telling herself that it was only a twenty-minute run to the outskirts of the city, and at least she'd be able to talk to him about Chloe.

Country music was surging from the speakers in the back. He turned it down a little.

'You don't like me, do you?' he said conversationally.

'I should have thought that was fairly obvious by now,' she said. She'd meant to be the one to launch the attack. The plush-covered seat was making her legs feel sticky. He kept one hand lazily on the steering wheel, while the other rested on the gear lever. The backs were scattered with coarse black hairs.

'Yet almost everyone else gives me the benefit of the doubt. If I had any debt to society I've repaid it. Or are you jealous because I like your sister? Is that why she didn't come back to the party?'

'Jealous?' said Georgia incredulously. The colossal vanity of his accusation momentarily stunned her. 'There's nothing to be jealous of. I took her home because there was crack in your house.'

'Crack? Surely not? You must have been mistaken.' He turned a sardonic gaze on her. 'Perhaps you'd had a little too much to drink.'

'You know I wasn't mistaken. Chloe's had enough problems in her life. I don't want her to have any more.'

'We're all concerned for Chloe at the Sanctuary,' he said smoothly. 'I can't think that your behaving in this authoritarian way is going to help her.'

'I mean it,' Georgia said. 'If you have anything to do with her outside the Sanctuary I'll tell the police what I saw at the weekend.'

'I can assure you they'd find nothing wrong at my house. You'd simply be making life even more difficult for me, for no valid reason, just when I've been trying so hard to persuade Bron to forget the past and accept me fully into the family again.'

'You weren't doing much to convince him of that by the river the other day.'

'Bron never was very likeable, and an army training hasn't improved him. I'm beginning to think I shall have to find some other way to convince him. It's a pity when Nico is so co-operative.'

'What sort of other way?' said Georgia.

He didn't answer, but turned his head and smiled at her. 'So what do you want me to do about your sister? Never speak to her again? That would be rather difficult since she comes so regularly to the Sanctuary.'

'Just don't pay her any special attention from now on. Leave her to Brighid.'

He drew up at the lodge, and gave a long blast on the horn. Mr Meads stumped out to open the gates, glowering at Morrigan.

'Poor old Meads,' said Morrigan imperturbably as the car speeded along the lane leading to the village. 'If I were Bron I'd have made a clean sweep of all the pensioners long ago. But I'm afraid nothing's going to save Merlinslade now except a sizeable injection of cash. He's taken too big a gamble there.'

'He seems to be doing quite well to me,' said Georgia.

'I wish he'd take my advice on the publicity for the opening of the estate to the public next year. But he's not as reasonable as Nico. He was difficult even as a child.'

They'd already reached the village. Morrigan accelerated through it, gunning the engine with a roar which brought a game of cricket on the green to a stop. He'd scorched a few hundred yards along the road leading to the main highway when a tractor pulling a cart laden with manure emerged from a side turning and began to trundle slowly ahead of them.

Morrigan slammed on the brakes. The driver had failed to notice that a loose tail gate was scattering dollops of evil-smelling slurry across the tarmac. Morrigan couldn't slow his car in time. It began to squelch through the manure. Georgia could hear it splattering against the sides. The stench was appalling.

Morrigan started to blare the horn violently and flash the headlights. After a maddening and, Georgia was certain, deliberate delay, the driver turned. It was Mr Samms. After another very long pause he finally pulled in to the side.

Morrigan accelerated past like a drag racer, so close that he came within an inch of ripping off his nearside wing mirror. In spite of the stench blasting over the car Georgia wanted to cheer Mr Samms.

'That'll teach him to hog the road!' said Morrigan through gritted teeth.

He only began to slow down as they approached the garage on the village boundary, but Georgia's relief turned to dismay when he swung into the forecourt. The middle-aged woman who staffed the pay booth rushed out when she recognised him, and complied like a star-struck teenager as he asked her to bring him a token for the car wash.

Another car was already being cleaned. He parked behind it and turned to Georgia as if settling down for a long chat. She tried to conceal her impatience. They could have been well on their way to Bath by this time.

'I'm planning great things for the Disciples. Chloe's going to play an important part.'

'What do you mean?' said Georgia, watching the brushes revolve busily over the car in front.

He pushed a button. The radio aerial silently retracted. He moved his hand again, and the wing mirrors swivelled neatly inwards.

'The group's badly organised at the moment. It's too low-key. It needs shaking up. I intend to start with a massive fundraising campaign. Chloe's going to be the focal point of the publicity drive.'

Georgia's first reaction was to protest angrily that she wouldn't allow it. But then she remembered that since the party the likelihood of Chloe's agreeing to anything she suggested had been severely reduced.

Morrigan touched the control panel once more. The roof of the car began to close slowly over their heads. 'Chloe's got a photogenic quality which I'm afraid Brighid, poor darling, will never have,' he continued. 'Those extra pounds of hers don't come over well in photographs. Chloe possesses that innocent waif-like look which the public finds so appealing just now.'

'Chloe doesn't have time for any fund-raising campaigns,' Georgia said. 'She's going to be fully occupied once she takes up her A level courses again in September.'

The car in front had just splashed away, and Morrigan switched on the engine.

'As long as Brighid agrees, Chloe will almost certainly do as I suggest.'

He slotted the token into a control box, and eased the car forward between the two high panels which formed the sides of the washing bay. He pressed another button on the dashboard, and the windows began to close. The conversation had been relatively low-key up to now, but, as at the river with Bron, she had the distinct sensation that he was issuing a challenge.

'We might come to some arrangement,' he said smoothly. 'It's been a source of great concern to Brighid that you've refused to join the Disciples when you so clearly need their support. You could change your mind, and take Chloe's place.'

The red stop light flashed. He switched off the engine. Jets of water began to engulf them, followed by a moving bar which travelled ponderously backwards across the car, dousing it in a curtain of streaming suds. Morrigan's eyes were fixed on her in the half-light.

Georgia, her mind already racing over the implications of what he'd just said, started to feel panicky as the two huge green brushes began to whirl across the bonnet, swinging together like a couple of crazy ballet dancers. The wrap of her skirt had fallen slightly to one side, and Morrigan's hand moved from the gear stick to her bare knee.

'For that, and for a little more friendliness, the sort of friendliness you give to Nico, there would be no problem about persuading Chloe to leave the Disciples at the end of the summer. In fact, I could guarantee it.'

The brushes swept inexorably over the windscreen and along the sides of the car, which was rocking gently to their motion. Morrigan's skin took on a strange tinge of reflected green. She pressed herself back against the door, clutching the sisal bag so tightly that the contents bruised her breasts.

His hand moved again. He began to walk his index and second fingers up her arm. Outside everything streamed with water. She stared in appalled fascination at the progress of the two shining, manicured nails, like tiny faceless masks.

The brushes loomed up against the rear window. His fingers stopped at the back of her neck, and began to massage the top of her spine. The brushes reversed, and tossed into a forward dance, flowing against the glass behind his head. Water whispered hypnotically all around them. The atmosphere in the car had become sinister and intensely erotic at the same time.

He swayed towards her, brought his mouth down on hers, and kissed her, the weight of his body crushing her bag against her breasts. Though he was as old as her father, she was still more unnerved when she found herself responding, not because she enjoyed it, but because the atmosphere was so compelling and because, like Nico, he was so perfectly self-assured.

For a moment she was as helpless as a rabbit in the middle of a motorway, until for once the emotional barrier she'd erected to shield herself since the divorce came to her aid. Helplessness began to be replaced by an icy disdain. Over his shoulder, in the make-up mirror attached to the sun-visor, she saw another car moving up behind them. Coldly and analytically she told herself that even he wouldn't dare go any further now. She willed herself to stay calm.

A moment later he tensed, and she knew he'd seen the other vehicle through the rear window. When the brushes paused at the end of their first cycle, and the car was silent again, he let her go.

'So it's a bargain?' he said, taking her silence for agreement. He tilted the driving mirror towards him, smoothing down his hair with a self-satisfied smile.

She struggled to control herself. She could still hardly believe he'd made such an offer. Every move she considered had some potential for disaster. His vanity was so colossal that she was sure he'd never forgive her if she rejected him, and he knew how easy it would be to hurt her by hurting Chloe. Blake had offered her the same deadly option before the divorce: sacrifice herself emotionally, or lose him. Now she was being asked to sacrifice herself or lose Chloe. But Blake had been an adult who could in theory look after himself. Chloe was so vulnerable still, and Morrigan could so easily ruin her life.

Smaller brushes began to vibrate along the sides against the wheels as she desperately juggled her choices. The strange atmosphere inside the car was making it difficult to think in any logical way.

'So we'll expect you at the Sanctuary this weekend,' he said, clearly thinking his performance had been irresistible. 'I knew you'd agree.'

His sweeping disregard for her feelings made up her mind. She hadn't gone through all those months of agonising readjustment after the divorce only to walk willingly into another trap. She couldn't sacrifice herself even for Chloe. She'd just have to find some other way to protect her sister.

'I've agreed to nothing,' she said angrily. 'I want to get out, now.'

She fumbled for the door handle, forgetting that it was centrally locked.

Morrigan didn't move. 'Playing hard to get, are you?' he said, smiling as though he hadn't understood one word she'd said.

She looked distractedly at the array of controls on the dashboard, and realised she'd never find the button to open the door. To her despair the metal arm started to move over the car again, this time drizzling a coat of yellow, mucus-like polish over the bodywork. In a moment the brushes would swing into action once more, shielding them from the gaze of the car at the back. Frantically she wondered if she could possibly break the window without hurting herself.

But as she watched the relentless advance of the polish bar, she saw that he too was staring at it. The expression of revulsion on his face made her remember his capitulation when he'd thought she was going to be sick. Suddenly she thought of a better way to escape. She scrabbled in her bag, pulled out the can of rubber solution, and levered off the lid, covering her fingers with the stuff and almost tearing her thumb nail in the process. She held it poised over the glove compartment on her side.

Her heart was hammering so violently that she could hardly speak. 'Open the door,' she said, 'or I'll tip it all over the car. And believe me, it isn't easily removed.'

His gaze fixed on the rubber solution. The surface, grey and viscous, trembled in the motion of the brushes, which were beginning to slide over the bonnet again. His expression of disgust deepened. She tilted the can.

'Go on, let me out!'

Reluctantly he pressed a button on the dashboard. She waited for the brushes to move to the back of the car before she opened the door.

'I hope you realise I shan't make the offer again. So you'll just have to take your chance over what happens next, won't you?' he said viciously.

It was an open challenge at last, but for the moment she didn't care about anything, as long as she could get away from him.

She stumbled from the car, splashing through a huge puddle, and rushed towards the front of the garage. As the brushes folded away for the last time, Morrigan's car rocketed out of the bay. His tyres left gleaming tracks on the tarmac. Leaning weakly against a petrol pump, she saw him disappear in the direction of the main road.

Georgia was shaking too much to get the lid back on the can, and threw them both into a litter bin. She managed to wash the rubber solution from her hands at a tap by the compressed air machine. Her heart was still beating like a crazy castanet, but she doggedly squelched out of the garage forecourt in her sodden shoes, and started to trudge up the road to the bus stop. She was within twenty yards of it when the last bus to Bath hurtled past.

Chapter 11

As Georgia sat down in the shelter to empty the water from her shoes, she tried to concentrate on the problem of how to get home. But the menace behind Morrigan's parting words, and the ferocity of his look, still hung in her mind as clearly as the imprint of an exploding flash bulb. She could hardly bear to think of what might happen if he deliberately tried to gain control over Chloe.

Eventually the coldness of her feet made her realise she was still sitting there, staring into space, with the shoes dangling from her hands, and no decision made about how to get home. She decided that activity was, as usual, the best remedy. Luckily the storm had not materialised, and rather than ringing for a taxi from the village, she'd walk the mile up to the main road where buses ran half hourly into Bath.

She tried to make herself think about the designs for the next play as she trudged along, but after a while her shoulder bag began to feel like a sack of bricks. She flopped down for a rest in the waist-high grass and hogweed lining the verge, dumping her load behind her.

The sun had dropped behind the clouds still piled along the western horizon, rimming them with gold. She pulled off her shoes, which were still wet and beginning to chafe her feet, and leaned back against her bag, gazing up through the parasols of hogweed flowers at a squadron of swifts chasing the last insects of the day.

Bron, driving back to Merlinslade from a difficult afternoon in Bath, was too preoccupied to notice his surroundings. After a conference with the family solicitor about raising a loan until harvest time, he'd spent an unproductive couple of hours combing the local scrap yards in search of spare parts for the numerous pieces of decaying farm machinery awaiting his attention at Merlinslade. His mind was only half on the familiar road as he considered the most imminent problem of all, the visit of Imogen at the beginning of the school holidays, and it was a few moments before he realised that he really had just seen a familiar pair of legs sticking out from the verge.

He slammed on the brakes, and reversed. Georgia was sitting beneath the hedge, looking as if she'd just done a route march. He guessed she'd missed the last bus, but wondered why she should seem quite so tired. She gave him a startled smile, and scrambled to her feet, gathering up her legs like a colt. She tugged on her shoes, and came over to the open window on the passenger side. There was a scattering of creamy petals in her hair. She looked even more wan in close-up.

'Where's your car?' he asked.

'Being serviced. I missed the last bus, so I'm walking up to the main road.'

She looked at him as if daring him to say she should have organised things better.

'Couldn't someone have given you a lift?'

Her face became wary.

'I did have a lift, but it didn't work out.'

'Why are your shoes wet? It hasn't been raining here.'

'It was an accident.' She bent to pick up a bulging bag. 'I must go on, or I shall miss the bus at the main road as well.'

Bron drummed his fingers on the steering wheel. He suspected there was more to it than she'd said, especially as Morrigan's car had scorched past in the direction of Bath only twenty minutes earlier. The most basic courtesy demanded that he gave her a lift up to the bus-stop on the main road.

He knew he ought to offer to take her all the way home, but he'd missed lunch and was ravenously hungry. Even Mrs Meads' usual Friday evening offering, gobbets of anonymous grey fish in a lumpy sauce under a lumpier layer of mashed potato, which had probably been shrivelling in the oven since six, seemed more appealing than driving to Bath and back again. But as she slung the bag, which was clearly overladen, and had distinctly unsafe-looking straps, over her shoulder, something about her pale, determined face made him change his mind.

'Get in,' he said abruptly. 'I'll take you to Bath.'

Though hardly enthusiastic, the offer was too inviting to resist. Georgia climbed into the passenger seat. At least, she thought with a flicker of amusement, it was highly unlikely that Bron would try to make a pass at her.

Bron made a rapid U-turn. His shirt sleeves were rolled up, and he was wearing a sweater knotted round his shoulders, but as Georgia turned to the back seat to stroke Rusalka, she deduced guiltily from the tie and jacket tossed on to a heap of files that he must have been returning from a business trip to Bath.

He kept the speedometer hovering meticulously on the speed limit for most of the way, though she was diverted to see that he couldn't resist a certain amount of cutting in to traffic queues as they approached the city. He didn't speak at all, but his silence failed to bother her, for she felt almost too tired to talk.

It was eight o'clock when they drew up outside the Sophia Street flat. Georgia was longing to do nothing more than make herself some scrambled eggs and go to bed. But when she turned to thank Bron she caught a particularly bleak look on his face, and began to wonder if his uncommunicativeness could be due to tiredness as well, and not to annoyance as she'd supposed. She had the uncomfortable thought that the cold comfort of a Merlinslade meal wasn't much of a reward for the double trek into Bath.

'Won't you come in and have supper before you go?' she said impetuously.

He looked at her as though he couldn't quite believe the offer. 'I'd better not. Rusalka isn't used to town houses, and I can't leave her in the car.'

Georgia was already regretting the invitation, and yet some perverse inclination to penetrate his monumental reserve made her persist.

'That's no problem. She can run in the garden. And there's nothing she could harm in the flat. As you know, it's not very grand,' she added wickedly.

213

Bron looked uncomfortable. She was sure he'd refuse now. But unexpectedly he smiled.

'Thanks. Then if you're sure about Rusalka, I'd like that,' he said.

She led the way into the sitting room, and flung open the French windows. A wave of rapidly cooling air wafted in, bringing with it the scent of stock and tobacco flowers. She went to the cassette player. He'd probably hate whatever she chose, so she might as well have what she liked. She slotted in a Rodrigo guitar concerto. When she turned he was still standing by the door, silently taking in the room.

'No snipers here,' she said, 'so why don't you sit down? Would you like a drink? I've got some white wine.'

'Perfect,' he answered absentmindedly. He walked over to the tulip chair, and stood looking at it. She hoped he wasn't going to turn it upside down and criticise her for glueing the joints instead of dovetailing them.

'Well, do you approve of my room or not?' she demanded.

He actually looked discomfited. 'I was just thinking that it's like you,' he said.

This remark was so loaded that she couldn't even begin to work it out. Instead she went into the kitchen and uncorked the bottle of chilled Chardonnay which she'd been expecting to drink slowly over the weekend. Rusalka's claws pattered on the tiles as she joined her.

When Georgia had given the dog a bowl of water, she put the wine and two glasses on a tray with a dish of olives. She carried it into the sitting room, the daily paper tucked beneath her arm.

Bron was on the sofa, looking out over the garden. Dusk was gathering. Soon in the terrace of houses backing on to her garden the windows would start to come alight like miniature theatres, one by one.

She set the tray and the newspapers on a table by his side.

'Help yourself,' she said. 'I just have to water the flowers.' She couldn't resist another tease. 'Sorry the newspaper's not ironed,' she added.

'I thought you said there weren't any snipers here,' Bron answered, reaching for the Chardonnay.

She gave him a startled smile. She looked as though she hadn't considered him capable of a joke, he thought. And now he came to reflect on it, he hadn't made all that many over the last year. He tried a cautious sip of wine. The Chardonnay was extremely good, crisp and dry, with a faint tang of oak. And the stagy sofa was surprisingly comfortable too. He allowed himself to give way to the temptation to lounge back in its depths.

As he picked up the newspaper, and his eyes flicked over the latest news from Bosnia, he thought yet again how insignificant it made Merlinslade and all its concerns seem. If he'd stayed in the army he would have been there too, doing something useful. Much as he loved Merlinslade, he'd never expected to have to devote the rest of his life to preserving an anachronism.

He tried to distract himself by concentrating on his surroundings. The tranquil room was full of surprises. A palm in a terracotta pot arched over the French windows. A scarlet raffia parrot hung from one of its branches. Over the fireplace was a David Hockney reproduction of a road winding down through the vibrant reds and greens of the Californian hills, with a glimpse of cobalt sea beyond. Behind him a huge Venetian mirror in a rococo gilt frame reflected the garden in its shadowy glass.

Idly he poured himself another glass of wine, watching Georgia as she wandered round the small walled garden with a watering can she'd filled from the rain butt, tenderly retrieving fallen trails of greenery, pausing to turn up roses in the palm of her hand and inhale the perfume.

Rusalka, who'd followed her outside, finished investigating the garden, and returned to slump against Bron's knee, her tail gently sweeping the polished floor. Georgia began to move back towards the house. The smell of damp earth had joined the scent of the tobacco flowers. Moths were beginning to fly in the twilight. Bron thought sleepily that she looked rather like a moth herself in that soft grey-blue skirt, with her arms glimmering palely through the dusk as she bent over a bed of herbs near the door.

Georgia plucked a handful of mint and basil, the pungent leaves cool against her hands. The garden had calmed her, as it always did, and she was at last managing to put the episode in Morrigan's car into some sort of perspective. She told herself firmly that he'd probably been bluffing, simply getting some sadistic pleasure out of trying to rattle her. If she could just manage to keep her head he'd soon become bored, and transfer his interest elsewhere.

As she stepped back into the sitting room she braced herself to deal with Bron, who'd no doubt been storing up more enigmatic observations on his surroundings. But instead he was fast asleep with an empty glass by his side.

She remembered how Nico had made her feel he was taking over her space, and yet Bron, whom she'd considered the most territorial of people, and who was stretched across a good half of the sofa, didn't give her that impression. He was very unlike Nico physically too. The arm lying along the sofa back was long-boned with a solid ridge of muscle, the hand square and competent. Nico's hands were pale, narrow, almost double jointed, capable of expressing emotion almost as clearly as his face.

Thinking about Nico's hands was not a good idea. It too easily led to other more destructive memories. Instead she escaped into the kitchen with the wine, and made herself concentrate on dinner. Scrambled eggs most definitely wouldn't do. Bron was the sort of person who'd expect a steak and kidney pudding at the very least.

There were two salmon cutlets in the fridge, placed there that morning to defrost for herself and the now absent Chloe. She put them to bake in the oven with herbs and wine, scrubbed a panful of new potatoes, made some hollandaise sauce to go with the salmon, and filled a bowl with garlicky salad.

While the potatoes were cooking she laid the table with the assorted china she'd collected over the years. He was sure to notice nothing matched, but she'd had a large glass of wine herself by now, and really didn't care. The raspberries had miraculously survived Morrigan's onslaught, and would have to do for dessert with a wedge of Brie and some Bath Olivers.

As she was draining the potatoes Bron appeared in the kitchen doorway.

'Sorry,' he said. 'I didn't mean to be quite so useless as a guest. I'm sure Ned would tell you it's in character, though. He doesn't have much faith in me as a provider of entertainment.'

216

'You're not alone,' said Georgia. 'My sister classes me with Mrs Whitehouse.'

'Why isn't your sister with one of your parents?' he asked, going over to the sink.

The towel was distinctly ragged, she remembered, as he began to wash his hands, but at least it was better than letting him loose in the bathroom, where there was probably a tidemark of henna round the washbasin. She dragged her mind back to his question.

'My father's in Sydney with his second wife, and Chloe doesn't get on with her. When our parents split up Chloe and I lived with our mother in East Africa. She's a botanist, and too busy saving the rain forest just now to have much time for anything else.'

'So you're in charge?'

'Until Chloe goes to college next year. Or decides to grow up, assuming I can survive that long,' said Georgia, putting the dish of salmon on the table as he dried his hands and hung the towel neatly on the rail, displaying its holes to the maximum effect.

'I'm not sure I'm going to make it through Ned's adolescence either,' he said, taking the chair opposite her. 'I wasn't much good at dealing with my own. Nico and I saw very little of our parents when my father was sent abroad. We spent most school holidays at Merlinslade. Nico used to get some breaks in London with Morrigan, though.'

She slid a piece of fish on to his plate. In spite of her lack of attention, the tender pink flakes of salmon were still moist, and smelt deliciously of herbs and wine.

'Nico mentioned that you never got on with Morrigan,' she prompted, intrigued by this further lowering of his guard.

'I wasn't very demonstrative, and because I didn't respond to him instantly like Nico, he started putting me down. It was done very subtly, of course. When I was very young I could only cope with it by keeping out of his way.'

Georgia was silent as she passed him the dish of potatoes. It was easy to imagine the sort of blight Morrigan could cast over a small boy's life.

'But as I grew older I began to see how cleverly he manipulated everyone: the staff at Merlinslade, my parents, even my grandfather until he saw the light. When I was Ned's age we finally had a terrific confrontation.'

'What about?' asked Georgia, fascinated.

He hesitated. 'Well, to put it crudely, he was trying to have it off with my mother,' he said in a dry voice. 'She and my father were usually close, but they rowed about something. He was a civil engineer who was sometimes sent overseas on consultancy trips, and the next time he went abroad she decided to stay behind at Merlinslade.'

He began to pile potatoes on to his plate, while she pushed the salad bowl towards him.

'At first I was pleased,' he went on, 'until I gradually began to realise that she wasn't happy. Then Morrigan turned up, somehow sussed out the situation, and made a play for her. I don't think it meant much to him. He just had to prove he could get anyone he wanted, but his pestering made her wretched. I grew up very fast in a few weeks. I decided I had to stop him.'

'What did you do?' asked Georgia in awe. It was hard enough for an adult to stop Morrigan.

'Something bloody stupid. I heard Morrigan chatting up my mother in the tack room. I took my grandfather's shot gun. It was usually locked away, but a fox had been taking the peacocks, and he kept it handy in his study. When I got back to the tack room I saw my mother leaving in tears. Morrigan was still there.'

He put down his knife and fork. His face was sombre.

'I was in a crazy, adolescent rage. I suppose I was partly jealous of his influence over my mother, though I didn't think of that till I was older. I threatened to kill him if he didn't leave her alone. I let off the gun at his feet. As soon as I'd done it I was terrified, but he was even more scared. He shot out of there like a rat out of a drain. He never bothered my mother again.'

'Didn't he tell your grandfather about the gun?' said Georgia, entranced. It was wonderful to think of Morrigan being so thoroughly discomfited, though she would never have imagined the self-controlled Bron as the lead in such a drama.

'No. I think he decided it was too risky.' He smiled and started eating. 'It was sheer luck he didn't lose his toes.'

'But how could you let Nico bring him into the theatre company, when you knew what he was like?' Georgia asked. It was something which had been puzzling her ever since the incident by the river.

'Because to be absolutely fair, in some ways he's had a rotten deal. My grandfather bought off Morrigan's mother with a miserable allowance to keep her out of the way. Morrigan's always bitterly resented that. And though my grandfather allowed Morrigan to come to Merlinslade, he tended to treat him as a second-class member of the family, though he was his eldest son. A lot of Morrigan's behaviour probably stems from early insecurity. It doesn't make me like him any more, but he's made such a big thing out of his conversion that I feel I ought to give him the benefit of the doubt. Sometimes, too, it's very hard to say no to Nico, as you know.'

'I'm not going out with Nico any more.'

He gave her a steady glance. 'I gathered that. He's on the phone to Esther Hallen at the rectory at least twice a day. I hope she can cope.'

'I think Nico may have met his match at last. And besides, Esther's already got a highly suitable boyfriend.'

'Then we'd all better put on our flak-jackets. He's going to be hell to live with if things don't work out for him,' said Bron cheerfully, helping himself to more potatoes. He was already halfway through the fish. 'This salmon's good. Sometimes we have trout from the river, but there's been no time for fishing lately.'

'The best sea-food I ever had was in the States. Baltimore crab cakes are out of this world.'

'I was in California a few years ago to take a look at the latest heavy plant. West coast cooking can be pretty good too.'

They talked about the States through the rest of the first course. So far the meal had been more relaxed than she'd expected, but as she was clearing away the plates he made a casual remark which almost threw her.

'I'm surprised you didn't want to stay in America. From what Nico tells me, work in the theatre's far better paid over there.'

Suddenly she wasn't hungry any more. Always the subject of

her failed marriage came up at the worst possible time.

'I was married in Baltimore, just for a few months,' she said, in the distant voice which usually put a stop to any further enquiries. 'I stayed till the divorce went through, but after that I just wanted to come home.'

To hide her distress she began to gather up the plates and stack them by the sink. When she came back to the table with the raspberries and a jug of cream he'd poured her another glass of wine, though he'd drunk very little himself during the meal.

'I know the feeling,' he said. 'You needed to go to ground for a while.'

'I thought I had gone to ground, until Chloe and Nico turned up,' she said with a rueful smile.

'Things do get better.'

It was his only comment, and he was silent as she arranged the cheese and biscuits on a board, and set the coffee to brew. She didn't look at him as she sat down and began to dish out the raspberries. Because he'd said nothing more she suddenly found herself talking about it after all.

'It was such a muddle at the time,' she said. 'Nothing was straight in my mind. That's partly why I didn't want to go on with Nico, because it still isn't straight. I keep having this feeling that it'll go on being like that until I can stop resenting Blake. I suppose that sounds unbalanced to you.'

'Even now it's hard not to resent Imogen for what she's done to Ned,' he said, pouring cream over the fruit, 'though I think he's beginning to settle down at Merlinslade. He never stops going on about the wonders of your flat. I should be studying it for future reference. God knows if I'll ever pull the house into shape.'

She took a long draught of wine in her relief that they'd got off the subject of marriage.

'The farm I can just about deal with,' he went on. 'The house feels more and more like a millstone every day.'

'But the house is marvellous! I mean, it could be,' she added more temperately. 'Take the great hall, for instance. If you toned down that clinical white paint, moved the furniture around a little, had some less formal flower arrangements . . .'

She broke off, gazing at him suspiciously. He looked as if he was trying not to laugh.

'I'm afraid I chose the clinical paint in desperation. I simply wanted the place to look clean. And I'm sure Nico's told you Mrs Meads does a nose dive every time we try to move things. I'm still trying to think of a way to get round her. Something has to be done before we let the public in.'

'You really need a professional interior designer,' she said. 'There are some good ones in Bath.'

'We can't afford it yet.'

'But the house has so much potential. A professional could make all the rooms look as good as the red boudoir, and then you'd have a winner on your hands instead of a millstone.'

'Ah, yes, the red boudoir.' A different note entered his voice. 'I forgot Nico took you upstairs.'

She tensed. They were entering dangerous ground again, and she was beginning to feel immensely tired after the long day, but unexpectedly he let the subject drop.

'How did you become interested in stage design?' he asked. 'I don't suppose there were many theatres in your part of Africa.'

'My grandmother was a theatre addict. I used to go with her when we were home on leave. The first play I ever saw was a pantomime at the Theatre Royal here in Bath when I was six. I was immediately hooked.'

She tried to conceal her fatigue as she went to fetch the coffee. He'd demolished most of the Brie and biscuits by the time she'd finished telling him about her training and the productions she'd worked on before she went to the States. He'd even seen one of them.

'I was stationed in London for a while,' he said. 'I've still got a flat there. I ought to sell it, but the only way I can stay sane is by going up there now and then, and taking in some concerts.'

She was trying to spin her coffee out to keep herself awake. Suddenly he pushed back his chair. She stared at him, wondering if her sleepiness was so evident that he was offended.

'Are you going? You really don't have to. I've got some brandy somewhere if you'd like it. Or are you worried about Ned? I should have asked you if you wanted to phone him.'

'It's all right. Nico's holding the fort. They're probably watching some highly unsuitable video together. But I'd better not have any more to drink before I go, much as I'd like to. I was going to suggest that I did the washing-up, while you finished your coffee in the sitting room.'

She began to protest.

'I won't break anything, I swear,' he said with a grin. 'I once washed up for a whole platoon for a week when I was on basic training. Go on, you look as if you're about to keel over.'

She was too tired to argue. She went into the sitting room with her coffee, switched on the ten o'clock television news to keep herself awake, and watched in a half-doze. He reappeared after the weather forecast, rolling down his sleeves. Rusalka, who'd gone to sleep after obligingly disposing of some left-over moussaka, looked up expectantly.

'It's been an excellent evening, but I'd better get on my way,' Bron said. 'Nico'll be feeling the strain soon, and Rusalka needs a walk before bed.'

'Thank you for bringing me home,' she said, as they went into the hall.

'I think I've had the best bargain.' He paused at the door. 'And I wonder if you'd do me yet another favour.? We've some old clothes stored in the attics at Merlinslade. Some of them go back a long way. Could you spare the time to take a look at them next week? I have to decide which to sell, and which to put on display.'

'Of course,' she said. 'I'd love to. It'd be fascinating.'

He said goodbye briskly and went up the steps two at a time. When he'd gone she returned to the kitchen. The dried plates were neatly stacked on the table, the cutlery ranked next to it with military precision, even the dishcloth wrung out and folded on the draining board. The saucepans had been scoured until they were as bright as the day they were bought.

She sat down and surveyed them. For some odd reason she felt like crying. The window sash was open at the bottom, and the movement of the curtains caught her eye. The empty milk bottle stood on the ledge, washed and gleaming too, and in it he'd stuck one of the Japanese sunflowers. She began to laugh instead.

★ ★ ★

The production period was well under way. Georgia always found it exhilarating, for then her designs started to have an existence of their own. She was at her busiest, constantly monitoring the workload, solving endless problems, and generally trying to keep both her staff and the actors happy.

After her next visit to the Sanctuary, Chloe defiantly told Georgia that she'd taken part in a preliminary photo session for publicity. With a superhuman effort Georgia managed not to make any critical remarks. She knew it was vital to rebuild her bridges with Chloe before Morrigan's next move. She engineered a costume call for Sean when Chloe next came to work in the wardrobe, hoping that he might provide another bulwark against Morrigan. Chloe too made an effort at rebuilding bridges, and at lunch went off with Sean to The Mortal Man.

Georgia ate some sandwiches while she made a few last-minute adjustments to Redvers' costumes before his second fitting that afternoon, when he would see them made up in the actual fabrics. Zelda had agreed to come along too as a trouble-shooter.

She appeared promptly with a Redvers who looked irritable and tired.

'Here we are,' she said in a bright voice, as though she was bringing a fractious three year-old to a party he didn't want to attend. 'We're longing to see the real McCoy, aren't we, Redvers?'

He gave a gloomy grunt. 'It's the cloak I'm worried about still. No one seems to have grasped quite how significant it is.'

'Why don't you wait till you've seen it made up?' said Georgia. 'I've laid everything out in the fitting area. We'll wait in the office while you change.'

As soon as Georgia had shut the office door behind them, Zelda rushed to a window and flung it wide open.

'Phewee!' she said, searching for her cigarettes. 'If tobacco doesn't kill me, the power surges will – they come on all the time when Redvers is so damn' negative. I've been doing my best to put him in a good frame of mind for this fitting, but he's been in one hell of a mood all day. Morrigan was in the theatre this morning, and Redvers got incredibly uptight while he was around.'

'Perhaps he's having a late male menopause,' said Georgia with a smile. 'Things can't be easy for him with Morrigan stealing his thunder.'

'I don't know why Redvers is so paranoid about him. The rest of the company think he's great, and his music's wonderful. Anyway, it's good that the wardrobe's quiet for the fitting. Where are the others?'

'Annie's gone to London on a shopping trip, Jenny and Kevin are in the dyeing room, it's Sumitra's day off, and Chloe's still at lunch. I'm not too pleased about that. She ought to have been back half an hour ago. She hasn't been in the best of moods lately.'

'What's wrong with her?'

'*I'm* what's wrong.'

'Thank God I'm not that age again. But in another two years you'll probably be worrying because she's too well adjusted.'

When they entered the fitting area Redvers was standing with his back to the mirror in the long velvet robe and cloak, his arms outstretched, glaring at his image over his shoulder as if Popeye was staring back at him instead of Prospero.

'You look magnificent, Redvers, truly Dante-esque,' said Zelda, in a voice which made it very clear that she'd done enough shoring up of the male ego for one day.

'Dante-esque is right,' said Redvers scathingly. 'Much as I admire your talents, Georgia my dear, this cloak appears to have been constructed in the inferno.'

Georgia stood back to study it, trying not to let him undermine her judgement. She knew he would instantly exploit any diffidence on her part.

'The material gives a wonderful rippling effect,' said Zelda nobly.

'Don't forget it'll look quite different when the embroidery's finished. You have to trust us a little,' Georgia said.

'I don't feel happy about it. I'm never going to be able to relax into the part while the cloak's wrong,' said Redvers fretfully. He sank on to the sofa, holding his hand to his brow. 'And it's been a beast of a day. Couldn't we discuss this another time?'

224

'Won't you at least try on your court costume while you're here?' Georgia coaxed him.

'I'm just not in the mood. You'd only be flogging a very dead horse.' He intercepted an exasperated glance from Zelda to Georgia. 'I know you'll both think this is simply an old man's histrionics, but I'm beginning to feel I've made a dreadful mistake taking on the part at all.'

Zelda appeared to be on the verge of spontaneous combustion.

'I've had enough of this, Redvers. Everyone's supporting you, and the rest of the cast couldn't be more enthused about your interpretation of the part. You must try to cultivate a more positive mental attitude.'

As Redvers began to do another imitation of a tortoise, and Georgia realised they'd now lost all hope of his trying on the court dress that afternoon, Zelda's paging machine went off in her pocket. She leaped up from her seat on the arm of the sofa, looking as if she'd been let out of the dentist's chair.

'Right, they need me for the next rehearsal. I'll leave you to go on with the fitting, Redvers, and I don't want to hear one more word about the cloak. It's perfect, you're perfect, and the sooner you accept that fact, the better for all of us.'

She almost toppled a dummy dressed in Miranda's wedding gown in her haste to escape. As Redvers began to fumble with the clasp of the cloak a pulse was beating heavily in his neck. He looked worn out and dispirited.

'So strong-minded, American women,' he said in a fading voice.

'Let's give the court dress a miss today,' said Georgia. 'If you'd like to come into the office when you've changed, I'll make you a cup of tea.'

'Real tea?' said Redvers, looking fractionally more cheerful. 'Zelda made me try some hideous herbal brew the other day. It tasted like goat's piss.'

'Nothing but the best Assam,' said Georgia, 'and there are some chocolate biscuits too.'

As she made the tea she saw Chloe slip back into the workroom.

'Who's that pretty little thing?' Redvers asked. 'She was in the pub at lunchtime.' He was sitting in the arm chair, and looking less hard done by.

'My sister, Chloe. She's helping us with the jewellery.'

'A nice child. Young Marchant clearly thinks so too.'

Georgia gave him his tea, and the tin of biscuits. She'd even managed to find a proper cup and saucer, which were usually reserved for Mrs Meads, who'd taken to coming into the wardrobe from time to time to reminisce about the good old days.

'First drinkable tea I've had in this place,' said Redvers. 'Better than that witch's brew from the machine in the green room.'

'Mrs Meads would make a pot for you in the kitchen if you asked. She's your most devoted fan. She saw you several times at the Theatre Royal.'

Redvers brightened still more. 'Ah, that generation, they still appreciate real acting.'

'We all do,' said Georgia firmly. 'And I know you're too much of a pro to let the cloak throw you at this stage. But of course I'll redesign it if you still feel it's wrong when it's finished.'

Redvers seemed not to have heard. 'There's a decent atmosphere in here,' he said. 'That bloody green room is hell sometimes. Full of chattering children.'

'Children who admire you tremendously,' said Georgia, wondering just how thickly she dared lay on the flattery. 'And you have so much to teach them. They're all in awe of you.'

'Morrigan isn't. Nico must have gone off his rocker when he decided to employ him. I warned him, but he wouldn't listen.'

'Has Morrigan been getting at you again?'

'His usual two-edged remarks. "I loved the way you purposely hammed up that speech, Redvers." "What a fascinating interpretation, Redvers, to portray Prospero on the verge of senile decay." And today, "What poignancy you gave the farewell speech, Redvers, when you made them last words of a defeated old man." Impudent beggar! Whatever else Prospero may be, he'd not defeated, and nor am I.'

'Then don't let Morrigan get you down,' said Georgia wishing she could take her own advice. 'He's jealous. He gets his effects partly through manipulation. Everything you do is pure art.'

'Do you really think so?' said Redvers.

'Of course I do. We all do. You've just got to believe it.'

Redvers began to look brighter. He took a Jaffa cake, and crunched into it.

'Do you know, I think I might manage to try on the court dress after all.'

'Thanks for keeping in the background while Redvers was here,' Georgia said to Chloe afterwards.

'I remembered you said it made him jumpy to have an audience during a fitting,' she answered, her head bent over the necklace she was making for Miranda's wedding dress. Her expression had gone from winter to summer since returning from the pub.

'Did you have a good time with Sean?'

'Not bad,' said Chloe nonchalantly, as she carefully glued tiny pieces of lace sprayed with gold paint to simulate filigree to imitation drops of pearl.

'That's not bad either,' said Georgia, as Chloe laid the necklace carefully to one side to dry. 'You really do have a gift for this sort of thing.'

'I'm working on something for Sean next,' said Chloe eagerly as she assembled the pieces for a jewelled belt. She'd cut the linked shapes from industrial felt, stiffened them with sizing, and with a glue gun was about to draw a design on them, to which she'd fix imitation silver leaf.

Georgia watched critically as she applied the leaf. 'That's fine. Just let it cool a bit before you go on, and don't forget to remove the surplus leaf with a hard brush, not a soft one.'

'It's great working here,' said Chloe, looking up with a confiding smile. 'Loads better than Fruits of the Earth.'

Georgia wondered if she dared push her luck a little further and mention the Disciples.

'How are things going at the Sanctuary?' she asked, trying to sound as though she didn't care what the answer was.

'The plans for the Foundation are really coming on. Morrigan's asked all the Disciples in work to contribute half their income to the fund, just temporarily of course. The group's a bit short of cash at the moment.'

Georgia bit back an exclamation of outrage just in time. She

227

didn't want to rebuild more ruined bridges.

'That seems rather a large slice,' she said. 'The church steward-ship scheme Esther runs only asks for ten per cent at the most.'

'The Church of England doesn't need any extra,' said Chloe in an aggrieved voice. 'Everyone knows it's rolling in dosh. You've only got to go in a church to see what I mean – the altar's always groaning with silver chalices and candlesticks. I don't think it's right when there are so many poor people around.'

'I'm sure Esther would tell you it's not as simple as that,' said Georgia. 'They can hardly pay the bills at the rectory.'

'Brighid doesn't make a penny's profit from the Sanctuary,' Chloe went on. 'She's an absolute saint. Everyone says so. She needs every bit of help she can get.'

'What does Natty think of all this?'

'She's not going there any more. She's taken up astrology classes in Glastonbury instead.'

'And is Morrigan giving half his income to the foundation?' Georgia asked, wishing Chloe was safely casting horoscopes too.

'Of course he is! He told us that yesterday.'

'Then I don't understand why you have to give as well. I should have thought his contribution alone would be quite enough to start with.'

'It's the principle of the thing, so that we're all on the same footing, all sharing and sacrificing together. The group's meant to be based on trust and fellowship, after all. You're getting twitchy again, Georgy, I can tell.'

'I am not twitchy,' she said through clenched teeth, 'but I should like to know exactly how you'll be able to check what he does with your money. You know how loosely the group's organised.'

'You're wrong again!' said Chloe proudly. 'Morrigan's going to have rules. He says they're essential if we want to be successful.'

'Rules? What sort of rules? Don't you know that's always when the trouble starts in this sort of organisation, when one person begins to impose rules on the rest?'

'You're putting me down again!' Chloe's hands shook as she glued a loose piece of filigree back on a pearl. 'You're making the Sanctuary sound stupid and sinister, when it isn't. I'm not going to discuss this any more. Brighid says I have to learn to shut off from things that upset me.'

'How convenient,' said Georgia, thinking how wonderful it would be if she could shut off too.

Chloe got up with a look of wounded dignity. 'I can't work when you're like this,' she said. 'I'm going to have tea in the green room with Sean.'

In desperation Georgia decided that her mother would have to take over responsibility for Chloe. Giving away so much of her income was bad enough, but Morrigan's imposing rules on the group sounded ominous in the extreme. Next morning, after Chloe had gone to Fruits of the Earth, Georgia made a hugely expensive peak time phone call to Africa, which did at least stand some chance of catching her mother in the research station.

Astoundingly the switchboard operator at the station managed to run her mother to earth in the herbarium. She sounded infuriated by the interruption. Georgia could imagine her as she'd seen her so many times, impatiently holding the phone in one hand, and minutely examining some hapless plant with the other.

'I really don't see why you're wasting your money,' she said snappily. 'There's absolutely nothing I can do at such a distance. You know Chloe's crazes. She'll soon get tired of this Sanctuary place.'

'It's more than a craze. She's really serious. I think there's a strong chance she'll decide to throw over college next year in favour of the group.'

'That wouldn't be so disastrous, would it? Lots of students take time out, and it might help her to learn about the real world.'

'The Sanctuary's nothing like the real world. The woman running the teaching side is all right, but there's a man who's recently taken over the administration who's bad news.'

'What do you mean "bad news"? Do try to be more specific.' Her mother's voice was at its most brisk.

'He's got a very strong personality. He's a great manipulator. He's persuaded Chloe to give part of her salary to the group, and she earns little enough as it is. He's talking of setting up rules, as well. I don't like the sound of it.'

As she spoke she was aware of how lame her objections sounded.

Beatrice gave a dry chuckle. 'It'd do Chloe good to have a few rules in her life. And once she finds she doesn't have enough money for new clothes she'll soon stop giving it away. Be fair, Georgia. What you've just told me certainly isn't serious enough for me to drop everything and fly home.'

'She's your child, not mine, and at the moment she needs you, not me. You haven't seen her for almost a year. You've got to believe this is serious. You must come and talk to her.'

There was a long silence at the other end. Georgia, wound up like a spring with frustration, could imagine her mother deliberately weighing up her options. She always tried to reduce her life and everyone else's to the level of an emotional game, a game which it was perfectly easy to win if one simply made the most rational moves.

'Well, I was planning a very quick visit early next month,' her mother said. 'Just to bring some plants to Kew, and talk to one or two of the key conservation charities. The negotiations to turn the forest into a reserve are at such a critical stage that I daren't stay away for more than a couple of days. I won't be able to get to Bath, but if you bring Chloe to London we could meet for lunch.'

'Couldn't you come to Bath for one night?' Georgia pleaded. 'It'd be so much better for you to talk to Chloe in the flat.'

She wasn't even sure if her mother was listening to her. She could hear her talking to someone who seemed to have just come into the laboratory.

'And anyway, I'm not certain I could persuade Chloe to leave Bath at the moment,' Georgia persisted. 'She's so absorbed in what's going on here.'

Her mother's voice sounded tinnily across the miles again. 'I must rush. We're expecting a visit from the Environment Minister this morning. I'll send you a date when I've been through my diary. Don't worry – we'll all meet in London next month, and I'll sort Chloe out then.'

Chapter 12

It was raining when Georgia next saw Bron. Heavy clouds had driven across the escarpment, blurring the landscape and filling the river with a turbulent brown flood. She'd only just arrived at the workshop, and was shaking out her umbrella when he called her on the extension, a call so business-like that their supper together might never have happened, to ask if they could look at the clothes in the attic after lunch.

As she waited for him in the great hall she already regretted the arrangement. The house was cold and gloomy in the rain. When Bron arrived he was wearing a heavy checked shirt with a pair of Levis whose patched and faded state was completely authentic. He carried a carpenter's canvas hold-all, and looked as preoccupied as ever.

They went up to the first floor in silence, and took a back stair to a dusty corridor on the second floor which led to the servants' rooms. It was even chillier here. Georgia wished she'd brought a sweater to put on over her short-sleeved blouse.

Bron opened a cupboard-like door at the very end. Immediately in front of them was a wooden staircase. The worn and splintered treads creaked beneath their feet as Georgia followed him to another door at the top. He produced a ring of keys from his pocket. The door opened with a grating squeak.

They were in a long attic lit by small dormer windows paned with watery glass, and so shadowed that until her eyes became used to the gloom she could scarcely make out its contents. Trails of cobweb hung from every cranny. The poles of ancient battle funerary banners lay across the massive oak beams supporting the roof, their tattered webs of faded silk swinging gently downwards in the draught from a broken ventilation grille in the gable end.

With a fine disregard for conservation the household detritus of four centuries was stacked casually about the floor, like rubble left by a slow-moving glacier. Georgia's first glance alone took in suits of dented armour, a couple of crinoline cages hanging from rusty nails in the beams, a penny-farthing bicycle with a buckled rear wheel, an old knife-grinding machine, ramparts of broken furniture, and a stack of empty barrels against the gable wall. In the middle of the room was a billiard table. Its sturdy rounded legs peeped like a Victorian music hall dancer's from the make-shift dust cover of a lace-edged banqueting cloth.

She felt as if she'd strayed into some bizarre antiques gallery. As the wind whined through the rafters, the thought came to her that if the kitchen had been perfect for *Cinderella*, this could easily double as a set for *Dracula*. She almost burst into giggles, imagining Bron as the villainous Count. He'd look splendid in a caped cloak and riding boots. She encountered a suspicious look from him, and to divert his attention went to examine one of the crinoline cages.

As she swung its whalebone hoops towards her, dislodging a cloud of dust, she heard a scrabbling noise on the beam above her head. She looked up, and saw the ghostly form of a barn-owl sitting in the gloom. It looked like some hoary and inscrutable sage. One yellow eye was open, staring at her. It winked sleepily and shuffled along the beam, tucking its head sideways into its feathers.

'We've always had owls up here,' said Bron. 'They get in through the grille. Nico and I used to think they had something to do with Merlin when we were young.'

'I thought you said the Merlin tradition was nonsense,' said Georgia, much amused that he'd let this reminiscence slip. 'I'm surprised you haven't blocked the grille.'

'The owls keep the mice down,' said Bron stonily, going over to a zinc steamer trunk and an ancient oak chest which had been hauled into the centre of the room. He took the keys from his pocket again, and opened the trunk. 'This is the first batch of clothes. They were part of my grandmother's trousseau, so they date from the thirties. The older stuff is in the chests.'

He sat down on the chest, notebook in hand. 'If you describe everything briefly to me, I'll make notes as we go along.'

The atmosphere was intensely distracting: the tattered banners swinging in the draught, the empty helmets that seemed to stare at her, and the owl presiding above it all like a totem on the beam. Yet Bron looked as if he was about to compile nothing more exciting than a list of agricultural supplies.

'How can you sit there as though – as though this is some DIY warehouse?' she demanded impulsively. 'It's incredible. It really is like Merlin's hideaway.'

He put down the notebook, and slowly looked around him. His expression thawed.

'This was our favourite place when we were children. Nico and I used to put on the hauberks and helmets, and have tremendous battles in here on rainy days. I'm surprised the owls didn't leave us for good.'

Georgia lifted the lid of the trunk, and was met by the haunting scent of L'Heure Bleu, rising from tissued layers of perfect evening garments, exquisitely sewn, adorned with diamanté and swansdown and fringes of bead, and bias-cut to move with the wearer as she shimmied through the dances of the day.

She rolled away the covering from the billiard table, laying the garments on the green baize surface and describing them one by one. Bron's face was impassive as he made punctilious notes.

'You could do a wonderful display with these if you set it up with your grandmother's portrait,' she said when she'd got to the bottom of the trunk.

'I suppose so.' His voice was almost bored.

For a moment she was annoyed. He seemed to have forgotten that he was getting her time and expertise for nothing. She was about to make a sharp comment when she remembered something Nico had said to her about Bron's closeness to his grandmother, and realised just in time that cataloguing these particular clothes was probably making the business of opening Merlinslade to the public even more difficult for him.

'It must be hard to put something as intimate as this on display,' she said. 'Do you remember your grandmother well?'

'I do. The house hasn't been alive since she died. But anything

233

that'll draw the crowds has to be done, or the estate won't survive.' His tone was a little too matter-of-fact.

She folded the clothes back into their layers of tissue, trying to treat them as gently as possible.

'What's Ned doing today?' she asked, in an effort at diversion as she covered the last dress. 'Haven't the holidays started?'

Bron got up to relock the trunk. 'I'm afraid so. We've already had a row because he doesn't think I've set up an adequate programme of entertainments for him. I had to say he could come up here when he'd finished helping Mrs Meads wash up, though I'm not keen for him to racket around in the attics on his own.'

Georgia began to laugh. 'But you did when you were young. You treat Ned as if he's an unexploded bomb. He's not as bad as all that.'

At last a smile lifted the corners of Bron's mouth. 'Don't you believe it. He was so turned on by the winter Olympics that he set up a luge run on the stairs last holidays. I caught him doing timed descents on one of those silver trays from the great hall. Christ knows how he didn't wreck himself, let alone the staircase.'

'At least Ned's inventive. Couldn't that be your genes coming out?'

'He doesn't stand much of a chance if they are.'

'He could help in the wardrobe, if you're stuck for things for him to do. I'm there most of the time, and Annie'll keep him in line if I'm not. He might like to make some of the props. Zelda's son worked for me for the whole of a summer vacation in Baltimore, and he was about Ned's age.'

The suggestion, made on the spur of the moment, was worth any potential problems just to see Bron's startled stare.

'Are you sure? Do you realise what you're letting yourself in for?'

'I know Ned fairly well by now,' said Georgia. He'd come to tea with her a couple of times since his first visit. 'He just needs to have a bit of lateral thought applied to him,' she added mischievously.

Bron pushed away the trunk, and manhandled the chest into a better position. He straightened, hands on hips, looking at her with amusement in his face.

'You're quite an organiser, aren't you?' he said. 'I wonder if I should consult you on some of my other problems? You've perhaps done some lateral thinking about them as well.'

'Perhaps,' she said. The tease had become promising. Bron in this different persona was to be encouraged.

'All right, then. See if you can solve this one. How can I persuade Mrs Meads to give up cooking the theatre company's lunches? She's convinced she's Merlinslade's own Prue Leith. She's so immensely good to Ned, to all of us, that I hate to upset her, yet Nico says the cast'll go on strike if they eat much more of her food.'

Georgia considered the problem. She'd been growing very fond of Mrs Meads, who had recently confided that she wasn't at all happy cooking for the theatre company but felt it was her duty to continue in that role. Life would be much easier for everyone if she could put her energies into doing what she knew and liked.

'Why don't you encourage her to go on some short residential course for professional museum guides, and get in someone else to do the lunch-time cooking while she's away? Presumably you and Nico can fend for yourselves for a few days.'

Bron gave her a quizzical look. 'I think we're capable of opening a can or two, or driving to the nearest take-away. But what about when she returns, and wants to take over again? The house won't be open to the public till next year.'

Georgia was suddenly inspired. 'You could have a knock-out of a uniform ready for her – maybe a sort of air-hostess outfit with a really imposing hat – and put her on to training her village friends as part of her team of official guides. She'd love it, and she could start by organising small informal tours of the house for the theatre audiences. That way she'd have no time for cooking.'

'Brilliant,' said Bron, now looking impressed as well as diverted. 'Except that there's no one else to do the company's catering. Mrs Samms is too old, and Nico hasn't enough cash to employ professional caterers.'

'I know someone who might help. Kim. She lives at the rectory. She's a terrific cook, and desperate for a job. She's not exactly a Sloane, though.'

He pounced on this instantly. 'And what makes you think I'd want a Sloane?'

She hesitated. 'Well, you do sometimes seem to be on a slightly different plane from the rest of us.'

He began to smile again. 'So if she's not a Sloane, what is she? Terrific cooks aren't usually desperate for a job.'

'She's on probation. She didn't do anything serious, though. She was just looking out for herself.'

'You'd better tell me about it,' said Bron, throwing open the chest.

Georgia wished now that she'd never mentioned Kim's past. She told him the little she knew. 'She was living with some travellers. The landlord fired her van, so – so – she beat him up. She didn't really hurt him, just gave him a black eye.'

Bron laughed outright. 'She sounds exactly what Nico needs. All right, if you ask her to come over, I'll have a talk to her.'

He'd been so surprisingly unjudgemental that she found herself rashly offering to make Mrs Meads a uniform as she delved into the chest. It held a fascinating hotchpotch of treasures: an eighteenth-century court dress which could have belonged to Letitia, brocade waistcoats, christening robes, a Victorian wedding gown with a veil of Honiton lace, and part of a trousseau to go with it. When Bron had noted down the contents, she began to put the garments carefully away.

'I really can't help you much more,' she said. 'You'll have to ask someone from the Museum of Costume in Bath to advise you on display.'

'At least I know what I'm dealing with now, thanks to you,' he said. He picked up the bag of carpenter's tools. 'While you finish here I want to take a look at the floorboards under the grille. The rain's been blowing in on them for years.'

He went down to the end of the attic, and began to do some vigorous rearranging among the barrels piled up against the wall. Georgia was so absorbed in her own work that she didn't notice that the attic had become unusually quiet until she'd finally closed the lid of the chest.

She wandered down to the gable end. Bron had moved most of the barrels, and was standing in the gloom contemplating the final one, which rested on its side against the wall. Apart from the age of its blackened oak staves it looked perfectly ordinary in every way.

'There's something odd about this,' he said. 'Listen.'

He rolled the barrel a few feet in her direction. She could hear something soft and heavy thudding about inside.

'It's the only one that's sealed,' he said. 'There's no bung hole, which is even odder, so it can't have been intended for cider or beer. These old barrels were so well coopered that they were completely airtight. It looks as though it was made specifically to preserve or hide whatever's inside. Perhaps even both.'

'And what do you think that could be?'

He looked up at her with an expression exactly like Ned's when he was about to embark on something he knew was forbidden. 'God alone knows. The ancestors'll probably turn in their graves, but let's have a look.'

As he trundled the barrel into the middle of the room, Georgia began to envisage all sorts of peculiar contents. She even wondered if one of the more eccentric Carwithens could have tried to preserve the body of some beloved pet in the barrel. She certainly didn't feel up to coping with a mummy.

Bron glanced at her as he upended the barrel.

'Would you rather wait downstairs?'

'Of course not!' she said recklessly.

With a hammer and chisel Bron began to force away one of the iron hoops which bound the staves together. As the hammer blows vibrated through the attic, puffs of dust drifted down from the beams. The owl launched itself from its perch, and flapped away through the grille into the open air.

The hoop finally clattered to the floor. Bron inserted the chisel between the staves, and they gently sprang apart. The top bounced to the ground and rolled away among the furniture.

He inserted his arm and withdrew a long, thin parcel about a yard in length, wrapped in an outer covering of leather, and tied with sealed linen tapes. Georgia began to relax a little. At least it didn't look like a corpse.

He laid it on the billiard table, and carefully sliced through the tapes with a pocket knife.

237

'It feels like fabric inside,' he said. 'Perhaps you should do the rest.'

Gingerly Georgia eased away the leather, disclosing layer upon layer of the finest lawn, rolled like tissue paper around something else within. She caught a kingfisher flash of embroidery. Holding her breath, she shook out the garment revealed under the final wrapping of lawn. A cloak, a river of indigo velvet, shimmered in her grasp.

She spread it on the billiard table, outer side upwards. The silky lustre of its surface reflected the light like a deep pool. On the back was embroidered the Queen of the Thrones of Water, wearing a robe stitched in every imaginable shade of lighter blue, from turquoise to lapis-lazuli, sapphire to aquamarine. Her hair flowed in golden streams over her outstretched arms to join the waves at her feet.

Bron's face was incredulous.

'Merlin's cloak! Exactly like the woodcut! So it really did exist.'

Georgia was reverently examining every detail – the exquisitely couched stitches, the shot silk lining, the filigree clasp. Finally she straightened, smiling at Bron.

'It's in marvellous condition, mainly because of the way it's been stored,' she said. 'It was embroidered in the eighteenth century, I should guess. Obviously it's a copy of the cloak in the woodcut, but even so it's a magnificent piece of work.'

'I wonder if Letitia could have done it before the original was destroyed?' said Bron slowly, still staring at the cloak.

Georgia leaned over it, smoothing out the last folds. Bron registered almost detachedly the soft forward slide of her hair, lustrous as the velvet beneath her hand. He was still trying to adjust to the existence of something he'd never expected to see. As he grew older and his marriage fell apart, he'd come to disbelieve in marvels of every sort. He wasn't sure if what he was feeling now was something to do with the cloak, or with her, or a mixture of both. Either way it was far safer to suppress it.

Her face was serious. 'I know I'm being completely illogical, and I know the cloak's only a copy, but doesn't it seem to you almost like the spirit of Merlinslade? It really would be hard to put something like this on public show.'

She was being illogical, he thought, and yet she was again offering him understanding as she had done over the contents of the trunk, and for a second time he was about to brush it aside, because he wasn't sure if he could handle what it might lead to.

'It's such wonderful work,' she said wistfully, still gazing at the embroidery.

The rain had increased, pelting against the windows as though someone was throwing handfuls of gravel against the glass. She shivered, and hugged her bare arms over her chest, defining the soft swell of her breasts beneath her blouse.

'You're cold,' said Bron. His voice sounded odd in his ears as he realised he was about to behave in a dangerously irrational manner after all, and that he wasn't going to be able to stop himself.

Georgia looked questioningly at him, wondering why his tone had changed so abruptly. He picked up the cloak, and wrapped it round her, lapping it across her breast. It was surprisingly light and immensely warm. As he did so she heard a soft, feathery rushing noise.

She looked up. The owl had returned. It gently passed above their heads, its pale wings cleaving the dusty half-light like the arms of a swimmer slicing through the sea. Bron's hands had stayed on her shoulders, and while she was still looking upwards he bent his head and kissed her.

It was a very brief salutation, over almost as swiftly as the owl's flight, and she was so startled that she made no attempt to draw back. Her first reaction was to think in a puzzled way that she didn't feel scared, though she was caught both by his hands and the cloak. She could smell the dust and sweat mingled on his skin. For a man who was normally so direct the kiss was surprisingly hesitant, yet she sensed the feeling behind it, just as she'd been aware of the banked-up fire in the unprepossessing range on her first visit to Merlinslade. And as if that hidden warmth, as controlled as it was, had communicated itself to her in some almost magical way, she realised she wanted him to continue.

The thought was so ridiculously unrealistic that even as he let her go she began to rationalise the event. The incident had simply been a chance product of the odd atmosphere in the attic, and the excitement of finding the cloak. It meant nothing at all.

The cloak slithered from her shoulders and dropped back on to the billiard table, the folds trailing down to the floor. She hastily retrieved it, and spread it out once more, still feeling as if her carefully directed life had gone into a violent skid. She was glad he couldn't see her face.

'That wasn't necessary,' she said, looking up at last after she'd spent a very long time rearranging the cloak.

He'd moved to the window, and was standing with his back to the light. 'I know. I'm sorry. It happened to seem right at the time.' His voice still sounded strange.

'And so you did exactly what you wanted,' she said. 'Just like Nico.'

She hadn't intended to be so aggressive, but it was the only way she could distance herself from the incident fast enough. Bron was far more unpredictable than Nico, and his marital track record was as poor as her own.

He turned, frowning. 'That isn't fair. You know it wasn't like Nico. It meant nothing, nothing at all.'

This Bron she could deal with more easily. 'Now you sound exactly like your brother,' she snapped back.

Another handful of rain pelted against the window. The wind had increased. The roof timbers were groaning like a sailing ship in a high wind.

'For Christ's sake, do you have to go on so? I've said I'm sorry. It won't happen again.'

'Good. So we've got things back in perspective, then,' she said in a voice as closely modelled on Chloe's ex-headmistress as she could make it.

She started to wind the tape into a neat bundle, dropped it, and began to wind it all over again. When she'd finished she looked up at him challengingly, expecting her last remark to have closed the subject for good.

He was still frowning at her. 'But I thought you'd just been trying to tell me they were never out of perspective,' he said.

'And I thought you wanted to drop the subject,' she snapped.

'You didn't give me a straight answer.'

Her reply died on her lips as the sound of the rain and the rattle of loose tiles was suddenly joined by a heavy thumping, which became the noise of feet on the stairs. Bron hastily began to put away the hammer and chisel. Georgia found herself winding the tape once more. A few seconds later Ned crashed through the door.

He was wearing a reversed baseball cap, and a baggy T shirt over Bermuda shorts. He gave them an accusing look.

'I knew you'd start without me. You might have waited!' he said, taking a flying jump over a stool made from an elephant's foot as he bounced up to the billiard table.

He came to an abrupt halt, braking his impetus with his hands against the edge.

'Wow! What's this. Seriously unreal!'

'It's a copy of the cloak in that old wood engraving I showed you in the library,' Bron said. 'And for God's sake don't start pawing it.'

'You mean Merlin's cloak? Mega, mega brill!'

Bron hauled him back by the scruff of his T shirt just as he was about to grab it.

'I only wanted to try it on,' said Ned in an aggrieved tone.

He had recently started to become interested in his appearance. Under the baseball cap was a startling new hair cut, shorn like a skinhead to the tops of his ears, then gelled forward into a jutting quiff. Georgia was sure he was wearing one of Nico's American T shirts as well.

'Definitely not,' said Bron. 'At least, not till Georgia's checked it over. And your hands don't look too clean to me.'

'Of course they're clean! Haven't I just been washing up? You've got dust all over your arms, and I bet you've both had a go.'

Georgia was now desperate to minimise any further risk of intimacy with Bron, to get everything back on to an ordinary footing, and banish the whole strange, surreal episode.

'I think we should take the cloak downstairs to check it in a better light. The table in the great hall would be a good place,' she said hurriedly, beginning to roll it up. 'If it still seems all right perhaps Ned can try it on then.'

'Ace,' said Ned. 'So what are you both hanging about for?'

He rocketed off towards the door. Georgia followed him down the stairs with Bron close behind her bearing the cloak in its lawn wrapping. Ned chattered to her over his shoulder, something about a scramble track which he and Jason were constructing in the woods. She scarcely heard him, and neither, apparently, when she caught a glimpse of his face, did Bron.

The great hall was empty, though a single bar of an electric fire as ancient as the one in the kitchen had been switched on, which meant that Mrs Meads intended to serve tea there shortly. When Bron had unrolled the cloak on the refectory table, Georgia began to examine it again, trying to ignore his presence next to her, and Ned's heavy breathing in her ear as he peered over her shoulder.

Nico's voice made her jump. He'd come into the hall unheard, and was advancing towards the table, wearing a scarlet towelling dressing gown over his rehearsal costume.

'What's all this? A jumble sale?' he asked. He stopped abruptly. 'Jesus! Do you realise what you've got there? It's Merlin's cloak! Georgia and I were looking at the woodcut only the other day.'

'We had managed to work that out,' said Bron.

'For Christ's sake, Bron, do you have to be quite so laid back? Where the hell did you find it?' Nico was still gazing disbelievingly at the shimmering fabric.

'It's not the original. Georgia says it's a late copy. It was sealed in one of those old barrels in the attic.'

'I've got to try it on. I've never seen anything so fabulous.'

'I'm first,' said Ned.

'You'd better join the queue, Nico,' said Bron. 'And anyway, Georgia's still examining it.'

'Lucky old cloak,' said Nico with a sidelong smile at her.

'Shouldn't you be at rehearsals?' said Bron.

Georgia was startled by the hostility in his voice.

'Redvers got a bit wound up by Morrigan, and since we both had a break in the script I asked Mrs Meads to bring some tea in here to give him a breather. He'll be along in a minute.' Nico looked up at the sound of rattling cups. 'And that'll be Mrs M now.'

Mrs Meads trundled in a trolley, which she brought to a stop by the fireplace. It was laden with egg-shell thin china, and a collapsed sponge cake. She cast a jaundiced glance over the extra people in the room, but luckily didn't see the cloak, which was hidden from her by the group at the table.

'You said there'd only be two of you, Mr Nico. Now I shall have to traipse all the way back to the kitchen for more cups.'

She scurried off, muttering under her breath, almost colliding with Redvers as she left the room.

'Come and see what's turned up in the attic, Redvers!' said Nico. 'If this doesn't take your mind off things, nothing will.'

Redvers ambled over to the table, his shoulders hunched, his hands in his jacket pockets. He stared in unfeigned amazement for several seconds until his professional instinct took over. He turned to Georgia.

'You've done it after all! You've found me the perfect Prospero's cloak. I must try it on!'

'I'm sorry, Redvers,' Bron said, 'but I really do think it's too old and valuable to go on stage.'

'At least let me try it,' he persisted. 'Surely that's not too much to ask?'

Georgia expected Bron to give a flat refusal, but he hesitated. It was yet another uncharacteristic piece of behaviour. The cloak was making everyone irrational. And why did they all seem almost driven to try it on? Her mind went back to her own response to Bron's kiss, which now seemed the most preposterous reaction of all.

'Would you let Redvers have first go after all?' Bron asked Ned, who'd found a coin wedged between the floorboards, and was playing shove-ha'penny on a corner of the table. 'I promise you can try it next.'

'I knew this would happen,' said Ned, looking up crossly. 'Oh, all right, I suppose so.'

He gave the coin a terrific thump, and sent it flying off the table.

'Dear, dear lad,' said Redvers, feeling in his pocket. Ned's expression of disgust was replaced by one of startled delight as a five-pound note was tucked into his hand.

Brown frowned. 'You didn't have to do that.'

'Boys always need money,' said Redvers, grandly waving aside Ned's awkward thanks. 'Now then, Georgia, on with the motley!'

'Please be very, very careful,' she begged, as she eased it over his shoulders.

Redvers walked to the oriel window, the cloak furled loosely about him, the silken lining rustling as he moved. When he stood in the full light, still with his back to them, he raised his arms so that the Queen of the Thrones of Water was displayed in all her blue and gold glory. Slowly he turned and launched into Prospero's speech. 'We are such stuff as dreams are made on', casting over his listeners a web of words so perfect that they were temporarily spellbound.

For at least half a minute no one spoke after the speech had faded away. Georgia was caught up in a brief dazzling image of Merlinslade in its great heyday, when Shakespeare's company had played in the hall. Even Ned was struck dumb.

The silence was broken by the sound of slow ironic claps. Morrigan stood in the doorway, dressed in black Levis, and a black leather vest against which his crucifix gleamed.

'Well, well,' he drawled, looking like a python who'd just swallowed something slightly too large. ' "Who would have thought the old man to have had so much blood in him?" '

Redvers twitched as if he'd been prodded with an electric goad.

'Don't ever quote that play again, Morrigan. Not the Scottish play. Not one word, for your own sake as much as ours.'

'Yes, cut it out, Ger,' said Nico, who was looking decidedly uneasy too. 'You know it brings bad luck.'

Redvers began to take off the cloak, but Morrigan didn't let up. He prowled round Redvers, taking in every detail.

'Why, I do believe that's Merlin's cloak,' he said as Redvers reluctantly handed it over to Georgia. 'I remember seeing a picture of it as a boy. Am I right?'

'It's a later copy of the one in the picture,' said Bron. 'It's up to you to decide whether the original was Merlin's. And it's about to go safely back where it came from.'

Redvers clutched his sparse locks.

'But haven't I just persuaded you how vital it is for me to have it in the play? Didn't you see the difference it made?'

'Even if Bron agreed, it isn't strong enough to withstand a six-week run,' said Georgia gently. 'We can make a copy of the copy, though. Sumitra's a genius at that sort of work. I'll take her off everything else if necessary. She's almost finished Ariel's costumes.'

'For the first night, then. One night only!' Redvers pleaded, beginning to look like King Lear at his most pathetic.

'Go on, Bron, let Redvers have it,' said Nico. 'You must have seen what it did for him.'

'A real pro wouldn't care what he wore,' said Morrigan evilly.

Georgia, more concerned for Redvers than the cloak, exquisite though it was, was surprised to intercept a look of deep sympathy for him from Bron.

'What do you think?' Bron asked her. 'Would the cloak stand it? Just for one night?'

'Ultra-violet light is the big problem. It fades these old fabrics so fast. But I don't think one evening performance under artificial light would make all that much difference, as long as Redvers and his dresser were very careful. I'd have to tack in a lining round the neck and wrists of course, and it should go to a conservator immediately afterwards.'

'Surely you aren't going to agree?' Morrigan said, sidling up to Bron. His voice was jeering. 'You, the cool cautious Bron, the one who always does the most sensible thing?'

'It's none of your damned business,' said Bron. 'It doesn't belong to you. Come to that, it doesn't belong to anyone. It belongs to Merlinslade.'

'You're wrong,' said Morrigan. 'It's meant to be mine.'

He placed his hand squarely on the embroidered figure on the cloak. Georgia wanted to scream at him to take it away, imagining the sweat and oil on his skin already filming the delicate threads.

'The Queen of the Throne of Waters is the goddess, the goddess who blesses our ceremony of baptism,' he went on. 'That's when it should be worn, by me, not by some sad, confused old man who'll rip it to pieces along with his performance.'

'You vindictive bastard!' said Redvers. 'You never could bear anyone upstaging you.'

245

'Judging by the activities of the Disciples on the estate, I'd have thought they were the ones most likely to rip it apart,' said Bron.

'I'd only use it on our most holy occasion,' said Morrigan reproachfully. 'You make no attempt to understand the Disciples.'

'I understand you, and that's enough.'

'I've asked for nothing from you up to now, Bron, except a little affection, and I'm even grudged that. Merlinslade is yours by the purest chance, and you know it. Your father wheedled his way into my father's affections while I was in prison, when I didn't have a chance to defend myself. I've lost everything. If you've any sense of justice, you'd let me have this one small part of my birthright.'

'You've got more in the bank than the lot of us put together,' said Bron, 'but Merlinslade's mortgaged to the hilt. You were never seriously interested in this place, except for the prestige of being lord of the manor. Nothing interests you except yourself.'

'If Merlinslade had come to me it would have been used for the highest purpose,' said Morrigan loftily, 'not thrown open for all and sundry to gawp at. I didn't make a fuss when I was swindled out of my inheritance, though I could have. I could even now. All I'm asking for is this one thing, the cloak.'

Bron was silent for a moment, glancing from Morrigan to Redvers, who'd collapsed into a chair with his head in his hands, and seemed to be in the depths of despair. Morrigan gave a triumphant smirk, clearly assuming from Bron's hesitation that the cloak was going to be his.

Ned had been anxiously following the exchange, shuffling from foot to foot with impatience.

'It's not fair,' he said mournfully. 'Everyone's going to get a shot at it except me.'

'Much good you'd do it,' said Morrigan, turning a baleful glance on poor Ned. 'It's not for children.'

'I'll be looking after Merlinslade one day,' said Ned indignantly. 'Why shouldn't I wear it? And I'm not a child.'

'You do surprise me,' said Morrigan with a sarcastic smile, giving Ned's ear a decidedly ungentle tweak which only just passed as a teasing gesture.

'Ow, that hurt!' said Ned.

Bron's face was stony. He put a hand on Ned's shoulder.

'Back off, Morrigan. You always liked strong-arming someone smaller than yourself, didn't you? But this time you're not getting your way. Redvers can wear the cloak for the first night. And afterwards it'll go on display here, at Merlinslade, where it belongs.'

Morrigan's sallow face became reddish-green with rage. For a moment Georgia thought he was going to launch himself at Bron.

'Just because you've never made it yourself, not with your career, not with your marriage, and now not even with Merlinslade, you want to fuck it up for everyone else. Not for me, though! I warn you, never again for me! This time I will have what's mine!'

He stormed out of the room, almost felling Mrs Meads on the way, and making the extra tray of crockery rattle in her hands. Ned's eyes were as round as marbles, and he was openly clutching the arm of Bron's shirt.

'Hoity toity!' said Mrs Meads comfortably, staring after Morrigan and shaking her head. 'He always did have a nasty temper, that one!'

Chapter 13

Georgia escaped to the window seat with her tea while Nico attempted to lighten the atmosphere with a flow of easy chat. Bron was completely silent, and even Ned hardly spoke.

Afterwards Nico and Redvers went back to the theatre. Georgia was about to follow them, when Bron, to Ned's open astonishment, suddenly offered to take him to the cinema in Bath, and to her even greater surprise asked if she'd like to go with them.

She made a lame excuse before returning thankfully to the wardrobe, though it was hard to ignore Ned's disappointed face. She was already disturbed enough by the incidents of the afternoon, without having to sit in a darkened cinema with Bron for a further two hours.

Luckily Annie, who'd lunched in Bath with a couple of other battle-scarred feminists, had brought back a reassuring fund of anecdotes about the unpredictability of the male sex. As Georgia listened to her in the familiar atmosphere of the wardrobe she began to persuade herself that Bron too had simply been thrown by the odd atmosphere in the attic. Yet the memory of being held by him still persisted over the next few days, though she hardly saw him, except sometimes in the distance, high on an old-fashioned reaping machine as it circled slowly round the first crops of corn.

Rehearsals were going well, and Redvers, now he was satisfied over the cloak, had become a model of co-operation, though he was still uneasy when Morrigan appeared. Morrigan himself had so far ignored Georgia, and she began to hope that his clash with Bron had diverted his attention from Chloe and herself. At least Chloe's relationship with Sean was recovering from the incident at Morrigan's party. When she wasn't at the Sanctuary she spent most of the time waiting for him to call her on the phone.

The date of their mother's visit was approaching fast, and Georgia still hadn't talked to Chloe about their proposed meeting in London. When she came in from the Sanctuary at the end of the week in an exceptionally confiding mood, Georgia decided to sound her out.

'It's going to be wonderful on Sunday night,' Chloe said. 'We're holding a Lughnasa ceremony at the stone circle.'

She was sitting at the kitchen table, surrounded by twine and bits of wire, attempting to make a circlet with a heap of foliage and flowers culled from the garden. Georgia hadn't dared ask yet what it was for.

'Lughnasa? What's that?' she said, wondering worriedly if it involved some peculiar Druid rite. 'And how long does it go on? Not all night, surely?'

'Do use your brain, Georgy. Brighid wouldn't let us stay out that long. And anyway, we're having a feast afterwards in the refectory. Brighid says I can stay overnight with her and the other girls. We're making ourselves crowns of flowers. Lughnasa celebrates the beginning of harvest time. It's terrifically important for the group this year, because Morrigan's going to make a special announcement after the feast.'

Georgia thought it sounded like a perfect recipe for trouble. But she'd learned not to argue with Chloe over what went on at the Sanctuary.

'Mother called last night while you were out,' she said. 'She's coming to London early next week, just for a couple of days. She wants us to meet her there.'

Chloe made a face as she wove a spray of rosebuds into the wreath. 'Do we have to? It'll be such a drag. She's not really interested in seeing us. She's only doing it because she feels it's her duty.'

'Of course she's interested. She wants to hear about your plans for next year,' said Georgia, strategically rearranging the truth.

'It wouldn't be so bad if we went shopping together, or somewhere interesting to eat, or anything other girls do with their mother. But I bet she wants to meet us in the Natural History Museum. It'll be swarming with kids.'

'Well, yes, she does, but only because she's so short of time. She's taking some specimens to Kew in the morning, and then she's arranged to do some research in the museum library.'

'Why can't we meet her after work?'

'Because she's having dinner with some conservationists who've promised to fund the new forest reserve. The next day she has to go back to Kew, and she's flying home in the evening.'

'Good of her to fit us in at all,' said Chloe, scattering leaves round her chair as she trimmed a piece of ivy.

'You and I can go shopping afterwards. I'll buy you a dress for the first night party. Nico's planning to hold it in the great hall.'

'The sort of dress *I* like?' Chloe asked, distrust written all over her face.

'Exactly what you like,' said Georgia rashly.

Chloe put down the secateurs with a martyred sigh. 'Well then, if it means so much to you both I suppose I'll have to say yes. But I hope you realise I'm putting my entire emotional well-being in jeopardy. Brighid says I'm on the verge of self-realisation, and I mustn't do anything to interfere with the process. And it'll be a disaster if Sean phones while I'm away, a total disaster.'

Just in time Georgia bit back a remark that she was sure he was capable of leaving a message on the answering machine. It was worth almost anything to keep her in a good mood till they'd been to London. Just thinking about the delightful prospect of handing over the problem of Chloe made her feel better. Their mother was unshakeable once she'd made a decision, and in the last resort Chloe usually obeyed her.

There was an unusually strained atmosphere in the workroom on the day following the Lughnasa ceremony. They were still frantically dyeing fabrics after a disastrous delay when the washing machine had been out of action for almost a week.

Annie was having trouble with her ex-husband, and accordingly bad-tempered. Jenny kept dissolving into tears because she couldn't get the hang of making ruffs, Kevin had lost his favourite scissors, and by ten o'clock Chloe still hadn't turned up from the Sanctuary.

At least when Morrigan came in for his second fitting he put Annie in a better mood. But he insisted on keeping the curtains open while she hovered around him, and constantly sent looks laden with some impenetrable meaning at Georgia through the window in the office partition.

Chloe ultimately appeared at eleven to be greeted by a huge dressing down, both from Annie for not clearing up after her last session in the wardrobe, and from Kevin, who'd discovered his scissors among her work materials. She went into a major sulk, and disappeared for much longer than she should have done at lunch.

As she drove Georgia home after work she complained bitterly about the unfair way the others treated her. By the time they reached the outskirts of Bath, and had become trapped in a stream of crawling traffic, Georgia could control her exasperation no longer.

'You're the one who's out of order. None of us can work in a muddle, and Kevin's been looking for those scissors for days. You were late for work, and away far too long for lunch as well. I didn't say anything earlier because the others had already told you off.'

'But I was talking to Sean at lunch,' said Chloe indignantly. 'I thought you liked me to be with him.'

'Of course I do, but not in working time, and especially not when we're so busy.'

Chloe stuck out her lower lip, and glared at a cyclist wobbling past on the inside. 'Well, I simply must have a long lunch hour tomorrow. He's taking me to The Mortal Man.'

'No,' said Georgia. 'We're too busy. Ask Sean if you can go to the pub after work. He's an actor. He understands about deadlines.'

It had been a horrible day. She'd been working all afternoon at a sewing machine with a flickering light, and had the beginnings of a migraine. Morrigan had come into the workroom again, suggesting several unnecessary alterations to his costume. He'd wasted Jenny's time by chatting to her for half an hour, briefly lifted Chloe's gloom by heaping praise on a neck chain she was making him, and sauntered out leaving Georgia with a real headache.

'Don't you see how difficult it makes things for me if I favour you?' she said. 'And you won't like it if the others start to resent you.'

Chloe's driving, which was still erratic, went to pieces altogether. She stalled the engine at some traffic lights, causing an enormous queue and rousing a symphony of protesting horns. Georgia felt still more frayed by the time they got home.

The flat was stuffy and she went to open the French windows. When she returned to the kitchen Chloe was making iced coffee. She looked up apprehensively, and Georgia, now she could relax a little, began to think more charitably that she'd nagged her sister enough. She sat down at the table, and eased off her sandals. The tiles were cool beneath her feet.

'How was the Sanctuary yesterday?' she said. 'You haven't told me what happened at the ceremony.'

Chloe put the jug of coffee on the table with a conciliatory smile. Georgia poured herself a glass. It wouldn't do her headache any good, but it would please Chloe. As the ice cubes tinkled in the jug she tried not to think that Chloe would almost certainly forget to refill the ice tray. She ran the cold glass across her forehead. Everything seemed to be putting her on edge just now.

'It was tremendous, out of sight,' said Chloe eagerly. 'We went up to the stone circle just before sunset. We sang hymns and Brighid gave thanks for the first fruits. Then we began to dance, widdershins to begin with, to undo all the harm in the world.'

'What's widdershins?' Georgia immediately imagined all sorts of bizarre proceedings.

'You really don't know anything, do you?' said Chloe, shaking her head with an expression of deep concern which would have made Georgia laugh at any other time. 'It's anti-clockwise, of course. Then we danced deosil, in the other direction, to raise the power of the goddess, to concentrate it in ourselves and give us strength, and to help heal all the suffering in the world. Afterwards we felt wonderful, so free and strong and light. We sat beneath the stones while the sun went down, and Morrigan sang to us. That was the best part of all. When it was almost dark we went back to the Sanctuary and had our feast.'

'And after the feast, what did Morrigan have to say?' Georgia asked, beginning to drink her coffee at last, and thinking that she needn't have worried about the ceremony after all.

'He said we had a duty to let the whole world know about Brighid and the goddess. He says the only drawback is our lack of funds. The group never makes much money, and most of it goes on the upkeep of the Sanctuary. He said that was all going to change now he's worked out the rules. He was – ' Chloe searched for a word – 'he was inspirational.'

'In what way?' asked Georgia, pushing away her coffee, and going over to the window to hide her concern. She threw up the sash. The bells were ringing in the Abbey. The evening was calm and still. Through the area railings, she saw a young couple go by, arms twined round each other.

Chloe's voice prattled on behind her. 'We're going to be organised into a chain of power. Each of us will have a personal mission to recruit another ten novices, and every novice who becomes a full Disciple – that's when Brighid baptises them in the Grail Well – is going to take a vow of poverty. Not permanently, of course, just till the Foundation's established,' she added quickly, catching sight of Georgia's expression as she turned back into the room.

'And how exactly is a vow of poverty going to help the group get rich?' Georgia asked. 'Or is Brighid adding alchemy to her other talents?'

Chloe's face fell. 'You don't have to be sarcastic. We've simply decided to donate all our income to the group for a while. And those who have them are going to give part of their savings too.'

Georgia gripped the edge of the table.

'How much of your savings?'

'As much as we can afford. It's a terrifically good cause. Brighid's put all her money into the Sanctuary, so it's only right that we should do the same.'

'Did she actually say that herself?'

'Not exactly. She'd gone to see to the feast. Morrigan was talking to us on his own. He wants us to surprise her, to pretend it was our idea. He says it would please her more than anything.'

'I bet it would,' said Georgia, trying to keep calm. 'At least you've nothing to give, I'm glad to say.'

'But I have! That's what's so extra wonderful. Have you forgotten, Georgy? Next month, when I'm eighteen, I get the money Grandma Baines left me. I'd rather it went to the Sanctuary than anywhere else.'

Georgia could hardly believe what she was hearing. Chloe became more ostrich-like with every passing day.

'Morrigan says no one's worthy of the name Disciple unless they make the sacrifice,' Chloe prattled on. 'I'm going to pledge my legacy the instant I'm eighteen.'

'You can't! Some of that money's to help with all the extras you'll need at art college. The parents won't be able to give you much. Dad's got a second family to support, and most of Mother's spare cash goes into the forest project. Grandma hoped you'd set up your own business one day, or put the rest of the money towards a flat. What's the matter with you?'

'Nothing's the matter! I'm sick of you pulling me to pieces. Every suggestion I make, everything I try to do on my own, you criticise. It's my money. I didn't tell you how to spend yours.'

'Can you imagine Grandma's reaction if she knew you were giving it all to Morrigan? Because that's what it really means.'

'You never trust anyone these days. Brighid says you're a deeply unhappy person.'

'Sod what Brighid says! I absolutely forbid you to do this. Even Mother'll say the same when we see her tomorrow.'

It was an unwise remark.

'I really don't know why I should bother to see her at all, if that's going to be her reaction as well. Why can't either of you treat me like a grown-up?'

Georgia's head, in spite of the migraine tablets she'd taken at teatime, felt as if she had a tank rumbling about inside it. The thought that Chloe had been discussing her with Brighid made her feel even worse. Instead of conciliating her, instead of making sure that she met their mother at all costs, she lashed back.

'We all try to treat you like a grown-up. It's a pity you don't behave like one.'

Chloe's eyes were flooding with tears. 'You never treat me like a grown-up! You still don't tell me anything about how you really feel, yet you're always needling away at me, trying to find out about Sean. And I don't see how I'm ever going to work things out with him if you won't even let us meet.'

Georgia sensed that Chloe was on the verge of a point-blank refusal to meet their mother. She became desperate to undo the damage.

'I'm sorry. Maybe I did go on at you a bit too much. Don't let's quarrel, I hate it. But you must come and see Mother tomorrow. She's expecting us, and she'll be so disappointed not to see you.'

'Who are you kidding, Georgy? She doesn't even seem like my mother any more. Brighid understands me better than she ever did, better even than you. I've never heard of anyone having so many dud relations as me.'

Tears were streaming down her face in an unstoppable cataract.

'I definitely won't go. I won't sit there with all those bloody dinosaurs, listening to Mother trying to sort me out in an hour before she goes back to her precious rain forest. You can if you like, but count me out!'

Extreme disappointment, fear of losing Chloe to the Disciples and Morrigan, the migraine, and the drug which was doing nothing for it except to make her feel strangely light-headed, pushed Georgia beyond caution.

'Then you won't be keeping your side of the bargain we made

when I agreed to let you stay here! You promised to co-operate. If you don't come and see Mother with me, I'll tell her I can't cope with you any more. You'll have to go back to boarding school next term. It's just too bad if you don't like it.'

'Tell her what you like.' Chloe was trembling like an aspen. 'But I won't go to horrible Brandon Lodge, or to live with Mother, or with Dad and bloody Karen, ever again. If you don't want me, there's someone who does. I'm going to Brighid, and I'm never, ever coming back!'

She rushed out, letting the door crash against the wall. Georgia heard her snatch up the phone and order a taxi, her voice thick with tears, then go into her bedroom, noisily opening drawers and sobbing as she began to pack.

Georgia was cold with horror as she realised she'd driven Chloe into Morrigan's snare more effectively than he could ever have done. She went into Chloe's room. She was rushing about like a whirlwind, stuffing her clothes into the kit bag, rolling up the coverlet, ripping down posters. She pulled the plug of the cassette player from its socket, tumbled her tapes into her suitcase, and started to lug everything into the hall.

'Please don't go, Chloe. Please. I'm sorry.' Georgia put her hand on Chloe's arm. 'At least listen to what Mother has to say, and I swear that if you don't agree with her you can come back to the flat and we'll forget all this ever happened. I didn't mean it about not staying on here, truly.'

'No,' said Chloe, rushing out to the bathroom and reappearing with a long ribbon of lavatory paper streaming behind her. 'I'd rather be up at the Sanctuary. At least they don't stamp on me there.'

'I've never stamped on you, ever,' said Georgia, now so frantic to make her stay that she was near to tears herself. 'You know I haven't!'

Chloe's eyes appeared like overflowing puddles from a bouquet of tissue as she blew her nose.

'If only you'd come to the Sanctuary with me in the first place none of this would have happened,' she said. 'You'd have found out how to be happy too. You don't know how awful it is when you look sad.'

Georgia shook her head, almost speechless at Chloe's concern. 'That won't make me happy, and nor will your leaving. Don't go. I'll miss you so much.'

'No you won't,' said Chloe, her sobs redoubling. 'You'll have your life back exactly how you want it, nice and tidy and no one to bother you. You know you don't really want me around. Nobody does except Brighid.'

'Sean does,' Georgia said frantically. 'I'm sure he does. Don't burn all your boats. At least keep on coming to the workshop. Please, Chloe.'

'I'll see,' she said, gulping. She had all her possessions gathered about her now, and Wooster wedged under her arm. She wrenched open the front door, looking up to the street.

'There's my taxi,' she said.

She heaved the duffel bag on to her shoulder, gathering up the cassette player and suitcase in her other hand. She looked far too slight to carry everything on her own. Georgia could hear the taxi's engine ticking over. It had all happened so quickly she could hardly believe it.

'Don't go,' she said again.

Chloe gave her a quick, defensive kiss. Her cheek was wet against Georgia's.

'Sorry, Georgy,' she said, her voice choking, 'but you've got to try to understand. The Sanctuary's the only place I'm ever going to find myself.'

She began to mount the area steps. Wooster's ears trailed down, his brown button eyes looking sadly out from under her arm. A minute later the taxi door slammed, and she'd gone.

As soon as Chloe had left Georgia began to miss her. The flat she'd so often longed to have to herself felt lifeless without Chloe's chatter and the songs of the whales, and it reminded her too much of the time Blake had finally returned to Lyn.

She looked in the fridge for some supper, discovered half a vegetable lasagne left there by Chloe, tried to eat it, and found herself again almost in tears. In the end she tipped the food in the rubbish bin, and took a strong vodka and tonic down to the studio to start working on the designs for the next play. As she surrounded herself with reference books she wished sadly that she could barricade her heart as well.

The vodka was unwise. Georgia worked until she was too tired to think any more, but woke soon after dawn feeling as if a vice was crushing her skull. She swallowed some painkillers, and tried to concentrate on the coming day, knowing she had to persuade her mother to come back to Bath to see Chloe.

She decided to visit the costume gallery at the V & A before meeting her mother at the Natural History Museum next door. After lunch she'd go over to the National Portrait Gallery in Trafalgar Square and research more costume details.

Although her mother wouldn't notice what she wore, she forced herself to dress carefully. London was full of actors, and she didn't want word getting around that she was losing her grip. She took more pain killers on the journey, arriving at Paddington in such a light-headed state that her brain felt as if it had been replaced by granules of polystyrene. Tiredness was beginning to catch up on her as well. She'd been sleeping badly ever since the incident in Morrigan's car.

She paused at the Brunel statue guarding the entrance to the underground, and decided to ring Annie at the theatre. There was still a remote chance that Chloe might be having second thoughts. She was supposed to be working in the wardrobe that afternoon, and if she turned up, Annie might be able to persuade her to go afterwards to the Sophia Street flat, for which she still had a key. It would be infinitely better than taking their mother to the Sanctuary.

Annie was nowhere to be found. Georgia tried the front of the house, the green room, and finally, in desperation the paint shop. She almost dropped the phone when Bron's voice answered. He was hardly ever in the theatre these days.

'What are you doing there?' she asked impatiently.

'I'm not checking up, if that's what's worrying you.' He sounded amused.

'I must speak to Annie. Is she there?'

'You don't seriously expect any of them to be up and about at this hour?'

'I certainly expect the wardrobe staff to arrive on time,' she snapped.

'Maybe there's a mutiny.'

'For Christ's sake, I've got to speak to Annie. Can't you go and look for her?'

There was a pause, during which she began to wonder if he'd refuse outright. Then she heard him put down the phone, and his footsteps leaving the paintshop. After what seemed like hours they finally returned.

'Sorry, but she's not about. Mrs Meads thinks all the wardrobe staff have gone into Bath.'

She felt sick with reaction. 'Oh God, I completely forgot. There's a lecture at the Museum of Costume this morning. I said they could go. Could you put a note for Annie in the wardrobe office? I'm visiting the National Portrait Gallery after lunch. Ask her to leave a message for me there if Chloe comes in. I can ring Annie back later.'

'Are you all right?' said Bron unexpectedly.

'Yes, of course I am,' she said, pitching her voice even higher above the din in the station.

'I'll leave notes everywhere,' said Bron. 'Sorry I can't do more. I'm just off to London myself. Are you sure you're all right?'

She began to panic in case he was going to suggest a meeting. Bron and her mother on top of a headache she could definitely not cope with in the same day. Deliberately she let the money in the coin box run out.

Georgia walked around the costume gallery in the V & A in a daze, worrying about Chloe and rehearsing a dozen different speeches to persuade her mother to come back to Bath that evening. Her headache was getting worse, and though the light in the gallery was subdued, the pencil lines of her sketch pad danced sickeningly as she tried to draw.

Her mother, coming from Kew, had arranged a late lunch, but Georgia still wasn't hungry as she walked up the steps to the Natural History Museum. She averted her eyes from the zig-zag tiling round the door, and the chequered mosaic of the entrance hall floor. In the cloakroom she took more pain killers in a final attempt to subdue the headache before the coming encounter.

The restaurant was too brightly lit and noisy for her present

State. Attendants clashed plates and cutlery together as they tried to clear the zinc-covered tables before more school parties descended. The bare wooden floors resounded with children's pounding feet. Scanning the room, she thought that it was typical of her mother to have chosen somewhere like this for an intimate discussion.

Georgia often wondered if she'd become a designer as a reaction to her mother's obliviousness to her surroundings. In all the years they'd lived in Africa, even with her father, her mother had never bothered to soften their ugly public works issue furniture with so much as a cushion. Ornaments only arrived by pure chance, donated by grateful patients of her father, or sent by Grandma Baines.

Though it was next to the ever-opening kitchen door, and under two spotlights, at least her mother had found a corner table, Georgia thought, as she caught sight of her with her head bent over a sheaf of notes. She was absent-mindedly eating a sandwich, and probably had no idea of its contents.

As always Georgia couldn't help feeling a reluctant admiration for such single-mindedness. And she had to acknowledge that Beatrice had at least fostered in her a belief that she could accomplish anything if she tried hard enough, and a self-reliance which was more enduring than the most attractive of homes. She'd tried her best, too, according to her own standards, to sort out Georgia's childhood problems with a brisk mixture of basic psychology and commonsense. It had worked quite well when leavened with her father's somewhat unpredictable charm, and probably if he'd been around when Chloe was growing up, it would have worked for her too.

Georgia bought herself a black coffee, averting her gaze from the mountain of glistening sausages at the hot food counter, and went to join her mother. Beatrice was wearing a crumpled Laura Ashley blouse with a pie-frill collar, which she'd no doubt slept in on the plane, but that was her only concession to her urban surroundings. Her faded button-through skirt had a safety pin at the waist, and an old navy cardigan hung over the back of her chair. Her hair was wound into a knot at the back of her head, and her skin was meshed with fine wrinkles from sitting too long

261

in the sun. When she gave Georgia a quick hug she smelt as always of TCP.

'What have you been doing to yourself?' she demanded, after brushing aside queries about her flight and her hotel. She never had any small talk. 'You don't look too bright. Have you been letting Chloe put you through the hoop? And where is Chloe? Wasn't she to be the main purpose of this exercise?'

Georgia knew she must appear as zombie-like as she felt if her mother had actually noticed her appearance.

'Chloe refused to come at the last minute,' she said.

'It doesn't sound as though she's changed much. What went wrong?'

Georgia tried to marshal her thoughts. Her mother would instantly discount any over-emotional presentation of the facts. But it was difficult to describe Chloe's exploits without revealing her own intuitive antipathy to Morrigan.

Beatrice listened attentively as she poured herself another cup of tea.

'I agree with you that it's worrying about Chloe's money,' she said, when Georgia had finished her tale. 'But on the plus side this Brighid does seem to have a restraining influence on her. It's my guess that a controlling maternal figure is exactly what Chloe needs at the moment.'

This was too much for Georgia. 'But don't you see, that ought to be you? I'm sure if she felt you were a bit more interested in her, she'd give all this up. I'm too near her age to be much use. It's absolutely vital for you to come back to Bath with me and sort her out. If she's not at the flat we'll drive over to the Sanctuary this evening, and you can talk to Brighid, maybe even to Morrigan. You'll understand the problem at once when you've met him.'

She couldn't imagine Morrigan lasting more than five minutes under one of her mother's analytical interrogations. The sheer thought of it made her feel weak with anticipated relief. She hadn't realised till now quite how much she'd been depending on her mother for help.

Beatrice sighed. 'There's no way I can cut my meeting this evening. It's with one of the top conservation organisations, and they're on the point of pouring in massive funds. It would make me seem so unreliable and unprofessional if I didn't turn up just because my daughter was having a fit of adolescent histrionics. I daren't take the risk.'

'Tomorrow, then,' implored Georgia. 'Couldn't you postpone your flight by just one day?'

'No. I told the Minister I'd be back with a promise of funding by the middle of the week. If I can't deliver on time there are plenty of other people – loggers, developers – waiting to leap in. Heaven knows what could be going on behind my back. You have to understand how important this funding is.'

'But isn't Chloe just as important? She's on the verge of committing herself completely to the Disciples, I'm certain of it.' Georgia could hear the rising note of panic in her voice. 'You might save the forest, but you could lose a daughter.'

It was the kind of emotional appeal her mother disliked most. Georgia had been almost certain it wouldn't work, and she felt a leap of hope as Beatrice's expression became unexpectedly troubled. She fiddled with the spoon in the sugar bowl, stared round the room, searched for nothing in her bag with most uncharacteristic indecision, and finally looked up. To Georgia's astonishment her eyes were pleading.

'Darling, I'm sorry.' Georgia was even more astonished by the endearment, which Beatrice hardly ever used. 'But you've got to stop harrying me over this. It makes things unbearably difficult, just when I must concentrate all my energies on the new reserve. Chloe's had these crises before. They've always blown over when she's put us all thoroughly through the mill. You seem to forget that in another month's time she'll be an adult, and fully responsible for herself. I think you've got to let go of her too.'

'Chloe's nowhere near being an adult. She may be almost eighteen, but in lots of ways she's still a child.'

Georgia's mother clasped her hands before her on the table.

'I've never talked to you much about my divorce, have I? Perhaps now you've been through one yourself, you can under-stand how tough it was for me, especially with two children in tow. Building a solid academic reputation for myself, after all those years trailing round after your father on his contract jobs wasn't easy. I can't put it or the forest at risk simply for one of Chloe's tantrums. Otherwise nothing in my life will have worked, and that's an awful way to feel at my age.'

Georgia, battling with a mixture of sympathy and despair, was thrown still more off balance when, in an uncommon gesture of tenderness, her mother put her hand over hers.

'And we've never talked properly about your divorce, have we? You probably think I'm callous about that too. But I do know how you must be feeling. Exactly as I did after your father left me. As if you've had enough emotion for the rest of your life.'

Georgia thought sadly how rare it was for her mother to discuss anything so intimate, and how true her words were. Since the divorce she'd craved nothing but peace. Nothing else, that is, till Chloe's arrival and she'd started to work at Merlinslade.

'I've felt that way ever since your father left,' her mother went on. 'And now I'm older, and need all my energy for the forest, I can see that it's the best thing that could have happened. I know I've not been much good as a mother, but if there's one thing I can pass on to you, it's that one's better off alone. Think about it, Georgia. We're very alike in some ways, you and I.'

Georgia stared at her mother. She'd never remotely thought that they were alike. Feverishly her mind went back to Zelda's warning that she mustn't stay in the freezer forever, then to Nico's taunt about not wanting to take chances any more. She suddenly saw with awful clarity that she was truly becoming like her mother, and turning into a sort of emotional dinosaur. Her lack of physical response to Nico and even to Morrigan was simply further evidence of what was happening to her. The thought was so overwhelming that she could hardly speak.

'You really do look awful,' said her mother.

'It's just a migraine,' said Georgia.

'Oh, a migraine,' her mother said dismissively. 'Nothing too bad, then.'

She so rarely gave way to illness herself that a headache had to be caused by cerebral malaria at least before she'd recognise it as serious. She looked at her watch.

'So that's settled then. I'm glad we've got things sorted out at last. And I've still got half an hour. I want to hear more about you. We've spent far too long on Chloe, as usual. How's your business doing?'

Georgia had had several phone conversations with her mother since leaving Blake. When Georgia made her first halting announcement that the marriage was over she'd listened attentively, but made little comment beyond saying that it was Georgia's decision entirely, and asking her if she needed any money. Georgia had been thankful for this practical non-interference. It was far better than the over-concern of her father and particularly of Karen, who fancied herself as a counsellor.

'I'm all right,' she answered. 'I've too much to do, but it suits me.'

'I was just the same after my divorce. Work's the only thing in those circumstances. You never did tell me exactly what went wrong between you and Blake. I gathered he had someone else, but that didn't seem to me at the time quite good enough a reason for such a rapid break. Jim wasn't blameless in that area before he met Karen, but I kept thinking he might improve. When I think of the years I wasted!'

The cafeteria had quietened in the lull between lunch and tea. Georgia went to get herself another cup of coffee before continuing the conversation. On the way she passed a mother, a very ordinary-looking plump woman in her early forties, sitting patiently with two little girls while they inexpertly filled in the pages of a colouring book. She looked as if she was prepared to sit with them for hours if necessary.

'So, you were going to tell me about Blake,' Beatrice prompted, when she returned.

'I didn't realise what he was really like till I married him.' Georgia hesitated.

'But you knew him for some time beforehand, didn't you?'

'Yes. He was an actor though, good at hiding how he really felt. But in the end not even he could keep up the pretence.'

'What pretence?' Beatrice looked at her watch again. 'Come along, Georgia, don't talk in riddles. I hope you aren't trying to tell me he became violent.'

'No, never violent. If he had been it would have terrible, of course, but I think I could have found it easier to break with him.

He was just sad, so sad at the end. Because he'd hurt me, and he never wanted to. Yet he couldn't hurt Lyn, the other person, either.'

'The times I've heard Jim say the same, and believed him,' said her mother.

'Lyn needed sympathy in a particular way,' said Georgia. 'Even I could see that, but it still hurt.'

She wondered if her mother would follow up the hint, would ask more, but she didn't.

'It sounds to me as if you're well rid of Blake,' Beatrice said in her most practical voice. Georgia wondered she was scared of learning more, scared of having to produce more sympathy than she felt able to give. 'I'm sure you'll bounce back. The first year's the worst you know, just like a bereavement. You'll be laughing at all this by next summer.'

'So everyone keeps telling me.'

'Think of those poor African women who can't divorce at all. You're better off than they are.'

If her mother wanted to pretend she understood, let her, Georgia decided. At least it left one of them feeling happy. And the pain killers were working at last, so that as Beatrice proceeded to regale Georgia with tales of the local people near the research station, she began to feel wonderfully detached, almost as if she were listening to their conversation from a great distance. Eventually Beatrice looked at her watch again.

'I'm glad we've been able to have this little talk,' she said. 'You must stop worrying about Chloe. I'm sure she'll tire of the group very soon. Once the reserve's sorted out I plan to come back to the UK to collect my results from Kew. I can spend a day or two with you in Bath then.'

'But by that time Chloe will have been formally baptised into the group. I don't feel she's likely to give it up after that.'

Beatrice shook her head. 'You feel, but you don't know. You should try not to over-react. Let's not jump to conclusions before it's absolutely necessary. And I really must go off to the library now, or I shan't get everything done.'

She got up, tucking her blouse unsuccessfully into her waistband, and gave Georgia another TCP-scented kiss.

'Chin up,' she said. 'It'll all blow over, you'll see.'

When Beatrice had left Georgia felt as if her last remnants of optimism and self-confidence had gone with her. The sense of being deserted was even more profound than when Chloe had left.

She sat for a while gazing at the debris of her mother's meal, and the empty cups, telling herself she was being ridiculous, that she'd just have to get over this as she'd got over everything else. Eventually, when a harassed-looking attendant began to clear away and push a sodden cloth over the table, she got up and forced herself to go back through the bright noisy streets to the underground.

She had to change at Piccadilly. As she waited on the platform the dusty wind gusting through the tunnel, the scraps of paper blowing aimlessly about the line, the people who so carefully avoided eye contact as they hurtled from place to place, made it seem a limbo of purposeless activity, the sort of limbo in which she herself was trapped. She felt so odd that she began to wonder if she'd make it to the National Portrait Gallery, but she had to, in case there was a message from Annie.

The attendant at the main desk of the gallery didn't have a message for her. He stared at Georgia as he gave her the news. She began to feel as if Chloe had died, but made herself go down to the cloakroom, and splash her face with water and tidy her hair. She looked like a victim from an Elizabethan tragedy of revenge, she thought, as she gazed at her distraught expression in the mirror, but at least the headache was still muffled. She gulped down two more tablets to make sure it stayed that way.

She went like an automaton into the refurbished modern galleries. It was the first time she'd been there since the alterations, and the new lighting affected her eyes like the flash of a blade. One of the portraits unexpectedly and devastatingly reminded her of Chloe. She found a seat, saw an attendant give her an odd look, and hastily moved on.

She began to climb the stairs to the upper galleries, where it was darker. When she arrived at the top she couldn't remember exactly how she'd got there. As she walked past the sixteenth-century portraits she came upon a portrait of a courtier in a black cut velvet doublet whose baleful gaze reminded her exactly of Morrigan. Something salt trickled into her mouth, and she realised she was crying soundlessly. She saw another attendant watching her, and speaking into a mobile phone.

She got the tears under control, went down a floor and wandered through the galleries there, wondering as she did so if she'd become completely paranoid. Every minute or so one of the attendants who were normally so friendly and helpful patrolled past, giving her stares which seemed increasingly suspicious.

Finally she came to rest in the Victorian section before a portrait of Lord Cardigan at the charge of the Light Brigade. He sat on a charger in a jacket resplendent with gold frogging, directing his troops, and wearing an expression which was so like Bron's at his most imperious that she only just managed to suppress the laughter rising in her throat.

She walked unsteadily into the next room, where a sympathetic-looking woman attendant sat in a corner chair, and drifted around the portraits. One of them, an Edwardian cavalry officer lounging on a sofa, had exactly the same quizzical look as Nico. The thought made her want to cry and laugh at the same time.

She sat down in the centre of the room on a curved banquette padded with crimson velvet, her back firmly to the cavalry officer. But now she faced a painting of a puddingy Queen Victoria handing a Bible to an African potentate, who appeared to be wearing the contents of the Balmoral dressing-up box. It became even more difficult not to laugh. The attendant came over.

'Don't you feel well, dear?' she said. 'Would you like a glass of water?'

Water, cool, flavourless, reviving, suddenly seemed the one thing which might make her feel better. Georgia nodded wordlessly.

'Then why don't you just come downstairs with me?' coaxed the attendant. 'We've a nice little rest room there.'

From the corner of her eye Georgia saw the other attendant, the one with the mobile phone, appear in the entrance. He was looking at her as though she was about to burst into flames. She focused hazily on the woman again. She too was staring oddly, not at Georgia's face, but at her bare arms. She couldn't understand why for a moment, then at last she understood. The woman was looking for bruises. They thought she was some crazy junkie out to harm the portraits. Instantly she began to panic. All she could think of was escape.

She rushed for the exit, almost slipping on the polished floor. The woman tore after her, and caught her shoulder bag. It tugged from her shoulder. Frantically Georgia snatched it back, and then felt her shoulders being so firmly grasped that she could hardly move. She looked up in despair, expecting the police, and found it was Bron.

Chapter 14

He was gazing at her with a face so grave that it made her want to laugh all over again. He gave her a little shake. She felt as if her knees were going to buckle.

'Is this lady with you, sir?' said the man, as if he didn't believe she had anything to do with someone who looked so immensely reliable.

Bron was still holding on to her arms. 'Are you?' he asked her. There was a flicker of amusement in his voice now.

She nodded. If she opened her mouth she knew she'd start laughing, and she wasn't sure she'd be able to stop.

'Of course she's with me,' said Bron in a brisk, clipped tone.

The attendant still looked dubious. 'Are you sure, sir? She seemed quite alone earlier on. We were concerned about her. She's obviously not well. She needs looking after.'

Bron's voice became even more peremptory. 'That's exactly what I'm about to do, just as soon as you let us have a few moments to ourselves.'

Georgia began to feel sorry for the attendant, who no longer seemed the inquisitor of ten minutes ago, but an ordinary, middle-aged man who looked as if he'd coped with enough visitors for one day. He gave them a doubtful smile, and walked slowly away to the far end of the room, where he still kept his eyes firmly fixed on them. As Bron propelled her back to the seat, she started to laugh.

'What's so funny?' he said, sitting next to her. 'And what *is* the matter with you? For Christ's sake, calm down. It'd be a lot harder to bail you out a second time.'

She said between gusts of laughter which she was only just able to control, 'Cardigan, Lord Cardigan! The portrait in the next room! Your expression was exactly the same just then! Only you could have been quite so high-handed! They do have to be careful here, you know. There are far crazier people than me around.'

He began to smile. 'Not Lord Cardigan. Anyone but him,' he said. 'He was the biggest botcher in the history of the British army.'

Reaction began to engulf her. The woman attendant had resumed her seat, and was gazing benevolently at them. The gallery didn't seem such a hostile place after all. If she could sleep for a little while she might just begin to feel better.

'How did you know I'd be here?' she asked.

'You told me yourself, on the phone this morning. Don't you remember? You sounded upset. I came along to see if you were all right.'

He was gazing at her as if she were some faulty engine whose machinery he couldn't quite work out.

'There's no need to look at me like that. I had a migraine, and took some pain-killers, that's all. I'm all right now.' She leaned her head back against the seat and shut her eyes.

She felt his hand on her arm. 'Don't go to sleep, Georgia. Not yet. How many did you take? You don't get like this after a couple of aspirins.'

Slowly she managed to work it out. 'It's all right. Only eight tablets of codeine, I think, and the first were very early this morning. But I had a lot of black coffee too, and I haven't been sleeping well.' She opened her eyes and smiled at him. 'Sorry, I suppose it was a bit stupid.'

'You're bloody right it was. And when did you last eat?'

Dreamily she thought about it. 'Lunchtime yesterday, I think.'

'Jesus, no wonder you're freaking out.'

Bron was at a loss for one of the few times in his life. She was leaning against the backrest of the ridiculous over-stuffed seat looking like a crumpled flower. Her eyes were closed, the lids smudged with the same tender violet-blue as the flowers on her dress, which reminded him of Monet's water-lilies. It was made of some soft, drifting material, against which her bare arms lay, her hands resting with loosely curled fingers in her lap.

She was normally so much in charge of herself that it was odd to see her defenceless. Odd, and yet seductive, making him feel as if the only natural thing to do was to look after her, to hold her. It was the same sort of irrational impulse he'd had in the attic at Merlinslade. He took her hand. The attendant he'd just spoken to began to look less suspicious, and walked slowly away into the next room. Bron thought that it was probably more than he deserved after his earlier outburst. He turned his mind to the problem of getting her out of the Gallery without another scene.

'Could you walk downstairs?' he asked. 'I can get a taxi outside.'

'Of course,' she said sleepily. 'Then I'll go home. I need to go home. I must speak to Chloe.'

Her eyes flew open. She sat up with a startled movement that stopped a couple of old ladies dead in their tracks. Her hands began to shake. She clasped them together.

'But Chloe's gone,' she said. 'No one ever stays.' She attempted a smile. 'I suppose Zelda would say I'm socially misaligned.'

Her voice stumbled over the phrase. She looked as if she was about to cry or laugh, or even worse, both together. The attention of the woman attendant focused on them again.

He put his arm round her. 'Forget Zelda. Let's concentrate on getting you out of here.'

He hauled her to her feet, and grabbed her bag with his spare hand. As he half carried her down the marble stairs, past the gaze of curious sightseers, and out into Charing Cross Road, he prayed she'd stay upright until he got her into a cab.

Providentially one had just finished disgorging passengers on to the pavement. He bundled her inside, and she flopped limply into a corner with her eyes closed. It was only too clear that she'd never make the journey home in her present state. He told the driver to go to Holland Park instead.

For some minutes she seemed to be asleep. He began to relax until a sports car with a broken silencer roared past. Her eyes flew open. In the comparative darkness of the interior they looked enormous. She stared out of the window as if she still couldn't focus properly.

'But this isn't the way to Paddington,' she said.

'I know. We're going to my flat.'

He tried to make it sound like a statement of incontrovertible fact. She seemed so untogether that he half expected her to wrench open the taxi door suddenly and disappear into the crowds. But to his consternation she began to laugh again, long shuddering laughs which rapidly began to peal out of control.

'Oh, Bron, I never met anyone else who was able to be quite so strong and silent and bossy all at the same time!' she said, gasping for breath.

The taxi halted at some lights. The driver, a shaven-headed heavyweight with rolls of fat round his neck, who up to now had seemed mesmerised by the bikini-clad doll hanging from his mirror, slid back the dividing window. He looked at them distrustfully.

'Better keep her quiet, mate,' he said to Bron, 'or I'll have to put you out. I don't carry druggies.'

Georgia was momentarily sobered. 'I'm not a druggie!' she said indignantly. 'I'll report him, I'll take his number!'

'For God's sake, just be quiet for another five minutes,' Bron said.

She opened her mouth to protest again, and found that he was kissing her. At first the situation seemed even funnier, until it suddenly began to take on quite a different aspect.

Bron, now still more concerned in case the driver imagined he was kissing her against her will – which was almost certainly true, he thought grimly – had put his arms around her in a further attempt to halt her muffled gasps. Her skin was warm through the thin dress. His hand moved before he knew it to her hair. It filled his fingers with a run of silk. She became quiet. The driver, satisfied at last, slid the glass partition shut. The taxi moved forward.

The sensation of being enclosed together in the half-lit interior of the taxi was intensely erotic. The kiss became far more than the diversionary tactic he'd originally intended. Her mouth was as soft as her hair. To his astonishment he felt it open beneath his. In a movement deliberate as a ballet dancer's she put her arms round his neck, and began to kiss him back languidly yet with great intensity. Her body was relaxed and heavy in his arms.

Bron struggled with feelings of a kind he'd deliberately avoided since the end of his marriage. The women he normally chose to take to his flat had, like himself, usually been divorced for some years, and were settled into comfortable single life-styles which they had no intention of giving up. They never stayed more than a night, and their couplings were always a sophisticated game, never a consummation. To make things worse, in her present state he couldn't even be sure that Georgia's reaction meant anything at all.

He had just enough sense left to glance out the window, and establish that they were leaving Holland Road. There was still a little time before they reached his flat. Abandoning every shred of long-ingrained caution he let his hand move to her breast. She sighed and pressed closer to him. Her mouth tasted slightly of coffee, like the most soft and delicious mocha ice-cream. His tongue explored the indented furrow of her upper lip, while his hand made a reconnaissance under the neckline of her dress, and he felt her breast slip into his palm like a heavy fruit.

The partition squeaked back.

'Here you are, mate, Ordnance Place,' said the cabby's voice. 'Can't wait long. There's a lorry behind me.'

Bron hastily withdrew his hand and sat up as he caught the driver's interested gaze. Georgia was lying back in the corner, smiling, with her eyes closed. She already looked half asleep.

In a complicated manoeuvre worthy of an officer's selection test he got her out of the taxi, holding her up with one arm, her bag crammed under the other, while he searched for the fare. Georgia's head drooped on to his shoulder.

'Right little cracker you've got there,' said the cabby.

'I think so,' said Bron with an answering grin, wondering why he felt so light-hearted all of a sudden. Recklessly he gave the driver a ten-pound note for the six-pound fare, and told him to keep the change. He was desperate to get Georgia inside before she went to sleep on the pavement.

Colonel Fawcett, the owner of the ground-floor flat, and so old that, to Bron's undying envy, he'd been a volunteer in the Spanish Civil War, was shakily looking through the afternoon

275

post in the entrance hall, a glass of brandy in his hand. Bron nodded non-committally and started to propel Georgia up the stairs. The colonel lifted his glass to him.

'That's right. Go for it, my boy,' he said, tottering off to his own entrance door.

Bron got her up the steep flight of stairs, and into his flat, where he hesitated briefly, wondering where to take her. He decided it'd have to be the bedroom. His sofa was built on less ambitious lines than hers, and in any case was covered with books he was sorting out to take to Merlinslade.

He steered her into the bedroom, which led off the sitting room, and like it looked over a square set with plane trees round some balding grass. With his free hand he dragged back the coverlet, and lowered her on to the bed.

She gave a deep sigh, flung one arm across the pillow, and immediately fell into a profound sleep. Her body was half turned, the shadowy valley between her breasts clearly defined. He went to the window, and drew the curtains partly across. When he came back to the bed she'd changed her position again, and moved fully on to her side. The lowest buttons on the skirt of her dress were undone, and it had rucked up and fallen apart over her thighs. She was wearing stockings with a pearly sheen. The skin above the lace tops glimmered in the half light. He'd intended to remove her sandals, but now he no longer trusted himself at all. He pulled the coverlet over her, and silently left the room.

Georgia was woken by the sound of taxi doors slamming in the street beneath. Dusk was gathering. Through the half-drawn curtains she could see tree tops and above them a fading sunset. She still felt leaden with sleep, but her headache had gone, leaving her mind in its usual curiously empty state after a migraine.

For a moment she couldn't remember where she was. The room, which was furnished soberly with some good old-fashioned pieces, held very few clues as to the character of the owner apart from the stack of CDs and a squash racket lying on a chest of drawers. But as she looked more closely and took in a framed opera house poster of Maria Ewing as Salome about to cast off the seventh veil, hanging next to a group photo of wooden army officers who looked incapable of casting off anything, she knew she was in Bron's flat.

Everything came back to her. She recalled with stinging clarity the gallery, the taxi ride, and the kiss. Then, worse than that, kissing him in return as though she was drunk, and worst of all hardly being able to walk up the stairs.

Hastily she left the bed, and went over to the window. There was only a short drop to the ground from the balcony, which ran along the front of the house, and contained a bay tree which needed pruning and a box of straggly geraniums. Her shoulder bag was on a chair, and for one mad moment she considered using the coverlet as a rope, and simply disappearing into the night. But even then she'd still have to face Bron at Merlinslade.

She peered at her watch. It was past nine o'clock. Her only other option was to pretend temporary amnesia, and make for Paddington as fast as possible. Still struggling with drowsiness, she found a bathroom leading off the back of the bedroom where she washed her face and tidied her hair. Then she went in search of Bron.

He was in the sitting room sorting out the contents of a bookcase. There was a sofa covered in faded white linen, a red leather library chair with a sagging seat, and in the window a small and beautiful walnut Pembroke table. Over the fireplace hung a Victorian watercolour of Merlinslade. Rusalka lay sprawled on the carpet with her tongue lolling.

Bron looked up as she approached. 'Hallo. How do you feel?'

'Better, thank you.' She took a deep breath and advanced further into the room. 'I'm sorry about – about what happened in the Gallery. I don't remember much, but it must have been awful for you.'

'Terrible,' he said.

The undercurrent of amusement had returned to his voice. She relaxed a little.

'And it's so odd,' she went on. 'I can't recall a thing about how I got here.'

'Really?' he said. He dumped an armful of books in a carton.

'Would you like to eat?' he asked. 'I was so hungry I got a takeaway. There's some left.'

'Oh God, I'm sorry again,' she said, remembering his plans for the evening. 'You must have missed your concert.'

'It doesn't matter. I think Rusalka's about to whelp, so I probably wouldn't have gone anyway. That's why I brought her with me. Nico's not very strong on midwifery.'

Though he was making it easy for her, she felt now that she couldn't repay him by getting in the way. She looked at her watch again. 'I'd better go. Truly.'

'The last train isn't till half-past eleven. You've plenty of time. Sit down. You must be ravenous.'

It was easier not to argue, though she still had no appetite. She went to the table, where a place had been laid. He disappeared, and came back carrying a bowl of Basmati rice starred with cloves and pieces of cinnamon. It was accompanied by a dish of chicken in a lemon sauce flecked with fresh coriander leaves, and some cucumber slices in yoghurt.

She felt a small stirring of hunger. He went away again, and returned with a glass of Perrier and ice for her, and a cup of coffee for himself. He sat down opposite her.

'You can manage some rice at least,' he said encouragingly.

Slowly she began to eat, and then with more alacrity. He spooned some of the chicken and yoghurt on to her plate.

'Sorry I'm slow,' she said. 'It's very good, but I feel so sleepy still.'

It took a long time to eat half of what he'd given her. He chatted lightly for most of the time, remarks that didn't need much in the way of reply. She guessed he was trying to keep her awake. Eventually she pushed the plate away, feeling slightly more anchored to the ground, and took a plum from a blue Spode bowl. Bron fetched himself more coffee.

'You weren't like that in the gallery just because of the migraine, were you?' he asked, stirring brown sugar into his cup. 'Something else upset you. Was it to do with Chloe?'

The unexpectedness and accuracy of the question caught her off guard. She answered without trying to wrap up her reply.

'She's gone to live with the Disciples for good.'

She gazed out over the square, feeling his eyes upon her as she wondered how much to tell him. The trees were almost in darkness, but she could hear the leaves whispering in a rising wind. The air was heavy and humid, as if it might rain at any moment.

'What happened?' he prompted again.

Hesitantly she began to unravel the events of the past few months for him, beginning with Chloe's arrival at the flat. When she finished she looked at him at last. 'I mismanaged the whole thing, didn't I?' she said.

He smiled, and went to move some papers off the window ledge. 'I left home like that when I was seventeen,' he said when he came back. 'I had a major row with my parents. They wanted me to go to agricultural college because they knew I'd have to look after Merlinslade eventually, but I was set on the army. I took an old tent and a rucksack, hitched up to Wester Ross, and walked about on the hills for a week. It was November, and there was a lot of snow. I've never been so cold in my life.'

'What did you do?' said Georgia, caught up in the tale in spite of herself. She could imagine Bron doggedly sitting it out in a tent under some lowering mountain peak.

He grinned. 'I got mumps, God knows how. Any normal germ should have dropped dead in that climate. I woke up one morning with a face like a turnip, and longing for my mother. A sobering experience for a seventeen year old trying to be independent.'

'So what happened next?'

'I went to the local doctor. He was a nice guy. He took me to Inverness station, and lent me the money for a sleeper home. It was like the return of the prodigal when I got there. We were all on our best behaviour for days afterwards, and when I was better my father said I could try for a commission as long as I did a year at college first. Surrender on all sides! So possibly Chloe may not find life at the Sanctuary quite so appealing once she's there full-time.'

'Maybe you're right,' she said, smiling. For the first time that day things began to seem more in proportion. 'I wish my mother was as co-operative. I met her at lunchtime, and she wouldn't even come down to Bath for one night to see Chloe.'

'I thought your mother was in Africa.'

'She's over here fundraising for her forest reserve. To be fair the negotiations are at a critical stage, but when she next comes to the UK it'll be too late.'

'Why?' said Bron.

Haltingly she told him about the latest financial developments at the Sanctuary.

'Jesus,' said Bron. 'What the hell's Morrigan playing at? I'm not surprised you're worried.'

The relief of someone taking her seriously at last was enormous.

'The problem is that you're the only person who agrees with me. Everyone else in the theatre thinks Morrigan's the second coming.'

Bron frowned. 'But why does he need these extra funds? He's loaded. He could easily finance the Disciples himself.'

'I don't know. Perhaps he simply wants the power. I just wish it didn't involve power over Chloe, that's all.'

'Would you like me to go up to the Sanctuary and talk to Brighid? It sounds as though she doesn't know what's going on.'

She stared.

'You don't have to look quite so worried. I wouldn't rush in with a horse whip. I can be tactful sometimes, you know.'

Yes, he could be tactful, she thought. She should have realised it sooner.

'I'd better cope with it myself,' she said slowly. 'Maybe it'll blow over. Chloe's going out with Sean, and I'll see if he can talk some sense into her. Zelda may have some ideas too. I think she's becoming slightly disenchanted with Morrigan. He never stops getting at Redvers.'

'You're pretty close to Zelda, aren't you?'

'She was good to me when my marriage went on the rocks. What she says usually makes sense.' Georgia was feeling better as the food began to take effect. 'She'd approve of my being here.'

'Why's that?'

'She thinks I'm in a state of fearful repression.' Georgia smiled to herself.

'She would,' said Bron drily. 'And are you?'

'I don't think so – at least, not as much as she makes out. It was hard when Blake left. It wasn't like the usual marriage break-up. Certainly not the sort of thing you often read about in agony columns. I never told Zelda everything, partly because Blake asked me not to, partly because I brought some of the pain on myself. It was my fault.'

'You shouldn't say that.'

'But it's true. I didn't try to see or understand. I didn't want to know about – his other side.'

The minute she'd spoken she thought what a fool she was. Now Bron would be sure to ask what she meant, and she didn't have the energy to deal with anything else that night. But to her surprise he said nothing. Instead he went over to the CD player and put on a disc. The voice of Callas, liquid and perfect as a nightingale's, stole softly into the room.

It was almost dark, but he hadn't turned on the lights. He stood for a moment with his back to her, seemingly absorbed in the aria. She thought what a strange mixture he was, usually so distant and self-controlled, yet able to give himself so unreservedly to the music. It was yet another puzzle, one she almost wanted to solve. But she'd already decided not to take any more risks, and lethargy was overwhelming her once again.

'I'd better go,' she said. 'If I don't, I'll fall asleep before I get to the train.'

'I'll take you to Paddington. Just let me clear the table first. It's too much of a temptation for Rusalka.'

She went over to the window while she waited. The sky was nearly dark, and rain had just begun to fall, pattering gently on the leaves of the plane trees lining the road, mingling the scent of greenery with the dusty smell of wet pavements. A couple, oblivious of the weather, went into the square and disappeared among the shadows. She waited for the usual aching sensation of loss, but it didn't appear.

She turned. Bron was standing in the doorway, looking at her. Callas launched into a new aria, this time the 'Habanera' from *Carmen*, the words, 'L'amour est enfant de Bohème' so strangely appropriate, the music haunting, tantalising, seeming to mock her for running away yet again. And suddenly she knew she didn't want to escape. The knowledge hit her like some lightning transformation scene, as if all the scenery of her mind had been shifted in a single second.

He came to her side and took her in his arms. He began to move about the room with her in time to the music. Her body moved closer to his. She put her hands behind his head, and began to kiss him as they danced. Hazily she heard Callas again. '*Et si je t'aime, prends-garde à toi.*'

'And if I love you, beware.' Bron was automatically translating the words to himself, thinking with his last rational thought that the words were so banal yet so true. The situation had the elements of everything he distrusted nowadays, purely emotional response, unconsidered action, and yet he found himself toppling over the edge of desire.

He manoeuvred her into the other room and on to the bed, feeling as if he'd just been given leave after years at the front. Her kisses were slow and sleepy, more tantalising than the 'Habanera' in their promise of future joys. Her tongue slid into his mouth as deliciously as a peeled grape, though her body was beginning to feel increasingly languid. He wondered if he was going to be frustrated yet again, and had the despairing thought that this was becoming like some never-ending test of knightly virtue.

Rapidly he began to undo the buttons of her dress. She let him slip it away like a child being undressed. The rest of her clothes were just as easy to get rid of. Her breasts fell free, shadows made by the light from a street lamp filtering through the leaves playing an erotic game of hide and seek, now revealing nipples a deep dusky rose, now flickering across a hip curved like a dune sculpted by the wind, now leading his eyes to the deeper shadow between her legs.

He began to undress, kicking away his shoes and socks beneath the bed, tearing off his trousers, wondering if he'd manage anything beyond the most basic of performances in his present state.

He heard her say his name drowsily, and went to sit by her, still wrenching at the buttons on his shirt.

'Bron,' she said, 'just hold me for a little while. I need you to. There's something I must tell you first.'

'Christ,' he muttered to himself. She'd be asking him to sleep with a sword between them next. She was probably going to tell him she'd slept with Nico, and that'd be almost as bad, though he'd guessed it long ago. But short of taking her against her will, there was nothing he could do until he'd heard her out. Patiently he lay down by her and took her in his arms once more. Her head fitted into the space between his shoulder and his neck like a bird settling into its nest.

'So, what's this great revelation?' he said, kissing her eyelids, and smoothing back her hair.

Georgia struggled not to give in to the infinitely persuasive ministrations of Bron's lips and hands, trying to detach her mind before she was completely lost.

'You must wait. You have to know what went wrong with me and Blake. It wouldn't be fair not to tell you.'

At least she didn't have to look at him while she spoke. She took a breath like a diver about to plunge into an ocean trench.

'Soon after we were married I discovered Blake wasn't – wasn't like most other men. He wasn't heterosexual, I mean.' Her voice stumbled. 'He'd had a secret affair with a man in New York before he met me. It was his first gay relationship, though he'd known for a long time that he was attracted to men as well as women.'

For a moment she couldn't continue as she remembered Blake almost in tears, trying to explain to her how he felt, and her own frozen disbelieving silence as she listened. As frozen as Bron's silence now.

Desperately she faltered on. 'It was difficult for him not to feel guilty about it – he'd had a strict religious upbringing – and eventually he decided he'd be happier as a heterosexual. He deliberately broke off the relationship with Lyndon, the other man. Blake told me nothing about any of this before we were married, and I never guessed. He was a marvellous actor.'

She was silent for a moment, still trying to gauge Bron's reaction, but he said nothing.

'Just a few weeks after our marriage Lyn came to Baltimore and told Blake he had Aids. Blake fell apart. He couldn't hide the relationship with Lyn any more. He had to tell me.'

She stopped again, remembering Blake's pale, anguished face, and her own feelings of horror and pity and betrayal. Bron remained completely silent. A car went by in the street, its tyres hissing on the wet tarmac.

'All he wanted then was to be with Lyn and look after him. Of course I couldn't stop him. As well as being frantic with worry about Lyn he was also terrified for himself. So terrified that he refused to have an HIV test. He said he couldn't bear to know if he was positive. So – so I didn't know whether I was positive either.'

She felt sick as she uttered the words, half expecting Bron to abandon her instantly, knowing too well how some people reacted to Aids as though it was the plague.

'Go on,' he said quietly.

'I went to the doctor. He told me it could take three months from the last time I slept with Blake for the virus to develop. So I had to wait from July to October to find out, and I couldn't tell anyone, not even Zelda.'

She began to shiver, and then she felt him move at last. His hand started to stroke her hair again.

'What made the waiting even worse was that I felt almost as though our relationship had never existed, as if I'd just been some incident along the way. Blake was completely absorbed in looking after Lyn. And on top of it all I felt so guilty, because I was jealous of Lyn even though he was dying.'

She turned up her head to look at Bron, but his face was in the shadow.

'Do you think that's very selfish of me? It seems like the ultimate act of meanness now. Yet I still can't forgive Blake.'

Bron, feeling as if he were treading through a mine-field, not wishing to hasten the story which was clearly so hard to tell, yet wanting to know the result more than he'd ever wanted to know anything in his life, thought that there was only one selfish person in all of this.

'I can understand why he had to go back. But to refuse to have the test, when it could have given you instant reassurance – I find it hard to forgive that myself.'

'Yet I wish I could,' she said. 'That's part of the trouble still.'

Her body was taut with stress. At first he'd wondered how he'd cope with his own reaction if she went on to tell him the test had been positive. But that thought had been rapidly overwhelmed with his own pity and horror at what she'd gone through, pity and horror which would only make her feel far worse if he expressed them openly. All he could think of was getting her through the confession as easily as possible.

'Hush,' he said. 'I'm not going away. Take your time.'

Softly he began to stroke the back of her neck and spine, forcing his hand not to stray.

Georgia felt the movement as a delicious, long repetitive caress. Gradually she relaxed. The relief of having told someone about Blake was immense. The drowsiness she'd been holding at bay for so long began to wash irresistibly over her, yet as she drifted into unconsciousness she remembered she had to tell him one thing more.

'The test was negative,' she said, and fell fast asleep.

Bron had never felt so wide awake as his mind raced over what she'd just said. He was still holding her naked body, and smelling the scent of her skin and hair, and yet he was unable to make love to her as if he were in chains. She didn't even stir as he got up, and pulled the coverlet over her.

He turned off Callas, who was now throbbing out 'Casta Diva', and went into the bathroom. As he opened the cold tap on the shower to its fullest extent, he thought with grim humour of how his Victorian ancestors would have approved. When he was dressed again, he poured himself a very large whisky, and sat thinking for a long time in the dark. He didn't move until almost midnight, when Rusalka began to whimper and move restlessly about.

Georgia woke to the sound of running water in the bathroom. She could see a line of light under the closed door. It seemed to be the middle of the night judging by the darkness outside and the lack of noise in the road. When the water ceased the only other sound was the distant hum of a city which never completely slept. The room was dimly lit by a street lamp. The curtains billowed gently in a light breeze. The rain had stopped, and the air smelt clean.

As her mind ranged back over the events of the previous evening, and she remembered she'd told Bron everything, the last vestiges of drowsiness abruptly vanished. She sat bolt upright as she realised she still didn't know his real reaction to her confession.

Then there was no more time to think about it as the light snapped off in the bathroom. She saw him emerge and pause to become accustomed to the dim light. He was naked except for a towel round his hips. His hair, damp from the shower, curled into the nape of his neck. She pulled the coverlet across her breasts.

'Bron,' she said, 'come and talk to me.' The matter had suddenly become so urgent that she couldn't wait.

He started, then walked over to the bed on bare feet, and stood looking down at her. A few drops of water on his shoulders glittered in the light from the street lamp. His stomach, flat and heavily muscled, tapered down to narrow hips beneath the towel. She was caught by a surge of lust as unnerving as the sudden drop of a plane in flight.

'I didn't realise you were awake,' he said. 'How are you?'

'I'm very well and very awake,' she said, stretching out her arm and taking his hand. 'Won't you come to bed with me?'

He didn't answer at once. The pause seemed to go on forever.

'I'm not so sure that's a good idea,' he said eventually. His hand was unresponsive.

Depression began to roll in again like a suffocating fog.

'Why not? At least tell me why.'

'Let's just say I don't want another cold shower,' he said. 'Two in one night are quite enough.'

'Two?' She didn't understand.

'One after you went to sleep, and one now. Rusalka had her pups an hour ago.'

'How many were there?' Georgia just managed to keep her voice as level as his own.

'Six, and she's fine.'

'How lovely,' Georgia said brightly, like a society hostess trying to cover up an awkward moment, while her mind continued to worry frantically over the real reason for his remoteness. And then she couldn't keep up the pretence any longer.

'You're like this because of what I told you. I shouldn't have done it. It's far too much to unload on anyone. I didn't even tell Nico.'

She was gabbling in her eagerness to reassure him that she'd told him the truth, that she understood his reaction, that she didn't mind.

'I really am clear, you know. You don't have to worry. There's not the slightest risk, but of course I understand why you don't want to go on. I should never have dumped on you in the first place.'

She struggled with the coverlet, trying to wind it round her before she stood up.

'If you call me a taxi I'll get the first train home. I think there's one just after five.'

Still he was silent, and an even worse thought struck her. 'Oh God, perhaps you thought I was leading you on just for the hell of it. That's what Nico thought too.'

Now she'd virtually admitted sleeping with his brother, and Bron was so bloody honourable he'd probably look on it as incest at the very least. Or perhaps he thought she was secretly still interested in Nico. She got up, almost tripping over the coverlet.

'You have to believe me. Though I slept with him there wasn't anything to it. Not – not as there might have been for you and me.'

At last the wariness left him. A moment later she was in his arms.

'Christ, Georgia, you've just given me the worst night of my life. You keep me on tenterhooks about the result of the test until I want you so much that I'm about to ravish you. Then you go to sleep on me yet again, though not before kindly informing me that you'll never get over your divorce.'

He paused to kiss her.

'After that I have to wait half the night for you to wake up, which gives me ample time to wonder if your behaviour is entirely due to some sort of mental freak-out and you don't mean any of it. Lastly I've had to act as obstetrician to an unstable prima-gravida, and when you do wake up you tell me you've slept with my brother. Then you're surprised I'm not totally enthusiastic for more punishment!'

'So you do believe me?' she said, though he was already unwinding the coverlet. 'And you're not worried about – about what happened in the States?'

'The only thing that worries me is whether I can do as well as Nico. I've a handicap of four extra years and two cold showers.'

Joyfully she responded to the amusement in his voice.

'I feel sure you'll manage,' she said.

Her fingers edged under the towel. It fell to the floor, and then they were on the bed once more. His unshaven skin was harsh against hers, but she hardly noticed it. He moved over her, his body blotting out the light. His mouth went swiftly to her nipples, his lips on the delicate flesh rousing in her a violence of response that made her forget almost everything. Almost but not quite. As always there was one more thing that had to be said.

And then, as she hazily heard him reach for something in the drawer of the bedside table, she realised he'd forestalled her. She sat up, gazing at him anxiously in the dim light.

'I haven't exactly lived like a monk since the divorce,' he said in a wry voice, 'but I had a blood-test recently too, and it was clear. I guess you'll want to feel safe, though.'

She put her arms round him. 'I trust you,' she said between kisses. 'You don't have to spare my feelings.'

This time there was laughter in his voice, laughter and deep tenderness together.

'Sparing your feelings is the last thing I'm about to do.'

His mouth and hands moved across her body, advance messengers telling her that her state of siege was over at last. His lovemaking was not at all the same as Nico's, and even more different from Blake's, powerful yet imaginative, yet holding intimations of even greater depths of passion to come. Soon he was invading all of her, taking her with him to the furthest outposts of desire, until all at once, as if spring had reclaimed a waste land, she felt her body flower, and she surrendered to pure delight.

When Georgia woke there was a stripe of sunshine across the floor, and she could hear a milk van rattling down the street.

Bron lay across her, still deeply asleep, his head on her breast, the sheet pushed down to his waist. She looked at her watch, and found it was past ten o'clock.

Bron didn't move as she left the bed. She had a shower, appropriated his discarded shirt as a makeshift dressing gown, and decided to make some tea in the small, galley-like kitchen. An old gentleman with a decidedly military look was dead-heading roses in the back garden below with a fearsome pair of secateurs. He caught sight of her and waved. While she waited for the kettle to boil she went to greet Rusalka, who was ensconced in her basket with her squirming litter, looking as if she wasn't quite sure about the overnight change to matron from coquette.

When she took the tea tray into the bedroom, Bron had moved on to his back to sleep. She bent over him, tickling his cheek with her eyelashes, blowing gently on his closed eyes. Still he slept. She slipped her hand under the sheet, across his hip bone, across the flat hard stomach, and mischievously on. His eyes opened, and she skipped away to pour out the tea.

He smiled at her. 'Not more tests?' he said.

'Just seeing how the Iron Duke is this morning.'

He hauled himself up against the pillows, and grinned. 'Ever ready,' he said.

She brought him a mug of tea, and sat on the edge of the bed, sipping her own. Lazily he put his free hand inside the half open shirt, and caressed her breasts.

'Rusalka and the puppies are fine,' she said. 'And an old man who looked just like Kitchener waved to me in the garden.'

He almost choked over his tea. 'Jesus, the colonel! I bet he did! He probably hasn't seen anything so exciting since he liberated Paris.'

He put the tea on the side table. His other hand was doing things which were making it impossible for her to fetch her own cup. He started to kiss her again.

'I think you should come back to bed right away,' he said softly in her ear. 'You shouldn't risk getting the colonel too worked up.'

At noon Bron went down to a Greek store on the corner and brought back newly baked sesame rolls, honey, butter, and coffee fresh from the roaster. Georgia, sitting at the window table after the meal, felt as lazy and contented as Rusalka looked.

She couldn't even be bothered to telephone Annie, and her other self who'd worried so frantically over Chloe seemed almost a stranger. It was probably all a false sense of security, and yet secretly, watching Bron through the kitchen door as he made another pot of coffee, she thought that it wasn't. Yet they'd discussed nothing about the future, and if the relationship was to continue, conducting it under the interested eyes of everyone at Merlinslade was not going to be easy.

Bron brought in the coffee. 'I feel as if I've scythed the whole of the great meadow single-handed. How about you?'

'Do you know what was the best of all?' she teased him. 'You didn't once mention marching through Georgia. Not even Nico could resist it.'

'So I was better than Nico?' he said. 'I've actually got you to admit it. Then won't you stay one more day? I'll ring home and say I can't move Rusalka yet. We can drive back to Merlinslade very early tomorrow, and miss the rush-hour traffic.'

Losing a day's work, which earlier would have been unthinkable, now seemed the easiest thing in the world. 'Are you sure they can manage at Merlinslade without you to keep them in line?' she teased him.

'Ned and Jason'll have a wonderful time beating up the estate on their bikes, and Nico can take all the hot water for his bath. I've been railroaded by the locals into letting them hold a Civil War re-enactment in the great meadow towards the end of the month, and I ought to be working on the arrangements. But they can wait, and I'll ask Nico to go to the parish council meeting instead of me tonight. He won't mind if it means he sees more of Esther. The affair's having an excellent effect on him.'

'An affair?' said Georgia. 'You mean Esther's actually slept with him?'

'That'd be almost as astounding as your sleeping with me, wouldn't it?' said Bron with a sidelong grin. 'No, not yet, though apparently Nico's working on it. The other day Mrs Meads heard him trying to get her into the Red Boudoir by telling her it was Letitia's private chapel. Mrs M was outraged.'

Georgia started to laugh, but quickly sobered. 'It'd be pretty serious for Esther if she did sleep with him. Being ordained is still more important than anything to her, and even if Nico's serious too, acting and the ministry wouldn't easily go together.'

'Stop worrying about everyone else,' said Bron. 'How about us? Are we serious?'

He gave her a look which made it even hard to say her next words. She'd been burnt so badly by her divorce that this time she had to be absolutely sure.

'I want to be more than anything. But let's not go too fast, and let's not tell anyone yet. We can easily keep it a secret if you come to my flat.'

'All right,' he said slowly. 'If that's what you really want.'

'I daren't tell Chloe yet. I don't know how it would affect her, and I must get her back. Then there's Ned. He likes me, I know, but having to accept me as a rival for your affection is quite another thing. I remember how difficult it was when my father began to see someone new. And then – then – ' She hesitated.

'Then what?' he said. 'Nothing you've said seems insuperable so far.'

'Then there's Imogen.'

She hadn't been mentioned so far. Indeed, since Georgia had known Bron, she'd only heard him refer to Imogen briefly a couple of times, but she remembered Nico saying he thought Bron might be holding a torch for her still. Georgia knew how destructive jealousy could be. She couldn't ever go through that again.

Bron frowned. 'Imogen's over. We're divorced. What's she got to do with us?'

'Bron, you have to understand,' she said desperately. 'It'll be quite hard for me. You won't ever have to meet Blake. He's in a different continent, a different world, and he wants to see me as little as I want to see him. But Imogen's still around. She's coming to see Ned soon: he told me so himself.'

'I'll cope with Imogen. And anyway there's no need for you to worry about her. She rang to say she's too busy to come to Merlinslade after all. She's negotiating an offer of a partnership in the States.'

'I'm sorry,' she said. 'It's just that I haven't felt as happy as this for a long time. I couldn't bear anything to spoil it.'

His face cleared. Her hand was lying on the table. He took it, turned up the palm, and kissed it.

'Nothing's going to be spoiled, I promise. But if it makes you happier we'll keep things quiet just for a little while.'

Afterwards they walked in Holland Park, and later Bron got some last-minute tickets for the opera, which she sat through in a state of heightened awareness, both of his presence and of the music. She was glad to have a private breathing-space to adjust to the almost overwhelming intensity of this new relationship.

Next day Bron, closely attended by an anxious Rusalka, transferred the puppies to the Range Rover, and they set off for Merlinslade. It was too early even for joggers. The Wiltshire downs were shrouded in dawn mist, and in Bath, where they stopped at the flat for breakfast and for Georgia to change into working clothes, only the newspaper shops were open.

Changing her clothes led to more lovemaking, but it was still only nine-thirty when they arrived at Merlinslade.

Mr Meads opened the lodge gates with his usual phlegmatic stare.

'Let's hope he assumes I picked you up at the bus stop,' said Bron cheerfully, 'because if Mrs M gets wind of this we don't stand a chance of keeping it quiet.'

She put her hand on his thigh, and gave him a sidelong smile. 'I'm almost beginning to think I wouldn't mind.'

The Range Rover performed a spectacular swerve across the drive. He just straightened it in time.

'Jesus,' he said, 'don't do that. Otherwise I'll have to take you into the rhododendrons here and now.'

Cows were grazing in the water meadows, scattered like dominos through the grass. The avenue of limes had darkened to the deep green of high summer. Bron stopped the car in front of the house. Georgia leaned from the car window to enjoy the scent from the banks of lavender by the door.

Bron took her hand. 'I very much doubt if I'm going to be able

292

to look as if nothing's happened, but I'll try. Kiss me before we go in.'

She'd begun to move towards him when she heard the front door creak open. She shot away to the side of the car. Ned came tearing down the steps, rushed across the courtyard, and stuck his excited face through the window.

'Hi, Georgia. Hi, Dad.' He craned over Georgia's shoulder to look in the back.

'Has Rusalka had her puppies?' he asked, his words tumbling out.

'Six of them,' said Bron. 'You can choose which one you like. But don't handle them yet.'

'Open the back door, please,' pleaded Ned. 'I must see.'

Bron went round to the rear to unlock the hatchback. Ned was bouncing up and down in a fever of impatience, but as he climbed into the car he remembered something.

'I almost forgot to tell you,' he said casually over his shoulder. 'Mum's here. She drove down last night. She says she's staying till September.'

Georgia switched her gaze in dismay back to Bron, and saw that he was staring at someone behind her with a mixture of wariness and resignation.

'Well,' said a clear, confident voice. 'I can see Ned's rapidly losing whatever social graces he once possessed. And for God's sake, Bron, haven't you reminded him how I hate to be called Mum? It's so suburban. He'd learned to call me Imogen in London.'

Georgia turned. At the foot of the steps stood a woman a few years older than herself, with silver-blonde hair cut in an ultra-short geometric bob. Her mouth was glossed with a shade of deep magenta which would have made anyone less sophisticated look like a refugee from a twenties movie. Her clothes were an Italian version of country house wear, mushroom-coloured silk jacket, crêpe de Chine palazzo pants, and a long Hermès scarf.

'Hallo, Imogen,' said Bron, walking slowly towards her. 'I thought you told me you were busy.'

'I decided it wasn't a problem after all. I've brought a fax machine and my PC with me, and Jasper's looking after things in

London. The partnership offer's gone off the boil, and I couldn't bear the thought of disappointing Ned.'

'Really,' said Bron.

'Don't look so grumpy,' said Imogen. 'You ought to be pleased. I can help you sort out the house.'

She kissed him lightly. Over his shoulder her Alpine blue gaze fell on Georgia as she climbed down from the Range Rover dressed in her shabbiest shirt and jeans because she was going to work on the special effects machinery.

Imogen lowered her voice, but not quite enough. 'And who's this, darling? Have you taken my advice and hired a proper cleaner to replace Mrs Meads at last?'

Chapter 15

'You'll jump to conclusions once too often one day, Imogen,' said Bron coldly. 'I'd like you to meet Georgia Tremain, our costume designer. Georgia, this is Ned's mother, Imogen.'

'I do have other functions besides motherhood, Bron, but you never liked to recognise that,' said Imogen, nodding at Georgia with a smile that had all the radiance and artificial warmth of a log-effect fire.

Georgia could almost see Imogen's thought processes as she took in her working clothes and tied-back hair: no competition sexually, and from her appearance probably not a success professionally either.

'I recognise it only too clearly,' Bron snapped back at her. 'Motherhood's always been second best for you.'

Imogen ignored his remark. 'I do think you might have made a little more effort with Ned. He looks a complete scruff. And the friend who was here with him yesterday evening, Jason something or other, was even worse. I can't think why you sent Ned to a comprehensive school. He'll be picking up a local accent next. You know I'd have paid for him to go somewhere decent.'

'He's there because it's what he wanted. I don't give a damn how he speaks as long as he's happy.'

'Be realistic, Bron. One hears the most horrific stories about comprehensive schools. If you don't get Ned focused on achieving now, he'll drift into some totally dead-end job. He hardly talks about anything except cars and machinery as it is. He'll end up as a used-car salesman at this rate.'

'He might make a bit more money than me, then.' An abrasive edge had crept into Bron's voice.

'Don't be so bloody flippant,' said Imogen. 'You know exactly what I mean. In another few years Ned'll be out in the world. At a decent school he'd get the right contacts, the right attitude. It isn't easy like the eighties any more.'

'We've been all through this before,' said Bron. His voice was beginning to sound weary. 'Your idea of the right attitude isn't mine. It hasn't been for a long time. In fact I doubt if it ever was.'

Georgia hated the way she was being forced into the role of unwilling witness, and equally she couldn't bear seeing Bron so swiftly revert to the tense, irritable person she'd first met in the kitchen at Merlinslade.

She made herself manufacture a smile as synthetic as Imogen's. 'It hardly seems fair to base your views on comprehensive schools on hearsay. I went to one myself, and it was excellent.'

Imogen looked at her properly for the first time. 'Really?' she said, with a wealth of disbelief in the word. 'Forgive me for saying so, but doesn't your present job bear out what I've said? Merlinslade isn't London or New York. I want Ned to fix his sights on a wider horizon.'

'I've just spent two years working in America. A state education wasn't a drawback there, and it hasn't been here. Surely it's best for Ned to be happy now, and make his own decisions when the time comes.'

Imogen was beginning to look slightly ruffled, but Georgia only had a few moments to enjoy the effect of her words before Ned came tearing over from the car, kicking up a shower of gravel and almost cannoning into his mother as he skidded to a halt.

'The puppies are ace, Mum! You've got to come and see them.'

'Imogen, please, Ned. How many times have I told you?' His hair was sticking up at the back, and she smoothed it flat. 'Have you brushed your hair today?'

He flushed and jerked his head from her hand. 'I want you to come and see them. Please, Mum – Imogen, I mean. I know you didn't like Conan because he chewed up your shoes, but these pups are different, truly.'

'Sweetie, puppies grow up, and if they're not trained properly they become a nuisance just like Conan.'

She looked meaningfully at Bron. Ned's gaze rushed anxiously between his parents' faces. Georgia guessed he was torn between wanting the new puppy, and trying to keep Imogen happy.

'Anyway you really don't have time for puppies now you're at secondary school,' Imogen went on. 'You should be thinking about more serious things. Now go inside and tidy yourself up. I want to have a nice long talk to you this morning.'

'Please, Dad.' Ned's voice was desperate.

'I think you'd better do what your mother says,' said Bron in a level tone, 'but you can carry the basket with the puppies into the kitchen first, if you're very careful.'

Ned dashed off to the Range Rover to fetch the puppies before Imogen could object. The battle of emotions on his face had been so patent, the tug of divided loyalty so evident, that Georgia began to feel uneasy about herself and Bron all over again. She remembered how she felt when her father announced that he was going to live with Karen, knowing she ought to be fair to her, for it was long after the divorce, yet being utterly and unreasoningly on her mother's side. Ned didn't need more problems, especially when he'd just started to settle down at Merlinslade.

'Don't be cross, darling,' said Imogen to Bron. 'You should be able to relax more now I'm here to cope with Ned.'

She put her hand on Bron's shoulder and kissed him lightly on the lips, as if to demonstrate that she still had rights over him. He stood motionless, seeming to will himself to resist the caress.

Ned, proceeding proudly towards the house with the basket of puppies, saw the kiss as he passed, and gave his parents a hopeful, longing look which disturbed Georgia even more.

'Tell Ned to come and see me in the library,' Imogen said to Bron. 'I've set up my PC and fax machine there. The first input for the day should be coming through from Jasper. You really ought to turn the PR for Merlinslade over to me, you know. I'd reduce my rates for you and Nico. I've never heard of this Bath firm you've hired.'

'We're fine as we are,' said Bron.

Imogen gave an elegant shrug. She wasn't wearing a blouse beneath her jacket, and Georgia's eye caught the curve of a small, high breast contained by only the briefest of bras. She had a sudden devastating vision of Bron making love to Imogen, and then a wave of jealousy of the sort she hadn't experienced since Blake left her.

'I'll see you at lunchtime, then,' said Imogen. 'Nico says you've got some amazing local girl to cook for you. It'll make a change from poor old Mrs M. You really have to retire her, Bron. You'll never get the house pulled together until you do.'

She glided away, throwing her scarf over her shoulder in an immensely elegant gesture. With her lithe perfectly groomed body and enormous self-confidence, she seemed to charge the atmosphere, as though her mere presence could make some sort of change occur in those around her.

Bron gazed after her in silence.

'The same as ever,' he said. He smiled at Georgia and took her hand. 'Couldn't you change your mind about keeping things secret? It's going to be even more difficult with Imogen here. It'll be like having the CIA in the house.'

He moved his hand up her arm. She tried to concentrate, still more certain that they must have time for their relationship to develop. It was far too delicate at this stage to expose to Imogen's predatory gaze, though she longed to shout out her happiness to the whole world.

'You said originally that you didn't want Imogen at Merlinslade, so why don't you just send her away?' she asked, knowing it was a useless question even before she'd voiced it.

'I wish I could, but I can't for Ned's sake. He hasn't started to view her critically yet, though that'll probably come quite soon. He's growing up fast. But for the moment he accepts her inconsistencies, and I think she loves him too in her own odd way.'

Georgia was silent. She was under no illusions that she'd have to share Bron with Ned and Merlinslade. She'd share him willingly with Ned, of whom she already felt almost as fond as Chloe, and she'd try to share him with Merlinslade, though she suspected this would be much harder. But she had no intention of sharing him with Imogen.

Out of the corner of her eye she could see Mr Samms approaching through the gate in the hedge. In a moment there'd be no chance of speaking freely to Bron for the rest of the day.

'Let's have a little time to ourselves without everyone knowing and watching and commenting,' she said. 'It'll be like some awful royal engagement otherwise.'

The tension left Bron's face. He grinned. 'I hope you don't equate the Carwithens with the House of Windsor,' he said. 'Right, we'll keep it quiet until after the first night of the play. But not a moment longer.'

When Georgia arrived at the wardrobe she discovered that Chloe had still not appeared for work. Before she began to tackle the long list of problems waiting for her, Georgia decided that she must ring the Sanctuary and try to re-establish communications. She was infuriated to be told firmly by Brighid that Chloe was incommunicado because she was on the verge of self-realisation.

During her final months in the States Georgia had had to train herself, for the sake of her professional survival, to put Blake and the problems of the divorce out of her mind. That training stood her in good stead now as she refused to let herself think of anything except the final fittings, which were scheduled to begin at the end of the week.

Hems needed to be checked, closings aligned for a perfect fit, hats and wigs adjusted so that they sat easily together. She spent over an hour with the actor who played Trinculo, watching him turn somersaults round the room, and then patiently altering seams until they were both convinced that his costume couldn't possibly fall apart. She was so absorbed that she didn't go over to the kitchen for lunch until almost half past two.

Georgia had hoped to avoid Imogen. But as she entered the kitchen, she knew instantly from the atmosphere that she was in the room, even before she saw her sitting in the Windsor chair at the other end of the table from Bron, unconcernedly slashing on lipstick with bold, confident strokes.

Nico was there too, forking up the last of a slice of gooseberry pie, and keeping a watchful eye on Zelda, who was clearly upset. Her Power Book was on the table, and she was stabbing at the keys, her face as flushed as Ned's had been earlier on. And Kim was standing at the work top by the window, flour powdering her black canvas jeans, glaring belligerently at the assembled company, and beating a bowlful of cake mix with her arm going like a propeller.

On the way Georgia had stopped to speak to Mrs Meads, who was polishing in the great hall, and she'd entered the kitchen from inside the house. As she paused by the dresser Bron sent her a smile which was half conspiratorial, half apologetic.

Imogen shut her compact with a click like the rap of a conductor's baton, and sent her vivid smile round the table.

'I knew you'd see it my way in the end, Bron. So it's agreed that I'll take over the publicity arrangements for the re-enactment, and the catering for the first night party? There's still time to get in touch with all the right people. I'll sort out some party entertainment as well, since Zelda isn't quite up to putting on a little private masque for us as I suggested.'

'Damn right I'm not!' said Zelda. 'I've more than enough on my hands.'

'Zelda works the hardest of us all,' said Georgia, coming over to the table, 'and the wardrobe staff are stretched to their limit.'

'I quite understand,' purred Imogen. 'You mustn't worry about it, Zelda. Some women have to set their sights a little lower as they mature.'

'You'll be lucky if you've half my energy in twenty years' time! I'm not about to waste it on something that isn't in my contract.'

'The sort of entertainment I have in mind will be perfectly easy to arrange,' said Imogen, powering on like a runaway lawn-mower.

'An interesting little demonstration of knee-capping, perhaps,' said Nico sotto voce to Georgia, as she slid into the seat next to him.

'As Kim's made it very clear that she's not interested in catering for the banquet, I'll hire a professional firm,' Imogen continued. 'It's probably for the best. We don't want anything too rustic.'

Kim glowered at her over the mixing bowl. Imogen pushed back her chair and stood up.

'And before you start to say yet again that the estate can't afford it, Bron, I'll pay.'

She smiled at Kim.

'That was a delicious meal, my dear. Perhaps a shade too much seasoning in the paella, but very well done, all the same. If ever you think of setting up in business on your own, do let me know.'

She passed by the back of Zelda's chair, leaned over her shoulder and deleted a typing error with a scarlet-tipped finger. 'I expect you forgot that schedule isn't spelt with a k over here,' she said sweetly, and proceeded towards Bron.

Georgia, watching him covertly as she took some paella, saw the shutters come over his expression at her approach.

'I want you to come to the library with me now, Bron, and look at some ideas I've roughed out for reorganising the main rooms,' Imogen said. 'It won't take long.'

'Sorry, but I'm busy this afternoon. And in any case I have my own ideas for the house.' Bron's voice was brittle with suppressed irritation.

One of the points of his shirt collar had become folded under, and Imogen smoothed it flat in a gesture which she made both wifely and proprietorial, letting her hand remain on his shoulder.

'It's because you're so busy that I feel I must concern myself. And we have to face it, interior design really isn't your thing, darling.'

Deliberately he removed her hand.

'Let's get this clear now, Imogen. I don't want any changes.'

Imogen seemed unperturbed. She walked towards the door, but as she was about to go through, turned. 'I'll just move one or two things around in the hall this afternoon – Ned can help me – and put up a few fabric samples I found in Bath this morning. You can see what I've done at teatime. But of course if you'd just spare ten minutes to look at my plans now, you could be sure that you liked it beforehand. And then afterwards I might feel like going to see the puppies with Ned.'

Bron's face darkened at the blatant blackmail. As Imogen whisked out of the door he stood up angrily and crushed his table-napkin in his fist.

'Damn you, Imogen,' he said in a low voice, as he threw the napkin down and followed her from the room.

There was a long silence.

'Christ,' said Nico. 'Sorry, everyone. Bron's going spare over her. He's only letting her help with the battle to keep her quiet.'

'I want it crystal clear that she's not to come within a hundred miles of the theatre's PR,' said Zelda. 'Otherwise I'm on the next plane back to the States.'

Georgia took some salad. 'And if Zelda goes, I go too,' she said recklessly. She'd never broken a contract, but carrying on at Merlinslade with Imogen and without Zelda would be impossible.

Nico was rooting round in the bottom of the dresser. He straightened, producing a bottle of Armagnac. 'I knew I had this left over from my duty frees,' he said. 'I think we all need a strengthener.'

He brought some antique spiral-stemmed glasses from the cupboard, and set them on the table.

'Come and sit down for a moment, Kim,' he said. 'You must have pounded that cake mix to death by now.'

She scraped the contents of the bowl into a baking tin, slid it into one of the ovens in the range, dragged her apron over her head, and pulled up a chair, still scowling. Nico passed round the drinks. Zelda shut her laptop, and leaned back in her seat, her eyes closed, breathing deeply.

'I'm going to need every Zen exercise in the book to help me survive that bitch,' she said.

Nico moved behind Zelda, massaging her shoulders. 'Don't worry about Imo. I confidently expect her to start missing London in a week or two.'

'She'd better not spend too much time on my patch, either, or I'm off as well,' said Kim, downing half her brandy in one gulp.

'It's my bet you'll hardly see her in here at all,' Nico soothed her. 'It's much too low-key. She'll be away to the Veneziana for lunch most days. You can't desert us now, Kim. The morale of the company's gone up a hundred percent since you took over the cooking. Redvers said that toffee pudding you made the other day was worth a Michelin star.'

Even Kim wasn't impervious to Nico's blandishments. Her face lit up with pleasure.

'That's something else I need to talk to you about, Nico,' said Zelda, who was also reviving under his ministrations. 'I thought Redvers' self-confidence problem would improve as he eased into the part, but Morrigan's been going too far lately. I think Georgia was right about him all along.'

Georgia stared at Zelda. It was the first good news she'd heard since arriving at Merlinslade that day.

'I know, I know, Georgy,' said Zelda, 'You've every right to look at me like that.' She turned to Nico, who'd taken a seat next to her. 'Morrigan never lets up on trying to undermine Redvers. It's not just an ordinary case of professional jealousy, as I thought at first. It's got an undercurrent I don't like, and when Redvers is upset the whole cast reacts badly. You've got to tell Morrigan to lay off.'

'I'll try to have a word with him,' said Nico easily. 'But you have to admit the music he's done for us is out of this world. And it'll give Redvers more confidence if he learns to deal with Morrigan on his own.'

'Maybe,' said Zelda firmly. 'But I'd like him to have some help along the way, so please do it, Nico.'

'Right,' said Nico, who was starting to look as if he'd had enough problems for one day. 'I'd better go back to the office, then, if everyone's OK now. I've got some overseas calls to make.'

'Thank God you've seen what Morrigan's really like at last,' said Georgia to Zelda, as soon as Nico had gone. She helped herself to some more salad.

'He's becoming a first-class pain in the ass,' said Zelda. 'He hates taking direction. He slips out of line if you take your eyes off him for a second.'

'I wish Esther would see the light over Morrigan as well,' said Kim. 'She will keep making allowances for the slimy bastard.'

'She's too busy seeing the light over Nico,' said Zelda, 'though I'm not so sure he's entirely good news for her. I thought he'd help her loosen up, but she's got very jumpy lately.'

'Yeah, she even shouted at the kids at the rectory the other day. The rest of us yell at them all the time, but normally Esther never does,' said Kim.

'I bet you don't bawl them out the way Imogen does Ned,' said Zelda. 'She sent the poor kid to finish his meal in the stables just because he spilt a glass of water. Boy, does she think she's the big enchilada!'

'It must be tough for Bron having her around. When you're over a relationship you want out for good,' said Kim. 'He's an OK guy – it's a shame.'

'I thought you didn't like him,' said Georgia.

'He's straight, and he's paying me a decent wage. He laid it on the line when he took me on, about no punch-ups on the estate, but I did too. I told him I wouldn't hack it if he tried any upper-class rubbish with me, and he hasn't. I wouldn't like to mess with him, though. I should think he could be heavier than a ton of bricks if he wanted.'

'Not with Imogen,' said Zelda. 'Did you notice? No one knows better than me about keeping in with one's ex because of the child, but I think there's a tad more to it than that. He could shut her up a lot more thoroughly. He does everyone else when he wants to.'

'Maybe he's thinking he ought to try to get it together again for Ned's sake,' said Kim. 'Poor sod if he does.'

Georgia pushed away the helping of salad unfinished. 'I'd better be getting back to the wardrobe. We're only just on schedule,' she said.

Kim got up and retrieved her apron. 'I must bugger off as well, and start the washing up,' she said.

'How was your trip to London?' Zelda asked Georgia, as Kim retired to the butler's pantry. 'Did you take in any plays?'

'Not this time. I had to talk to my mother about Chloe. And I had a migraine.'

'Doesn't sound much like a bundle of laughs. Are you sure you aren't holding out on me? You haven't looked so relaxed for a long while.'

'I had to rest a lot because of the headache,' said Georgia, imagining Zelda's screech of horror if she knew where she'd been resting. To deflect any further detective work she added quickly, 'Chloe moved out of the flat to the Sanctuary just before I met my mother. I'm terrified she'll join the Disciples permanently. They've got a baptism ceremony coming up soon.'

'Christ!' said Zelda. 'What's your mother going to do?'

'Nothing. She's still convinced it'll blow over. And Chloe refuses to talk to me on the phone or meet me, so all I can do is hope she sees what Morrigan's really like before it's too late.'

'I'm not surprised you had a headache,' said Zelda. 'I'd go crazy if Howie got involved with a set-up like that. In fact now I've seen how Morrigan operates on Redvers, I'm beginning to think he's seriously out of gear. Have you spoken to Sean about Chloe?'

'Yes, after I'd phoned the Sanctuary. He's pretty upset. She didn't even want to speak to him.'

'Can't you ask the police to do something?' said Zelda.

'What exactly? Chloe's over sixteen. She's a free agent, and she hasn't been harmed physically at the Sanctuary. Brighid's had a good reputation up to now for helping young people. I've nothing concrete to complain about.'

'Then I guess it is just a case for hoping for the best. When's the baptism taking place?'

'Chloe said it's a secret.'

'Maybe you'll pick up a lead somewhere. And you know, Georgy, you really do look great after your break.'

Imogen was everywhere as she took over the publicity for the re-enactment, scattering her business cards like poisoned confetti, infuriating Zelda with continued unwanted advice, making Mrs Meads look permanently put-upon with her demands, and creating a general atmosphere of tension. It reminded Georgia of the end of dry seasons in Africa, when lightning crackled along the horizon all night, and the air seemed permanently charged with electricity.

Bron managed to visit Sophia Street most evenings. He was often on edge when he arrived, but Imogen was rarely mentioned by either of them. Georgia assumed he was as reluctant as herself to discuss the past. And all she wanted at the moment was to try to build on the relationship they'd begun to establish in London. It would be easier and safer to talk about Imogen when she'd left Merlinslade.

And once Bron had unwound, once they'd talked, and he'd made love to her with his own particular blend of tenderness and strength which always held an irresistible hint of even deeper passion, as though he still hadn't quite lowered all his defences, she felt too thankful for her present happiness to want to do anything to endanger it.

As the re-enactment approached, Bron became increasingly disenchanted with it. A few days before the event he arrived at the Sophia Street flat seething with annoyance.

'It was supposed to be an informal local affair,' he said, when Georgia had brought him a very large whisky, 'but I've been so busy with the harvest that Imogen's been able to arrange all sorts of extras behind my back. She's publicised it as far away as Bristol. God knows how many visitors'll be pouring on to the estate, and we don't have enough experienced wardens to deal with them.'

Georgia had begun to water the house plants in an effort to keep herself calm. She was becoming increasingly resentful of the way Imogen kept Bron on a permanent slow fuse. She watched him through the fronds of the palm. She knew his face as well as her own by now, but because they'd talked so little about their marriages there were other things about him that she didn't know at all.

Each evening he'd leave the flat looking relaxed and cheerful, and yet when Georgia saw him next day he'd be as tense as a gundog again. He almost exaggeratedly avoided any physical contact with Imogen, but she touched him as much as possible: perching on the arm of his chair, pressing her long toffee-coloured legs against his, resting her chin on his shoulder as she leaned over to show him her sheaves of plans. Georgia couldn't understand why he didn't shrug her off, or why he so often let her have her own way.

'You must have known this was likely to happen when you let Imogen loose on the PR. I've never understood why you agreed,' she said.

Her own day, spent bringing the costumes to a state of perfection for the dress rehearsal, had been just as long and hard as his, and she wasn't able to stop a note of exasperation creeping into her voice.

'It would have been worse if she hadn't had the re-enactment to occupy her,' Bron said. 'She'd have focused all her energies on Ned. As it is he's been able to have a fairly carefree holiday.'

'But why do you give in to her so often? The more she gets, the more she wants. Don't you see that?'

'Of course I do,' said Bron, coming over and taking the watering can firmly away from her. 'But if you still want to keep this secret, the best way to stop her becoming suspicious is to keep her busy. I just have to deal with the fall-out as best I can.' He pushed aside a frond of palm which hung between them. 'And stop frowning at me through this overgrown aspidistra. You always rush off to the plants when you're upset.'

'You know very well it's not an aspidistra. It's a very fine Kentia palm, and it's perfect just there.'

He began to kiss her. 'It's not perfect if it keeps us apart. Stop being suspicious of me and Imogen. One of the reasons I love you is because you're so unlike her. You never make demands.'

As usual their lovemaking was acting like some magic balm, smoothing out the day's irritations, making her forget everything except the present moment.

'I believe I'm going to make some now,' she said, starting to unbutton his shirt. It was only much later, as they lay on the sofa in a state of lethargic content that she remembered he hadn't fully answered her question.

The afternoon before the re-enactment Georgia returned to the wardrobe from a rehearsal to sense a different feeling there, and a different scent from the usual one of bales of new fabric, ironing and spray starch. Imogen was giving the room a leisurely examination, pulling back covers from racks of costumes, tweaking at trims, and inspecting Georgia's designs on the display board, while Annie hovered round her with an infuriated look on her face.

'I'd no idea you had such an ambitious set-up,' Imogen said when she saw Georgia. 'Nico's sung your praises so often that I thought I'd come and see for myself.'

'It would have been helpful if you'd let me know in advance, then I could have arranged to show you around properly,' said Georgia, as Annie melted discreetly away.

'I just wanted to be friendly,' said Imogen with a disarming smile. 'Nico made me think I might have offended you in some way.'

Georgia was still suspicious. 'It would have been better not to jump to conclusions about me,' she said brusquely.

'I really am sorry,' said Imogen, examining a lace ruff. Her voice was friendlier than it had ever been before. 'Do you like Nico?'

'It would be hard not to like him, as I'm sure you know.' Georgia took the ruff from her before she wrecked it.

'Only too well,' said Imogen, in a way which hinted all sorts of things Georgia refused to think about. 'I'm very impressed by what he's been telling me about you. How did you start up?'

This was an Imogen Georgia hadn't seen before, warm, and apparently genuinely interested. She began to understand why she had such a good PR reputation, and how hard it must have been for Bron to resist her when they first met, if this was the side she'd shown him. Nevertheless she remained wary, even when Imogen made a couple of business suggestions that Georgia had reluctantly to accept were inspired.

'If you ever decide to expand your business and need some publicity, I'd be only too happy to help.' Imogen put one of her ubiquitous business cards down on a table. 'Perhaps I could have a quick look at Ned's costume for the battle while I'm here. He seems remarkably keen on it. I only wish he were as enthusiastic when I ask him to wear a jacket.'

Bron had given reluctant permission for Ned to take part in the re-enactment, and Georgia had been working on a costume for him in her few leisure moments, trying to make it look as dashing as possible while cutting out anything that could possibly be construed as girlish. It hadn't been easy. As she laid out the costume for Imogen to see, she rearranged the trim on the hat, which sported an immense ostrich plume he actually approved of. She was certain he'd lose it in the battle, but it was essential to cover up his hair, which he'd refused to grow to the required Cavalier length.

Again Imogen heaped Georgia with praise.

'I gather from Ned that he helps here sometimes. I do hope he doesn't get in the way. He's going through such a clumsy phase.'

Ned had helped to make some giant papier mâché shells for the beach set, but lately the weather had been so good that he was spending most of his time out of doors with Jason.

'He's not in the way at all. He's good at practical work.'

'And he tells me he's had tea several times at your flat. It's very kind of you to take so much trouble over him.'

The level, silky voice sounded utterly sincere.

'I like Ned,' said Georgia shortly. 'It's been a pleasure.'

'I nearly died when he was born,' said Imogen. 'You can't imagine the agony. We had to get a full-time nanny from the start, and so I never had a chance to bond properly with him. I'm sure that's why he's difficult to manage now.'

She slipped Georgia a let's-be-girls-together glance through long black lashes. The contrast between them and her ash blonde hair was so marked that Georgia, coldly resisting the look, thought with sneaking satisfaction that one or the other must be dyed.

'Bron was most unsympathetic, of course,' Imogen went on, poking at a heap of fabric scraps with the toe of her elegant green leather shoe, 'and he's become even harder over the years. He's never really been able to give himself wholly to anyone. That's why we parted. But there's still a certain chemistry between us.'

She gave a complacent smile. Georgia forced herself to appear unmoved.

'I often wonder if I should consider coming down here for good, and trying to make a go of things with Bron again,' Imogen went on relentlessly. 'Ned obviously needs me. What would you advise? You must know him quite well by now.'

'That's your business entirely,' said Georgia. 'He's your child, not mine.'

'Yes, he is, isn't he?' said Imogen sweetly.

The implication that Georgia had overstepped the mark in befriending Ned was clear. She wondered if Imogen was simply jealous, or if there was more to it than that, and she'd somehow picked up on Bron's interest in her as well. She could be trying to goad her into giving something away.

'Well, I'd better not waste your time any more,' said Imogen graciously, after a long pause during which Georgia forced herself to remain silent, though she longed to retaliate.

She rose from the sofa with much jangling of bracelets and her usual elaborate redeployment of her scarf. 'I'm so sorry you won't have time to come to the re-enactment to see Ned in his costume – Annie tells me you'll be too busy but I can't tell you how much I admire the effort you put into your work. I'll certainly try to put business your way. I have an excellent contact in youth theatre in the north.'

She wandered away, looking like a model departing from the catwalk. Georgia felt like picking up the scissors and hurling them at her back. She tried to persuade herself that Imogen had probably been on one of her usual ego trips, veered round to wondering if Bron really was still attracted to her, went off in another direction as she reminded herself that she was perfectly free to go back to her peaceful single existence, and in the end, exhausted by her scurrying thoughts, acknowledged that she couldn't bear to break with him. The only decision she did make was to go to the re-enactment after all. Imogen couldn't be allowed to have everything her way.

On the day of the battle Georgia occupied herself with last-minute alterations in the wardrobe until the noise of the public address system, which was booming out military marches between announcements, finally forced her to put down her work, and make her way to the great meadow. It was a perfect summer's day, and she'd put on the dress she'd worn in London, partly because Bron liked it, partly because Imogen had never seen her in anything except work clothes.

The perimeter was crowded with spectators, held back from the arena by a double barrier of ropes set several feet apart. Behind them were ranks of stalls selling programmes, souvenirs, and fast food. The smell of hamburgers and rancid chip fat hung in the air, obliterating the scents of the countryside. Litter blew about the field. The grass had been bruised and flattened by hundreds of feet. Georgia could imagine Bron's reaction. This was not the way he'd meant visitors to see Merlinslade, and it was not the way it should be seen.

The two armies, Royalist and Parliamentarian, were lined up

310

on opposite sides of the field, ready to begin the advance into battle, each behind a phalanx of leather-coated footsoldiers bristling with sixteen foot pikes. At the back of the pikemen were ranks of musketeers, and in the rear cannon were being trundled clumsily into position.

Jason's father, in a glamorous and wildly inaccurate costume, and riding a flashy grey hunter, commanded the Royalist cavalry. With him were Jason on a lively piebald pony and Ned, with a slightly quieter mount. Mr Samms, on a sedate old mare whose barrel ribs perfectly accommodated his bandy legs, was looking cross and determined in a badly fitting costume and a hat much too large for his small, bald head. He had clearly been appointed Ned's minder.

Georgia found a relatively quiet spot for herself between two outside broadcast vans near the commentary stand, and soon caught sight of Bron patrolling the perimeter of the field on a heavy bay built like a police horse. He was wearing riding breeches and a Lovat tweed jacket. The clothes suited him, but made him look distinctly county, and she wasn't sure she liked the effect.

She continued to watch him as he stopped to greet some country notables, very much in the role of owner of Merlinslade. Not for the first time she was uneasily aware how different their backgrounds were, a feeling which had lately been intensified by Imogen's constant name-dropping and references to the local aristocracy.

Georgia had caught a glimpse of her earlier through the entrance to the publicity tent, with a whip tucked under her arm, wearing a pair of pristine jodhpurs which fitted her like cling-wrap, and a tight-waisted couture version of a hacking jacket. The outfit made her look an upmarket dominatrix, and was helping her to reduce the hardboiled press contingent to the consistency of scrambled egg. Now she'd moved on to the commentary stand, where she was flirting with a presenter from Avon Television. Wistfully Georgia's eyes went back to Bron, wondering how much of this slow torture she'd be able to endure.

★ ★ ★

Nico had been chatting up Mr Samms' grand-daughter, who was taking part as a camp follower, until she'd had to return to the battle. He was loping round the side of the field, in search of other diversions, when he caught sight of Georgia standing disconsolately between two vans, looking like a sweet pea in a soft clinging dress which reminded him again of what he'd lost when she refused to go out with him any more.

He crept up on her, wondering who she was watching so intently, and as he followed her gaze was not altogether surprised to find it was Bron. He'd suspected for some time that there might be something going on between them.

He put a casual arm round her shoulders, wondering if he could surprise her into an admission. 'That's a distinctly lustful look you're giving my big brother. And don't think I haven't noticed the way he watched you – just like Ned eyeing the last piece of cake.'

Georgia made a startled movement at his touch.

'Don't be ridiculous. You're imagining things.'

'Am I? He's been away from home almost every evening lately, and lots of villagers have seen him driving towards Bath. Esther told me he even cut the last church committee meeting.'

Mentioning Esther was a mistake. Georgia instantly used the reference to move the conversation on.

'I'm surprised she's not here this afternoon. Most of her parishioners are.'

'She's gone to a diocesan training session this weekend. I never met anyone so determined to do her duty.'

'What on earth do you expect? She's going to be ordained shortly.'

Nico decided that a little gentle repayment for Georgia's crossness wouldn't do any harm.

'I wonder?' he said. 'I keep telling her it'll be a criminal waste of acting talent if she signs on with the God squad for good. I've been trying to take her mind off that dull boyfriend of hers. I really think I may be getting somewhere at last.'

He'd been cultivating Esther hard, partly because he was determined to recruit her for the rest of the season, partly because it amused him to try to break down her resistance to his charms. The look of alarmed concern on Georgia's face jolted him.

'Nico, you mustn't! It's not fair to influence her. Can't you see what a disaster it'd be if she made the wrong decision?'

'How do you know it'd be a wrong decision? She comes alive on stage. If she did a few more months with the company she might even turn into a normal human being.'

'And who are you to say what a normal human being is?' demanded Georgia. 'Life in the theatre isn't exactly normal, either. Don't hurt her, Nico, please. It's so easy for you to influence people, but I don't suppose Esther would ever get a second chance to be ordained.'

Nico was silent for a moment, feeling suddenly contrite over his not very gallant reception of Esther's refusal even to kiss him when he'd taken her home after their dinner at Veneziana.

'You don't have much faith in me, darling. I'm the one who's likely to be hurt. I don't think I ever went out with anyone so good. It's agony keeping up to her standards for a whole evening.'

'I don't think you understand how much ordination means to her. She really feels she's called by God.'

'She's got a God-given talent in her acting, a talent that would bring her a hell of a lot more fulfilment than all this self-negation she goes in for at the moment.'

'She and John are planning to work together in Leeds. She is unofficially engaged to him, or had you forgotten?'

'What's he doing letting her out of his sight, then?'

'You still don't understand. He lets her go because he's as good as she is, and he trusts her.'

Nico, watching Georgia's grave, concerned expression, and the soft set of her lips, suddenly wanted to kiss her. He said more mildly, 'You really do believe in that sort of thing, don't you?'

'Yes,' said Georgia, her eyes going back to Bron, who was patrolling near Ned. 'I suppose I do. Or I used to, anyway.'

Nico followed her gaze again. 'There's someone else who's too damned noble,' he said treacherously, thinking that Esther would make him do a hundred penances if she could hear him. 'Bron's been so bloody long-suffering with Imogen ever since she arrived that I really do think he's holding a torch for her still. I wouldn't like you to be hurt either. Because you have been seeing him, haven't you?'

He gave her waist a little squeeze. Georgia tensed, and pulled herself away from his arm.

'Yes, I have,' she answered angrily, 'but there's nothing serious about it yet, and if you breathe a word to anyone I'll leave the theatre now, first night or no first night. You'd better believe me, Nico.'

He smiled triumphantly. 'I knew I was right! There's no need to throw a wobbly, darling. I won't tell anyone, I swear. But I mean it about Imo and Bron. And I honestly don't think he's right for you. He's too bloody serious and uptight. I was talking to an ex-girlfriend of his the other day, one of those women he used to invite to his London flat. She said there's a part of his mind one never really gets to know, almost as if it's never completely been reclaimed from Imogen.'

'I'm not interested in what other women think about Bron. I'll make my own decisions,' snapped Georgia, trying not to reveal how much this new information had dismayed her.

She was rescued by the Royalist cavalry performing a spectacular wheel on the left flank as it took up a position at the back of the pikemen and musketeers. Nico was instantly diverted by the sight.

'They're almost ready to start another charge. Don't they look terrific? I'd be out there myself, but Zelda was convinced I'd get run down and have to play Caliban in plaster. Why don't we watch from the commentary stand?'

'You go. I'm fine here.'

'You're not upset, are you?' he said. 'You did say you weren't serious about Bron.'

'Of course I'm not. For heaven's sake, Nico, you're going on as though I can't look after myself.'

'If you're sure, then. I'll buy you a drink later on.'

He loped off after giving her a kiss. Georgia had never felt so alone now her most pessimistic thoughts about herself and Bron had been fully confirmed. If she hadn't wanted to betray her feelings to Nico, she'd have made straight for the bolt-hole of her flat.

There was a breathless, expectant air over the battlefield. Orders were shouted at last, drums began to beat, and on either side the troopers began to move forward at a steady march, pennants fluttering from their pikes.

More orders were yelled from the commanders in the rear. The pikes rippled downwards as the troopers levelled their weapons. The two lines broke into a steady run, and met in a clash of wood and steel. They swiftly disintegrated into shifting struggling knots, and began to fall in tumbled heaps. The musketeers came forward, and as one man dropped back to reload, another in the ranks behind took his place.

In the background cannon began to thump, filling the air with clouds of smoke and the smell of gunpowder, discharging the wads of straw with which they were packed over the field. The cavalry horses, not yet deployed, became increasingly restive with each explosion.

Eventually the centre of the field began to clear. The commanders on both sides called a temporary retreat, and camp followers dragged away the wounded on hurdles. The crowd round Georgia thinned a little as some of the onlookers went in search of refreshments. She was about to leave herself when Bron appeared, now walking beside his horse.

'So this is where you've been hiding,' he said. 'I was looking for you everywhere.'

'Ned seems to be having a good time,' she said, casting round for a safe remark, 'and he hasn't lost his hat yet.'

'I've put him on the quietest pony we've got, but he's much too inclined to treat it like a souped-up Ferrari. At least he has Mr Samms with him. He taught him to ride, and Ned usually does what he says.'

'I thought you'd be out there leading the Royalists,' Georgia teased him.

He smiled. 'I don't play at battles, especially ones as disorganised as this. It's nothing like the Sealed Knot. The commanders still haven't got their act together.'

'Imogen seems to be enjoying herself at least,' said Georgia, unable to resist the remark.

Bron glanced swiftly over to the commentary stand, where

Imogen was sharing some very private joke with Nico and the commentator. Standing so close to Bron that she could catch the tang of leather and the scent of his freshly ironed shirt, yet being unable to touch him, was unnerving enough, Georgia thought, without having to dissemble for a whole afternoon under Imogen's laser scrutiny. Her presence would have put an enormous constraint on their relationship even if they weren't keeping it secret.

'I should never have let her publicise the battle so widely,' he said. 'There are far too many people here. It was meant to be just a local affair.'

'I'm not sure how much longer I can carry on being polite to Imogen. I hate all this pretence.'

He looked at her in a way which made her feel like one of the melting ice-creams being demolished by the crowd.

'The sooner she knows, the better as far as I'm concerned. And she probably will if I stand here much longer eyeing you up in that dress.'

His gaze was drawn back to the field, where the footsoldiers were reforming the front lines for a second advance, and lowering their pikes to the attacking position. The cavalry had become even more fidgety, sidling towards the centre of the field, and Mr Samms had his grasp firmly on the reins of Ned's pony.

The battlefield was still comparatively quiet, apart from the occasional accidental clash of weapons and the whinnying of horses, and a tune began to filter into Georgia's consciousness, one she'd heard in a quite different place, and what now seemed like years ago.

The words that went with it, *Amazing Grace*, were becoming clearer all the time, and in another few seconds its singers appeared. A slow column of white-clad figures carrying banners was progressing straight towards them across the field in the space between the two armies. It was led by Brighid in her usual flowing draperies, with a willow wand in her hand. Morrigan was by her side, guitar slung before him.

'What the hell are they up to?' Bron burst out. 'Don't they realise this isn't an interval? Why haven't the stewards stopped them?'

As the Disciples came closer Georgia could see Chloe behind

Brighid. She looked as if she were in a trance, as did all the other Disciples. Brighid and Morrigan continued onwards, Brighid holding her wand in front of her like Moses commanding the Red Sea to part.

Morrigan stopped a little ahead of the column, in the very midst of the field. It was a publicity stunt bordering on the suicidal. He held up a hand for the others to be silent, and began to sing on his own. His voice flooded the field so clearly that Georgia knew he must be wearing a radio microphone tuned to an amplifier somewhere on the far side.

The pikemen and musketeers were just disciplined enough to remain motionless, but the crowd, which had become absolutely silent under the spell of the music, suddenly began to move forward towards Morrigan and the Disciples, almost as if it were collectively walking in its sleep.

As it inexorably broke through the first barrier of rope, Bron remounted so fast that Georgia hardly saw him move. At the same time one of the cannon went off prematurely, and the Royalist cavalry leaped forward into an undirected flanking dash straight towards the heart of the Parliamentarian ranks, a path which seemed as if it would take them straight through the Disciples.

Morrigan's song abruptly ceased. The column behind him wavered and halted. The crowd ceased its lemming-like advance as it reached the second barrier of rope. Just in time Jason's father managed to steer his troop away from the Disciples. Even so the horses hurtled past within a yard of Morrigan, who had held his ground and grabbed the banner to defend himself, eyes shining, head thrown back, looking as if he were in the grip of some berserker madness.

Ned was at the back of the cavalry, seriously hampered by Mr Samms, who was hanging on to his charge's reins like a drag anchor. As Ned came level with the Disciples, Morrigan brandished the banner at him and let out a blood-curdling yell.

The pony shot forward from Mr Samms' restraining grasp and bolted, with Ned, his plumed hat gone as well as his grasp on the reins, clinging to its neck. At the same time the rest of the cavalry reacted to the yell by again disastrously changing course, sweeping Ned with them towards the pikes.

Chapter 16

'Christ! They'll kill themselves!' Bron exploded.

He too shot off in the direction of the Commonwealth pikes, making his heavy horse move like a Derby runner, churning up huge divots of turf, and taking a path which took him at right angles to the oncoming advance.

It was a cold-blooded act of bravery, and Georgia felt sick as she watched. She was absolutely certain he'd be mown down. His mare was on a collision course with the cavalry. He pulled it up to a thundering halt, deliberately placing himself and his horse sideways to the charge.

Miraculously they were deflected. They began to stream harm-lessly away, wheeling in a huge circle back to their original station. Ned's pony still came hurtling on, and Bron just managed to grab its reins before it impaled itself on the pikes.

The second phase of the battle ground to a halt almost before it had started. Morrigan had disappeared into the crowd as effec-tively as an eel into a bank of weed. Bron led a hugely excited Ned from the field and handed him over to Nico, then went off to talk to the commanders of the two armies. Stewards rushed forward and began to shepherd Brighid and the Disciples towards the first aid tent. Georgia caught a glimpse of Chloe, deathly white, the crown of flowers on her head awry, the skirt of her robe torn, supporting another girl who was in tears.

Frantic with anxiety, Georgia began to make for the first aid tent as well. She'd managed to get halfway towards it, consider-ably impeded by spectators milling round the field, when through a gap in the shifting crowd she caught a totally unexpected distant glimpse of Bron and Morrigan. Bron was leaning down from his horse, his hand twisted into the collar of Morrigan's shirt, almost dragging him from his feet. Georgia couldn't hear what he was saying, but both men's faces were white with fury.

Still sickened by the incident, she turned her head from the sight, and made for the first aid tent again. It was stuffy and crowded inside. A hysterical Disciple was being calmed by Brighid, and another was having a bandage put on a sprained ankle. The rest of the group appeared miraculously unharmed.

Chloe sat on a bench, drinking some water. Her hair, which had been pinned up under her crown, was tumbling down, but surprisingly she wasn't in tears. She rushed to Georgia when she saw her.

'Oh Georgy, I thought we were going to be pushed straight in among the pikes!'

Georgia could feel Chloe's heart thudding against her ribs. She sat down with her on the bench, pushing back her hair and gazing anxiously into her face. Chloe cast herself at her yet again.

'I thought I was going to die. And all I could think of was you and Sean, and how I'd never see you again!'

'You were nowhere near dying,' said Georgia, lying with every ounce of sincerity she could summon, and soothingly patting her back, though she felt weak with shock at how close she'd come to losing Chloe.

'You didn't see those pikes close to.' Chloe shuddered. 'Brighid says it was only because she prayed to the goddess that we were saved.'

The Disciple in hysterics went into a fit of noisy sobs. It was extremely hot in the tent, and the emotional temperature was even higher.

'Let's go outside for a moment,' coaxed Georgia. 'You'll feel better away from this heat.'

They sat under a tree on some empty cases which had held equipment for the battle. Chloe was still making a most unusual effort to control herself, sitting with her hands clasped in her lap, and only now and then drawing a shuddering breath. Georgia saw that she'd lost weight again. Her thin white arms looked as vulnerable as bluebell stems pulled carelessly from the earth. She ached to protect her.

'Won't you come home with me, just for a little while, just to get over the shock?' she asked.

'I can't. Some of the others feel much worse than me. Brighid'll need me to help. I mustn't let her down.'

Georgia, astounded and encouraged by this rare thought for others, tried another tack.

'Chloe darling, don't you see that most of what happened was Morrigan's fault? I'm sure it wasn't Brighid's idea to march on to the battlefield like that. How can he truly care about the group when he put you all at risk? And Ned could have been killed.'

'Morrigan was in the first aid tent just now till some awful PR woman called him away,' said Chloe, busily twisting the ribbon sash of her robe into a knot. 'He told Brighid he thought there was going to be a long interval. He said that Ned couldn't control his pony. He didn't see him until it was too late. Brighid says he simply made a mistake.'

'Anyone less trusting than Brighid would have checked whether it really was an interval. And I'm sure he intended to make Ned's pony bolt. I couldn't have had a clearer view. Are you absolutely certain you're still happy at the Sanctuary with him there?'

Chloe looked round nervously, as if Morrigan might pop out from behind the tree.

'He hasn't been quite so nice lately, we all think that. He gets so angry when we don't keep his rules. I don't like being in the group as much as I did.' Her voice was almost a whisper. 'But I've promised Brighid I'll stay till the baptism, and she's done so much for me that I can't go back on my word. She says that's when I'll fully find myself.'

'Do you know when it's going to be?'

Chloe started twisting her sash again.

'Well, yes, but Morrigan's made us swear not to tell. Don't ask me any more, Georgy, please. And I really ought to get back to the others.'

'At least have a cup of tea first,' she said, desperate to prolong the conversation.

She leaped up before Chloe could object and went over to a stall about twenty yards away where a woman in a cheerful plastic apron was filling polystyrene cups from a metal urn. Georgia was waiting for a family in front of her to be served when she saw Bron swiftly weaving in her direction through the other stands. He looked impatient and worried as he came up to her.

'Have you seen Chloe?' he asked. 'How is she?'

Georgia was instantly thrown by his presence. She'd had no time to reconcile her growing unease about their relationship with the terror she'd felt when she thought he was going to be killed.

'She's over there, under that tree. I'm getting her some tea. She's all right now.'

'What an afternoon – the whole event's been a wipe-out. I was a total fucking idiot to let Imogen anywhere near it.'

'Bron, Bron!' said a high, imperious voice. 'I want to talk to you!'

'Christ, not again!' he said tiredly.

He swung round to face Imogen, who was approaching over the trampled grass looking as if she'd just swallowed a Martini with too much bitters. By her side was Morrigan, his sunglasses flashing in the sun.

'How dare you cancel the rest of the re-enactment without consulting me?' Imogen demanded. 'Do you realise how much work I've put in on it? And you must be insane to offer a ticket refund. You'll make a huge loss.'

'Do you realise how many people were nearly killed this afternoon, including Ned? I'm not risking a repeat performance. And I'd rather make a loss than have people saying they were cheated at Merlinslade.'

He turned a withering gaze on Morrigan. 'And as for you, do I have to tell you the score again? You should have been out of here ten minutes ago.'

'Don't be ridiculous, Bron,' said Imogen. 'I didn't see the incident myself – I was in the press tent at the time – but I've heard enough from Morrigan to know that you're making a huge fuss about nothing. Ned's fine. I've just been talking to him. He seems to have enjoyed his little escapade thoroughly.'

'And it's not my fault if you can't control your child,' said Morrigan.

'What have I been saying, Bron?' Imogen's voice was triumphant. 'None of this would have happened if he was at a decent school with some proper discipline.'

Georgia was tired of keeping quiet.

'It wasn't only Ned who might have been killed. Chloe and the Disciples were almost driven in among the pikes.' She felt shaky as she said the words.

'Chloe? You mean your odd little sister? Does she belong to the Disciples too?' said Imogen, who'd been looking decidedly chagrined as she took in Georgia's appearance in non-working clothes. 'In my opinion the only thing they were suffering from was hysteria.'

Georgia felt Bron's hand on her shoulder. He was so taut with anger that she sensed he'd done it unknowingly, but Imogen didn't miss the gesture. Her eyes narrowed. She tucked her arm through Morrigan's. Bron's fingers dug into Georgia's flesh.

'I'm giving you five minutes to leave, Morrigan, and if you aren't away from here by then I'll throw you out myself,' he said.

'You're so gloriously physical sometimes, darling,' said Imogen. 'It does remind me of the good old days.'

Bron ignored her as he continued to concentrate on Morrigan. 'You're damned lucky that I haven't called the police and made a formal charge. I'm letting you stay on at the theatre till the end of the play for Nico's sake, but after that I don't want to see you at Merlinslade again.'

'There's nothing to charge me with,' said Morrigan. 'The event's been so poorly organised that you're the one likely to be charged. I've no wish to hang around this disaster area a moment longer than I have to.' He turned to Imogen and smiled lazily at her. 'I'm sure you must feel the same, darling. How about coming back to Bath with me? Don't forget we have business to discuss.'

'Perfect,' said Imogen. 'You go on ahead to the car. I just want to have a few more words with Bron.'

Morrigan cast a smug look at him, and sauntered away, pausing en route to sign an autograph for the woman at the refreshment stall, who had been staring fascinatedly at him while she let the cups of tea overflow.

'Now,' said Imogen, speaking to Bron in a voice like an infant school teacher telling off an over-aggressive five year old, 'I want to know why you keep on being so unutterably bloody to Morrigan? Someone's got to tell you about it. You consistently over-react when he's around.'

Bron's expression became even harsher. 'Perhaps you'd better tell me why *you've* become so concerned about him.'

'Because I know what it's like to be on the receiving end of your disapproval, and because he appreciates me. He's just asked me to take over the publicity for the Disciples and I've agreed.'

'You've *what*?' demanded Bron.

'You heard,' said Imogen sweetly. 'I know you'll be glad for Ned's sake. It means I won't be going back to London for some time yet.'

'The only thing that concerns me at the moment is that Chloe and Ned were almost killed,' Georgia burst out. 'Certainly not your squabbles. I'm going back to Chloe.'

She knew she hadn't been entirely fair to Bron, but she was in such despair at Imogen's latest pronouncement that she didn't care. She swung away so abruptly that she had only a moment to take in Imogen's satisfied smirk, and Bron's look of consternation.

She felt angrier still when she found Chloe had become tired of waiting and gone back to the first aid tent. She was deep in conversation with Brighid, and it was obvious that there wouldn't be another chance to talk to her. When Georgia emerged from the tent near to tears in her frustration at the lost opportunity, and discovered Bron waiting outside for her, she was in no mood for making allowances.

'I'm sorry,' he said stiffly. 'I shouldn't have let you get caught up the backlash of our argument.'

'No, you shouldn't,' she snapped back, searching in her shoulder bag for the car keys. 'I've just missed the only chance I've had in days of a proper talk with Chloe. All you had to do was tell Imogen to sod off, but you didn't, of course.'

She found the keys, and started to march towards the official car park.

He fell in by her side. 'So are you telling me to sod off too?'

'It just makes me so angry that you keep placating her.'

'A public row with her was the last thing I wanted.'

On the far side of the field a children's carousel had started a relentlessly manic tune. Bron was already retreating into his formal distant self, as he always did when he was hurt, and this time she couldn't be bothered to do anything about it.

'That's becoming very evident,' she said bitterly. 'Things aren't easy for me, either, you know. The dress rehearsal's only a few days away, and Chloe's about to commit herself to the Disciples for good. I don't need any more problems. I think we should stop seeing each other for a while, at least until Imogen's gone. You obviously find it hard to concentrate on us both at the same time.'

Bron's jaw was so set that she could have drawn a right angle with it.

'Is that what you really want?' he said slowly.

She felt like shouting at him that what she really wanted was for him to hold her and kiss her and simply tell her she was more important than Imogen. She might have done so even then, if she hadn't seen the chairwoman of the local WI bearing down on them, obviously longing to get Bron to herself.

'Yes, I do,' she said, and walked away without looking back.

Georgia half hoped Bron would come storming round to the flat when she got home, but he didn't. After supper she switched her phone to the answering machine, and shut herself in the studio to work on the designs for the next play. When she came back upstairs at midnight he'd left no message. She went to bed trying to persuade herself that if he cared so little about her she was well out of the affair. By two o'clock she still hadn't been able to make the ache in her heart go away, and finally fell asleep wondering how she could have been such a fool as voluntarily to get on the treadmill of jealousy all over again.

Over the next few days she was so involved in last-minute work for the dress rehearsal, and Bron so occupied with harvesting, that their paths never crossed. Once when she came to work early she saw him harnessing the carthorses in the stable yard, and once he appeared in the orchard with Mr Meads to inspect the progress of the apples, but though he must have been aware of her he never looked her way.

The weather became breathlessly hot. The roadside hedges

were grey with dust, and the woods behind the house had begun to take on a faint tinge of bronze. Shortly before the dress rehearsal Nico put up a notice backstage asking for volunteers to help harvest the Forty Acre field the following day, and promising them a picnic supper afterwards.

'Bron's going spare over this particular crop. It's wheat for thatching, and he's expecting to pay off a loan on the strength of it,' he said later to Georgia, as she checked some alterations to his costume. 'He needs the extra help because the sheaves have to be stacked by hand so as not to damage the stalks. But I expect he's told you all about it.'

'I haven't seen Bron for a bit. We've both been too busy.'

'Doing his usual distancing trick, is he? I did warn you.'

'We simply agreed to have a break until Imogen goes. It's not easy when she's around.' Georgia heroically refrained from saying something a good deal more acid.

'That's putting it mildly. Everyone's feeling the strain here, especially Bron. Imo nags Ned too much, he reacts by not co-operating, and then Bron gets the fall-out from them both. Are you sure you couldn't offer him just a little Sophia Street R and R? He's been in a terrible mood lately.'

'I told you, I'm too busy. And unless you want me to miss some vital stitches, and risk having your seams give on the first night, you'd better drop the subject now.'

'That'd interest the fans!' said Nico. 'But I know you wouldn't. You've still got a soft spot for old Nico. I wish you'd let me take you out. I could cheer you up in no time.'

It was true, Georgia thought, though she didn't reply. He was a lot easier to understand than Bron, he was kind in his way, and she had no problems adjusting to his world. At times like this, when everything seemed to be going wrong, it was only too tempting to take up his offer.

Before Georgia left the flat next morning she stuffed a long-sleeved shirt into her bag to protect her arms just in case she decided to help with the harvest, though she had no serious intention of joining in. The workshop was too busy, and in any case she still wanted to avoid Bron.

But it was the hottest day of the year, and by mid-afternoon everyone was tired. Jenny had just finished dyeing some fabric in the twin-tub, and Kevin was filling the room with choking clouds of fuller's earth and spray paint as he distressed Trinculo's costume. Annie had flopped on to a chair after a session styling wigs, which she'd patiently set and dried, then stored on blocks in a dust-proof cabinet. The atmosphere in the wardrobe was like a Glasgow steamie. Georgia, looking out at the orchard, and seeing a breeze stir the grass, suddenly decided that everyone had done enough for that day, and announced that they could all go home or help with the harvest, as they wished.

Like the others she decided on home, but as she was locking up she suddenly had an uncomfortable thought that it would look rather poor-spirited if no one from the wardrobe take part at the harvest. Bron would be far too busy commanding his troops to talk to her, and she need only put in a token appearance for an hour or so. Quickly, before she could change her mind, she pulled on the long-sleeved shirt over her vest top and jeans, and made for the Forty Acre field.

It was bounded on one side by Merlinslade woods, and on the others by hedges of hawthorn and spindleberry, with an occasional sentinel oak. Two-thirds of the crop had been cut, leaving a golden island in the centre. The trees cast long blue shadows across the stubble. Bron sat in the high iron seat of the reaping machine, guiding the carthorses as the great revolving sails of the cutter bore down into the corn. Mr Samms perched at his back, keeping an eye on the binder which was steadily flinging out fat sheaves of wheat to the helpers who toiled in its wake.

Georgia soon found that it wasn't easy to hoist a bristling sheaf, and stack it neatly with five others to form a stable ridge through which the drying wind could blow. About a quarter of the cast were there, including Zelda, who kept stopping to take photos and enthuse over the quaintness of the scene. Ned and Sean were working like demons with Mr Meads. Nico too was doing surprisingly well, apart from a tendency to burst into excerpts from *Oklahoma* every now and then.

Even Imogen was present, wearing a pair of fragile sandals which precluded any close acquaintance with the stubble, and calling out suggestions for the better disposition of the sheaves which everyone ignored. Morrigan had made an appearance, and was being allowed to stay, presumably on the strength of his membership of the theatre company, and because Bron was too busy to send him away. He spent most of his time in the shade of the hedge with Imogen, very occasionally sallying forth to construct a few ridges of wheat which almost instantly collapsed.

At last there was no corn left. The remaining rabbits had made desperate dashes to the safety of the hedge, and the fiercest heat was beginning to leave the sun-baked stubble at last. Georgia straightened her aching back. Her arms were scratched even through the long-sleeved shirt, but she found it surprisingly satisfying to survey the long rows of bronze-headed sheaves.

Mrs Meads and Kim appeared with baskets of food tucked away under red and white checked cloths, and while Mr Meads went to retrieve two flagons of cider which had been cooling in the river, they gathered in the shade of the largest oak.

Georgia had planned to go home immediately the work was over, but the food looked so delicious, and she felt so thirsty, that she decided to stay, counting on the presence of the others to prevent any serious conversation with Bron. She needn't have worried, for he hardly spoke, and after the meal sat silently with Ned and Imogen, a battered and frayed Panama hat tilted over his eyes as he whittled at a stake destined to mend a gap in the hedge. His arms were a deep Indian brown, and Georgia was suddenly afflicted by a disorienting desire to touch him, to feel his skin against her own. She hastily tore her gaze away, looked up, and found Imogen watching her.

Ned, who'd gone to give Mr Samms' dog a piece of sandwich, came back to his parents and threw himself down by Imogen, slumping against her in exactly the same way that Rusalka flopped against the nearest friendly body when she wanted to rest. Imogen, who seemed to have mellowed after the cider, for once didn't complain, and let him stay there. Seeing them so close made Georgia again feel uneasy at the prospect of any upset to Ned.

People began to revive and chat. Nico and Zelda lit cigarettes to keep off the midges. Swallows were wheeling high overhead, prophets of more fine weather. Morrigan picked up the guitar he'd brought with him and very softly began to play.

Georgia, made slightly less critical of him than usual by the cider, thought how strange it was that someone so sinister could produce such heavenly sounds. Even Imogen was affected by it. She sighed, stretched out her elegant limbs, and put her arm round Ned. Georgia's gaze was drawn back in spite of herself to Bron. He'd thrown aside his hat, and was watching Imogen and Ned with an expression of profound sadness.

Morrigan began to weave the words of a folk song into the music. He sang so quietly, almost it seemed for himself alone, and Georgia was so occupied with her thoughts that she hardly heard them, until their meaning filtered at last into her consciousness.

> ' "*I leaned my back against an oak,*
> *Thinking it was a mighty tree.*
> *But first it bent, and then it broke,*
> *Just as my love was false to me.*" '

She looked towards Bron again. Imogen moved closer to him, and put her arm through his. He didn't move away. Ned smiled up at his parents. They presented a perfect picture of a united family.

Georgia couldn't bear to watch or listen for a moment longer. She got up blindly, caring about nothing but escape. She had to force herself not to break into a run as she struck across the stubble and the lumpy hard-baked earth, making in desperation for a stile in the hedge which led to the cool anonymity of the woods. It was the same stile she and Esther had crossed together on her first visit to Merlinslade.

She hit her shin on the crossbar of the stile, but was still too distraught to register any pain. She broke into a run along the sunken path which led to the beech hanger, pounding up the slope until almost breathless, as if the activity could drive away her thoughts.

Sheer fatigue finally forced her to collapse on the bank. The foliage had grown thicker in the sunken track since she was there with Esther, and it was like a green tunnel. A thrush was pouring out a rapturous evening song in the tree above her head. It seemed to contain all the pent-up feeling in her heart. Bron's ambivalent attitude to Imogen, Ned's obvious fondness for his mother, and Imogen's affection for him, which though spasmodic appeared genuine enough, and her own jealousy, were all driving her to the conclusion that she'd again made a disastrous mistake.

She longed to be back at the time before she came to Merlinslade, when her life had some balance. She had a childish urge to run away from it all, there and then, even to throw up her commission and risk the ruin of her professional reputation.

A glimpse of blue shirt behind overhanging branches lower down the path caught her eye. She looked round for somewhere to hide, but the banks were too high for escape. And then Bron came into full view, walking fast and purposefully in spite of his long day at the harvest, last winter's fallen twigs crackling beneath his feet like miniature explosions. Hastily she began to retie the laces of her canvas boots in an effort to appear unconcerned.

Bron halted and stood staring down at Georgia. His mind was full of anger with himself at the way he'd mishandled things at the re-enactment, exasperation at the way she was still refusing to be rational about Imogen, and Imogen's evident determination to stir things up.

As he gazed at Georgia sitting among the mossy roots of the overhanging limes, her long brown arms, scratched in spite of the shirt she'd been wearing earlier, spangled with coins of light falling through the leaves, he remembered the time he'd come across her on the river bank. She'd seemed dryad-like then, as if she might disappear at any second. Now he felt even closer to losing her.

He sat down and gently pulled away one of her hands from its task, turning her arm so that the white inner skin, laced with scratches, was exposed.

'Poor arm,' he said, and kissed the soft crook of her elbow. Her skin tasted of salt. 'I'm sorry about what happened at the re-enactment. We've got to talk, you know.'

She pulled her arm away.

330

'What's wrong?' he asked.

Still she didn't answer, and he almost began to wonder if she was using one of Imogen's ploys, a malicious, paranoid refusal to speak, sometimes for two or three days at a time, which used to drive him insane with frustration before he learned to deal with it. But suddenly she spoke in a rush.

'Bron, I think we should finish this now. Completely, I mean.'

She wouldn't look at him. The part of his mind that always remained detached, that had done so ever since Imogen's first spectacular attempt to wreck their marriage, and he'd decided to never let himself be so hurt again, registered it as a bad sign.

'Why?' he asked, wondering what further minefields the brief question would reveal.

'I know you so well by now, and you do feel something for Imogen. You may not realise it yourself, but there's still some attraction.'

She looked at him at last. In astonishment he saw that she really meant it.

'All I feel is the most profound relief that we're divorced. What brought on this fantasy?'

'It was so hard, so hard just now,' she burst out, 'to see you all together, like – like bloody happy families, to see Ned really at ease with you both.'

'Happy families?' Bron couldn't stop an edge creeping into his voice. The last years of his marriage had passed in a permanent state of warfare. 'If you believe that, you'd believe Lady Macbeth had a happy family!'

'I felt excluded, and even worse, jealous. Just as I did whenever I saw Blake and Lyn together. And now it's happening again!'

'Do you think I don't know what it's like? But I don't want Ned to have parents who fight all the time even after their divorce. That's the only reason I sometimes go along with Imogen.'

'Sometimes! It seems like always to me.'

He put his arm round her, but she didn't respond. Her body was tense with suspicion. He'd felt for a while that he should tell her the full story of his marriage, which not even Nico knew. It would certainly convince her that he had no interest in Imogen.

But the break-up had been so cataclysmic for him, had so nearly led to the loss of his self-respect, that he still felt diminished simply by thinking about it. He knew he was being stubborn, perhaps inordinately proud even, but he couldn't bring himself to whine to Georgia. It couldn't possibly help either of them.

'Let's walk for a bit,' he said, trying to play for time.

She got up, keeping well apart from him, and they began to walk on up the path in silence. By the time they got to the beech grove he'd decided that there was only one other way to convince her.

He stopped and put his hands on her shoulders. Her expression was angry, troubled and suspicious, not at all a good omen for what he was about to say. He took a deep breath. He'd intended to broach the subject more cautiously than this. She guarded her independence so fiercely that he'd wanted to make certain she wouldn't be frightened off. But it had become too late for subtleties.

'I think we should get married,' he said.

For a moment Georgia thought he was joking. She stared at him.

'Marry you?' she said slowly.

She'd always assumed that Bron, like herself, wouldn't want to marry again. For him the financial risk of a second marriage was huge. If it didn't work, and she claimed maintenance, he'd lose at least a third of the estate.

'Don't sound so horrified. Ned and Chloe will adjust, I'm certain, and I can guarantee that Imogen won't want to come anywhere near Merlinslade once you're living there. She never could bear to share anything.'

Now Georgia was even more shocked.

'Live at Merlinslade? Give up my flat?'

'You don't have to make it sound quite such a death sentence. I couldn't really run the house and farm from Bath.'

He was trying to pin her down to a decision. Frantically she thought that she was going to be trapped like the rabbits in the field of corn. For the first time she realised fully that to take Bron was to take the whole estate as well as Imogen and Ned. Merlinslade could never be a home for her. It was too cold, too unwelcoming. If she gave up her flat she'd lose her only refuge. The package was too daunting for her to deal with.

'You could rearrange the house as you liked,' said Bron. 'I know your own work might take you away from Merlinslade sometimes, but we could cope with that, at least until—'

He bit off the words, but she knew he'd been going to say until she had a child. And then she'd be still more tied.

'I must think about it,' she said feebly, not looking at him. The disappointment she knew she'd find in his face was more than she could take.

'What is there to think about? We love each other, we're both free.'

'You're not free. Not really free. And nor am I. I've too much baggage from the past to be a good risk. And you've still got a stake in Imogen.'

'How many times do I have to tell you I feel absolutely nothing for her? Stop being so negative.'

'Why don't you stop patronising me?'

They were suddenly glaring at each other, as if they were enemies instead of lovers. It reminded her that she'd never felt she'd completely fathomed his character. There had always been some ultimate reserve, as Nico said. Perhaps it was something to do with his class, or his code, she thought despairingly. If it was, they had even less chance of putting things back into perspective, especially now that he seemed to be demanding a decision.

'You want it all mapped out like some military operation,' she said. 'But it can't possibly work like that. It has to evolve gradually. We've had hardly any time to get to know each other in a normal kind of way.'

'I know I love you,' he said, with a look that made her feel dizzy. 'You've said you love me. All we need is a measure of trust.'

'I can't decide on something like this to order,' she said obstinately.

'You have to make some allowances,' he said, beginning to sound desperate himself. 'Can't you see how many different things I'm trying to hold together? The estate's on a knife-edge financially, Morrigan's a loose cannon threatening to go off at any second, Ned's still unsettled. The simpler things are, the easier. This prolonged uncertainty's beginning to affect my concentration and judgement, just when I most need to keep a firm grip on things. Christ, I've hardly slept since the re-enactment!'

She knew emotional blackmail was far from his mind, but she still felt as if she was being pushed right to the back of her corner.

'Chloe,' she said, remembering her almost with relief. 'I can't because of Chloe. I have to get her sorted out before I can decide.'

'That might take years. You don't seriously plan to arrange your happiness round Chloe's?'

'Aren't you arranging yours round the estate and Ned? I don't see the difference.'

She felt exhausted by the argument, and Bron looked almost as dispirited, his expression harsh and set. The still air was laden with the dry bitter scent of straw rising from the fields below. The escarpment and the towering trees seemed to hang menacingly over them, as if the great weight of rocks and branches and leaves might all suddenly come toppling down.

'There's no point in going on like this,' she said wretchedly. 'All we do is hurt each other. Let's finish it now.'

He stood for a moment absolutely motionless. She'd expected him to react with instant anger. His look of stunned defeat was far worse.

'Finish it? You really want to? I never thought you'd give in so easily.'

'There you go again, talking about it as though we're on a battlefield,' she said wildly, desperate by this time to finish the conversation in any way she could.

'So it's over, just like that? Are you absolutely sure? Because I won't ask you again.'

'You don't have to. All I want is to work out my life in my own way in my own time.'

'I thought I was the one who was supposed to need everything cut and dried,' he said. 'But you're going to make no concessions at all.'

He kicked violently at a loose stone. Her heart began to thud in her chest as she watched it ricochet down the hill in a series of tumbling bounds. She wavered between hysterical laughter and wanting to cry. He looked exactly like Ned when something hadn't gone his way. But this was different. She and Bron weren't children.

She caught at his arm. 'Please, Bron, at least let's stay friends.'

'Friends!' he said derisively. 'For Christ's sake, Georgia, I want more than that! I want all of you, or nothing at all. Friends! You sound like a bloody agony aunt.'

'And you're still going on like a bloody general, as if I'm a military objective you for once can't take!' she blazed back, glad to be angry with him, because it dulled her pain.

He stared at her, then wrenched his arm from her grasp. Without a word he headed downwards through the trees, ignoring the path, driving in his heels like a scree runner, dislodging showers of pebbles and dried beech husks. In another ten seconds he'd picked up the sunken track, and disappeared.

She staggered to a beech stump, and sat down, scarcely able to absorb the swiftness of the break. Yet that directness was completely characteristic of Bron, and one of the things she loved about him, she thought, near to tears again.

She waited a few minutes to get herself under control, then started to walk back soberly down the path, telling herself furiously not to be a fool, that she'd got exactly what she wanted, and now she could get her life into balance again. But the lecture had no effect at all on her heart, which continued to feel as if it had turned to stone. As she climbed over the stile into the Forty Acre field and began to walk along the verge back to the picnic spot, she scarcely noticed the grasses in the hedge, heavy with pewter seeds, or the hazelnuts ripening in frills of green.

Most of the harvest helpers had drifted away, including Nico and Zelda, but Morrigan and Imogen were still there with the Meadses and Kim. Mr Samms was helping Bron unharness the horses from the reaping machine, for it was to be left in the field to make a quick start on a neighbouring crop of oats the next day.

Imogen was fastidiously picking pieces of straw from her skirt before getting up. Morrigan strutted over to her like a flamenco dancer about to sweep his partner into some wild display. As he took her hand to pull her to her feet, Georgia saw his other hand stuff a piece of folded paper into his pocket. It looked suspiciously like a used wrap of cocaine.

Morrigan plucked a bunch of scarlet briony berries from the hedge, and tucked it into one of the combs holding back her hair. They matched her lips exactly. They made a handsome, predatory-looking pair.

Georgia began to help Mrs Meads and Kim collect up the last of the paper and plates and cups, still covertly watching Morrigan who had not released Imogen's hand and was laughing a little too loudly at something she'd just said. She was absolutely certain now that he was on drugs again.

Bron had just returned to the group, and Morrigan dropped Imogen's hand, a little too late. Bron's face hardened. Imogen looked around her at the tranquil country scene.

'We've been talking about a harvest bonfire for the Disciples here next month, to celebrate the solstice,' she said to Bron. 'The setting's perfect. Think of the PR potential for Merlinslade. You could have a special opening of the house at the same time, as a sort of trial run. I don't mind organising it, now I'm staying on. Don't you think it's a good idea?'

'It's bloody stupid,' said Bron. 'The fields are like tinder already. Another disaster like the re-enactment would turn the public off Merlinslade for good.'

Morrigan took a packet of cigarettes from his pocket while Imogen was talking, and put one to his lips. He stood with a match poised ready to strike as he listened to Bron's reply.

'Lack of imagination's always been your problem, hasn't it, Bron?' he said, glancing meaningfully first at Imogen, then at Georgia. 'You've never known what to do with a good thing.'

The match spluttered into life. Morrigan lit his cigarette, held the still burning match between his thumb and forefinger, smiled challengingly at Bron, and flicked it into a heap of straw a couple of yards away.

Georgia watched in appalled disbelief as a tongue of flame instantly licked out of the straw. Morrigan stood gazing at the flames, his face exultant yet totally undisturbed, as if he'd done nothing more alarming than set off a firework. Bron snatched up the rug where Mrs Meads had been sitting, shoved Morrigan violently away, and with it began to beat out the flames.

The incident was over in a few minutes, leaving only acrid fumes of smoke, and a blackened patch of stubble. Imogen flapped languidly at the smoke with an expression of distaste. By her side Morrigan, on an even greater high at the result of his actions, picked up his guitar and played a final triumphant chord. He didn't see Bron, his hands blackened, his shirt scorched by flying sparks, approaching him until it was too late. He grabbed Morrigan by his jacket, and shoved him back against the trunk of the tree, almost crushing the guitar between them.

'Not even you could have been so stupid as to have started that fire by accident,' he yelled at him, in a voice hoarse with anger and smoke. 'If I find you anywhere except the theatre in future, you'll leave so fast your feet won't even touch the ground. I'll get an injunction slapped on you as well. I don't care what the reason is!'

The Meadses were staring in open-mouthed fascination at this latest development in the family saga. Kim and Ned looked as if they'd like to throw a punch or two at Morrigan as well. Imogen watched with an expression which indicated very clearly that she considered herself the real object of contention.

The smile never left Morrigan's face. As Bron's grip finally slackened, he twitched himself away and stepped neatly to one side.

'That's the third and last time you've put me down in public, Bron! You've no right to bar me from Merlinslade. I'm going to do what I should have done when my father died. I'm going to contest his will!'

The silence among the onlookers became so absolute that Georgia could hear the rustle of oats in the next field.

'You think I can't,' said Morrigan with a manic grin. 'But you're wrong. I've already been to a lawyer. The will can be contested up to six months from probate, and you only got that last February.'

'On what grounds?' Bron rapped back. 'Old Edmund had every right to leave his property as he wished.'

'I'm a poor man. I told you so some time ago, but you chose not to believe me. I've a half million mortgage on my Royal Crescent house, and it's just been foreclosed. I've given the rest of my capital, such as it was, to the Disciples. I'm entitled to support from the family estate.'

Bron's face was the epitome of contemptuous disbelief.

'I can well believe you've mortgaged your house, but only as a part of some enormous tax scam. You've got funds stashed away everywhere. Swiss bank vaults must be bursting with them.'

'That's a dangerous thing to say in front of witnesses,' said Morrigan. 'I think I might sue you for slander too. Adequate provision was never made for my maintenance in my father's will, and that's what I'm going to claim. Maintenance in my accustomed style, which includes a suitable home. My London lawyers tell me I've an excellent chance of getting the house at Merlinslade and a large slice of the estate.'

Georgia, in sympathy with Bron over this at least, could see that he was as tense as an overstrung bow with fury, anxiety and absolute determination not to give an inch to Morrigan.

'Your lawyers? If you're so poor how can you afford to hire London lawyers?'

'They're only too keen to take on such a cut and dried case, especially with such excellent publicity value!' Morrigan was dancing from foot to foot now in his delight at Bron's discomfiture, goading him like some lunatic matador. 'What a dog in the manger you are, Bron. You can't bear to share anything, can you?'

'You never showed the slightest interest in the house while old Edmund was alive. That was another reason why he willed it away from you. What the hell do you want it for now? And where would you find enough money to maintain it if you're unable to earn? I can hardly keep it going myself.'

'I don't want Merlinslade for myself. It's for Brighid and the Disciples, so that they have somewhere worthy to live. And once the Fountain Foundation's established there'll be more than enough money to maintain Merlinslade!'

Chapter 17

Morrigan smiled at his stunned audience.

'Well,' he said genially, 'I think I've done enough for one afternoon, and this smoke's getting to my voice. I'll be off now. Does anyone want a lift into Bath?'

For once even Imogen was at a loss for words. Morrigan shrugged, and sauntered away through the stubble like a glossy black jackdaw in search of better pickings. Everyone watched in frozen silence until he'd clambered over the stile into the lane where his car was parked. The moment it had roared away Imogen turned furiously to Bron.

'I told you not to be so heavy-handed with him. You really asked for that. Where the hell are you going to find the money to contest the action?'

'Obviously not from you,' said Bron, who looked haggard with anxiety.

'You're absolutely right. Why should I pour capital into a lost cause? I might once have been interested in Merlinslade, but not any more, not the way it's going now. In my opinion it'll be the best thing that could happen if Morrigan does get it. Then Ned won't be stuck with a white elephant for the rest of his life, and he'll have a chance to make some real money, unlike his father.'

Ned was chewing his thumbnail. His gaze alternated between Imogen and Bron as if he were watching a tennis match where the ball was his future.

'Dad said Merlinslade would be mine one day. What's going on? I don't understand.'

'Your mother's the one who doesn't understand,' said Bron. 'And didn't I hear you promise Mr Samms that you'd help him stable the horses? What are you doing here still?'

'But I want to know what's happening. It's not fair!'

'It's not fair if you don't help Mr Samms. I'll tell you later what's happening. Go on, now.'

'But it isn't fair, is it, Mum, I mean Imogen?' said Ned in a rising whine, employing another well-tried tactic of divide and rule.

'I said go on,' Bron snapped. 'Otherwise there'll be no Castle Combe this weekend.'

Ned looked as if he was about to burst into tears.

'You just want me out of the way so you and Mum can go on being shitty to each other!' he said. 'Well, see if I care!'

He shoved his hands in his pockets and mooched sullenly away towards the field gate, deliberately scuffing his trainers and registering resentment with every step.

'Do you have to put Ned through it as well?' said Bron angrily to Imogen. 'This is the worst place to explain to him what's going on.'

'You're the one who puts him through it. No wonder he's a bundle of insecurities. The whole afternoon's been a nightmare.'

Georgia was feeling increasingly sickened by the argument, but the Meadses were watching avidly, their sympathies clearly all with Bron. Kim had been quietly getting on with stowing away the used paper plates and cups in the baskets after Morrigan's departure, and was ready to go. She looked towards Mrs Meads to see if she was ready to return to the house, shrugged as she realised she was still engrossed in the drama, and set off on her own.

Georgia grabbed at the chance to slip away in her wake. She took one of the baskets, and they began to walk across the stubble.

'I could see you were as pissed off as me by all that aggro,' said Kim, when they were safely out of earshot. 'Imogen's a right ball-breaker, and Morrigan's really screwed things up for Bron now. Poor guy – what the hell's he going do?'

It was a question Georgia had been turning over in her mind as she tried to subdue a sensation as severe as it was illogical that she'd somehow deserted Bron, even though her decision had been made well before Morrigan's threat.

'I don't know,' she said slowly. 'He's tough, but he's already got a load of problems. I can't see how he's going to deal with this on top of everything else.'

The financial implications of the court action were huge. If Morrigan was successful Bron would probably have to sell the rest of the estate to pay the legal expenses. In any case, the land without the house would lose most of its attraction for visitors.

'Bloody Morrigan! How can a guy who's made his sort of money say he's skint? It's obvious he's doing it to try and wipe Bron out.'

Kim glanced at Georgia as they trudged towards the gate.

'And what was going on before that, when you bunked off and Bron shot after you? Imogen was gob-smacked. Have you been having it off with him? I didn't think he was your type.'

Georgia opened the gate, allowing her hair to swing forward and conceal her face as she wrestled with the catch.

'He's not. We did go out a few times, but it was just a casual thing.'

'It didn't look to me as if Bron thought it was casual.'

'You know Bron. He takes everything seriously,' said Georgia, feeling still more like a traitor. 'And he's got such a hell of a lot of extra baggage, what with Ned and Imogen, and now this. It's the last thing I need just now.'

'I know how you feel,' said Kim. 'I miss having a man, but not the hassle. Once I've enough dosh for a place of my own I might start looking around for someone new, but it'll be on my terms, not his.'

That was the trouble with Bron: everything had to be on his terms, Georgia thought, as they walked on towards the house and Kim talked about her plans for buying a new van. Yet though Kim's comments had helped to put the sense of guilt in perspective, Georgia couldn't dismiss a feeling that perhaps she'd jettisoned something much more important than she'd realised.

All the cornfields had been reduced to stubble by the day of the dress rehearsal. Georgia arrived early, but when she walked over to the theatre Bron and his henchmen were already at work with the threshing machine in the stableyard. The huge box-like contraption which separated the corn from the stalks and chaff was rocking and groaning on its wheels as it spewed grain into a trailer.

Georgia hurried past and Bron did not acknowledge her, though Mr Samms, who was stacking the surplus straw into a rick, gave her a cheerful wave. Georgia felt as if she'd been in a threshing machine herself. The news of Morrigan's impending legal action had spread like wildfire among the theatre company, everyone had taken sides, and she was constantly canvassed for her opinion as she dealt with last-minute fittings.

She was torn by conflicting emotions: desperately sorry for Bron, bitter because he'd made their parting so difficult, and still troubled by her sense of loss. Her worries about Chloe had increased as well, for Kim had met one of the Disciples in the village, and discovered from an unguarded remark that the baptism ceremony was imminent.

To crown it all, the technical rehearsal the previous day, or tech as it was usually called, the first with the sets and lighting fully installed, had been a disaster. Not without reason were they also known as stagger-throughs. At them the actors were concerned not with interpretation but with the mechanics of adjusting to lights and scenery. The process of integration always produced frayed nerves and panic.

Things had not been helped by Bron, to whom she hadn't spoken since the picnic, deciding to make a sudden safety check just before the tech began. He'd looked gaunt with worry, but he had been so icily distant that she didn't dare to offer sympathy. His problems hadn't stopped his carrying out a detailed inspection which did nothing to increase anyone's confidence. The backstage staff were incensed by what they felt was an insult to their expertise.

Morrigan, on the other hand, seemed unaffected by the tense atmosphere. He coolly supervised the setting up of the background music tapes he'd made in his studio, and afterwards sat in his place at the side of the stage, ostentatiously practising meditation while he waited for the play to start. His performance at the tech was oddly downbeat and unco-ordinated, and Georgia became still more certain that he was permanently back on drugs. The knowledge doubled her fears for Chloe.

Though Bron had found no faults, things went worryingly wrong throughout the tech. Several of the flats, which had run perfectly up to now, jammed when gravel mysteriously appeared in their grooves. A vital connecting screw vanished from the wind machine, so that the opening storm sounded like a gentle breeze. The position of the spots on a lighting gantry had inexplicably become altered, and several bulbs blew, sending the lighting designer, whose first commission it was, into near hysterics.

The one saving grace, Georgia thought, as she went through the stage door and made her way past the green room to the wardrobe, had been that they'd had time for separate technical and dress rehearsals at Merlinslade. A combined rehearsal was a nightmare for the costume designer. Actors tended to sit around for hours waiting to go on, their costumes becoming crumpled and food-stained, and having to be cleaned at the last minute when there was no time at all.

Nico, preparing himself with a percolator of coffee and a cigarette in the green room for the rigours to come, was about to settle down with the newspaper before the others arrived when he saw Georgia pass by on the way to the wardrobe. She looked as gloomy as he felt, and he called her in to share the coffee.

'I loathe dress rehearsals,' he said. 'The tech was quite bad enough, especially with my dear brother's safety inspection thrown in. Do you know why he went so over the top? Everyone realises he's worried about the court case, but that wasn't any reason to come on quite so strong.'

'Why should I?' she asked crossly. 'I gave up trying to work him out ages ago.'

Nico wondered what was going on now between his brother and Georgia. Mrs Meads had made a dark reference to Madam, by whom she meant Imogen, getting all uppity at the end of the harvest picnic, setting Mr Bron in a real twist, and giving that nice Georgia such a turn that she'd had to go into the woods for a breath of cool air. 'Mr Bron went after her to make sure she was all right,' Mrs Meads had added confidentially, 'and he came back looking as if he'd lost a shilling and found a sixpence!'

This was the understatement of the year, Nico thought. Bron had been so bad-tempered since the harvest picnic that he could have understudied Tamburlaine. Not even Morrigan's threat could be making him this grouchy. He must have split with Georgia.

'I don't know why you didn't tell Bron to get lost at the tech,' Georgia went on, irritably flicking over the pages of the newspaper.

'The more I suggested he kept away, the keener he got. He'd just had formal legal notice of Ger's court action that morning, which didn't improve his mood. Bron maintains Ger doesn't have a leg to stand on, but he's bloody worried all the same.'

'Aren't *you* worried, Nico?' said Georgia, looking up from the paper with one of the clear, cool looks which sometimes made him feel slightly ashamed. 'It's a pretty bad outlook for Bron.'

'Of course I am. I don't know what the hell Ger's playing at. But looking at it from the worst perspective, it's going to take a year at least to get a legal judgement. Even if it goes against Bron, we'll have got through the first season in the theatre. And Ger, thank God, doesn't seem to have it in for me personally. Anyway, I'm convinced it's yet another of his teases. This is the most massive wind-up of Bron he can think of.'

'I don't think it's a tease. I think Morrigan means every word of it. Surely you can see what it would be like if Merlinslade were in his hands?'

'I haven't got such strong feelings about the place as Bron. I'd prefer to stay here, of course, after putting so much effort into the company, but there are other challenges, other things I want to do. And anyway the theatre's my world, not Merlinslade. It's the same for you, isn't it?'

Georgia stopped turning the pages of the paper. 'I suppose so,' she said listlessly. 'I always thought it was, anyway.'

'Is that why things have gone wrong between you and Bron?' said Nico in his most cajoling voice. 'Have you split with him? Tell your old uncle Nico.'

Georgia sighed. 'You're obviously not going to stop till you find out,' she said irritably. 'All right, I have, but that wasn't the real reason. And I certainly don't want to discuss it now.'

'I guessed it all along!' said Nico. 'You know, darling, I honestly think it's for the best. All that reserve got too much for you in the end, didn't it?'

It was a lucky guess. Now he had her full attention.

'How did you know?' she asked with an astonished look.

'Don't you remember I warned you about it at the battle? If you'd come on the scene before Imo I'd have said he was perfect for you, even though I'd have been as jealous as hell. But definitely not now.'

They were sitting side by side on the dusty, lumpy sofa. The cleaner seemed to have missed the green room today, for it was still strewn with empty coffee mugs and overflowing ash trays, and smelt of stale smoke in spite of the open window. Not an ideal ambience for trying to get together with her again, but it was worth a go, he thought.

He put his arm round Georgia. 'Bron's not the right guy for a warm, loving person like you,' he said.

Even as he touched her, he felt her tense. The breeze from the window, ruffling the pages of the newspaper, had revealed the gossip column, and Georgia wasn't concentrating on him any more.

Nico followed her gaze. 'Morrigan claims his own!' the headline screamed, below a photo of Morrigan and another of Merlinslade, together with a fierce-looking shot of Bron taken on an assault course.

'Morrigan, the charismatic pop star of the seventies,' the piece went on, 'whose father willed the historic family estate, Merlinslade, away from him, is bringing a legal action for a share of the inheritance. The present owner, Morrigan's nephew, Bron Carwithen, who was unavailable for comment, won the Military Cross in the Falklands conflict. In an exclusive interview, Morrigan told this column, "I intend to be scrupulously fair. I am only claiming the house and part of the land. Bron will retain the rest of the estate, and my other nephew Nico, the well-known actor, will continue to run the theatre."

Nico grinned. 'At least I've got it in writing that Ger won't give me the sack.'

'Look at the rest of it!' said Georgia angrily.

Nico read to the end with a mixture of amusement and exasperation. 'Morrigan intends to use Merlinslade as a head-quarters for the Disciples of the Fountain, a group of green Christians whose influence is already widespread in the West Country. Bron Carwithen's ex-wife Imogen said when contacted today, "I always felt Merlinslade was in the wrong hands." This story should run and run.'

'I would have said the Disciples were a hell of a lot more pagan than Christian. But the last bit is true enough,' Nico observed, determined to make light of the piece, 'especially with Imo handling their PR. I bet this is based on her press release. If you'd been in the gossip columns as often as I have, you'd know there's no point in letting this sort of thing get to you.'

'But how must Bron feel when he sees something like this? And what about Ned? What's it going to do to him?'

'I thought you said you weren't interested any more? Bron can look after himself and Ned. I think you should start forgetting him, and have dinner with me tonight.'

She stared at him coldly, crushed the newspaper into a ball, and hurled it behind the sofa. It just missed his head.

'And I think you ought to be rooting for Bron. He stands up for you every time.'

She grabbed her bag, and shot towards the door, looking even more bad tempered than when she'd arrived.

'Oh, boy, have you got it badly still!' he called after her as her footsteps echoed away down the corridor.

But all the same he was left with an unusual feeling of penitence, which didn't quite clear until he'd had another cup of coffee and a second cigarette.

When Georgia reached the workshop she couldn't afford to think about anything but the dress rehearsal. Methodically she checked each item for the play against the costume plot, knowing that any omission could create a major crisis, and afterwards helped Annie push the wheeled racks of clothes over to the dressing rooms, where the actors were already making up.

As they began to get into their costumes Georgia hovered

discreetly in the background, watching for last-minute problems while trying not to interfere too much with Annie's direction of Jenny and Kevin, who were doubling as dressers. They were all on edge after the difficulties of the tech, and it required endless tact to keep everyone happy. Soon she had a notebook full of comments for things to put right in the workroom before the first night.

Once everything was under control in the general dressing rooms, Georgia went to check on Nico. He was already dressed, and so totally absorbed in perfecting his make-up that he scarcely acknowledged her. In their shared dressing room Miranda was going over her lines, and Esther sat composedly reading a commentary on St Luke.

Warily Georgia peered round the door of Redvers' room. He hadn't begun to dress, though all his costumes hung ready on their stand, including the original of the cloak, which was shrouded in a cotton cover. Bron, in another surprising demonstration of understanding which Georgia preferred not to dwell on, had given permission for him to wear it at the rehearsal as well as the first night.

Redvers was sitting in an old string vest and a pair of striped pyjama bottoms, smoking furiously, sipping barley water with an expression of disgust, and snapping at Edie, his dresser, who'd been brought out of retirement for the run. Georgia wasn't quite quick enough to avoid catching his eye in the make-up mirror.

'What wouldn't I give for a double Scotch! Even a single, come to that,' he grumbled at her. 'How I'm expected to give a deathless performance on soft drinks, God knows.'

Ash from his cigarette was sprinkling his vest, but Edie, whose small stout body was encased in a reassuringly nanny-like grey uniform, gave Georgia a cheerful smile. 'Always like this before a show, is Mr Monk. I'll see he's all right. He's pleased as punch about the cloak.'

'Stop talking about me as though I'm a bloody infant, and make me a cup of decent coffee instead of this hospital brew,' grumbled Redvers, thumping down the glass of offending liquid. 'Barley water's for weak-bladdered women.'

Sending up a fervent prayer that Edie would be able to brace

Redvers sufficiently to get him on stage, Georgia wished him luck, and went to the auditorium. She took a seat next to Zelda in the centre of the stalls, where they could view the play from an average viewpoint. Behind them were Kim and Sumitra, most of the estate staff and their friends from the village, and a bus load of senior citizens on a mystery tour from Cheltenham, who'd arrived to see the house and were so disappointed at finding it not yet open that Bron had asked Nico to let them into the rehearsal.

The atmosphere was charged with anticipation as the house lights dimmed, and the ancient theatre prepared to wake from a sleep of almost fifty years. A single spot slowly intensified on a high-backed chair at the side of the stage, draped with scarlet silk, on which lay a solitary lute. Morrigan's opening music, an ethereal amalgam of viols, citterns and flutes, synthesised to produce an effect never dreamed of by the Jacobeans, swelled softly through the theatre as he strode into the spotlight.

He was a disturbingly Machiavellian figure in his swirling cape and wasp-waisted black velvet doublet. The lace standing collar framed his dark hair and obsidian eyes like a web of crystalline ice. He took up the lute, fixed the audience with his glittering stare, and began to sing one of the simplest and loveliest of Dowland's late-Renaissance songs. His delivery was so hypnotic, and the accompaniment so bewitching that the audience was instantly caught in his spell.

As the song came to an end, the spotlight on Morrigan faded and the curtain rose to reveal Prospero's ship foundering on the island shore. Georgia's gaze was everywhere as she checked broken rigging and tattered sails, and made certain the sheet of black plastic with a fan blowing beneath it to simulate waves was correctly pinned to the floor of the stage.

Her mind was behind the scenes as well, with the stage hands who were working the thunder roll, and who would soon have to heave a new set of flats into place along the antiquated grooves. Most of all, though, her attention was on the clothes, the ease of the actors in them, and on the lighting which could so easily make one costume seem washed out and insignificant, and throw another into too high relief.

Everything was in order, and she started to relax a little. But the moment she was able to divert her attention from the stage, she began to realise that there was something very wrong with the audience. Morrigan's presentation of the opening music, which was supposed to ease the onlookers gently into the first scene, had instead focused their attention on him so firmly that the shipwreck held no interest for them at all. In spite of the noise and spectacle, they were already coughing and shifting restlessly in their seats.

The shipwreck scene ended, to be replaced by the first view of the island and Prospero's cell, heralding the entrance of Miranda and Prospero himself. By this time the audience should have been fully involved, but they remained restless and uninterested until the spotlight made an unscheduled return to Morrigan. The synthesised sound of waves which set the atmosphere for the opening of the scene was already pulsating through the theatre like a soft heartbeat. Morrigan, who was meant to accompany it in the dim light at the side of the stage, and only with music on his lute, began to weave in an unscheduled, eerie, wordless song. Once more his presence and his voice utterly dominated the audience.

Zelda turned furiously to Georgia as the spot faded.

'How the hell did that spot get on Morrigan again?' she hissed. 'And who told him he could sing just there? He's ruining the balance of the thing. Why didn't I pick this up before, for God's sake?'

'Because Morrigan never did it this way before,' Georgia whispered back. 'He was much more down-beat at rehearsals. It's not simply because we're seeing it all meshed together and in full dress for the first time.'

'You don't have to tell me,' groaned Zelda. 'If he goes on this way he'll make Redvers freak out completely.'

'At least Redvers is wearing the real cloak today,' said Georgia, grabbing at the only consolation she could think of.

'What good will that do? Morrigan's already got the audience exactly where he wants it. Look at how the bastard's altered his position as well!'

Morrigan, who was meant to stay unobtrusively at the side except when he was actually singing, had during the scene change

349

manoeuvred his chair forward a few crucial feet to a spot where he was only too noticeable. Miranda, who'd just made her appearance from the cave, was instantly aware of him, and in her nervousness fluffed her opening lines.

What Georgia had tried to warn Zelda and Nico about for so long was becoming disastrously apparent. Morrigan was a wrecker, she thought as she watched in helpless frustration, a greedy solo performer, who looked on all the other players simply as his backing group.

'Redvers'll never cope. I guess I'll just have to stop the play and have a showdown with Morrigan right now,' Zelda said in a low, furious voice. 'Christ knows what it'll do to my arteries.'

'At least give Redvers a chance,' Georgia whispered back.

Prospero had been standing in the dimly lit cave during Miranda's speech, half obscured by her, with his back to the audience. As her speech came to an end and she moved to one side, he slowly raised his arms like a butterfly extending its wings to the sunlight. A single spot strengthened on the Queen of the Thrones of Water, gradually deepening the spectacular richness of the embroidery.

Redvers turned to the audience. It was impossible for him not to see Morrigan, but for the first time he seemed oblivious of his presence. As his perfect voice launched into his opening words to Miranda, they took on a significance far beyond the play.

> ' "Be collected:
> No more amazement: tell your piteous heart
> There's no harm done." '

His appearance in the cloak was so magnificent, his technical and artistic mastery so flawless, that the eyes of everyone there were instantly and irrevocably locked on him. The audience gave the quiet collective sigh which signified the recognition of a great actor at the height of his powers, and happily settled down.

Morrigan tried to re-focus attention on himself, adding little runs of lute music and moving impatiently during Prospero's best speeches, but to no effect. Redvers' voice was at its most glorious, his presence benign, calming, belonging to a different person entirely from the anxious ageing man in the dressing room. The performance began to fly.

'That's better, that's better,' said Zelda eagerly, leaning forward on the edge of her seat. 'Thank God for Redvers. What a pro he is. But I'll take Morrigan apart after the play.'

After the dress rehearsal Georgia took the wardrobe staff back to the workshop for a marathon discussion of how the costumes had worked in the play. She gave everyone their assignments for the following day, when there was to be a final rehearsal before the opening, and managed to send them all home by seven o'clock.

She lingered on for a little while, making a list of her own tasks from her rehearsal notes. As she was about to pack up a movement in the orchard caught her eye, and she saw Chloe coming through the trees. A minute later she walked through the workshop door.

Her hair was furled neatly into a roll round her head, and she was wearing a simple brown-printed cotton dress. Though it was only a short time since Georgia last saw her, she looked older and more serious. She smiled bashfully, and advanced into the room.

'Hi,' she said, 'I've been having a drink with Sean at The Mortal Man. I was walking back to the Sanctuary by the field path, and I thought you might still be here. I just wanted to see if my jewellery was all right.'

'It's fine,' said Georgia, rushing to the cupboard where it was stored as she tried to think of more ways of keeping Chloe there. 'You'd almost completed it when you left,' she went on, setting the jewellery out with deliberate slowness on a length of black display felt. 'I only had to do the buckles for Sean's shoes in the betrothal scene, and one or two other small things.'

Chloe studied the pieces lovingly before rearranging them on the felt.

'I've missed you a bit, Georgy,' she said in a casual voice, her eyes firmly on a necklace.

Georgia felt as if she'd managed to entice some rare and timid creature into the workshop. She was terrified of making a remark that would scare Chloe away.

'I'm glad you've gone on seeing Sean,' she said.

'Morrigan hasn't been too pleased about it. Brighid isn't worried, but he doesn't really like the Disciples seeing people from outside. He says we should be focused on the Foundation, and nothing else.'

Georgia bit her lip in an effort not to make a sharp reply.

'The paint's got scratched on some of these pearls. Perhaps I should give them another coat,' said Chloe.

Georgia rushed off again to fetch paint and a brush, and a piece of board to work on.

'Morrigan's so peculiar sometimes,' Chloe continued, after she'd carefully detached the faulty pearls and begun to recoat them. 'I don't really know if I should take the final step at the baptism. He's got sort of scary lately, and if I do become a full-time Disciple there are going to be loads of national fund-raising tours, and I'll see even less of Sean.'

'Have you talked about it to Brighid?'

'Not about Morrigan being so weird, of course. But she's been sweet over my problem with signing up for good. She says do what you want, the most important thing is finding yourself. The trouble is that Morrigan makes me feel I'll be betraying Brighid if I'm not baptised into the group.'

Just in time Georgia managed not to point out that Morrigan was a specialist in betrayals of every sort. Instead she made a valiant effort to see the problem from Chloe's point of view.

'Brighid's right.' She'd never thought she'd hear herself say it, or that she'd actually be grateful to the woman for once. 'Your own development is the most important thing at the moment. Even if you don't become a full member of the Disciples, I'm sure you could keep on going to the Sanctuary if you wanted. And you've been so grown-up about getting together with Sean again that it'd be a pity to lose his friendship.'

The advice sounded horribly glib. Georgia knew that life hardly ever worked out in such a satisfactory way, but it was obviously what Chloe wanted to hear. Her face shone.

'Do you really and truly think so? That's what I've been feeling for ages, too. But I made such a mess of things with Matthew, and if I did with Sean as well I don't know how I'd bear it. You and Mother haven't been exactly successful with your relationships, and perhaps it's sort of in my genes to fail with them too. If I stick with the Disciples they're so terrific and loyal, and always there if you need them. Though it doesn't feel very grown-up to keep hanging on at the Sanctuary, it might be best in the long run.'

'Of course it's not in your genes. Mother's totally different from you. She's more interested in things than people. And I was just unlucky with Blake. Our marriage didn't stand a chance from the start.'

'What do you mean?' said Chloe, looking up from the pearls.

Georgia sat down opposite her in one of the paint-spattered chairs. She rested her chin on her fists and wondered wretchedly whether the time had come to tell the whole sorry tale. Chloe was almost bound to over-react to it, yet if she didn't take her into her confidence, she'd probably lose her anyway. She mustn't treat her like a child. That was the mistake she'd made before.

'Blake was different, and I didn't realise it,' she said carefully.

Her voice felt as if it was being smothered in her throat, and as soon as she'd spoken she remembered she'd broached the subject to Bron in much the same way.

'Different!' said Chloe, opening her eyes very wide. 'You mean he was nutty or something? But wouldn't you have known?'

'Different mentally, yes, but not how you think. It was because he wanted different things physically too.'

Chloe's eyes began to pop. 'He was a weirdo? Into S and M? That sort of thing?'

Georgia wondered how she could go on. She could feel her self-control slipping already.

'For Christ's sake, Chloe, what do you know about S and M? Just keep quiet and let me finish. It's hard enough as it is.'

Chloe subsided. 'I do know about S and M,' she said in a dignified voice. 'Natty went out with a guy who tried to get her to do it. Don't treat me like a child again.'

Georgia buried her head in her hands, struggling to restrain her irritation and despair, and was almost glad when she registered that the sound of high heels, which had been tapping down the corridor outside for the last few seconds, had stopped outside the wardrobe door. She'd expected the sound to pass on – backstage staff hardly ever wore high heels – but the door pushed open and Imogen appeared.

She was about to go home too, carrying a slender snakeskin briefcase initialled in gold, and dangling a remote control car key from her other hand.

'Am I interrupting something?' Imogen asked.

'Yes, we're busy,' Georgia snapped. She didn't give a damn about keeping Imogen happy now, because she didn't give a damn about Bron either. 'You'd better come back another time.'

'But I've brought a note from Morrigan. There's something wrong with his costume.'

She produced a piece of folded paper from the pocket of her long cashmere waistcoat.

'Right, leave it on the table, and I'll look at it later,' said Georgia curtly.

'But don't you think you should do something about it right away? After all, he is your star performer.'

'There's nothing wrong with Morrigan's costume.'

'If he says there is, my dear, I rather think it isn't your place to question him.'

'And what do you think my place is, Imogen?' said Georgia, who was feeling more and more like a fight.

'You're an employee, and I personally think rather lucky to work here at all, particularly as it's your first commission in the UK.'

'She had plenty of commissions here before she went to the States. I think her work's brilliant,' said Chloe, startling Georgia yet again.

'You would, sweetie. You're her sister.' Imogen's eye fell on the neck chain Chloe had made for Sean. 'This for instance. Isn't it rather overstated, melodramatic, almost vulgar, dare I say? It is a small, intimate theatre, after all.'

'If you'd bothered to come to the dress rehearsal you'd have seen it looked perfect under the lights. The sort of understated design you have in mind would be lost on stage,' said Georgia.

'Really? How fascinating it all is,' said Imogen, with a yawn. She turned to Chloe again. 'Anyway, I'm glad you've made it up with your sister. It's so distressing when members of a family fall out.'

'We haven't fallen out,' said Chloe. 'I've just been a bit too busy to see Georgy recently, that's all.'

'Not too busy to see Sean Marchant, though,' said Imogen in an arch tone. 'He's a nice boy. And I'm sure you're pleased your sister's got someone to go out with too.'

Chloe gave Georgia a puzzled look. 'Are you seeing Nico again, Georgy?'

'Good heavens, you are behind the times,' said Imogen. 'Your sister's been going out with Bron. I wouldn't be surprised if we heard wedding bells there. Didn't you know?'

The pearl Chloe had been working on rolled off the edge of the table and away into a dusty corner. She stood up clumsily, overturning the pot of paint. Georgia hardly noticed in her dismay at Chloe's expression. She looked hurt, rejected, betrayed, just as she used to when she was little, and their mother went away without her.

'Bron? You're going to marry Bron?' Chloe said to Georgia, in a voice like the last gasp of a bagpipe.

'Didn't you know, dear?' said Imogen. 'I'm sorry. Have I said something I shouldn't? But I'm sure you and Bron will get on wonderfully well.'

She put the note from Morrigan in a more prominent position. 'I can see I'd better leave you both to discuss things in private. Don't forget about this, will you, Georgia? It really is important, you know.'

Chloe stared at Georgia while Imogen's heels clicked away down the corridor.

'You didn't tell me!' she said. 'You didn't tell me! Again! And I thought we were starting to be real friends this time.'

Georgia felt as if the smell of paint would choke her. 'Don't be silly. We're not even going out. I saw him for a few weeks only, and it's all over. I didn't tell you because I thought you didn't like him.'

'There you go, still jumping to conclusions about me. I *do* like Bron. He was nice after the battle. He gave some of us a lift back to the Sanctuary in his Range Rover. Brighid says there hasn't been enough of the female in his life. She's said prayers to the goddess for him.'

'Bron doesn't need prayers! There's nothing wrong with him. How bloody condescending!' said Georgia angrily, her self-control again draining away like the paint now dripping on to the floor.

Unaccountably Chloe didn't respond by flying into one of her usual tantrums, but made Georgia feel even more unhinged by continuing to look at her with a patient, thoughtful expression.

'I thought you didn't like him. I thought we were having an OK talk for once. I thought I'd almost got things sorted out.'

She put the jewellery to one side, out of the way of the paint, with a carefulness that was again unlike her.

'You said it was a one-off when things went wrong with Blake, but you were lying because now you've messed up things with Bron as well as Nico. I was right. You and Mother are exactly the same.'

'That's not fair!' Georgia said frantically. 'At least let me finish telling you about Blake and the divorce.'

Chloe had already reached the door.

'I've got to have someone I can trust, Georgy. I've learned that much about myself now.' As she pulled open the door she looked more than ever like the five-year-old Chloe. 'And if I trust Sean I'll probably end up making the mistakes you and Mother made, so I might as well sign on with the Disciples after all.'

Chapter 18

Esther spent the afternoon of the opening performance at the local primary school. She arrived at the wardrobe after tea for a last-minute adjustment to a costume she'd thought perfect but which had produced some minor flaw at the final dress rehearsal not pleasing to Georgia.

Everyone in the workshop looked worn out. The atmosphere of first-night nerves was almost tangible. She'd forgotten how insidious it could be, and how much she disliked the way it threw everything out of proportion.

Life in the theatre had kept her on an emotional see-saw generally for the last three months. After her decision to give up acting, her work at the mission had called for so much energy and commitment that she rarely thought of the stage, and John's steady affection had seemed to fill any other needs. But very occasionally, when she was caught up in the drama of one of the great Church feast day services, or when she was listening to a tale of passion from one of the women at the refuge, she felt a disturbing desire to experience once again some of that passion and drama in her own existence.

It was a desire she'd found easy to sublimate in her ministry, until she joined the company at Merlinslade and began to experience the old treacherous feeling of coming fully to life on stage. She knew she could hold an audience far more easily than she held a congregation, but she mistrusted the means by which she did it. Indeed, she scarcely knew how it happened herself. And Nico was even more dangerous. He was everything she suspected morally, yet his touch had an effect on her which John never produced, and he found only too many reasons for touching her during the course of the play. She was fairly certain that Nico hadn't guessed her state of mind, but she still felt it was a betrayal of solid, kindly John.

She'd even found her attention wandering during services, and it had made her less attentive to the problems of others, to the problems of Georgia, for instance. She'd been looking wretched lately, and Esther suspected it was because of Bron.

The others had left for home while Esther was having the fitting, and when she'd finished buttoning herself back into her cassock, she went over to Georgia who was ironing out creases in one of Sean's shirts.

'Is something wrong, Georgy?' she asked. 'Is it because you've stopped seeing Bron?'

Georgia stared at her, the iron poised in mid-air above the board.

'Who told you? Nico, I suppose.'

'I just happened to mention that I was worried about you. I haven't told anyone else, of course.'

Georgia banged down the iron in a spurt of hissing steam. 'He hasn't got any bloody right to tell anyone. I wish he'd keep quiet. At this rate it'll soon be round the whole company.'

She started to push the iron angrily back and forth across the shirt, nevertheless still producing a perfect finish to the rows of tucks Esther had seen Sumitra stitching a few weeks earlier.

'I'm sorry,' said Esther. 'I think he would have been right for you.'

When she'd suspected originally that Georgia and Bron might be seeing each other, she'd thought what a good combination they'd make. Georgia would tease Bron out of his seriousness, and he would bring some much-needed stability into her life.

'Well, I don't!' said Georgia, working away at a non-existent crease.

'Why are you so upset, then?'

'I'm not upset. I'm just trying to finish my work in time to go home and have a bath before tonight.'

Georgia banged the iron down on its heel, switched it off, hung up the shirt, and stumped over to a sewing machine. She snatched up a skirt and furiously began to run the hem, which had already been tacked, under the needle. The machine almost took off. It was so unlike her usual controlled behaviour that Esther began to think the worst. She was behaving just like the under-age pregnant girl who'd appeared at the refuge the other night.

'You aren't – you aren't going to have a baby, are you?'

The machine stopped abruptly.

'I'm not that stupid! Anyway, you should be pleased, instead of giving me this third degree. Doesn't the church disapprove of divorced people remarrying?'

'Not always. Sometimes it's better than persistent unhappiness.'

'Let's get one thing straight,' said Georgia, coming to the end of the hem, and snatching up some scissors. She began to rip out the tacking. 'I am not unhappy. So why don't you go and practise all this Relate stuff on your parishioners instead?'

Georgia held out the skirt as she gave the hem a final inspection. She shook its folds irritably into place, and yanked the waist loops on to a hanger, thinking that Esther would choose today of all days for her homily.

'You seem to be having rather an extreme reaction for someone who's not unhappy,' Esther said mildly.

'OK, what would you advise? You're obviously longing to tell me. To get myself all over again into an impossible situation? At least Blake didn't come with a power-crazy wife, a disturbed child, a derelict house, and a mountain of debt. And now there's Morrigan's threat to add to everything else.'

'Aren't you exaggerating a bit? Imogen's selfish and neurotic, I agree, but I think she's rather pathetic as well. And Ned's no more upset than most children who have to adjust to a broken marriage. As for the house and the debt, Bron's more than capable of dealing with them. Morrigan you'll just have to leave to the Lord. I'm afraid I didn't realise quite how sick his mind was till recently. But I do think you and Bron should give yourselves another chance.'

Georgia slammed the skirt on the rack. She'd completed the last task of the day. Now she could go home and forget about everything for a few hours, just as soon as she could escape from Esther.

' "Charity suffereth long and is kind",' Esther quoted, with one of her sweetest smiles.

'A man wrote that,' said Georgia. 'There's no need for women to go in for masochism any more. And anyway, aren't you making John suffer by going back to the stage? Isn't he worried that it might put you off ordination, or even off him?'

She knew the question wasn't fair, but couldn't think of any other way to change the subject.

To her surprise Esther went bright red. 'Sometimes I wonder that too,' she said slowly. 'I often feel I'll never know all the answers about myself. I still don't understand why I let myself become involved in acting again. How can two such different things as the church and the stage have such a strong hold over me?'

Her distress was so genuine that Georgia felt even more guilty for her question. Esther was at least being sincere in her comments, but all she wanted to do was wound people these days. It seemed to be the only thing that alleviated her own heartache.

'Perhaps you hadn't really worked out the answer when you made your original decision to leave the stage,' she said in a gentler tone. 'You were quite young. Perhaps you should have had a bit more experience of life.'

'I had plenty of experience of life at the mission.'

'But it wasn't your life, it was other people's.'

'I suppose not. But at least I was doing good there.'

Now Esther looked as if she wanted to escape. She glanced at her watch.

'This conversation isn't getting either of us anywhere, is it?' she said regretfully.

Georgia didn't answer. She couldn't bear to upset Esther or herself any more.

Esther smiled. 'I can see you've had enough, and if I don't go now, I shan't have time for supper. Zelda wants us in our dressing rooms by seven at the latest. I'm sorry, Georgy. I haven't helped much, have I?'

Georgia gave her a swift hug.

'I think I'm past helping,' she said equally ruefully. 'Good luck for tonight, anyway. We're both going to need it.'

After going back to Sophia Street, having a bath, and changing
into the dress she'd worn at the Veneziana, Georgia felt more like
facing the long evening ahead. As she drove back to Merlinslade
she thought without much hope that perhaps Chloe might come
to the party after the performance, since Sean was bound to be
there.

The sun was dropping towards the horizon. Flares lined the
drive up to the house, ready for lighting when darkness fell. In
another hour the paddock which had been turned into a car park
would be almost full.

Young girls chattered in clusters round the stage door, hoping
for a glimpse of Nico. There was a bevy of older admirers
watching out for Redvers, and a whole fan club lying in wait for
Morrigan.

Georgia was working her way through the throng when
Morrigan's car screeched to a halt on the opposite side of the
yard. His self-advertising swagger was more pronounced than
usual, almost a parody of itself, but the fans loved it, and
descended on him in a screaming horde. He started to sign
autographs with a dramatic flourish. His behaviour was so
exaggerated, even for him, that Georgia knew he was high.

She went into the theatre before he could catch up with her,
and walked through to the wardrobe. When she'd checked the
costumes for the last time, thanked all the wardrobe staff, and put
a celebratory bottle of champagne to cool in the workshop fridge,
she set out with Annie to trundle the racks of costumes down the
corridor to the dressing rooms.

She took especial care with Redvers' costumes, checking them
yet again before handing them over. His dressing room was
crammed with flowers from his legions of faithful fans. Edie was
wedging good luck messages into the frame of light-bulbs round
his mirror. Redvers smoked furiously while he put on his
make-up.

Now there was little more Georgia could do for the production,
except, she hoped, enjoy watching it. This was always a moment
of hiatus for the designer. After tonight her work on this play

would be over. For the actors and technicians every performance would be a new one till the end of the run, but her sets and clothes could evolve no further.

A seat had been reserved for her at the end of a row in the mid-stalls next to Zelda, who was still backstage. Many of the playgoers were in evening dress, among them a posse of London critics. She knew that good reviews from them could make her business take off so fast that she might even have to hire an assistant.

The excitement increased as a very minor royal couple whom Imogen had managed to corral for the occasion entered the main box. Imogen, who was with them, looked stunning, upstaging everyone in a Versace dress that revealed at least two-thirds more than it covered. Bron came in with Ned behind the main party, wearing a dinner jacket and an expression of extreme stoicism. Ned was in a formal jacket too, and looked excited and uncomfortable at the same time.

Everyone rose as the National Anthem was played, the auditorium doors were closed against latecomers, and at last the lights began to dim. When Morrigan appeared there was a massive round of applause before he'd even begun to sing. This time he stayed firmly at the side of the stage, but Georgia's gaze kept going back to him. His expression was just visible in the dim light, and during the second act, at the entrance of Redvers, who got an even bigger round of applause, Georgia could clearly see Morrigan's look of frustration.

Redvers was already casting his spell over the audience. So far, so good, thought Georgia. She looked over to the box to see the reaction there. The royal couple were as much engrossed as anyone else, but Bron was still standing at the back. Georgia wondered irritably why he didn't sit down and relax.

Redvers finally exited to more thunderous applause. He now had a whole act in which to recover from his initial ordeal. Stephano and Trinculo came on, and Georgia had just settled down to enjoy their clowning when she was distracted by a programme seller tugging at her arm, and feverishly whispering that there was an urgent message for her on the box office phone.

She crept out into the foyer, blinking in the bright lights, and picked up the receiver.

'Georgia!' said Zelda's distraught voice. 'Have you done something with Prospero's cloak?'

'What do you mean, done something with it? Of course I haven't. The cloak's either on Redvers or in his dressing room.'

'It's damn' well not. It's disappeared. You'd better get backstage right now. Redvers is freaking out. His next entrance is in twenty-five minutes. He says he won't go on again without it.'

Georgia had never moved so fast. She rushed outside and round the theatre to the stage door, hurtled past the alarmed stage door keeper, and burst into Redvers' dressing room.

Zelda was sitting grimly on the edge of the dressing table. In a corner Edie was crying. Redvers had slumped in his chair, staring into the mirror. His face was funereal under his make-up. At least he was still in the costume he wore under the cloak, Georgia thought. She'd half expected to find him back in his everyday clothes.

'I can't go on without it, you know,' he said, looking up at her dolefully.

'What did you do with it when you came off stage?' Georgia demanded.

'Gave it to Edie of course, just while I went for a necessary slash, and when I came back it had gone.'

'But I only left it for a moment while I fetched Mr Monk some coffee from the green room,' Edie moaned, rocking to and fro. 'Who could have done such a wicked, wicked thing?'

Zelda and Georgia stared at each other, and exclaimed in unison, 'Morrigan!'

They tore along to his dressing room, almost flattening one of the extras in their desperate haste. There was no sign of him or the cloak. His costume hung neatly on the rail, his dressing gown was on his chair and his own clothes had gone.

'Christ, that's it!' said Zelda. 'Did you notice Morrigan had left the stage, Georgy?'

'I was too busy watching the clowns. He must have taken the cloak. There's no other explanation.'

'I've got Redvers' understudy on stand-by, and we can just about manage without Morrigan. But the critics'll really get their knives out if Redvers lets everyone down for a second time. I knew Morrigan was a bastard, but I never thought he'd go this far.'

'We've still got the copy,' said Georgia.

'Georgy, you're a genius! How did I forget?' said Zelda, running her hands through her hair. 'I must be completely menopausal. For Christ's sake go and fetch it, while I try to talk Redvers round. At least we still have a little time.'

When Georgia returned to the dressing room with the copy bundled under her arm Zelda had not been successful. Redvers was fumbling at the buttons on his velvet robe, trying to get out of his costume. Edie hovered by him, pumping her hands anxiously together.

'A drink,' she was saying to Zelda. 'It's the only thing. A little nip of brandy'd bring Mr Monk round in no time. It's always worked before.'

Georgia looked at Zelda. They both knew that if Redvers didn't make it unaided back on stage, if he had even the smallest amount of brandy, he'd probably slip into alcoholism again. But there was no time for subtle persuasion. Over the tannoy they could hear the play progressing inexorably towards Redvers' next entrance.

'Edie's right,' said Redvers, allowing his arms to flop, and looking like a collapsed pantomime horse. 'It's the only way. I can't let my audience down again.'

'It's really too much for Mr Monk to cope with, *Scarborough Fair* and losing the cloak,' said Edie.

'*Scarborough Fair*? What the hell are you going on about now?' Zelda was almost screaming at Edie in her exasperation.

'It's a folk song, Miss Stein. Dreadfully unlucky it is, and Mr Morrigan was singing it to Mr Monk just before curtain up. He only felt able to go on because he had the real cloak.'

'You cannot be serious!' Zelda shouted at Redvers. 'You're freaking out because of a fucking folk song? I don't believe I'm hearing this. Do you know what Edie's talking about, Georgy? Is it some crazy British superstition?'

Georgia rushed through the words in her mind, which felt as if it had gone into permanent fast forward.

'There's a sort of veiled curse in it. It's about a false lover. Some people think it's unlucky if you sing it in a certain way. And Morrigan seems to make a speciality of lethal folk songs,' she added bitterly.

'He sang it to me once before,' Redvers volunteered in a mournful voice, 'the time I dried on stage in New York.'

'Morrigan was there then?' Zelda asked incredulously.

'He'd been recording a new album in the States. God, I'll never forget that night. And it's going to happen again.' The room was very hot, but Redvers was shivering. 'I've got to have a drink. Go and get me a double brandy at the bar, Edie, and I might just manage to crawl on stage.'

'Do that, Edie, and you're fired!' thundered Zelda. 'You listen to me, Redvers. I've laid my reputation on the line with this company, and I'm not having you put the skids under us just because of Morrigan. You're going to shape up right now, and that's an order!'

Redvers was staring at her as if the Statue of Liberty had come to life. Zelda grabbed him by the front of his robe, and hauled him to his feet.

'You've ten minutes to get your head together. Then you'll put on the copied cloak, and go out there and wow them! Is that understood?'

Redvers nodded bemusedly. As he did so an urgent call from the stage manager came for Zelda over the tannoy.

'Right, then. I've got to get back to the play. Other people need me too. I don't trust Redvers not to get round you, Edie, so you're coming with me, just till he's back on stage. And I'm relying on you to make damn' sure he gets there, Georgy!'

Zelda frog-marched Edie from the dressing room before Georgia could even open her mouth to protest at having this enormous and unwanted responsibility dumped on her.

Redvers still looked bemused, in spite of Zelda's tirade, but picked up his coffee cup and drank the almost cold liquid at a single gulp. Georgia began to refasten the buttons at his neck, thinking that was one positive thing she could do at least. The pulse was thudding in his throat again, just as it had done at the fitting with Morrigan.

'I won't make it, you know,' he said.

'Of course you will,' she answered calmly, though she felt like shouting at him as loudly as Zelda. 'There are actors in this company who've got their first big chance tonight. I know you won't let them down. Do you remember what it was like in your first acting job, when the star seemed almost god-like? That's how people like Sean and Fiona feel about you.'

'A god with clay feet.' His voice was bitter, but he smiled at her. 'My wife thought I was a god too. Christ, how I let her down! *Scarborough Fair* made me remember it all. Morrigan knew it would, damn him.'

He looked as though he was miles away. 'I was playing Faustus the night I fell apart.'

He began to quote in a low voice:

> *"Hell hath no limits, nor is circumscrib'd*
> *In one self place, where we are is Hell,*
> *And where Hell is, there must we ever be." '*

Over the tannoy Georgia could hear the opening words of the scene before Redvers' next entrance. She was longing to know more, but she knew it was no way to prepare him to go on stage.

'Wouldn't it be better if you told me afterwards?' she said gently. 'It's your cue in ten minutes.'

'It's the only way I'll get back there, the only way to exorcise it. And you're the only person I trust to listen and understand.'

He lit a cigarette. His hands were shaking so much that Georgia wondered if he'd ever pull himself round, but there was no stopping him now.

'We'd been married only a short time. We should have been happy. She was young and attractive, and far more sensitive than I deserved. But I – I –' He took a long drag on the cigarette, and exhaled with a sigh. 'I liked young men as well.' He gave another smile. 'I was a double-decker, as people called it then.'

Georgia gripped the back of Redvers' chair. This was a revelation she hadn't been prepared for.

'It was commonplace in the theatre then, and probably still is. It had never worried me. I even felt it helped artistically, gave me a deeper insight into human behaviour, but I knew I must give up that side of my life when I married. I was happy with my wife for a few months, until I heard that Rob, my former lover, had turned to drugs – drugs supplied by Morrigan.'

Georgia held on to the chair as if it were the only stable thing in the universe. 'Morrigan? How did he come into it?'

'Rob was part of Morrigan's backing group until he left to live with me. He was dying of heroin addiction, and he was alone. I had to go to him, and when I did I knew I should never have married.'

He stubbed out the cigarette half smoked, and automatically began to light another.

'My wife couldn't take it, and left me. Then I was forced to leave Rob, because I was committed to play Faustus on Broadway. I got the news of his death a few hours before the first night. I managed to get myself into the dressing room, but Morrigan turned up, ostensibly to wish me luck, and sang *Scarborough Fair* to me instead. I knew what the message in the song meant, and I knew he intended me to fail. He had a huge grudge against me because Rob had left his group. You know the rest. It's theatrical history by now.'

The story had been uncannily like Blake's, and yet Georgia found she didn't hate Redvers. She felt intensely sorry for him.

'So that's it,' he said. 'At least my wife found someone else who made her happy afterwards, but it's a sordid little tale, even for these days when anything goes. Don't you think so?'

Georgia could hardly cope with her own emotions, let alone Redvers'. But over the tannoy the scene was drawing into its final lines, and in a few minutes they'd hear his cue.

'I think you've punished yourself enough,' she said. 'You have to go back on stage and prove to yourself and Morrigan that you're still the greatest actor in the English theatre today. You can do it, Redvers. You know you're a trouper. This time you won't let the company down.'

She went over to the rack and picked up the copy of the cloak. She stood behind his chair and held it outspread, willing him to stand.

'A trouper?' he said, staring at his reflection. 'I wonder.'

As if in a dream he slowly rose from his chair, pushed it to one side, and stood motionless while she arranged the cloak round his shoulders. When she'd finished he took his cap from the dressing table, and gravely settled it on his head. Hastily she did up the clasp of the cloak, thinking almost inconsequentially that whatever else happened at least it wouldn't fall off.

'Perhaps it's too late to change,' he said. 'Perhaps there's no magic left.'

'Remember how many of us worked on this cloak for you,' she said in desperation. 'I copied the design, Kevin cut the pattern, Annie put it together, Jenny did the lining, and Sumitra almost wore out her eyes over the embroidery. We all put something extra into it because we knew it was for you. Don't you think there's magic in that as well?'

She'd touched the right chord at last. As the speech before his entrance drew to a close, he drew himself up straight, settled the cap more firmly on his head, and made for the dressing room door. He turned just before he opened it, and made her a deep, courtly bow. His only words were a final quotation.

' *"O wise young judge, how I do honour thee!"* '

And then he'd gone, hurrying through the door in a swirl of silk as the prompter called his name. A few seconds later Georgia heard him launch with every bit of his former confidence into his next speech.

She collapsed in his empty chair. She was still shaking with the intensity of her effort to will him on stage. The quotation and the story of his marriage had touched her deeply. She felt as if she'd just saved someone from drowning, and in a strange way she didn't yet understand, as if she'd been saved herself, for at last her resentment against Blake had begun to ebb.

Eventually Georgia felt calm enough to think of going back to the auditorium. She returned to the stage door, and began to walk slowly across the theatre forecourt towards the main entrance. Day had almost given way to night, and a full moon was rising above the curved gables of the house. From the branches of a cedar a barn-owl flew towards the fields on wings which blended invisibly with the dusk.

Georgia felt a moment of longing as she remembered the afternoon in the attic with Bron. She thought of the way Morrigan had tried to get Bron to give him the cloak in the great hall afterwards, and suddenly his words came back to her as though they'd blared through a loudspeaker.

'Don't you see, the Queen of the Thrones of Waters is the goddess who blesses our ceremony of baptism?'

She halted abruptly in the middle of the forecourt as she realised exactly why Morrigan had taken the cloak. The baptism was going to take place tonight, the night of the full moon, at the Grail Well, and she was about to lose Chloe for good.

She had a brief tussle with her sense of professional responsibility, and told herself that Annie would just have to manage if any problems came up. Chloe was more important to her at the moment than any play.

There was no time to change into sturdier shoes, even to grab a sweater or a torch from the workroom. She hurried in the rapidly failing light across the front lawn, through a formal parterre, and past the greenhouses, until she came to a wicket gate. From there a narrow track led to the path by the side of the Forty Acre field. A silvery mist wreathed upwards from the river, and the woods lay like a black pelt against the escarpment. As she climbed over the stile into the trees she saw a fox emerge stealthily from a covert.

Georgia began to stumble up the sunken path, which was in near darkness. Her footsteps sounded like a giant's. She could hear scuttlings in the undergrowth as she disturbed the creatures of the wood in their nightly rounds. Gnarled tree trunks loomed like distorted faces in the gloom, but she was too intent on reaching Chloe to be scared.

She emerged into the beech grove, and halfway through stopped briefly to rest. A faint wind was stirring the trees like a forest of masts. The moon slid in and out of the topmost branches. She was standing exactly where she'd had the argument with Bron. Some kind of madness seemed to have got into them both, she thought miserably, indeed into Merlinslade itself.

When she'd regained her breath she hurried on. Night had finally arrived, but the moon was bright enough to light her way. Soon she came to the yew thicket. Dusty branches caught her skirt and dragged with scrabbly fingers at her hair as she pushed her way through.

Moonlight illuminated the glade like a natural stage. Somewhere among the trees a night-jar chirred. The stream murmured in the background as it tumbled down the hill, but the surface of the pool was completely still, mirroring the moon in its depths.

From the downs above Georgia caught the sound of singing, and guessed the Disciples were on their way from the Sanctuary. But for once luck was on her side. Chloe was already at the pool, standing alone with her back to Georgia, absorbed in dressing the well head, packing every crevice with flowers from a basket at her feet. Candles were set in niches on either side of the squat figure incised on the standing stone. Their flickering light threw it into powerful relief.

Chloe wore her long white robe, and her hair was loose and unadorned. She began to wreathe flowers round the candles. Georgia walked softly towards her across the grass, and Chloe turned as she sensed another presence. A pair of scissors clattered on to the flagstones. Her hand flew to her mouth.

'Georgia! You scared me! What are you doing here?' she said in a panicky voice. 'You mustn't stay. The baptism's private.'

Georgia caught hold of her arm.

'I've got to talk you, to finish what I was telling you about my marriage. If you don't listen to me now it'll be too late.'

'You'll only say the same old things.' Chloe pulled her arm away. 'And anyway I'm not supposed to talk to anyone. I have to concentrate on my decision. That's why Brighid sent me ahead on my own.'

'I swear that once you've heard me I won't do anything more to stop you joining the group.'

Rough seats had been carved from the rock on either side of the standing stone. Deliberately Georgia sat down, trying to make their meeting less like a confrontation. Chloe hesitated, then very reluctantly came to sit by her side.

'Go on, then but you'd better be quick,' she said, folding her arms and looking deeply suspicious.

The cold from the stone seemed to strike into Georgia's bones. She knew Chloe felt it too, for she shivered, and moved closer. Georgia remembered times during tropical storms in Africa when the electricity failed, and she'd sit squashed in an armchair with Chloe, reading stories to her by candlelight. Now Chloe no longer trusted her, and was about to hear a very different tale. Georgia almost despaired at the enormity of her task.

'Try not to make it too hard for me, Chloe, please. It's so difficult to tell anyone about Blake. People can have such – such cruel reactions.'

'What do you mean, cruel?' Chloe's expression was puzzled, innocent, and still impatient.

Georgia felt she was having to drag the breath up from her chest before she could speak.

'Blake had a lover, a man, and I didn't realise it until after we were married.' The words when they came seemed to suffocate her.

Chloe's arms fell apart.

'He was gay?' she said in a wondering voice, 'And he didn't tell you? Why ever not?'

Disjointedly, stumbling through her story much too fast as the Disciples' singing came ever closer, Georgia told Chloe everything. All the time the sound of the stream threaded in and out of her words, and the figure of the goddess looked impassively on, hundreds of years removed from the confusion of the modern world. Georgia became colder and colder. She felt as if the chill would never leave her.

'So that's it,' she said, when she'd recounted everything, right down to the result of the test. 'My marriage failed mostly because of sheer bad luck. Nothing to do with genes, or because of any reason that's likely to affect you. You must never, ever think that way again.'

'What about Blake now?' Chloe asked.

Her face was grave. For once Georgia couldn't guess what she was thinking, even whether the story was likely to influence her decision at all.

'I don't know. He went to California with Lyn.'

Chloe looked graver still. Georgia began to wonder if the worst had happened, if Chloe like too many other people was so horrified by the illness that she couldn't bring herself to talk of it. Or even, most unbearable of all, whether she was condemning her sister. Desperation made her tell Chloe the one thing she hadn't meant to tell.

'I was so jealous of Lyn that I couldn't make myself ask for their address. Imagine being jealous of someone who was going to die! For ages I didn't care what happened to Blake either, he'd hurt me so much. That was almost as bad. Even now I've only just started to forgive myself for feeling that way.'

The face of the goddess wavered through her tears, and she thought hysterically that it almost seemed to smile. To her amazement, Chloe threw her arms round her, pressing her own wet face against Georgia's, and hugged her so tightly she could hardly breathe.

'It's all right, Georgy. Don't cry. I understand. Truly. I only wish you'd told me ages ago, and then I could have helped.'

Georgia felt helpless with relief, but she still struggled to retain her self-control. The singing was so close that the Disciples must be about to enter the glade. She needed to be completely sure she'd won Chloe over.

'So do you understand that there's no longer any reason for you to join the Disciples? The Sanctuary isn't real life. Don't opt out.'

Chloe hesitated. Georgia began to shiver again as much with apprehension as the cold.

'I know how difficult it was for you to tell me about Blake.' Chloe took Georgia's hand. 'But there's still a little part of me that thinks the Disciples' way might be best. Brighid said I wouldn't really find myself until the baptism ceremony began. She said the presence of the goddess alters everything.'

The singing was now on the edge of the glade, and at last Chloe herself became aware of its closeness.

'They've arrived, and I'm not supposed to be talking to anyone!' She flew up from her seat. 'Morrigan will be so angry if he finds you here. You must go, Georgy. You must let me make this last decision for myself.'

'I don't care what Morrigan thinks.' Georgia clutched Chloe's arm. 'All I care about is you. You've got to come home with me, before it's too late.'

'But I care about Brighid and the other Disciples. They've done so much for me. If you stay it'll ruin the ceremony for them all. I want you to go. I told you, I need to make this final decision alone.'

Her face was imploring in the moonlight. Georgia released Chloe's arm and pulled herself up from the stone seat. She knew finally that she'd lost, and she felt almost too exhausted to move.

'Hurry, hurry!' Chloe urged her.

Slowly Georgia began to walk back across the grass towards the yews. The air was heavy and humid, and still seemed to clog her lungs. But in spite of her exhaustion she remained in the shadow of the trees, some last stubborn impulse making her determined to see the episode through to the end.

Clad in their white robes, and led by Brighid bearing a long wooden staff, the novice Disciples filed slowly into the glade. They had an air of innocent simplicity like angels in an infants' nativity play. Morrigan struck the only jarring note. He swaggered by Brighid's side in Merlin's cloak, the moonlight glimmering on its gilt embroidery. He looked as alien as a peacock butterfly among a collection of drab wood moths.

The singing ceased. Chloe joined the end of the procession. It moved silently in a clockwise circle round the well, until Brighid brought it to a halt at the head of the steps down to the water. Soberly the Disciples lined up on either side of her.

Morrigan remained next to Brighid. It was the first time Georgia had seen them standing close together since the Roman Baths, and again she was struck by the look of devotion on his usually sardonic face. It was almost childlike in its openness. She remembered Kim's remark about his adoration of his mother.

Slowly Brighid raised her arms and began to half chant, half sing an invocation to Gaia. In other circumstances Georgia would have been amused by her slightly off-key contralto, but the surreal atmosphere in the moonlight glade, the utter sincerity and concentration of the Disciples, and above all the presence of Chloe, kept her completely sober.

The invocation ended. Brighid beckoned forward the first of the novices for baptism, and in words which at times oddly echoed the Christian marriage ceremony asked if she would remain faithful to the goddess and the Disciples for the rest of her life. When Brighid received an assent, she dipped her hand in the pool so gently that the reflection of the moon hardly trembled, and sprinkled a few drops of water on the novice's head.

So far the proceedings had been strangely impressive. The newly baptised disciples seemed to have acquired a sort of joyful calm. Their faces shone with a remote, other-wordly happiness which both impressed and disturbed Georgia.

Chloe was at the end of the line. As it came to her turn, and she moved forward to stand before Brighid, she looked like a sleepwalker. Solemnly Brighid asked her to take the final vow. Georgia felt sick with apprehension.

'If you firmly intend to love and honour the goddess, to obey the direction of her priests, and to dedicate your life to her service, repeat the pledge after me.'

The glade was absolutely silent apart from the sound of the stream. The noise of the water drummed in Georgia's ears as she strained to catch Chloe's reply. But at the very last moment Chloe finally seemed to connect with what Brighid was asking of her. She stared at Brighid, then to Morrigan and back again.

'There's no need to be nervous,' prompted Brighid gently. She began to lead Chloe through the promise, a few words at a time.

Chloe stammered out the first phrase, and then her voice faded uncertainly away. Brighid bent to scoop up the water. She stood encouragingly with it dripping from her hand.

'We weren't told we'd have to obey,' Chloe wavered.

Georgia couldn't bear to go on watching her bewilderment and distress. She rushed across the glade to the edge of the pool.

'Of course you mustn't obey! Don't do it, Chloe!'

A ripple of dismay went through the Disciples as they realised there was an intruder at the well. They turned uncertainly towards Brighid, looking for guidance. Morrigan's reaction was far more direct.

'This is a private ceremony,' he shouted at Georgia. 'What do you know of the goddess? Who are you to come here and tell us what to do?' His voice shattered the peace of the glade. He turned angrily on the Disciples. 'What are you waiting for?' he yelled at them. 'Make her go away!'

A couple of the male Disciples stepped hesitantly towards Georgia. Regret and disappointment rather than anger were uppermost in their expressions. They looked incapable of hurting anyone, but Georgia was sure Morrigan would be quite ready to take matters into his own hands if she didn't make an instant exit.

'The last thing the goddess wants is any kind of violence,' Brighid said sternly to Morrigan. She waved back the Disciples, and smiled at Georgia. 'You're welcome among us, my dear, as always. But you must let your sister decide for herself.'

Brighid turned to Chloe again, and scooped up more water from the pool.

'The way of the goddess or the way of the world, Chloe? The choice is yours.'

'Does the vow mean I have to obey Morrigan as well as you?' Chloe faltered.

'In obedience you'll find perfect freedom,' said Brighid, with another beatific smile.

Georgia thought despairingly how impossible it was to argue with Brighid when her meaning was obscured by this vague, semi-religious phraseology. Helplessly Georgia watched as Morrigan, goaded into action again by Chloe's inability to respond in the way he wanted, turned on her this time.

'You owe it to Brighid to obey. Hasn't she treated you like her daughter? Of course you must obey!'

'But I don't want to obey you,' persisted Chloe in a wobbly voice. She shrank back, looking as if she was about to collapse with the effort of opposing him.

He grabbed Chloe's wrist. 'Obedience to me is necessary for Brighid's protection, if she's not to be worn down by the demands of ignorant children like you.'

'I told you, no violence, Morrigan! The goddess forbids it.' Brighid's bland tones were at last beginning to alter.

'It's not just having to obey. I feel I've changed. I don't think the group's right for me now.' Chloe was breathless with distress.

'You'd be useless without us, and you know it!' Morrigan

taunted her. 'What would you do? Go back to your sister, who's even less capable of running her life?'

Georgia hardly heard the insult. She was feeling increasingly indignant with Brighid for being so slow to take control, for not better protecting the Disciples in her care. She could just imagine the bracing douche of commonsense her own mother would pour on such a scene if she had to deal with it. She had the unexpected thought that perhaps she was like her mother after all, in this at least. The idea was so astonishing that it suddenly made her determined that Brighid should know and face up to the real Morrigan.

'Who are you to judge anyone?' she accused him. 'Why should Chloe obey a man who's wrecked so many lives? You almost ruined Redvers. You killed his lover by supplying him with drugs. You deliberately destroyed his self-confidence, made his existence so unendurable that he became an alcoholic. And you've just tried to destroy him all over again by stealing the cloak as he was about to go on stage.'

Morrigan retreated a step, but still kept his nerve and his grip on Chloe. 'You're simply repeating the same old slanders. You've no evidence,' he blustered. 'You're like all the rest of them, trying to pin on me something I never did.'

Georgia ignored him. 'You'll do the same for the Disciples once they have to obey you,' she went on. 'Isn't that the idea? To set up a network of addicts dependent on you for drugs, whom you can force on to a treadmill of fund-raising to fuel your life style and their habit?'

'I'm used to rising above this sort of filth by now,' he answered grandly, though the sweat was beginning to glisten on his forehead. 'Don't listen to her, Brighid. She's lying, like all the others.'

Brighid didn't answer. Her face was slack with astonishment.

'Come back to Merlinslade with me, Brighid, and ask Redvers and Bron for yourself,' said Georgia, only just keeping her voice steady. 'They'll tell you if I'm lying or not.'

Brighid stared at Morrigan as though she was seeing a face in a hologram change before her eyes.

'Is this really true? That you did all those terrible things, that you even stole the cloak when you told me Bron had given it to you?' she said slowly.

'They all hate me,' he yelled. He was shaking with rage. 'Don't you see, they say it because they hate me?'

He made a sudden pounce towards Chloe.

'It's your fault! All this has happened because of you. You must promise, promise to obey!' he shouted, hauling on her arm, and dragging her to the very edge of the pool.

In a travesty of the baptism, he began to scoop up water and throw it wildly at her, like a child playing a splashing game.

'Stop it, stop it this instant!' Brighid sounded exactly like a nanny rebuking the same child. 'This is no way to honour the goddess.'

Georgia was momentarily frozen by her fear of Morrigan becoming more violent if she tried to intervene. Brighid, galvanised into action at last, had no such qualms. Moving with surprising speed for so large a woman she made a dive for Chloe's other arm, so that she was trapped in a bizarre tug of war. Morrigan lost his footing on the slippery edge of the pool, teetered on the brink, and with flailing arms toppled backwards into the water.

As he hit the surface the moon's reflection shivered into a thousand pieces. Beneath the cloak he was wearing a leather jacket and trousers, and high suede boots. He went under for a long time. When he finally surfaced he was thrashing his arms under the cloak like a fish in a net. His hair hung round his face, and a bald patch, formerly concealed, gleamed whitely on top of his head.

Momentarily he struggled up until he was half out of the water, then lost his foothold on the weed covering the sunken ledge and went under once more.

'I can't swim, I can't swim!' he shrieked as he disappeared.

Several of the Disciples hurried forward to help him, but again Brighid stopped them with a gesture. When he came up next time he'd managed to free one arm, but was increasingly hampered by the cloak as it absorbed more and more water. He clung precariously to the parapet, trying to keep his balance on the submerged ledge as he attempted to drag himself out.

'You've defiled the presence of the goddess.' Brighid's voice was loud with indignation. 'You've desecrated her holy place.'

'What the hell are you talking about? Just get me out of here!' Morrigan yelled, struggling to release his other arm from the cloak. His feet slipped, he inhaled a mouthful of water, and went down spluttering again.

Georgia still hadn't moved. His humiliation was too enjoyable, and she hadn't thought for a moment that he was in real danger. The water was only waist deep at the edge of the pool, and if he'd kept his head he would have been able to pull himself out eventually.

But things were different now. He'd panicked as his heavy clothing increasingly hampered his attempts to escape, and he was starting to choke. The cloak by this time was completely saturated, dragging him backwards towards the dangerously deep water in the centre of the pool.

Brighid had again relapsed into a state where she seemed to be waiting for some sort of inspiration. The Disciples seemed unwilling or unable to move without her permission. Impatiently Georgia grabbed the staff from her. Grasping it in both hands, she held it out over the pool, standing at the head of the steps, and keeping it just beyond Morrigan's reach as he came up again.

'Nearer, nearer!' he gasped, flailing at the end of the staff with his free arm as he found he couldn't regain his foothold on the ledge.

'Tell me it's true!' Georgia shouted at him. 'Admit you're on drugs again. Admit you planned to use the Disciples as cover for dealing.'

'You must be mad,' spluttered Morrigan. 'Just give me the staff!'

He took in another mouthful of water. His face had become a livid purple. Georgia knew she daren't leave him there much longer. The water was icy cold, he was drugged, and he clearly didn't have the strength to get back on the ledge. Slowly he began to sink once more, until the water crept up to his chin, and she was beginning to think her bluff had failed.

'All right,' he screamed, only his head and one desperately

searching hand visible now. 'It's true, it's true! But you must let me explain.'

She let him grasp the staff. Laboriously he hauled himself along its length till he reached the steps, and began to drag himself out of the water.

Brighid had been standing with her hand clutched to her breast, her face aghast, but as Morrigan staggered up and threw off the cloak, letting it fall in a streaming heap at his feet, she made a visible effort to pull herself together. Suddenly she wasn't just a kind-hearted, muddle-headed woman with a religious obsession which had made her temporarily blind. She took on a dignity Georgia had never seen in her before.

'You've betrayed the goddess and you've betrayed those in her care, Morrigan. You've lost the right to be one of us. I forbid you to visit the Sanctuary again.'

Another wave of dismay went through the Disciples. One of the girls started to cry. Georgia felt almost sorry for them for having lost so many illusions in one night.

'You're sending me away? Me, of all people?' Morrigan clearly still couldn't quite comprehend what Brighid had said. 'But don't you understand I had to admit it, or I'd have been drowned? You've got to believe me.'

Brighid looked coldly at him. 'I believe now that you've lied and cheated to gain our trust. There's no more to understand.'

Morrigan's bravado deserted him. He fell to his knees. His hair clung round his bald patch like seaweed to a stone. Water streamed from his boots.

'But you're my mother. I need you,' he babbled.

'If you treated your mother as you've treated us, her life must have been sad indeed.'

The simple comment seemed to affect him more than anything she'd said before. He shuddered, looked imploringly at her, and when he saw that she was still unmoved, stumbled to his feet.

He gazed at Brighid one last time for some sign of forgiveness, and then, white-faced, turned away from her, his boots squelching as he limped across the grass, and plunged into the yews. Slowly the sound of his footsteps crashing through the undergrowth faded away.

Georgia found she was clutching Chloe as if she might disappear at any moment too. Her legs felt so weak she could hardly stand. Brighid was staring after Morrigan. There were tears in her eyes.

'I thought I knew him. Poor, poor man,' she said. 'To betray so much trust surely denotes some deep unhappiness I never guessed at. But I betrayed the goddess too by letting him persuade me to change our ways.'

Her voice was shaky. She pulled a large white handkerchief from a pocket in her robe, and wiped her eyes.

'You've got to go back to the Sanctuary and ring the police,' said Georgia. She was deeply sorry for Brighid, who had suffered the severest disillusion of them all, but she desperately needed to recall her to the realms of reality. 'You must tell them what's happened. Morrigan must be stopped before he does something even worse.'

'The police?' said Brighid. 'Oh no, my dear. I can't add revenge to everything else.'

'But he's dangerous. He's freaking out. Don't you know what that means?'

'Leave Morrigan to the goddess. Let her deal with him in her own way.' She glanced at the Disciples, who were looking utterly dispirited. 'I must care for my flock. And you should take Chloe home to rest.'

'Yes, let's go, Georgy, please. I don't want to stay here now,' Chloe whispered urgently, tugging on her arm. 'My robe's wet, and it's getting so cold.'

Georgia was shivering too. A chill breeze was invading the glade, her shoes had been soaked by Morrigan's struggles, and arguing with Brighid was like arguing with a marble pillar.

She decided that Chloe and the play had to be her most important immediate concerns. She must get Chloe down to the wardrobe and into dry clothes, then try to catch the end of the performance at least, before she decided what to do about Morrigan.

Brighid folded Chloe in her ample embrace.

'I'm proud of you,' she said. 'You made a hard decision tonight, but I think you'll find it was the right one. Just remember we're always your friends.'

380

Georgia picked up the cloak, which was still lying where Morrigan had abandoned it on the edge of the pool, and gently rolled it up, squeezing out as much water as she could. Then, taking Chloe by one hand, and the parcel of sodden fabric in the other, she set off for Merlinslade.

Chapter 19

As they hurried through the yew thicket Chloe could talk of nothing but the events at the pool. Georgia kept up a series of soothing comments, but her mind was still concentrated on Morrigan. The wind had increased, and it gave Georgia the odd sensation that even the natural surroundings were disturbed by his presence, that he might at any moment burst out on them through the undergrowth.

When they reached the beech grove the gale was seething in its upper branches. The trees seemed to vibrate like huge tuning forks. The slope was strewn with the trunks of fallen giants from past storms, and Georgia was so anxious to regain open ground that she almost dragged Chloe downhill. In the sunken path the air roared behind them, spinning leaves about their heads, like a huge hand pushing them towards Merlinslade.

Yet as Georgia waited for Chloe to climb over the stile into the Forty Acre field, the wind had already begun to subside as unexpectedly as it had started. The water-meadows were bathed in silver calm, and beyond them the house and theatre, floodlit for the performance, seemed to float like a mirage. By the time they'd crossed the field not a twig stirred. Georgia half expected to see Morrigan's dark figure hurrying fox-like through the fields intent on some final mischief, but the atmosphere was now so tranquil that she began to relax, feeling intuitively that he'd gone. She decided that he must have picked up his car and returned to Bath.

Redvers' revelations and the events at the pool were still haunting Georgia, but Chloe had temporarily talked the Grail Well out of her system, and began to chatter happily about Sean and the party after the play, which she seemed determined to attend. Georgia had planned to drive her back to the flat after the play, but now she started to think that an evening with Sean would probably do Chloe far more good than an early night. She wouldn't have to put in more than a token appearance at the party herself, for Sean was bound to give Chloe a lift home.

When they reached the theatre Georgia took her straight to the wardrobe to borrow a dress from a rack of sixties clothes she'd been collecting for a future production of *West Side Story*. While Chloe had a shower in the women's dressing room Georgia turned her attention to the cloak. Until she was able to get it to a conservator the following day all she could do was let it dry naturally on unbleached paper spread over one of the cutting tables. At least the well water had been pure, and held no chemicals to weaken the fabric further.

Chloe returned, and excitedly began to try on dresses. Georgia wanted to stay with her, but professional pride drove her back to the auditorium. Still at the back of her mind was a niggling fear that even now something could happen to disrupt the play.

The Grail Well episode, which seemed to Georgia at the time to go on forever, had in reality only taken a couple of hours. There had been a long interval halfway through the play, and she slipped back into her seat in the stalls just in time to catch the end of the closing scene.

'Where've you been?' Zelda whispered from the seat next to her. 'You've missed Redvers' best performance ever. The critics were raving about it in the interval. They loved your work too.'

'I'll tell you afterwards,' Georgia whispered back, as she settled down to enjoy the closing minutes of the play. The set and costumes looked perfect, nothing was out of place, the familiar poetry calmed her, and she began to relax.

Redvers came on stage to speak the epilogue, the farewell of the old enchanter who has finally renounced his arts. When the last words faded the audience sat in silence for a long moment before bursting into a storm of ecstatic applause. Georgia joined in out of pure relief. She could hardly believe the evening had finished so well.

As the minor members of the cast came forward to take their

bow the audience began to go wild with delight, shouting bravos, and stamping on the wooden floor until the auditorium resounded like a drum. Sean and Fiona appeared to surges of applause, then Nico and Esther, Esther radiant as Nico led her forward, and gave her centre stage.

Now all the audience had risen and were calling for Prospero. No one seemed worried about Morrigan's absence, not even the members of his fan club, who were all demanding Redvers as well. The occupants of the royal box were shouting with everyone else. Georgia had tried to avoid looking at Bron because every time she did so her sense of loss surfaced again, but she couldn't resist watching his reaction. He was at least applauding, but he still looked preoccupied.

Redvers came on, took a dozen bows, and joined hands with the rest of the cast to lead them forward for the final curtain. The clapping petered out as it fell for the last time, and the house lights came on. Relief flooded over Georgia. Now there really was no need to worry any more.

Slowly the audience began to filter away, leaving behind a litter of programmes and confectionery wrappers. Zelda went off to speak to the press in the foyer. Georgia, experiencing another wave of reaction, felt almost too tired to move. She decided to wait where she was until everyone had gone, and took her notebook from her bag to jot down a few reminders for the wardrobe the following day.

By the time she'd written the last note the ushers had finished collecting the worst of the debris and retrieving forgotten wraps and purses. They dimmed the lights again before leaving. As the auditorium doors closed behind them Georgia briefly caught an excited babble of conversation from the crowd still in the foyer.

The stage-hands had raised the curtain, and all the props were cleared away. The stage was empty apart from the flats set up for the next performance and a trolley stacked with rigging for the shipwreck, but Nico had asked the stage manager to leave a few rehearsal lights on in case the first-night party decided to migrate there later that evening. A movement caught Georgia's eye in the wings, and she was startled to see Bron there, apparently making yet another of his endless checks. Irritably she wondered if he ever let up.

Luckily he hadn't seen her. She knew she ought to go and speak to him about Morrigan, but she couldn't face the prospect. It would be so much easier to tell Zelda first, and let her relay the news. As she slipped unobtrusively into the aisle to go in search of her, she heard the auditorium doors swing open. She looked towards them and saw a cameraman and news reporter from Avon Television whom she recognised from an earlier publicity session.

Georgia sighed. Zelda must have told them where she was. She'd have to manoeuvre them back into the foyer. It would be impossible to cope with a media interview with Bron looking on. Nevertheless out of sheer habit, and in spite of Bron's presence, before she went to intercept the television crew her own gaze returned to the stage, checking it one last time. Everything was in place, and she was about to turn towards the doors, when another movement caught her eye, this time at the back of the vista stage.

To her alarm a series of grating creaks filled the air, a sound which she instantly knew heralded the descent of the laden cradle with the winch unattended and the counter-balance left to control the load alone. Only too vividly she could picture the whole structure juddering under the strain. Frantically she wondered if one of the stagehands had celebrated too well too soon, and was playing some drunken game with it.

In a series of violent jolts, Juno's chariot began to progress towards the stage. She was still more astounded to see Morrigan standing in it, holding on to one side. He'd changed back into his costume. His damp and tangled hair was pushed roughly back from his face, his standing collar was awry, and his doublet gaped at the chest. Most horrifyingly of all, he was carrying one of the lighted torches from the drive.

By some miracle the cradle lurched safely to the ground, and Morrigan stepped out. He didn't see the onlookers, who had all been momentarily startled into inactivity. He began to meander round the stage in what appeared to be some bizarre tour of inspection, the torch held high above his head. His movements were so erratic and unco-ordinated that Georgia was terrified he'd touch the scenery with it. Though the curtains and the flats had been treated with fire retardant, it wasn't sufficient to resist a concentrated onslaught from a lighted torch. The ropes of the hoist, and the centuries-old wood of its scaffolding hadn't been treated at all, and would act like a tinderbox on the rest of the stage.

The reporter was the first to collect his wits. He rushed forward to the front of the stalls.

'For God's sake stop fooling around with that torch, Morrigan. We've got the message that you're here.'

Morrigan's only answer was to whirl the torch at arm's length, spinning his whole body with it so close to the reporter's head that the draught lifted his hair. He hastily drew back and began to retreat to the comparative safety of the side aisle where Georgia and the cameraman were still standing.

'That's right,' shouted Morrigan. 'Keep away. Don't you know this theatre belongs to me?'

'Christ, I do believe he's freaked out!' said the reporter ecstatically in Georgia's ear. 'No wonder he didn't show up for the rest of the play! What a story!'

He dropped on to all fours and with the cameraman began to inch back towards the stage, keeping close to the cover of the seats. Bron had temporarily disappeared, and Georgia prayed that he'd gone to call the emergency services on the backstage telephone. It was abundantly clear that any direct confrontation with Morrigan would be a disaster.

He began to strut about the stage, sweeping the torch as if he were painting pictures of fire. The cameraman, unable to resist such an opportunity, started filming with his camera pointing above the edge of the proscenium, like a sniper over a parapet. Georgia fully expected the action to trigger Morrigan into still greater excesses, but he seemed to welcome the attention this time, for he stopped, smiled delightedly, and even struck a pose.

In that moment of inattention, Bron suddenly reappeared from the wings into the centre of the stage. Her heart began to beat like an over-active metronome. If he attempted any kind of physical heroics she was certain it would tip Morrigan into extreme violence. Bron had no knowledge of what had happened at the Grail Well, nothing to give him a clue to understanding Morrigan's state of mind. The psychological as well as the physical advantage was all on Morrigan's side.

It took only a moment for him to be aware of Bron. He seemed unsurprised, almost as if he'd been expecting him. Bron, still in evening dress, looked as wary as a wrestler searching for a grip. Morrigan threw the torch into the air again. It soared upwards, and as he caught it he swept it so close to Bron's face that he must have felt the heat on his skin.

'Why are you doing this, Morrigan?'

Bron's voice was as calm as a father trying to soothe a hysterical child. The theatre was so silent that every syllable could be heard. The reporter poked up a microphone like a periscope, not wanting to lose a syllable of this scoop which would surely supplant everything else in the next day's newscasts. It was publicity of the first order, Georgia thought distractedly. Not even Imogen at her most inspired could have dreamed up something like this.

Morrigan's voice dropped to a murmur. He began to quote from the play, speaking more to himself than Bron. ' "This island's mine, by Sycorax my mother, Which thou tak'st from me." '

'So does this have something to do with *your* mother?' Bron prompted quietly.

Georgia began to relax a little as she realised that he wasn't going to hurl himself at Morrigan as he'd hurled himself at the oncoming cavalry during the re-enactment.

'No one wanted her,' said Morrigan. He and Bron might have been alone. 'No one knows how she suffered when my father abandoned her to bring up a child alone. Or how I suffered when he stole Merlinslade from me, just as he stole marriage from her.'

His voice rose as he lashed himself into an orgy of self-pity.

'The best thing I ever did was to make the last years of my mother's life happy, to provide for her in the way my father never did.'

He gave the torch another flourish. Bron had inched a little nearer during his soliloquy, but was forced to retreat again.

'She died when I was on my way home,' Morrigan went on. 'I

wasn't even able to say good bye to her. So now I'm alone. All alone. Not even Brighid wants me now. No one listens to me.'

Georgia saw Bron tense almost imperceptibly. Her breathing eased. Morrigan had given him a lead at last.

'But I'm listening to you,' said Bron. His voice was still unruffled.

'You never wanted to before,' said Morrigan in a doubtful tone.

'I told you, I'm listening,' said Bron. 'Tell me what happened to make Brighid not want you any more.'

'I forget,' said Morrigan, his face becoming vague. 'I don't understand. We were going to do so much good together. Why did she send me away?'

'Would she call this good?' Bron asked.

'It's for a greater good. I must have Merlinslade. For my mother's sake.'

'Then perhaps we should talk about letting you have the estate after all. Now seems as good a time as any.' Bron sounded so casual that he might have been going to discuss the harvest with Mr Samms.

'You'd give it back to me?' said Morrigan. 'You'd really give it back?'

His expression was incredulous. Bron inched a little nearer again.

'Why not? There'd be conditions, of course, the same conditions under which I inherited it. You'd have to take it with all its debts, all its traditional responsibilities, and run it as my grandfather would have wished.'

Georgia was nearly as incredulous as Morrigan. Even as a gamble the offer was insane. She couldn't begin to imagine why Bron had made it. The shock seemed to sober even Morrigan. His next words were almost rational.

'Why should I concern myself with tradition and responsibility? I'm an artist, a free spirit, not like you. You're in no position to dictate terms, Bron, and you know it. If you don't give me Merlinslade, I'll win it in court.'

'But you still haven't told me why Brighid sent you away. Wasn't it because she didn't like something you'd done?'

An edge was creeping into Bron's voice at last.

'Wasn't it something that would make a judge think you were asking for Merlinslade for all the wrong reasons?' he persisted. 'Something that would make him decide you were the last person to take on the responsibilities of the estate?'

Morrigan shook his head like an animal maddened by flies, and swept the torch in a semicircle in front of him. It passed so close to Bron this time that he had to duck to avoid it. A piece of the torch flew flaming to the floor of the stage, smouldered and mercifully went out. Georgia felt sick with fear. Bron was playing a lethally dangerous game, and she didn't see how he could win.

'I've told you everything you need to know,' Morrigan shouted. 'One more stupid question, and you'll see what I can do.'

'But I haven't told *you* everything yet,' said Bron levelly. 'About your mother, for instance. Did you know she didn't want you to have Merlinslade?'

The torch wavered in Morrigan's hand. Almost imperceptibly the balance of the confrontation began to alter.

'Didn't want me to have it? Of course she did. Who told you such a lie? How can you know something about her that I don't?'

Bron hesitated. Georgia got the impression that he didn't relish what he was about to say.

'I went to see her when I inherited Merlinslade, just before she died. I wanted to make sure she had enough to live on.'

'How dared you visit her without my permission? Why didn't you tell me this before? I had a right to be told.'

'Because nobody knew exactly where you were at the time, and also because I had some thought for your feelings, though you probably won't believe that either.'

'How can you suggest I wasn't looking after her? She was living in luxury, thanks to me.'

'Yes, she was, I agree. The nursing home was comfortable enough – comfortable and impersonal, as you'd have found out if you'd ever visited her there. All she wanted was to see you sometimes, yet she didn't even have your address. The fees for the home were paid by your bank.'

'Huge fees, huge fees!' muttered Morrigan incoherently.

'Nothing was too good for my mother. I was all a son should be.'

'Until she was old. She said that when she became slow and forgetful and couldn't wait on you as she used to do, you had no more use for her. The last time you met, when you told her she had to go into a home, she realised you'd never be able to handle responsibility of any sort. She told me that in spite of what my grandfather had done to her, she was glad he hadn't left you Merlinslade. She didn't think you deserved it.'

'It's not true! You've no proof!' said Morrigan, the torch wavering ever more wildly.

'She wrote to me afterwards, saying much the same thing,' said Bron.

'You're lying!' Morrigan yelled. 'Why does everyone tell lies?'

'The letter's in the library. If you put that torch down you can come and see for yourself.'

Bron's voice was flat and unemotional, but his eyes never left the torch.

'Even my mother,' Morrigan said. The torch began to droop. His voice was almost inaudible. 'Even my mother deserted me.'

He began to shiver like a dog in a storm. Bron caught the torch just before it hit the ground. He rushed it into the wings to extinguish it in a bucket of sand. When he returned Morrigan was rocking back and forth, pumping his clasped hands together. He looked as abject as Caliban deprived of his island.

'I don't know what to do,' he said in a thin, high wail. 'For God's sake tell me what to do.'

Bron hesitated, then put his arm round his shoulders and quietly led him off the stage.

Even the reporter and cameraman were stunned by the private drama they'd witnessed. There was a long silence, as there had been at the end of the play, until they suddenly remembered that they had the scoop of the year on their hands. Only then did they make an excited dash for the doors. They rushed past Georgia, the interview with her completely forgotten, leaving her alone once more in the empty theatre, not elated as they were, but struggling with a profound sadness over what she'd just seen.

When she went backstage the company was in tumult as it

391

celebrated the play's success and discussed Morrigan's sensational downfall, which had been leaked by the television crew. It was hard for Georgia to join in. In her state of fatigue and disillusion Morrigan's final disintegration still seemed pathetic rather than a cause for rejoicing. She was exhausted after the events at the well, and by trying to cope with the regret which had been growing since her talk with Redvers, for she knew now that she'd allowed bitterness over her divorce to rule her attitude to Bron.

Nevertheless, the post-performance party was an event she couldn't duck out of. Back in the wardrobe she made a pot of very strong coffee, admired Chloe's choice of dress, a short tunic of silver paillettes, and waited while she turned her face into a work of art with borrowed make-up. When Chloe had finished Georgia tried to paint a mask over her own weariness, but merely ended up thinking gloomily that she was looking more duenna-like every day.

They walked together through the terrace garden to the great hall. It was already crowded. Music throbbed from the minstrel's gallery, where Ned was helping a DJ from a Bristol disco mastermind a tape deck. The early music consort engaged by Imogen had let her down at the last minute.

She'd solved the problem of the decor by simply throwing money at it. Overpowering arrangements of white and pink lilies, bird of paradise flowers and trails of waxen orchids stood in the fireplace and the window bay, their scent cloying the air. Lengths of immensely smart striped black and white silk had been pinned and draped over the faded brocade curtains.

Her version of a light buffet supper adorned the refectory table: a whole smoked salmon, red and black caviare set in bowls of ice, a Bavarian chocolate cake four layers deep and as large as a dustbin lid, and a pyramid of cream-stuffed profiteroles held together with a web of spun sugar. The food was presided over by Mrs Meads, who looked as if she would much prefer to be at home with a cup of tea and a digestive biscuit.

Imogen herself darted like a humming bird about the room, greeting the notables from the audience who'd been invited to attend the party. In spite of her friendship with Morrigan she seemed stimulated rather than sobered by the evening's events, as though they'd all been part of the general entertainment.

Georgia got herself a drink from the bar by the door, and went to sit on an iron-hard sofa which at least had the merit of being half hidden by one of the flower arrangements. Chloe was deep in conversation with Sean. Bron, to Georgia's relief, hadn't appeared, and she presumed he was still with the police.

Nico appeared round a spray of orchids, looking unusually subdued. He sat down by her, and confirmed her unspoken thoughts.

'Poor old Bron. It's not much of an evening for him. He rang to say he had to go to the hospital after he'd finished with the police. Ger went completely round the twist when he left here, and the doctors needed Bron's consent as the nearest relative to put him inside.'

Georgia shivered. It wasn't an end she would have wished on anyone.

'I know,' said Nico. 'It's a bloody awful finish to Ger's career. But thank God we've got his recorded music for the play. And even though we're having to do without him for the rest of the run, the publicity will more than compensate, in a gruesome kind of way.'

He took an enormous gulp of his vodka and tonic. Georgia guessed that Morrigan's descent into madness had hit him perhaps harder than anyone there.

'I know you and Bron loathed him from the start,' Nico went on, staring at the twist of lemon in his glass, 'but when I was young, before fame started to screw him up, he could be terrific company with people he didn't feel threatened by.'

He took another gulp of his drink as Imogen went by with one of the sponsors in a cloud of Opium and cigar smoke.

'Bron used to be good company too, before Imo screwed him up. Just look at her. On an even bigger ego-trip than usual, in spite of everything that's happened. I reckon she's got something up her sleeve, she's looking so smug, but I'm past caring now the theatre's safe. I've decided the only thing to do is get steadily smashed.'

He finished his drink, and while he made a bee-line to the bar to replenish his glass, Georgia went back to watching the crowd. The DJ put on an unfashionably slow tape. People groaned, but started revolving round the room in couples. Chloe, dancing with Sean, seemed drunk with happiness. Georgia felt older than her grandmother as she watched.

Redvers was teaching Zelda the foxtrot. Esther, dancing with the actor who played Trinculo, looked almost beautiful. Georgia had persuaded her to buy a new party dress of carnation red ruched silk which made her skin glow and rounded her slight figure. John was to visit the rectory the following day, and Georgia wondered what he'd make of this new Esther.

Ned, finally tired of helping with the music, gravitated back to the hall. He didn't see Georgia, and for once she was glad. She watched him go over to Mrs Meads and attempt to filch a profiterole. He was trying to conceal his yawns.

Georgia retreated further behind the flowers when Bron at last appeared, looking extremely grim. He got himself a very large whisky at the bar, where he was immediately besieged by people wanting to know more about Morrigan. Nico, who'd delayed proposing a toast to the company until Bron's arrival, leaped on to a chair and called for silence.

Esther came to sit by Georgia as he made a drunken and brilliant speech. It included a wicked impersonation of Prospero which Redvers applauded as loudly as anyone, but Nico saved his most lavish praise for Esther. When he finally raised his glass for the toast she was as red as her dress with pleasure and embarrassment.

Afterwards he came over to her. His step was decidedly unsteady, his hair flopping over his forehead, and his tie askew.

'Now you're a star you've got to learn to stop hiding away, sweetie. I'm about to make you an offer you can't refuse.' He smiled mischievously at her. 'It's a contract for the rest of the season, and I forbid you to turn it down.'

The colour drained from Esther's face.

'It's no good saying you'll think about it. I want you to decide now,' Nico went on remorselessly. 'This is a once-only offer. If I let you go away and pray over it, we'll never see you again after *The Tempest*.'

Esther stared from Nico to Georgia and back.

'There's no need to look as if you've seen Banquo's ghost,' Nico jollied her. 'It's the best thing that's ever happened to you. You know you don't really live until you're on the stage. Isn't that true?'

Though Nico was half drunk he'd by no means lost his wits, Georgia thought. Esther could never lie to anyone, not even Nico, who manipulated the truth every day of his life.

'Yes, I admit it's true,' Esther said. Her voice shook. 'But that doesn't mean it's right.'

'If you were completely decided about the church you'd have turned me down at once,' said crafty Nico. 'You can't go on deluding yourself like this.'

'I am *not* deluding myself,' said Esther. It was one of the few times Georgia had ever heard her sound angry. 'You don't have the slightest idea what such a decision involves.'

'Be fair, Nico,' said Georgia. 'You've got to let Esther have a little time.'

'She must know this has been coming. I've dropped enough hints. Haven't I, sweetie?'

'Well, yes,' said Esther, once more helpless in the face of his questioning.

'People in our profession have to make quick decisions. There are too many others waiting for a chance.'

'John,' said Esther in desperation. 'John'll be here tomorrow. At least let me talk to him first.'

'That'd be fatal. It's a one-off, now or never offer.'

'It doesn't have to be like this, Nico, and you know it,' said Georgia angrily. Esther looked dazed with distress.

'It does with Esther. If I let her go and wrestle with her conscience, then talk to John and the Bishop, she'll persuade herself in no time that she must do what her conscience dictates. She ought to follow her heart for once. God, I sound like a Hollywood musical, but I mean it.'

Georgia had never actually seen someone wringing her hands, but Esther was doing it now, twisting them in an agony of indecision.

'You sound to me as if you're being bloody cruel. I didn't think you were like that,' Georgia snapped at him.

Nico relented a little.

'All right, I'll give Esther till midnight. It'll be a great opportunity to announce that she's joining us for the whole year, and the break just gives me a chance to soak up some of this vodka first.'

He ignored their dismayed protests, and wandered off to the buffet as carelessly and confidently as if he'd just asked Esther to change her mind over where she went for her holidays. Georgia glanced over to the longcase clock ticking away sedately near the fireplace. It was ten minutes to midnight. The demand was typical of Nico, dramatic, thoughtless, selfish, and yet she couldn't help feeling that in some ways he was right about Esther.

Bron was standing near the clock, still drinking whisky, with Ned by his side. Every time Georgia saw him she still felt as if there were some invisible wire of attraction stretched between them. She hastily switched her gaze as she saw Imogen bear down on him and take his arm. She forced herself to concentrate on Esther, whose face was strained with indecision.

'What do you think, Georgy?' she asked. 'I can't believe I'm finding it so hard to decide. Three months ago I'd have laughed if you'd told me this would happen.'

'Perhaps it means you're changing,' said Georgia cautiously. It would have been fiendishly difficult to advise anyone, let alone Esther, over such an enormous decision. 'You could always postpone your ordination for a year. No one's going to be angry with you.'

'But I should be so angry with myself. I went through all this before at Oxford. I'd be breaking a commitment I made long ago. I can't help feeling this is a final test of my purpose.'

'Would it be so terrible if you didn't go into the Church?'

'The world of the stage has nothing much to do with everyday life, everyday suffering. And seeing what happened to Morrigan made me realise how badly things go wrong when fantasy takes hold of the mind.'

'Things don't have to go wrong. Fantasy can enrich life too. An actor teaches just as effectively as a preacher. And aren't the parables a form of drama, after all?'

'Perhaps, but the world's falling apart these days, and society with it. I can't abandon it just for the sake of my own personal fulfilment. So I know the decision I have to make.'

Her hands had become peaceful at last, and lay quietly in her lap. She smiled at Georgia.

'Don't look like that, Georgy. I won't regret it.' She glanced at the clock and smiled. 'And I've decided with a minute to spare. I'll go and tell Nico now, before he starts embarrassing me all over again.'

Georgia's eyes followed her through the crowd as she went up to Nico, and spoke to him. His face was so disappointed as he listened that Georgia began to wonder if he'd been seriously attracted to Esther. But in the end he smiled, shrugged, and exchanged a decorous kiss with her. She slipped unobtrusively from the room with the expression of someone who'd just escaped from the four horsemen of the Apocalypse.

Nico came over to Georgia.

'Well, that's it. I've lost,' he said with a wry grin, sitting down by her and taking her hand. 'Instead of playing Beatrice to my Benedick, she'll be making John's bedtime cocoa and looking after delinquent teenagers. But in an odd kind of way I admire her for holding out.'

Georgia had never liked him as much as she did then. She squeezed his hand sympathetically. As she did so she saw Imogen walking purposefully towards them, followed by a sleepy-looking Ned, and Bron with a face as stony as the courtyard outside. He gave Georgia a distant nod.

'What are you two talking about?' said Imogen brightly. 'They're very confidential, aren't they, Bron?'

Bron's eyes had a strange, hard glitter. He said nothing, but looked at Georgia in a way that made her feel as if she'd just got out of Nico's bed.

'Esther's turned down my offer of a permanent place in the company,' said Nico lightly. 'It was the chance of a lifetime.'

'Obviously she didn't think so,' said Bron. 'I don't blame her.'

'Then you make a good pair, Bron,' said Imogen. 'You never take chances, either.'

'Cut it out, Imo,' said Nico, who'd begun to look very drunk indeed. 'Bron took a hell of a lot of chances tonight, but you still keep slagging him off. You've done nothing but stir things up since you got here.'

Imogen's face was outraged.

'How dare you talk to me like that, Nico? Whose money's paying for the party tonight? Who's got you more sponsors than you ever dreamed of? And *don't* call me Imo. I'm not a box of soap-powder.'

Ned had thoroughly woken up by this time. He watched tensely as Imogen turned on Bron.

'Make him apologise! I demand that you make him apologise!'

Bron looked at her with an expression of contempt Georgia had never seen him use on anyone except Morrigan before.

'You demand?' he said coldly. 'Do you ever stop demanding?' His words were infinitesimally slurred, and Georgia realised he was even more drunk than Nico.

'How dare you speak to me like that?' she hissed.

'Because I'm tired of your demands, Imogen. We're all tired of them. We've had enough. So I suggest you fuck off to London and leave us in peace.'

Imogen's face became as hard and angular as her hair style. 'Don't be ridiculous. You know very well you need me here. It's obvious you can't manage on your own.'

'We all managed a hell of a lot better before you turned up.'

'You're telling me to go?' said Imogen. She ran her long manicured fingers beneath the black chiffon scarf round her throat. 'Just like that, without even a word of thanks?'

'Just like that,' said Bron. 'In fact I'll drive you to the station myself.'

Imogen's normally composed and self-satisfied face was twisted with fury.

'So you want me to go! All right, I will, but only because it happens to suit me. And you won't like it one bit, I promise you!'

She gave Bron a look so vindictive that Georgia quailed.

'That partnership in New York's come up after all. I'm leaving at the end of the month, and Merlinslade can rot for all I care. You and Nico have never showed the slightest appreciation for my help.'

Ned clutched at Imogen's arm, looking as if he was on a sinking ship.

'You're going abroad? But you promised me you wouldn't.'

He began to gnaw the knuckles on his other hand.

'That was before I realised how unreasonable your father was going to be. When you've grown up you'll realise promises can't always be kept. But this is even better, because I've arranged things so that you can come with me! That's what I was holding out for.' She shot a glance of pure triumph at Bron. 'There's a fabulous apartment with the job, and you'll love the States.'

Ned stopped biting his knuckles and began to twist his hair instead, gazing suspiciously at Imogen. 'How do you know? It might be really crap there.' He looked up at Bron. 'And I'd have to leave Dad and Nico and Merlinslade.'

'Your father won't mind. He's said all along that now you're older, where you live should be your decision. Haven't you, Bron?' Imogen demanded in a voice like ground steel.

Bron was taut with anger, but his voice was gentle as he put his hand on Ned's shoulder. 'Of course I'll mind. I don't want you to go, Ned. No one at Merlinslade does. Your mother's right, though. You're old enough now to decide for yourself where you want to live.'

'But why can't you and Mum stay together?' he burst out despairingly.

Bron went very white. 'That's just not possible. I've explained it all to you before. It wouldn't be any better for you if we did.'

'Stop upsetting him, Bron,' snapped Imogen. 'You'll like it a hundred times more in the States than here, Ned. You'll be able to go to all the latest movies, baseball matches, Indy car racing, anything you like.'

'Indy car racing?' said Ned, looking slightly more receptive.

'Of course. Rocco'll take you. He loves it too.'

'Who's Rocco?'

'A really nice man, Ned, a fun person, one of the other partners in my new firm. He'll be living with us. He'll take you Indy racing every weekend when you're home from school.'

Ned began to frown. 'You mean I'd have to go away?'

'Any inner city school in the States is a jungle. But Rocco

knows of a really good private place in Connecticut. You'll adore it. You can play American football.'

'I don't like American football. I like Bath City. And I'd have to leave Jason and Rusalka too. I bet you wouldn't let me take the puppy, either.'

'Don't be silly, Ned. You can't keep a setter in a New York apartment.'

Ned stared from Bron to Imogen, and then for some reason which Georgia couldn't quite fathom at her. He looked as if he were trying to solve a problem in his maths homework that wouldn't work out. His fist was rammed in his mouth again. Georgia felt a rush of sympathy as she realised he was trying not to weep.

Bron put his arm round Ned's shoulders. 'It's all right, Ned. Take it easy. You don't have to decide tonight. And you don't have to do anything you don't like.'

Ned pulled his fist from his mouth. His face was scarlet. His nose was running and tears were pouring from his eyes.

'I hate you, I hate you,' he yelled at Imogen. 'You made me cry in front of everyone! I won't go with you. I want to stay at Merlinslade!'

He hurtled across the room, pushing unceremoniously through the dancers, and flung himself into the arms of Mrs Meads. She cast a startled glance towards Imogen and Bron, instantly took in the situation, and valiantly led the still weeping Ned outside to calm down.

Imogen looked suddenly shattered. 'He said he hated me. He never said that before. How can my own child hate me?'

'A good question,' said Bron coldly. 'Perhaps you'll think it over when you're in the States. And you'd better think hard, because if you don't you're going to lose Ned altogether.'

'What do you mean, lose him? Don't be stupid.' Imogen was rapidly regaining her self-control, but her voice was still uncertain.

'I let him live with you, much against my better judgement, when my father died because I thought he ought to have a chance to live with his mother. Don't forget you were the one who signed over custody of Ned because you wanted to live your own life.

Our marriage ran way beyond injury time long ago, Imogen, but you still don't seem to realise that Ned's the casualty. Whether you mend your relationship with him is now entirely up to you.'

He turned brusquely. His sleeve caught the flower arrangement in passing, almost toppling it.

'And this is Merlinslade, not a bloody jungle,' he flung at her as he made for the door to the outer hall.

'What does Bron mean? Those flowers were done by a top Knightsbridge florist,' said Imogen wildly, appealing to Nico, who was beginning to laugh. 'And he makes it sound as though I don't want the best for Ned. Of course I do. Why else would I offer to take him to the States?'

'Just put a sock in it, Imo,' said Nico. 'Why don't you go and give the duchess an earful instead?'

Imogen was finally rendered speechless. She stood glaring at Nico for a moment, then stomped away on her high heels. A few seconds later she was flirting defiantly with one of the local JPs.

'Bron did it! He really told Imo to piss off at last!' said Nico in delight, stumbling drunkenly over the words. 'This definitely calls for another drink. Then I'd better go and see how Ned's doing. Poor kid – what a way to have to decide.'

Georgia watched him weave uncertainly through the room. He was delayed by admirers at the bar, but eventually made it through the door. She felt a destructive wave of loneliness when he'd gone. Bron had sent Imogen away too late to help their relationship, but he'd always have Nico and Ned. Soon she'd have no one. Chloe was wrapped up in Sean, Esther would shortly be joining John in the north, and Zelda was going back to the States in a few months' time.

She told herself to stop wallowing in self-pity, that she was only feeling like this because she was tired, but the lecture had no effect. She looked round at the other party-goers, whose celebrations seemed to have less and less to do with her, then up at the impassive pictures of the Carwithens on the walls, and suddenly thought that she never wanted to see Merlinslade again.

On legs she had to force to move, she made her way back to the wardrobe, which was quiet and empty now. She took Chloe's dress from the tumble drier and put it on a hanger, then went into her office and sat down at the old manual typewriter she'd had since college days. Slowly and carefully she typed out a letter giving Nico a month's notice of her resignation from the company. If she hadn't been so tired she would have cried as she did it.

She put the letter in an envelope, still hardly able to believe that she'd just negated all her professional principles. She could only hope Nico would understand and not bad-mouth her throughout the theatre world. If he was generous, and if *The Tempest* had good reviews, she might just be able to hold on to her business reputation.

She went over to Nico's office and slipped the letter under his door. Now there was no turning back.

Chapter 20

A month later Georgia again set out early for Merlinslade. It was her last day at the theatre, and she intended to gather her personal belongings together unobtrusively before the rest of the wardrobe staff arrived.

They'd been dismayed by her resignation, and she felt a traitor at leaving them. Nico, though, once he found he could neither charm nor manipulate her into changing her mind, had been surprisingly sympathetic, and remained so.

'I still think you're crazy, especially after your designs for Merlinslade had such fantastic reviews, but I do understand,' he'd said only the previous night over a farewell drink in The Mortal Man. 'I once chucked in a year's contract halfway through the run because the director thought I was having it off with his wife.'

He tore open a packet of peanuts and offered her one, looking at her teasingly over the top of the bag.

'The way Bron's behaving at the moment, I think he'd like to chuck everything in as well. I thought he'd be more cheerful once Imogen was out of the way.'

'That's his business,' snapped Georgia.

'No need to get stroppy with me too,' Nico drawled. 'I certainly don't blame you for wanting out as far as he's concerned. It's a pity, though. Bron was quite human again for those few weeks you two were an item.'

'Tough,' said Georgia. 'I'm not a rescue service.'

Nico gave an elegant shrug. 'Only an observation, darling. Anyway, you've still got time to change your mind, you know.'

He and Zelda had argued for the last three weeks over Georgia's replacement, and were interviewing a short list of applicants that afternoon. She'd worked non-stop to see that the costumes for the next production, *The School for Scandal*, were well advanced so that the new designer would be able to slip easily into her place.

Zelda had been much less accommodating over Georgia's resignation than Nico.

'I don't know what's wrong with you. Just when you're back in the boat, you go overboard again. And for such a damn' fool reason, too – that you don't like the atmosphere at Merlinslade any more. Supposing I let myself be thrown by atmosphere? I'd never do another day's work in the theatre.'

'It's not only the theatre,' Georgia had replied lamely.

'You're going to end up in serious shtuck if you carry on this way.'

Georgia felt that what she said was probably only too true, and that she didn't deserve it when Zelda, in spite of all her reproofs, generously offered to find her work in the States.

Of all the company, she'd miss Zelda most, Georgia thought. She smiled as she drove through the entrance gates to Merlinslade, remembering Zelda's remarks about the stone griffins before her first visit. Then it had been early summer but now there was autumn in the crisp air and yellowing leaves.

Too much had happened in the intervening time, she thought. And as if he were there specifically to make the contrast more painful, when she approached the bridge over the river she saw Ned sitting by the road in his school clothes with his bike propped beside him. He was eating what looked like a bacon sandwich. His face split into a smile when he saw her.

She stopped the car, and leaned over to open the window. She'd hardly seen him since the beginning of term, and when she did he was always with Jason. Bron too had been absent from the house, occupied in long days of ploughing, and then away at agricultural shows.

'Hi,' Ned greeted her. 'I thought you might come along around now. Nico told me you'd be making an early start.' With some difficulty he composed his face into an attempt at Bron's gravest expression. 'I wonder if I could have a word with you?'

Georgia's timetable that day scarcely allowed for drawing

breath, let alone intimate conversations with Ned. She still had a hundred loose ends to tie up in the workshop. But this was clearly more important than checking the size of a farthingale, or making sure Jenny really did know how to curl an eighteenth-century wig. She pulled the car over to the side and got out.

'Won't you be late for school?' she asked.

'Only a little.' He looked anxiously in both directions. 'Could we go down by the river? Someone might come along and hear us.'

Suppressing a smile, Georgia followed him down the slope to the river bank, and sat by his side on a fallen tree trunk. The air was still cool, and she rolled down the sleeves of the blouse she was wearing with her old wrap-over skirt and tried to look suitably serious.

'What's wrong?' she asked. 'New term blues?'

Ned stowed the last of the sandwich in his mouth, chewed vigorously, swallowed, and went bright red.

'It's not that. I've been back nearly a month now. It's – it's you and Dad!'

A moorhen with an almost fully grown brood came bobbing by like clockwork toys, but Georgia scarcely saw them. She felt herself blushing with him.

'What about us?' she asked.

Ned started tugging at a loose thread in his trousers.

'I know he was seeing you. I got a bit worked up one night because he was always out, and Nico told me.'

'Nico! He'd no right to tell you anything,' said Georgia, so annoyed that she forgot she wasn't talking to another adult.

Ned left the thread dangling, and began to bite his nails instead. He looked almost as if he might cry again.

'What are you getting angry for? I thought it was great until Dad suddenly started acting like the Terminator, and Nico said it was all off between you. Why, Georgy? It would have been ace.'

Georgia was overcome with contrition for snapping at him. She was also struggling with amazement at Ned's declaration. She knew he was fond of her, but in spite of Bron's assurances she'd never been able to believe that Ned would actually welcome her as a stepmother. She put her arm round his shoulders. His chin was sore, as if he'd been trying to scrape at a non-existent beard, and he smelt of Nico's aftershave. That made her want to cry as well.

'You really ought to talk to Bron about this, not me,' she said.

'He'll just say some other time. Please, Georgy.'

Georgia plucked a withering spray of willow herb and ran her finger and thumb along one of the seed heads. As it neatly unzipped and the down floated away across the river she wondered what to tell Ned.

'We simply decided it wouldn't work out,' she said lamely.

'You at least might have told me what was going on. I never have any say in things, and I'm nearly grown-up now.'

He was echoing exactly Chloe's eternal complaint. Georgia remembered how disastrous not treating her as an adult had been, and decided that she must tell Ned at least a little about what had happened. If Imogen and Bron wouldn't communicate with him that was their affair, but there was no reason why she shouldn't explain her side of things.

'My first marriage was pretty difficult,' she said, continuing to split the seed heads one by one. 'Not in the way that your parents' was, but bad all the same. I decided in the end that I couldn't risk a second one.'

'Didn't you love Dad, then?' said Ned.

'Your mother wasn't happy about my seeing him,' said Georgia desperately. 'I didn't want to make things any more difficult for you and Bron.'

'We wouldn't mind. We're used to her,' said Ned, brightening. 'And anyway she's gone now. Dad said I can visit her at Christmas if I like, but he's not having her at Merlinslade again.'

'That wasn't the only problem,' said Georgia. 'Your father wanted me to live here, but I need my own home. I decided I couldn't give it up. You'd feel the same way about leaving Merlinslade, wouldn't you?'

'I suppose so,' said Ned reluctantly. 'But we'd have made Merlinslade home for you. What you're doing seems a bit like chickening out to me.'

His voice was trying to be matter-of-fact, but there was a wobble in it. She gave his shoulders a comforting squeeze.

'Sometimes it does to me too, but I still think it's better than a second bad marriage. I just wish I could make you believe how sorry I am.'

'You would have made the house look great as well,' he went on. 'I bet you'd even have persuaded Dad to let me have a party of my own. Couldn't you give it another go, just once, please?'

The conversation was bringing her still closer to tears. She knew she'd have to finish it.

'I'm sorry, Ned, but I must get on,' she said, throwing away the piece of willow herb, which was just a bare stalk now. 'I've a busy day ahead. You know you can come and see me any time at the flat when I've left Merlinslade. We're friends, and we always will be, I hope.'

'You haven't answered me,' he said, his voice even unsteadier.

'It wouldn't work. You'll just have to believe me.'

'I don't believe you. I never in a million years thought you could be as pig-headed as Dad! And I thought you were one of the really grown-up grown-ups, too.'

He tore himself away from her arm and rushed blindly up the bank, crushing more of the long-suffering willow herb. He grabbed his bike and flung himself on to the saddle.

As he pedalled furiously away in the direction of the village she heard him shouting again and again, 'It's not fair, it's not fair!'

There was still a lump in her throat as she drove into the courtyard. She had to force back her tears, and blow her nose purposefully before going into the workroom. Once there she gathered together her work tools, the bits and pieces from her desk, the posters and books, and dumped them into a couple of cardboard boxes.

In her mail she found a letter from the conservation department at the V & A, with the news that the cloak was almost back to its original condition, and could soon go on display at Merlinslade. That was something to be thankful for, Georgia told herself firmly, and so was Chloe's current exemplary college attendance. She occasionally went to the Sanctuary at weekends, but spent most of her spare time with Sean.

When Georgia had read the rest of her mail, it was still only nine o'clock. She went to the window and stood looking into the orchard. The grass under the trees was saturated with dew. Mr Meads had spent all the previous day wheeling barrow loads of apples to the old cider house which stood at the back of the stables. Scores of windfalls lay among the grass. On the branches a few late Blenheims and Worcester Pearmains were ripening in the October sun.

It was a mellow, peaceful scene, so peaceful that it was hard to imagine how she could have been disturbed by anything to do with Merlinslade. Yet again she had the unsettling feeling that perhaps she was doing something very stupid by leaving.

She slammed the window shut. They'd all worked late the previous night, and the others wouldn't arrive until about ten. Though she had so much to do, she decided to go over to the rectory. It was safer than becoming dangerously introspective on her own.

She carried the boxes to her car, stowed them in the boot, and decided to walk through the fields. There was no chance of meeting Bron. Mr Meads had told her that they were working together today on the first pressing of cider.

All evidence of summer had gone from the fields. They were now a uniform brown, ribbed by the plough, and waiting for next year's seed. The hedgerows were full of pink spindleberry lanterns and glossy rosehips. The woods looked utterly benign, not a tree moving in the morning air, and their leaves tinged with russet and gold.

No one answered Georgia's knock on the rectory front door. She went into the back garden, skirting a huge line of washing. The lawn was strewn with plastic toys, and was almost bald where the children had been playing football. A strong smell of vinegar and spices wafted through the open kitchen door.

Kim's rubber-gloved hands were plunged into a sinkful of dishes. Radio One was belting out the Simon Mayo show as she stacked plates streaming with hot suds on to the draining board. On the stove a pan of chutney heaved and bubbled.

Kim waved a thinning dish mop at her. 'Hi. Esther's out parish visiting.'

'I didn't especially want to see her. I just wanted to talk,' said Georgia lamely.

Kim gave her a curious look. 'No problem. I'll be with you in a minute. There's some breakfast coffee left.'

Georgia found a wiping-up cloth even more tattered her own, and began to dry the dishes. In spite of the music and the sunshine flooding into the room, she still had a lump in her throat. When all the dishes were stacked on the dresser, Kim wrung out the mop, letting the water gurgle noisily away.

'It's your last day, isn't it?' she said. She turned off the radio, and when she'd inspected the chutney poured two mugs of coffee from a percolator on the side of the stove. 'I know you're not sorry, but we'll all miss you.'

'I've just started to realise how much I'll miss it too,' said Georgia.

Kim began writing labels for the chutney jars with one of the children's felt pens.

'So why are you going, then? I know the official reason, but it sounded like a lot of flannel to me. Was Bron hassling you?'

'It was just a bit of everything,' said Georgia feebly. Kim was getting a little too near the truth, as she had after the harvest picnic.

'Come off it, Georgy. Who are you kidding? You were both doing OK together until bloody Imogen and Morrigan put the boot in. It's my guess you'd had enough and just wanted out.'

'How did you know?' said Georgia in amazement.

'Put it down to experience,' said Kim. 'The same kind of thing happened to me. When things got bad over that bastard who was trying to throw us off his land, I chucked out Dave, the guy I was living with. I was so uptight I couldn't think straight any more.'

She grinned ruefully, dumped brown sugar in her coffee, and stirred it into a whirlpool. 'I'm not sorry for duffing up the farmer, but I do regret Dave. I wouldn't have minded getting back with him now I've got a job, but then I heard he's shacked up with another woman over Glastonbury way. So I reckon I've had that.'

'I'm sorry,' said Georgia, with a rush of sympathy. 'Things must have been tough for you lately.'

409

'Yeah, they haven't been much of a laugh. Everyone seems to have gone crazy this summer. Look at Esther. Anyone can see she really lives when she's on stage. Yet she's turned down Nico's offer, and decided to do a Sister Wendy for the rest of her life.'

'It's not quite like that,' said Georgia.

'I still think she's doing a runner. But you – you're the last person I'd expect to mess up your life deliberately. You've been around, you know the score. Imogen and Morrigan have gone, and Bron hasn't got anyone else. So what's to stop you getting together with him again?'

'All sorts of things,' said Georgia wretchedly. She wished she'd stayed in the workshop. 'The class business to start with. He gets so uptight about his responsibilities sometimes, and he's so bloody reserved. And then the set-up at Merlinslade, the whole heritage scene. It's all too much.'

'He can't help his class. And you couldn't blame him for being uptight when he was getting so much flak from Imogen and Morrigan. As for Merlinslade, everyone freaks out because of its history, but what is it really but a pile of old bricks and some rundown land? Nothing much to be scared of there.'

She began to line up empty jam jars at the side of the stove.

'I think he's an OK bloke, and they aren't easy to find. He's just had a bit too much to cope with recently, like you.'

Georgia didn't answer. Though the subject had an awful fascination for her, she couldn't bear to go on listening to Kim when she'd already made up her mind.

Kim had just embarked on another diatribe on the subject of Esther's recently announced engagement to John, when Maureen appeared looking for her screaming toddler's dummy. In the ensuing rush to find it Georgia finished her coffee, and thankfully made a tactful exit.

She returned to Merlinslade a different way, walking along the river bank. Someone, Bron she supposed, had replaced the section of broken handrail on the wooden sluice bridge, and cleared the choked irrigation ditches. Fallen leaves glided slowly down the stream. It was hard to believe the angry encounter there between Morrigan and Bron had ever taken place.

When she entered the main courtyard to return to the theatre through the terrace garden, Rusalka lay at the top of the steps to the front door. Conan Two, Ned's puppy, was rooting about in the lavender bushes. She looked up at the façade of the house and realised with a jolt that it now seemed almost as familiar and unimposing as her own.

On an impulse she went up the steps into the great hall. It had reverted to its usual shabby self. The clock was ticking away quietly. Mrs Meads' flower arrangements, this time of funereal mauve chrysanthemums and white aster spikes, stood stiffly on the refectory table. The room had a forlorn air, like a beautiful actress badly dressed, as if it still waited for some transforming hand.

Even the portraits which had seemed remote and proud on the night of the party had reverted to perfectly ordinary paintings of farmers and soldiers and their families, just an older version of the family photo album. She went up to the fireplace, and looked at the portrait hanging over it of Miles Carwithen, a Royalist officer in a buff jacket and scarlet sash whom she'd always thought was a little like Bron. Today the face of the portrait seemed simply amused rather than arrogant.

Slowly she went outside and stood on the step next to Rusalka, listening to the doves on the roof and the church clock ringing the hour. The impulse she'd been trying to resist all morning she couldn't resist any more. She had to say goodbye to Bron before she left, however difficult it might be. She owed him a dignified farewell, and at least in Mr Meads' presence there would be no danger of renewed arguments.

The cider house was at the back of the outbuildings, a small barn with a stone-tiled roof and a pair of ancient entrance doors on collapsing hinges. They were normally locked, and Georgia had never been inside, but today one of them was slightly ajar.

The smell in the barn hit her at once, acid and fruity, the heavy fumes almost tangible in the air, a mixture of fresh apple juice and cider from earlier years fermenting in oak barrels stacked against the walls on wooden racks. It seemed to Georgia as if the essence of all that long strange summer had been concentrated into the one place, a summer which would end forever when she'd said goodbye to Bron.

Above and to her right was a half loft where she guessed the apples were stored and roughly crushed before being poured down a chute to feed the press. Mr Meads had told her that this was his part of the operation, but when she peered up into the cobwebby darkness he wasn't there, and neither was Bron. She supposed they'd both gone to fetch more apples from the orchard. Now, she thought resignedly, she'd have to wait around until they got back.

She forgot her apprehensiveness in her interest in the machinery. A massive iron screw set in a frame of age-silvered oak operated the press itself. The apples were sandwiched between heavy boards and filters of layered straw. Though the press was at a standstill, amber juice still trickled along a runnel into a deep stone trough.

Behind the press was a high-sided box stall piled with straw for replenishing the press, with a silent portable radio poised on one of the crossbars. Georgia caught her breath as Bron unexpectedly emerged from its recesses with a bundle of straw in his arms, and dumped it in an open rack. He was wearing a blue sweatshirt covered in pieces of chaff, his old denim jeans and turned-down Wellington boots shiny with apple juice.

At first he didn't notice her. He was too busy starting up the press again. It was operated by a winch, a long bar of oak which slotted into the screw and was laboriously pushed round by hand to lower the press a few inches at a time. For a few moments the only sounds were the squelch of his boots on the wet stone floor, and the creak of wood mingled with the slow trickling of cider. She hadn't been near him since the party, and in the intervening time he'd assumed Mr Darcy-like dimensions in her mind. But now he looked perfectly normal, frowning only because he was concentrating on his work.

Eventually he paused for breath, resting his forearms along the top of the winch handle. He looked up and caught sight of her at last. She advanced a little way towards him over the slippery floor.

'Be careful,' he said. 'The whole place is awash.'

'Where's Mr Meads?' She couldn't think what else to say.

'Gone for coffee. He'll be back soon.'

There was a long silence.

'So, what do you want?' he asked. He clearly wasn't going to smooth the meeting with light conversation.

'Just to say goodbye, that's all,' she said lamely. 'I thought it wasn't – it wasn't right to leave without speaking to you.'

He continued to gaze at her, still resting his arms on the winch handle. The smell of cider was so strong she felt almost light-headed.

'Why wasn't it right?' he asked.

'I don't have to give you a reason.'

'I think you do. You've never properly explained what went wrong between us, not even after that catalogue of my faults on the day of the harvest.'

She felt her face growing hot.

'I thought I made it very clear. And in any case, I didn't come here to start arguing again.'

'Good. I don't want to argue either. But since you're here I'd like to sort a few things out.'

'There's nothing to sort out. It's exactly as I told you in the beech grove.'

'Really?' he said in a disbelieving voice that irritated her intensely.

She pulled some straws out of the rack, and began to plait them together. 'All right, if that's how you want it, let's go into some of your motives. Why did you wait so long to give Imogen the push? You must have realised she was trying to break us up.'

'You know exactly why,' he said. 'Because of Ned. I couldn't do it while there was the slightest chance that Imogen might begin to show some long-term interest in him.'

'But I was hurt too. Didn't you see what it was doing to me, to both of us?'

'Of course I did,' he said roughly. 'But, of everyone, Ned was the least able to stand being hurt. You didn't want to hurt Chloe either, if you remember. Or perhaps you prefer to forget.'

'Of course I don't prefer to forget. It wasn't only that, though. You never told me what really went on in your marriage. You

413

seemed to expect me to understand intuitively. But I felt you were deliberately shutting me out.'

He slowly shook his head. 'Not for any sinister reason. Only because the failure of our marriage was such a wretched tale I didn't care to repeat it.'

Georgia already felt she'd never be able to drink cider again. She longed to go outside, but he was making her so angry that she stayed firmly where she was.

'What do you mean, you don't care to repeat it? Have you any idea how alienating that sounds? And how bloody pompous, too? You're talking to me, Bron, someone who loved you, not a solicitor or a bank manager. That's been your problem all along. There's always a final barrier you never quite let down. If you'd really wanted me to believe you, to understand you, you'd have told me everything, no holds barred. Just as I told you.'

Bron gazed down at his hands clenched on the winch. His knuckles were white against the grey wood. She thought he'd respond with anger, but to her astonishment he didn't.

'All right. No holds barred then,' he said slowly. 'But afterwards you have to promise to tell me something too.'

'Go ahead,' she said recklessly. 'I promise.'

There was another long silence, broken only by the sound of some small birds scrabbling about on the roof tiles. Eventually he raised his head and looked at her.

'Imogen started agitating for me to leave the army even before Ned was born,' he said. 'It was a difficult birth, and she found it hard to feel any affection for him. She hired a nanny at once, which meant she had still more time to be bored. I refused to resign. If she'd had some vocation which army postings might have hindered, I'd have given way. But I didn't see why I should just for the sake of her social life.'

He paused, as if the story was being wrung from him with as much difficulty as the cider from the press.

'I think now that I should have been more understanding after the birth. But her constant complaining got me down, and I was glad to be sent to the Falklands. For a while Imogen enjoyed the role of wife to an officer on active service. It impressed her friends enormously. Then she got bored again, and had an affair, at the depot. Not only that, it was with a corporal.'

Georgia sat down on a barrel as she continued to listen, so engrossed that she hardly noticed her surroundings now.

Bron smiled wrily. 'The British army isn't noted for its understanding of fraternisation between officers and men, and that applies to wives too, particularly unfaithful ones. The corporal got a new posting, and I was given compassionate leave to sort things out. Imogen was delighted to have found such an effective weapon. She threatened to go on having affairs unless I left the army. She knew exactly how damaging they'd be to my career. As it was, it was one hell of a loss of face, to have the men you were commanding knowing exactly what was going on. Being a Carwithen made it even worse. The name's a bloody menace at times, especially in the army. Everyone expects twice as much from you.'

Georgia was astounded. Up to now she'd always assumed he was completely hung up on family tradition.

'I was so frantic to get back to my command,' Bron went on, 'I persuaded myself Imogen was bluffing. I was pretty sure the army wouldn't do anything too drastic while I was on active service. I took a chance, told everyone it was sorted out, and got back to the Falklands on the next plane.'

He looked levelly at her. 'In a way it was cowardice,' he said. 'At least, it's how I see it now.'

'That's ridiculous,' said Georgia heatedly. 'How could it be cowardice? You got the MC, for heaven's sake.'

'Because it was the easy thing to do, far easier than trying to sort out Imogen. Usually I was terrified as I went into action, but the next time I simply felt a terrific elation. I didn't care if I died, because I thought it'd solve everything. The honour of the Carwithens would be satisfied, Imogen would be free, and I knew my parents would look after Ned.'

He let his hands fall to his side. His thoughts were obviously still far away, and Georgia realised there was even more to come.

'We captured an enemy position, but we were still under fire. The sergeant who was with me was wounded, and I didn't sober up till I knew I had to get him out. He might not have been wounded at all if I'd gone in more cautiously.'

There was a long silence during which Georgia didn't dare speak, terrified in case he clammed up for good, and she lost the end of the tale.

Finally Bron continued. 'The most ironic part was that when I got home Imogen had already dumped Ned on my parents and left me, so I'd let emotion affect my professional judgement for nothing. Luckily the sergeant recovered, but it's not a story I'm especially proud of.'

At last Georgia could understand the reason for Bron's reserve over his marriage. The conflict in his mind after the real battle must have been almost unendurable. But his pig-headed refusal to accept that a slight amount of weakness was normal was so typical that she couldn't hold back her exasperation.

'Do you always have to be so hard on yourself?' she burst out. 'We've all got something we're not proud of. Considering how young you were, knowing what Imogen's like, knowing that you were on active service, it was perfectly understandable to act as you did. You've exaggerated this out of all proportion.'

'Isn't that what you did with your marriage?' he asked drily.

'All right, I know I can't talk,' she said furiously. 'But you've got to stop distancing yourself because of something that happened so long ago. It's not good for you or anyone round you.'

'I was trying to stop, when I asked you to marry me.'

She pushed back her hair in a gesture of frustration.

'But don't you realise the difference it would have made if you'd told me this then?'

He was silent for a very long time. Until he spoke again she began to have a glimmer of hope that perhaps he might be on the verge of understanding at last.

'So are you going to answer my question now?' he said.

'Yes, I suppose so.' She wondered what was coming. She'd almost forgotten her original promise.

'Have you been sleeping with Nico again?'

She stared at him. 'You've no right to ask me that now.'

'You're a fool if you are. Nico's all wrong for you.'

He looked so like Ned when he was about to proclaim that something wasn't fair that she had a hysterical desire to laugh, but it was swiftly overcome by a more basic need to retaliate.

'And you're jealous!' she countered.

He pushed the winch handle forward so there was no barrier between them. The wheel which operated the screw shuddered and groaned into life as the clamp descended another inch, and apple juice again began to flow into the runnel.

'Of course I'm not. But after that little display of together-ness at the first night party you can hardly be surprised,' he replied.

She'd said he was jealous to taunt him, but now as she remembered Nico briefly holding her hand, she knew her words were true.

'Anyway,' he went on, 'I thought you'd only come to say goodbye. I've wasted enough time and I'm missing a good concert.'

He turned to the radio and switched it on. As usual it was tuned to Radio Three. Holst's *Planets* suite reverberated through the barn.

Angrily she darted past him, nearly losing her footing again on the slippery floor, grabbed the radio, and hurled it over the side of the stall into the straw.

He looked at her coldly and silently, and went into the stall to retrieve it. She followed him. He began to search for the radio, which was pounding out 'Mars, Bringer of War' in the depths of the straw.

'The only thing you really care about is music, and I'll tell you why,' she shouted at his back. 'Because you can control exactly how you feel about it, because you know just what's coming next. You're putting up the shutters again, but this time I won't let you!'

He'd found the radio while she was talking, and straightened with it in his hand.

'You nag almost as much as Imogen,' he said sardonically, replacing the radio on the edge of the stall.

Her arm shot out to hurl it back in the straw, but he grabbed her wrist.

'Don't you dare stop me!' she yelled at him. 'And don't dare compare me with fucking Imogen! She didn't love you. I do.'

She tried to pull herself away, but her foot slipped on one of the apples which were scattered everywhere, and she crashed back against the wooden slats of the stall.

Bron caught her and began to kiss her with a mixture of fury and tenderness that she found instantly arousing. She felt drunk on the cider fumes. Her hair had scattered across her face. He pushed it away, gazing down at her, and started to smile.

'For once you're wrong. Imogen never liked fucking,' he said.

She struggled not very whole-heartedly to escape, but only succeeded in retreating further into the heart of the straw, until he had her pinned against the back of an untied bale. The straw scratched her legs. She was almost submerged in a golden, springy nest.

Bron had already undone her blouse and was loosening her skirt, tearing it away with her underwear. He stood for a moment, dragging off his own clothes and kicking his boots into a corner, then dived into the straw, pulling her down beside him. He began to make love to her with a devastating intensity she'd never experienced before.

The suddenness of it all, combined with the illusion of being in their own entirely safe world, was more than she could take after the tension of the previous weeks. Tears began to spill from her eyes. He kissed them away.

'Don't,' he said. 'Don't cry. Just listen for a moment. It's Jupiter now.'

She caught her breath. The music had changed to a glorious uninhibited surge of joy.

'I hope you like the background effects this time,' he said with a smile even more persuasive than Nico's, as she went back to making love to her, building with the music to a climax in which all the constraint and distrust of the past weeks vanished at last.

When she opened her eyes again the radio had finally succumbed to its rough treatment, the music had stopped, and they were almost hidden in the straw. She lay looking up at the dusty roof beams and a gap in the tiles, through which she could see a piece of blue sky and a wispy cloud.

The barn door creaked open. A crack of light penetrated the gloom. She sat up in alarm, pulling the straw over her breasts, thinking that Mr Meads would probably have a cardiac arrest if he discovered them like this. Bron lazily sat up too, looking more amused than concerned.

Footsteps squelched across the stone flags, and a moment later Ned's head appeared cautiously over the side of the stall. His eyes popped like billiard balls. For a moment he was rendered speechless.

'Wow! What are you and Georgia doing there, Dad?'

'What do you think?' said Bron with a grin. 'And why aren't you at school?'

'There was another teachers' training day. I had to come home. I forgot.'

Ned had answered automatically. He suddenly realised exactly what Bron had just said.

'Wow!' he said yet more fervently. 'You mean you've actually been doing – it?'

'Got it in one,' said Bron.

Ned's face began to crack into an enormous smile. 'So does this mean everything's OK?' he asked.

Bron looked at Georgia. 'Is it?' he asked.

'Very, very OK,' she said, 'if that's all right by you, Ned?'

'Geronimo! I'll say it is!' Ned shouted as he hurtled towards the door. 'Wait till I tell Jason this!'

Epilogue

Once more it was an early June day, and Georgia was on her way towards the village church in Merlinslade's ancient Rolls-Royce, recently resurrected by Bron and bedecked with bridal ribbons. Mr Samms, wearing the navy blue suit he kept for county shows, drove at a snail's pace in his determination to show off the pride of the Carwithen garage.

Nico had received Georgia back into the theatre company with flattering eagerness, only slightly marred by some outrageously chauvinist remarks on the subject of female unreliability. To begin with she went on living at the flat while she made sure Chloe was settled at college, but she hadn't been able to resist reorganising Merlinslade. In the end she spent so much time there that it seemed natural to move in with Bron, and then even more natural for them to marry.

They had wanted only the quiet register office ceremony they'd gone through earlier that afternoon, but the cries of dismay from everyone at Merlinslade forced them to change their minds. Esther, ordained at Christmas and about to move north, had, after an immensely long homily on the seriousness of marriage, agreed to officiate at a service of blessing of her own devising, based as far as possible on the church ceremony.

Georgia's father and Karen were too busy to attend, and sent instead a cheque and a set of table mats depicting scenes from the outback. Her mother, having also said that she was too busy, had unexpectedly appeared the previous evening hot foot from a trip to Kew. Zelda was to be Georgia's escort to the altar, and luckily Beatrice had shown no sign of wanting to take her place. Indeed she still seemed to be in a state of shock

421

at the idea of Georgia marrying at all.

Zelda sat next to Georgia now, making last-minute adjustments to a pill-box of black satin perched precariously on the front of her russet hair.

'Damned hat,' she grumbled. 'I wouldn't wear it for anyone but you, Georgy.'

The rest of Zelda was clad in a Donna Karan suit whose brief skirt revealed a pair of still extremely good legs. She'd been looking remarkably rejuvenated generally over the last few months, Georgia thought.

'The whole business is like something from the ark,' Zelda continued. 'Imagine, still handing over a woman to a man as though she can't look after herself! And to Bron of all people!' She then totally ruined the effect of her words by hugging Georgia, and saying huskily, 'He'd damn' well better take care of you, too!'

As the car rolled up to the west gate of the church, Chloe, who was now living in the Sophia Street flat with Sean, came forward to rearrange Georgia's dress. The wardrobe staff had insisted on making it. They'd copied an ankle-length long-sleeved Fortuny tunic in pearl grey chiffon over a pale rose underslip, caught at the shoulders and sides with Venetian beads. Sumitra had sewn a narrow band of silver embroidery at the hem and wrists. Georgia wore no veil, but lilies of the valley were woven into her upswept hair.

She paused briefly with Zelda at the door. The theatre company as well as the villagers had turned out in full force and the church was packed. Ned sat next to Bron's mother in the front row. At the altar steps Bron himself stood parade-ground straight with Nico beside him.

The organ thundered into the Bridal March from *Lohengrin*. Georgia couldn't help remembering her marriage to Blake in a Maryland justice's office, where the only accompaniment was the hum of a dilapidated air-conditioner, and the only witness a clerk who'd seen it all a hundred times before.

'This music is nothing but high octane schmaltz, but it's getting to me already,' whispered Zelda, as they began to move forward.

Georgia would have preferred something less obvious herself, but according to Mrs Meads all Carwithen brides for more than a hundred years had gone up the aisle to that tune, and nothing else would do. Altogether, she thought, while the heads of the women guests craned round to watch her like flowers bending in the wind, her wedding hardly seemed to belong to her at all. And yet she didn't mind, though this time six months ago the thought of such a ceremony in such a public setting would have terrified her.

When Georgia came level with the front pew, Ned scandalised his grandmother by waving at her. Nico gave her an enormous wink as she arrived at the altar. Bron simply smiled, and took her hand long before he was supposed to.

Esther, in a lace surplice, stepped gravely forward and the ceremony began. Georgia found herself making a far deeper commitment than she'd ever done in Baltimore, though the first time round she'd been blithely certain that nothing could possibly go wrong. Now, though she knew the risks by heart, as the organ pealed out Mendelssohn's 'Wedding March' and she walked back down the aisle with her hand tucked under Bron's arm, she felt only a serene optimism.

They stepped through the main door into bright sunshine and the jubilant clamour of bells. Rooks rose in protesting clouds from the churchyard trees. On either side of the steps leading down from the porch stood the gowned Disciples holding up an arch of green willow wands. At the foot of the steps Brighid, in a flowing broderie anglaise robe, beamed up at them.

'The blessings of Gaia on you both as you pass beneath her arch of fruitfulness and joy,' she called.

Bron, who'd so far not turned a hair, even when Nico gave Georgia an unusually long kiss after the ceremony, hesitated on the top step.

'I didn't know the Disciples were invited,' he said to Georgia in a low voice.

'They weren't, though Chloe wanted me to,' she whispered back.

Bron started to laugh.

'Well, since Brighid's got her best nightie on today, I suppose we'd better not disappoint her. But God knows how many little

Carwithens this may lead to!' he said, as they started to walk through the arch.

A wedding breakfast prepared by Kim was laid out on the table in the great hall. Redvers, in a jacket of mulberry velvet and a scarlet bow tie, insisted on augmenting Nico's speech, and completely upstaged him. For once Nico didn't seem to mind. Georgia, sitting next to Zelda, caught her looking at him with a good deal more than ordinary affection. Suddenly the reason for Zelda's rejuvenation dawned on her.

'Zelda – you and Nico – have you been holding out on me?'

'I only kept off as long as I thought there was a chance of you two getting together permanently,' said Zelda with her gravelly laugh. 'Then I thought it was a shame to let him go to waste. It probably won't last, but for the moment he's definitely got the edge on HRT.'

The occasion was crowned for Georgia by hearing Brighid, who'd managed to infiltrate the reception as well, saying earnestly to her mother, 'I've been wanting to talk to you all afternoon, Dr Tremain. I have the strongest feeling that you are not entirely a whole woman, that there's something missing in your life which only the goddess can supply. I do urge you to visit the Sanctuary before you leave . . .'

At last, in the early evening, they dragged themselves away, and set off from Merlinslade for Heathrow and their honeymoon. Bron stopped the Range Rover at the bridge so that they could shake the confetti from their clothes. Georgia waited by the parapet, watching the yellow kingcups sway in the stream while Bron removed the assortment of old shoes and tin cans tied to the back bumper by Jason and Ned.

Shadows were lengthening across the water-meadows and beginning to cover the Merlinslade woods with a cloak of blue. In the distance Brighid and the Disciples were slowly making their way home along the edge of the Forty Acre field, singing as they went. Bron came to stand with his arm round Georgia as the sound of the Disciples' favourite hymn floated towards them.

'It really was amazing grace,' she said softly, 'but where it came from, we shall never quite know.'